Baby, it's cold outside...

"Cinderella?" he croaked.

"Alex," she corrected. Her voice was smoky, like he remembered.

"Any chance you'll untie me, Alex?" His throat might be dry, but the rest of him wouldn't be if he didn't get some relief.

"Nope."

"Then you'd better get me a bottle. An empty bottle."

She quirked an eyebrow and tried not to smile. "And I don't even know your name."

"Tag."

"As in, 'you're it'?"

"Yeah, like I've never heard that one before."

She stood up. She had the body to go along with the sexy voice; it was the first thing he noticed, and he wasn't happy about it. Not about her body, but about the fact that he'd been sidetracked by it. So what if he caught the hint of some intriguing curves under her baggy sweatshirt and jeans? He needed to concentrate on the important things. Like what kind of woman she was. Her clothing was well-worn, for instance. So were her hiking boots; and the rest of her was no muss, no fuss, from her cropped, blond-streaked hair to her short fingernails. She was either practical or broke. Clearly a private woman. Tag could respect that, but it would be damn hard to read her, and if he couldn't read her, he would be in big trouble . . .

TAG, YOU'RE IT!

Penny McCall

BERKLEY SENSATION, NEW YORK

THE BERKLEY PUBLISHING GROUP
Published by the Penguin Group
Penguin Group (USA) Inc.
375 Hudson Street, New York, New York 10014, USA
Penguin Group (Canada), 90 Eglinton Avenue East, Suite 700, Toronto, Ontario M4P 2Y3, Canada
(a division of Pearson Penguin Canada Inc.)
Penguin Books Ltd., 80 Strand, London WC2R 0RL, England
Penguin Group Ireland, 25 St. Stephen's Green, Dublin 2, Ireland (a division of Penguin Books Ltd.)
Penguin Group (Australia), 250 Camberwell Road, Camberwell, Victoria 3124, Australia
(a division of Pearson Australia Group Pty. Ltd.)
Penguin Books India Pvt. Ltd., 11 Community Centre, Panchsheel Park, New Delhi—110 017, India
Penguin Group (NZ), 67 Apollo Drive, Rosedale, North Shore 0745, Auckland, New Zealand
(a division of Pearson New Zealand Ltd.)
Penguin Books (South Africa) (Pty.) Ltd., 24 Sturdee Avenue, Rosebank, Johannesburg 2196,
South Africa

Penguin Books Ltd., Registered Offices: 80 Strand, London WC2R 0RL, England

TAG, YOU'RE IT!

A Berkley Sensation Book / published by arrangement with the author

PRINTING HISTORY
Berkley Sensation mass-market edition / July 2007

Copyright © 2007 by Penny McCusker.
Cover photo of "Back View of Man with Gun in Pants" by Masterfile; "Portrait of Woman" by Thomas Schweizer / Masterfile.
Cover design by Rita Frangie.
Interior text design by Laura K. Corless.

ISBN: 978-0-425-21645-3

BERKLEY® SENSATION
Berkley Sensation Books are published by The Berkley Publishing Group,
a division of Penguin Group (USA) Inc.,
375 Hudson Street, New York, New York 10014.
BERKLEY SENSATION is a trademark of Penguin Group (USA) Inc.
The "B" design is a trademark belonging to Penguin Group (USA) Inc.

PRINTED IN THE UNITED STATES OF AMERICA

10 9 8 7 6 5 4 3 2 1

For Marie

chapter
1

ALEXANDRA SCOTT EASED THE BINOCULARS UP TO her eyes an inch at a time, barely drawing breath. She made no sudden movement, there was no glint of reflected light off the lenses, no sound, and still her quarry whipped around. Wild, piercing golden eyes, magnified a thousand times, seemed to stare directly into hers.

Excitement shivered down her spine, mixed with a healthy dose of fear. A full-grown male mountain lion was nothing to mess with, especially one half-starved from a brutal winter that should have eased into spring a month ago.

Good thing she was a mile away, and there was a mule deer between the two of them.

Alex waited until the cat went back to stalking its prey, then she carefully hung the binoculars from her horse's saddle, fielding the look the horse sent her. Equine impatience. "Just a couple of shots," she said, her hand moving over the rifle scabbard and stopping at the camera bag hanging from the saddle, "then we'll pack it in for the day." Jackass snorted, but he did it softly.

It was the plane that set everyone off. It wasn't unusual

for a small plane to fly through that part of the Rocky Mountain foothills without Alex ever seeing it, but the sound carried for miles. So did Alex's curse. The doe leapt away, the cat froze and swiveled again to peer at Alex, its yellow eyes like lamplights through the late afternoon gloom and heavily falling snow. It would have made a hell of a photo if she'd been able to fumble the camera out before the plane flew over the crest of the hill to her right and dropped into the wide, treeless valley between her and the cat.

Instead of taking off after its quarry, the cat froze. So did Alex, both of them watching the plane drop low enough to almost skim the snow drifts before it shot back up to about treetop level. The wings waggled back and forth, and there were a couple of pops that might have been the engines cutting out. Or . . . gunfire?

Nah, couldn't be gunfire, Alex thought, but just as she'd almost convinced herself it had to be mechanical trouble, a man fell out of the plane. She didn't believe it was a man at first, until he hit the slope right below her and rolled a couple of times, arms and legs—two of each—windmilling before he came to a crumpled stop.

The plane buzzed away to the east, the sound of the engine growing fainter and fainter. Alex watched it go, her mouth open, feet rooted to the spot, frozen in disbelief. But the second the mountain lion moved, so did she. In the same direction. Toward the man.

Alex was closer, but the cat was faster. And the cat was hungry. Not hungry enough to attack an able-bodied adult human, but an incapacitated one? Survival was one of those instinctive things that was hard for a mountain lion to ignore.

Alex reacted just as much from a gut level, no thought to her own safety, no idea if the guy was even savable. No clue what she'd do when she got there and had to fend off 120 pounds of starving mountain lion.

To save someone who might already be dead.

The protective instinct that had set her feet in motion

started to think better of itself, giving way to a feeling that was more along the lines of what-the-hell-am-I-doing?

Unfortunately the cat was only about twenty yards away, still barreling forward in full attack mode, and Alex had downhill momentum behind her. A conflict of some sort seemed unavoidable—then the satellite phone clipped to her belt rang, the sound shrieking through the stillness.

The mountain lion started to backpedal, sliding another few yards before he found the traction to bound away at a right angle.

Alex slid to a stop herself, looked at the readout, and wanted to run away, too. The mountain lion might be gone, but a conflict still loomed. She almost preferred the cat. She considered not answering, but that wouldn't work either. Moving two thousand miles away from her mother might have cut the apron strings, but it had notched up the guilt level to something approaching monumental proportions.

She peeled off a glove and whistled up her horse, then wrenched at the satellite phone, ripping her belt loop before she managed to get it loose. It was an outdated piece of equipment, but it did the job in an area that had no cell phone towers. And at the moment it was way too modern. "I asked you not to call me on this phone, Mother."

"Alexandra, thank heavens, I heard there was a blizzard in Canada, and I was so worried about you."

"I'm in Colorado, Mom. But you got the snow right." Big wet clumps of it had been falling all day, adding ten inches to the foot and a half already on the ground and reminding her that although the calendar said spring, Mother Nature was running the show.

"Oh, darling! Can you get outside? I mean, I know you have to go out to . . . Well, you must be careful not to get chapped," her mother lowered her voice, "you know, down there."

Right, she spent her days trekking in the wilderness, tracking an animal that could tear her to shreds inside of thirty seconds, and her mother was worried about her getting a chapped backside? "This isn't Siberia, Mom. My cabin has every comfort I could possibly need." Except indoor plumbing.

"Does it have a man?" Cassandra Shaw Scott Hanson Martindale Winston Hobbs demanded to know. "No. And you're not going to find one there. Especially since you won't use your title—not that it does you any good alone in that forest with no one around for three states."

Alex headed toward the guy in the snow, more warily now, shifting the satellite phone so her right hand was free. "There's a town about seventy-five miles from here, and the people who live there aren't impressed with titles."

Her mother made a sound that managed to be ladylike and derogatory at the same time. "I'm talking about *civilization*, Alexandra, not that little backwater filled with cowboys and farmers. You'll never find the right kind of man out there."

"I met the right kind of man once," Alex reminded her. "I didn't like it. Neither did he. And what he did to you—"

"Oh, well, water under the bridge," Cassandra trilled in the kind of voice that came with a dismissive wave of her hand. "You mustn't let one unfortunate experience stop you from looking."

"You've found the right man five times, so I'll take your word for it."

"Alexandra!"

"Sorry," she muttered, but really, it had only been a matter of time. She always had good intentions at the beginning of these conversations with her mother. Keep it cool, she'd say to herself, don't lose your patience. The torture would be over sooner if she could only keep her mouth shut.

She could never quite pull it off. This was why they were better off on different sides of the continent—a concept her mother always failed to grasp.

"Alexandra? Are you listening? You're not getting any younger, you know. It'll take simply forever in a salon to repair the damage all that sunlight and fresh air have done

to your skin. And then we have to ease you back into
Boston society, find a way to explain where you've been,
scare up some eligible men—"

"I wouldn't want to scare anyone."

"This is serious, Alexandra. Do you think a man is just
going to show up on your doorstep?"

"No," she said, stopping beside the guy in the snow. "He
missed by about half a mile."

"What?"

"Gotta go, Mom."

Alex disconnected midprotest and stood there, torn between concern for the man at her feet and a gut-deep sense
of self-preservation.

Concern won out, propped up on curiosity and bolstered
by the more immediate fact that the guy seemed to be out
cold—at the very least—and likely to freeze to death if the
fall hadn't killed him.

Alex's cabin sat at the head of a valley about a mile
wide and two long. She'd been a good half mile away from
home, collecting deadfalls, when she'd spotted the cat. Not
a long distance for an able-bodied woman wearing cold-
weather gear. Too far for an unconscious man without even
a coat.

She didn't know what kind of man he was, but if he was
still alive, she couldn't leave him to die. That didn't mean
she intended to be foolhardy.

Jackass had ambled down the hill when she'd whistled,
stopping not far away. Alex hung the phone over the saddle
horn—ignoring the fact that it was ringing again—and
pulled the rifle from its saddle scabbard. Jackass looked
back at her as if to say, *You really think you're going to need
that?*

"He dropped out of a plane," Alex said, racking the gun
so a shell was in the chamber. "I can come up with any
number of reasons for that. None of them are good."

Jackass snorted his agreement, waiting patiently while
she strapped on her snowshoes, untied the ropes, and
shoved the deadfalls she'd collected off the sled. Then he

followed without hesitation where she led. The perfect male.

"He's probably dead anyway," Alex said. "I heard something that sounded like gunshots just before I saw him drop. If whoever else was on the plane didn't kill him, I bet the fall did."

Jackass had no opinion about the likelihood they were standing next to a corpse, but it didn't take Alex long to find out. The man lay half on his side, twisted at the waist so he was chest down, both his arms beneath him and his left cheek resting on the snow. Alex stripped off her other glove and hunkered down beside him, hesitating when she got a good look at his face.

In all the speculating she'd done after he'd fallen, she'd never followed it up with the word "angel." He had the looks for it, though, jet-black hair, chiseled features, and a not-bad body to go along with the handsome face. Of course, Lucifer had fallen from heaven, too. If you subscribed to that sort of thing.

She kept her shotgun in her right hand, feeling with her left for the pulse in his neck. He still had one—which ruled out tying a rope to his ankle and letting Jackass drag him back to be stacked outside the cabin like cordwood. Dammit. She'd have to get him on the sled, and then she'd have to get him back to her cabin and lug him inside somehow. Alex had a feeling she wasn't going to enjoy any of that. He looked heavy. And he looked like trouble.

He didn't waste any time proving her right. She rolled him over and found herself looking down the barrel of a pistol. She went still, eyes crossed on a half-inch black hole that looked roughly the size of a cannon. It wasn't the first time she'd had a gun aimed at her. She'd never gotten used to it, and she was having the predictable reaction: ringing ears, pounding heart, the fight-or-flight spike of adrenaline.

It took a lot of effort to hold her ground and drag her gaze up to meet his, as piercing and feral as the cat's had been, although his eyes were blue instead of gold.

"Back off," he rasped, reaching for her rifle.

She handed it over, easing off a few steps.

He tried to clamber to his feet. He wasn't having much luck.

He wasn't looking very dangerous either, Alex decided the second time he sank to his knees. And then he got the brilliant idea to use her Winchester as a crutch. Alex stepped forward, but he waved her away. With the pistol.

"I'm trying to keep you from blowing your arm off," she said. "Or my head."

He'd made it to his feet, but he was obviously in pain and half out of it, weaving and fighting to stay conscious. He tucked the pistol in his waistband—on the second try—and pointed the rifle at her. Most of the time. Kind of hard to aim a gun when you could barely stand upright.

"You're practically unconscious," she said, although she wasn't quite brave enough to go for the gun. If it had just been the pistol he was holding on her, maybe, but a shotgun blast at fifteen feet was sure to hit her. "Put the guns down and let me help you before you freeze to death."

He blinked a couple of times, squinting fuzzily in her direction and mumbling something that sounded like "two to one."

"Either I've gotten really fat or you're seeing double," Alex said, reconsidering her decision to go for the gun.

He shook his head a couple of times, looking a lot more alert. "Just a girl," he said. "Not much of a threat."

"Neither are you."

"I've got the gun."

"And no coat, no idea where you are or how to get to safety," Alex pointed out, sounding a hell of a lot steadier than she felt. "You shoot me and we're both in trouble."

"I could take the horse."

Jackass swung his head around and nipped at him, just grazing his hip but sending him stumbling. He caught himself with the rifle, not giving Alex enough of an opening to try for either gun.

"Jackass doesn't let anyone but me ride him," she said,

"and even if he did, you're half-frozen already, not to mention you could be injured from falling out of the plane. Yep," she crossed her arms and nodded, "you're probably bleeding to death internally as we speak."

He slammed a hand flat against his chest, well, flat except for the pistol, moving it around like he was searching his insides for pumpers—until he caught her smirking. "Stop talking so much and get us out of here." He pointed the gun at her again, but he was clearly on his way back to oblivion, shivering uncontrollably and struggling to keep his eyes from rolling back in his head.

"Why should I help you? You can barely stand upright. All I have to do is wait . . ."

He looked up at the sky at the same time Alex heard the plane again. "That's why," he said, and then he fell on his face in the snow, unconscious.

This time Alex hesitated, weighing the intelligence of rescuing a man who'd just pulled a gun on her against the possibility he wouldn't survive the guys in the plane long enough for hypothermia to do him in.

She didn't debate for long. "He didn't even have the courtesy to collapse onto the sled," she said to Jackass, her voice shaking in the aftermath of having a gun pointed at her.

She forced herself to ignore the plane coming closer, to stop and take a few precious seconds to calm herself. Then she led Jackass around until the supply sled was lined up where she wanted it. She rolled the man over, took her rifle and stuffed his gun in her pocket, then shoved and tugged until he was sprawled on the sled, except his head and shoulders. She straddled him and the sled, fisted her hands in the front of his shirt and jerked him up and over in one fast Russian-weight-lifter move.

His head bounced on the wood, he groaned, and Jackass looked around at her. "He's dead weight and I'm doing the best I can," Alex said. "I'm not Wonder Woman, you know."

"Who are you?"

She looked down into those amazing, fallen-angel blue

eyes and experienced a minor, and completely internal, earthquake. He could probably stop most women in their tracks with one look from those eyes.

Alex wasn't most women. It took a whole lot more than a set of gorgeous eyes in a to-die-for face to get her attention. It even took more than a spontaneous orgasm.

It took character. Not being in possible mortal danger would be a plus, too.

The whine of the plane engine closing on their position reminded her that this man probably had a bad character. He looked like the kind of guy who'd charm old women out of their annuities and young women out of their trust funds—and their panties. The kind of guy who'd be dumped out of a plane by shady acquaintances.

And speaking of planes, the one she was currently hearing had just appeared over the crest of the hill. Alex peered through the still-falling snow; the angle was different, but she was pretty sure it was the same plane, and now that she got a good look at it, she had a bad feeling about it. The not-a-coincidence feeling.

The plane was an airvan, the kind of boxy, flying school bus used for skydivers. The type of plane with a door on the side that slid open really easily, with handy loops for the occupants to hold on to while they contemplated the chance they were wearing a working parachute versus the possibility of ending their life as a grease stain on the landscape. The loops also worked out well for guys with guns to grasp on to while they sprayed the ground below with bullets.

Great, Alex thought, suddenly sure the man on the sled had a bad character since his shady acquaintances had come back to finish the job. And she didn't think they'd care if she and Jackass got in the way. In fact she had a sneaking suspicion they'd prefer it.

She grabbed her shotgun, pointed it skyward in the plane's general direction, and squeezed off a couple of shots. She didn't have any real hope of hitting the plane, but she wanted whoever might be tempted to shoot at them to know she was armed. The plane veered away and up above the trees, but apparently she didn't pose that much of a threat because it went a ways off and started to loop back around. Which gave Alex all of ten seconds to make a decision.

She could cut the sled loose, hop on Jackass, and get away under cover of the trees while the guys in the plane took out their primary target. But she was already tugging at the horse's bridle. It went against the grain to leave someone helpless out in the open like a shooting gallery duck. Even after he'd stuck a gun in her face.

She was a good fifty yards from the trees, and her snow-shoes were made to walk in, not run. If she took them off she wouldn't be going much faster, not in a couple of feet of wet snow. All she could do was slog along at a shuffling trot, hoping like hell it took the homicidal plane a while to get back and that the guys inside would aim at the sled first. Okay, so she couldn't leave him out there like a big spread-eagle "shoot me" sign; that didn't mean she was prepared to give up her life for him. Or her horse's life. And since Jackass was the bigger target and more likely to get hit than either of the people around him, Alex stepped up the pace to a point where she was in danger of falling on her face at any second.

She managed to make it into the trees just as the first bullet kicked up snow behind the sled. The plane veered off again, and Alex threaded their way into the thickest part of the forest she could find, belatedly checking to make sure her cargo hadn't rolled off somewhere along the way. He was still there, and if she was cold and wet, he wasn't going to survive very long.

She would have preferred to stay out of sight a little longer, just in case, but again her only choice was to risk a run for the cabin. Thankfully it appeared the plane was fi-nally leaving, judging from the faintness of the engine.

She covered the half mile to the house as fast as she could, unhooked the sled by the front door, and took Jack-ass around to his nice, warm stable, wishing, for the first time, the horse was a man. Even her ex-fiancé, bastard that he was, would be welcome. Nope. There was never a good reason to think about Bennet Harper. If she were dying of kidney failure and he was the only living donor, she wouldn't want him back in her life. She'd have to find a way, all by herself, to get this guy inside before he turned into an icicle.

For once that day, something went right. He was awake—at least halfway, moaning and shivering and trying to get up. "C'mon," Alex yelled at him. "You can do it."

He made an effort, she had to give him that, but he just couldn't manage on his own. Sighing, she picked up an arm and tugged until he got his wobbly knees under him. Then she half dragged him inside, stopping just over the threshold and wondering what in blazes she was going to do with him.

And if the plane was going to come back and make the decision unnecessary.

chapter
2

TAG DONOVAN WOKE UP AND SAW LOGS. LOG ceiling, log walls, log door. He cast his memory back, trying to see where logs fit into the last twenty-four hours. There was a plane, there was shooting, there was a short fall and an agony-of-defeat landing. Nothing after that. Logic told him he ought to be looking at the sky. Or burning in hellfire, if he believed what his Irish Catholic upbringing had drummed into his head.

Somehow, though, he wasn't dead. He took another tour through his recollection of the last few hours and came up with the fuzzy memory of a woman with a smart mouth and no appreciation for danger. The only clear visual was a set of sharp eyes the color of storm clouds. The audio portion of the memory consisted of a voice, low, smoky, not the kind of voice that brought logs to mind. Not the kind voice that brought anything to *mind*, actually. What it inspired was more . . . visceral. And he was in no shape for visceral.

Maybe the woman with the smoky voice had been a figment of his imagination and he'd been rescued by lumberjacks. She'd been yelling at him, so it wouldn't be a complete tragedy if he'd invented her, because when she yelled at him his head hurt.

His head hurt when he tried to lift it, too, and when he stopped trying to lift it. And when he blinked his eyes. His head hurt all the time; it was just a matter of intensity. He reached automatically to cradle his skull and nearly forgot about the pain when he discovered his hands were tied. So were his feet.

He was lying on a bed made of logs; there was a pillow beneath his head and a blanket slung over him, and he was tied up. Except for his boxers he saw that he was naked, once he could think about more than how much everything hurt.

Now he was really hoping it was a woman who'd rescued him, because if it was lumberjacks, he didn't want to know how he'd gotten out of his clothes. He didn't like his odds of talking his way out of the ropes either. And he needed to get out of the ropes.

It was imperative in fact, so imperative he sucked up his courage and turned his head. It notched the headache back up to excruciating, but once he could get his eyes to uncross it was worth it because, sure enough, there was a woman watching him from the hearth beside a large fieldstone fireplace.

"Cinderella?" he croaked.

"Alex."

Her voice was smoky, like he remembered, and she wasn't yelling at him, which was hopeful. "Any chance you'll untie me, Alex?" His throat might be dry, but the rest of him wasn't going to be if he didn't get some relief.

"Nope."

"Then you'd better get me a bottle. An empty bottle."

She quirked an eyebrow and tried not to smile. "And I don't even know your name."

"Tag."

"As in, 'you're it'?"

"Yeah, I've never heard that one before."

"It's your name. Don't blame me."

"It's Irish," Tag said, because in his book that explained everything. "The bottle?"

She stood up, putting her face in shadow and the rest of her in the light. She had the body to go along with the sexy voice; it was the first thing he noticed, and he wasn't happy about it—not her body, the fact that he'd been sidetracked by it.

So what if she was tall and slim (healthy slim rather than starvation chic)? So what if he caught the hint of some intriguing curves under her baggy sweatshirt and jeans? He needed to concentrate on the important things. Like what kind of woman she was.

Her clothing was well-worn, for instance. So were her hiking boots; and the rest of her was no muss, no fuss, from her cropped blond-streaked hair to her sensibly short fingernails. She was either practical or broke. Or both. And she was strong, strong enough to somehow get 180 pounds of dead weight out of the snow and onto this bed. And it didn't stop there.

She took something off a shelf and crossed the room, her movements unhurried, efficient, effortless. And silent, except for the slightest suggestion of hollowness when her boot heels contacted the wooden floor. It was kind of unnerving how quietly she moved. Her face was quiet, too. It was an attractive face, not beautiful but strong, a face that would age well, he thought. The fine lines at the corners of her eyes only made her look calmer, more comfortable in her own skin.

Those lines must've been from the sun, though, because he'd yet to see her smile or frown, or do more than quirk an eyebrow. Cool, calm, and collected was the phrase that came to mind. If you didn't look her in the eye. Pure steel there—even the color, slate gray, made it seem like a storm was brewing inside her all the time, just waiting for some unsuspecting clod to come along and salt the clouds.

She was exactly the kind of woman Tag usually steered clear of. Unfortunately that wasn't an option this time. He was there for a reason, but aside from the snowdrifts that had saved his ass, he wasn't sure what he'd jumped into. Except he knew it was trouble.

Ordinarily he liked trouble. The right kind made things more interesting, not to mention exciting. At the moment, however, he had a very definite agenda, and getting tossed out of a plane into the lap of a strange woman with unknown affiliations wasn't anywhere on the list.

He fought for patience, but he knew he was losing it, hands and feet straining against the ropes, Alex's face disappearing behind a tide of red. This was supposed to be a fluff assignment, something to keep him busy while he got over the murder of his partner, and now this? He was stuck, powerless, dumped into a situation he knew nothing about except that he needed to gain Alex's cooperation if he had any hope of solving the case.

All he wanted was to get the hell out of there and find out who'd killed his best friend before the trail got too cold to follow. That brought on another surge of anger—which ended when he heard the distinctive sound of a shotgun being racked to slam a shell into the firing chamber. But it wasn't pointed at him, he noticed when he managed to focus on Alex again.

"You were looking a little hysterical," she said, holding up her Winchester by way of explanation. "This seemed a better solution than a slap in the face."

And a hell of a reminder that she had the upper hand. At the moment. Tag lay back, got his breathing under control, and let the anger settle like ice in the pit of his stomach while he put his head back into the game. The others would be waiting for him when he got out of this mess, he told himself, and if his handler thought time and distance would help him get over losing his partner, he was wrong. Revenge—now that would be a start.

"Your bottle."

He looked up, studied the pop bottle she was holding while he put the past back in the past. Better to focus on the present. In fact, focusing on the present was becoming a dire emergency. "Got anything with a wider opening?"

"Your aim that bad?"

"It has nothing to do with aim."

She dropped it beside him and crossed her arms.

"Fine. It's your bed," he reminded her. "You planning to stand there and watch?"

"I'm kind of curious to see why you think you need a bigger bottle."

"You undressed me. Don't you already know the answer to that?"

She held his eyes for a second, and then her gaze panned down, stopping at the body part in question. She looked like she had a pretty good idea what was inside his boxers, and her expression could best be described as unimpressed.

"I was cold," Tag objected, "and unconscious."

"Whatever you say."

Tag ground his teeth together, and then he noticed the way her eyes were sparkling. "I could do better than a visual," he said, looking at the ropes around his wrists. "Even with a handicap."

"Says the man with an inferiority complex and something to prove."

"I don't have an inferiority complex. And I don't have anything to prove."

"Good, then you won't mind if I take a pass."

"I'll mind if you don't untie me," he said, "at least long enough to test my aim."

She'd already started across the room. She stopped and looked back at him for a long moment, then returned, bringing the shotgun back with her. Tag added cautious to her list of character flaws.

"You really think you're going to need that?" he asked, his eyes on the Winchester. "I'm actually harmless."

"Now that I took away the pistol you stuck in my face."

He met her eyes, grinning. He'd thought he'd lost everything between the plane and the bed, but some of it was coming back to him—well, mostly what was coming back to him was him half-dead, and still trying to protect himself. "Not bad for a guy who just had a near-death experience," he said.

She rolled her eyes. "It was a toss-up whether you were going to shoot me or blow your arm off, since you were trying to use my rifle as a crutch."

"That's right, I took your gun away from you, too."

"And then you passed out, and I got both guns."

"I can see how happy that makes you. And since you have all the firepower," he held up his hands, "I promise I won't make any sudden moves."

"And I should believe you why?"

"I just fell out of an airplane. About all I can do right now is lie here and look pretty."

"Nothing wrong with your ego." She set the gun down on her left, away from him, the barrel resting against the side of the bed. She untied his hands, stuffed the rope into her back pocket, then picked up the gun again. Her eyes never wavered from his. "Except the way you came by it."

"Meaning?"

"At the expense of other people. Probably women."

She went back to the fireplace, leaving Tag to replay the conversation and wonder where it had taken a left turn from joking and sarcasm to her slapping him down. Must be a cynical streak hiding behind that matter-of-fact exterior, he decided. And it wasn't because of something he'd done. Not that he hadn't left a woman or two with a heightened level of . . . resentment. But he hadn't done anything to Alex. Aside from the gun thing. "I'll bet there's a man in your past," he concluded.

"You had a mission, remember?" She looked pointedly at the pop bottle, then confined her attention to the fire, poking around in it and adding more logs. The cabin was one room, big enough for a sleeping area and a living/work area, small enough to be warmed by the single fireplace. Barely manageable for bodily functions involving strangers.

Alex stayed by the fireplace, making cover noise by

poking at the logs but keeping him in her peripheral vision so he didn't try any funny business. He didn't know her story, but whatever it was it had left her pretty suspicious. He'd barely set the pop bottle down on the opposite side of the bed when she picked up the interrogation again.

"So what's your story?" she asked.

"You first." When she didn't answer, he popped up an eyebrow.

She mugged back at him, but he could see she was amused. She wasn't, however, wordy. "I grew up, went to college, and got a grant to come out here and study mountain lions," she said. "Just the normal stuff—except for the Miss USA thing." She did the royal wave. "But that was before I got my PhD."

Tag snorted. "You should tell people you were a stand-up comic. That I'd buy."

"You don't believe me?" She pressed a hand to her heart. "I'm devastated."

Her expression was so perfectly deadpan, Tag couldn't help but laugh.

"So?" she prompted. "What about you?"

"I don't know," he said, "I don't have anything as exciting as being a beauty queen to show for my life."

"Well, we can't all be gorgeous and talented, but you got dumped out of a plane without a parachute. You could start there."

"Is that coffee I smell?"

Up went that damn eyebrow. "Is that evasion I hear?"

"It's caffeine withdrawal."

"Then by all means, let's take care of that," Alex said. "Wouldn't want you to succumb to your addiction before you satisfy my curiosity."

She did some more stuff by the fire, then brought him a cup and a bowl. The bowl was filled with gray slop, which he promptly handed back to her. He'd had enough oatmeal in his childhood to stucco the Washington Monument. Besides, the cup was sending off little tendrils of steam that made his nostrils twitch in anticipation. She handed it to him. He ignored the headache long enough to lever himself up and take a healthy gulp. The minute it hit his tongue he opened his mouth over the cup and let the coffee trickle back out.

"Hot?" she asked.

"Crappy," he said. "Do you actually drink this stuff?"

"I did yesterday. I didn't get around to cleaning the pot before I went out this morning, so it's been sitting on the hearth for twenty-four hours, give or take."

"Give or take?"

She shrugged. "I figured a guy who could survive a header out of an airplane could drink day-old coffee."

"That's not coffee," Tag said. "I'm not sure it even qualifies as a liquid."

"Rocky Mountain espresso." She took the cup from him and set it down on a small table beside the bed. "No self-respecting cowboy would turn his nose up. But you're not a cowboy, are you? Or even a Westerner, for that matter."

"You're not exactly the kind of woman I normally associate with either."

"Why? Because I don't charge?"

"Because you carry a gun."

"So do you," she reminded him. "So where are you from and what do you do that you need one?"

He huffed out a breath. "Anybody ever mention dogs and bones around you?"

She raised her chin and looked down her nose at him, and Tag could feel his face heating. He knew that look. He hated that look. She might be broke and alone in the middle of nowhere, but she'd come by way of a society drawing room. Could be Washington, DC, could be New York, but every now and then he heard a hint of broadness in her vowels, so he'd put his money on Boston.

"You haven't answered my question," she said in a tone of voice that went with the expression on her face.

"It's not important."

She took her time digesting that. Her eyes were on him the whole while, and he had to battle the urge to fidget.

"Let's start with something easy," she finally said. "Do you have a last name?"

"Donovan."

"Good. No hesitation, and it goes with the Irish theme. Donovan might actually be your last name. Care to tell me why you fell out of that airplane? Or did you jump?"

"Why would I jump?"

"Gee, I don't know, because someone was shooting at you?"

"You've got good ears," Tag said. And a good brain, the kind that read between the lines instead of taking a story at face value.

"Well?" she said. "Why the gun, why the plane, and why did you get tossed out?"

"It's better for both of us if I don't answer those questions."

"Ignorance is bliss?"

"Something like that."

"Funny," Alex said, "it feels a lot like I'm the only one who's ignorant and you're the only one it benefits."

"I can't help that," Tag said. Even if he'd been a hundred percent sure she could be trusted, FBI protocol had to be followed. He was undercover; he couldn't break cover unless absolutely necessary, and he couldn't tell her the truth without breaking cover. Lying wasn't an option, either. He didn't know enough about her yet to feed her a believable story. "If I told you what was going on you wouldn't believe me anyway. All you'd have to go on is my word, and you've made it clear that's not good enough."

She opened her mouth, then snapped it shut again, and he knew he had her.

"If you don't mind, I'd like to get some rest." Tag let his eyes drift shut, but he could feel her watching him. Skeptically. It pissed him off. "I fell out of a plane, remember?"

"Yeah. I was there. You dropped thirty-five feet, forty at

most, into the equivalent of a twenty-inch-thick feather mattress. Not the softest landing, but you survived it. You weren't even hurt except for some bruises. If you're going to complain about something, maybe you should try crabbing about the fact that they came back and shot the place up, just in case the fall didn't kill you. Of course, you dodged that bullet, too. Literally."

"Wait, what?" Tag reared up, fighting his way past the stab of pain in his head. "They came back?"

"And shot at you." Alex folded one leg under her backside and sat at the foot of the bed. "You don't remember that part because you'd already fainted."

"Passed out," he corrected her. "I'm lucky my brains aren't permanently scrambled."

"You're lucky there was a couple of feet of snow this late in the season, although it almost got me killed. I don't think they cared if they hit me, as long as they got you."

Tag didn't say anything, busy looking at the situation in a whole new light. Unfortunately, the new light didn't provide any additional illumination. All it did was create shadows, and every one of the shadows was a complication that was going to take time to work through.

He wasn't in this position by accident. Okay, being tied up in Alex's bed wasn't exactly intentional, but he'd been dropped on her purposely, to gain her sympathy. That's what the guys in the plane had told him, right before they'd shot at him to convince him jumping was actually the smart option.

He figured the second round of shooting was for Alex's sake, but if that was the case she was being severely underestimated. She'd saved him, but she didn't trust him, and no amount of gunfire was going to change that. Not that he was jumping on the trust bandwagon, either; her being evasive about her past wasn't exactly giving him the warm fuzzies.

So far he'd been able to figure out she was from Boston, but that only sparked all kinds of new questions. Harder

questions, ones only she could answer, and she was clearly
not in a talkative mood. Ever.

He looked at Alex and found the same kind of specula-
tion in her gaze that must be on his face. And the same
wariness.

"They who?" she said.

He rolled his eyes, instantly regretting it. "You were
shot at and you still want to know what's going on? Jesus,
what'll it take to get through to you?"

"It's not like they're coming back any time soon. They
can't land a plane here. Maybe a helicopter, but they won't
risk that, seeing as it's almost nightfall. And they can't
come by land, not without someone to guide them. I'm not
exactly listed on the maps."

"So we have some breathing room. Not that you need
breathing room. You'll be safe once I'm gone." He fed her
the lie with an absolutely straight face. Of course she didn't
buy it.

"First," she said, "even if you had suitable clothing and
the first clue how to get to safety, you're not in any shape to
leave. Second, they tried to kill me once, just because I was
in the way. I don't think they're going to be too happy that
I rescued you. In fact, I imagine they consider me a problem, and they appear to be the kind of people who find permanent solutions to their problems."

Tag shut his eyes and lay back, really tired this time, exhausted by the day's events and the ramifications of the fix
he'd gotten himself into.

The mattress jiggled as she stood. Thank God she'd finally taken the hint because he couldn't think anymore,
and she wasn't the kind of woman he should be talking to
without the benefit of forethought. And then he felt her slip
the ropes around his wrists and realized forethought had
deserted him some time ago. She'd been sitting within
reach for the last ten minutes. Sure the rifle was right there,
but even with a killer headache and a sore . . . everything,
he could have gotten to her before she got to it. Before she
got it pointed at him, at any rate.

"You're cutting off the circulation," Tag said as she tightened the ropes. "Do you really have to do that?"

"Yes." She tied the knot off and tucked the ends of the rope between his wrists for good measure. "Unless you can convince me there's no reason for it."

He heaved a sigh. "I feel like I've landed in a Stephen King novel. There's not a typewriter around here, is there?"

She gave a slight laugh. "Fiction isn't going to get you out of those ropes, but you might try the truth."

"I'm not a threat to you," Tag said. "They were shooting at me, remember?"

"That doesn't prove anything. Maybe they were FBI agents and you're an escaped criminal."

"They're not FBI. They're not law enforcement of any kind."

"If they're not good guys, they're bad guys, and you knew that when you got mixed up with them."

"They didn't exactly give me a choice."

She thought about that for a minute, those wintry eyes steady on his face and searching. Then she shook her head. "You're not the kind of man who gets caught up in circumstances beyond his control."

"You sure about that, or is it just that you're the kind of woman who sees every man through a filter of bitterness?"

That eyebrow inched up again, but the mouth wasn't reflecting humor. The mouth trembled, just a bit, before she pressed her lips together. Worse, he could see the doubt in her eyes. Before he could identify what he was feeling as guilt, get past the shock, and decide what to do about it, she bounced back.

"Good try, Svengali," she said. "And thanks for convincing me I'm right. You knew exactly what type of people you were hooking up with, which tells me you're an ends-justify-the-means kind of guy. You ought to be more careful who you jump into bed with."

"Climb in here and give me a chance to improve my record."

She smiled then, for the first time, and Tag shook off the

feeling he'd seen her somewhere before. The smile took her face to pretty, even if what that smile said about him wasn't.

"The only thing I want from you is your absence," she said. "And since I don't trust you enough to let you loose, I guess I'll have to take care of that myself."

chapter
3

ALEX PUT THE GUN DOWN NEXT TO A TABLE SET under the single window by the door, and unhooked a radio microphone.

"Now what are you up to?" Tag wanted to know.

"Talking to you turned out to be a waste of time. That doesn't mean the questions went away." She held up the microphone, gave him a minute.

He just smiled at her, eyes sparkling, handsome as sin, looking so sincere she wouldn't have been surprised to see his eyetooth glint.

If he hadn't been shot at by questionable associates, fallen out of an airplane, and pointed a gun at her, she'd believe any sob story he dished up. And wasn't that pathetic, considering she'd almost married the biggest con man this side of Pluto?

"MLR1 to Casteel Base," she said, shoving her ex-fiancé back into the dungeon of her brain, where he was eternally tortured for his sins. Tag Donovan she was keeping right where she could see him.

"MLR1, this is Casteel Base. Hey Alex," Matt Harrison

said. "How's the wood holding up? I was worried about you with the snow."

"Has he actually met you?" Tag muttered.

She ignored him. "Everything's fine, Matt. How's the best sheriff this side of the Mississippi?" This time she slid a glance Tag's way. A smug glance.

He still looked like he could have cared less, but she knew he was thinking *crap, the guy on the other end of the radio is the local cop.*

"Great, now that I get to talk to you," Matt said, and her smirk turned into a heavy sigh.

They'd had a casual romance during the second summer of her four years in Colorado. She was still trying to convince Matt it was over.

"Listen," she said, "there's a man here, says his name's Tag Donovan."

"A man?" She could all but see Matt jumping to his feet, a scowl on his honest, square face, his protective instincts going into overdrive. "How the hell did a man get there?"

"You wouldn't believe me if I told you."

"Try me."

"He fell out of a plane." And before Matt could pepper her with questions, she told him the rest. He was predictably stuffy about it. And insulting.

Judging from the way he bit off each individual word, she suspected he might be angry, too. "You shouldn't have gone anywhere near him."

Nope, not angry, she concluded. Pissed off. "It's not every day a man drops out of a plane," she pointed out.

"So you're saying you were curious?"

"Isn't there some saying about curiosity and cats?" Tag asked, grinning.

"Mostly I figured there was a good chance he was dead so I didn't have anything to lose," Alex replied to Matt. Her response to Tag was visual.

"And when he wasn't dead, you felt compelled to save his life?" Matt asked.

"Would you have done differently?"

"I'm not a woman living alone with help a day away."

Alex took a second, the rage in Matt's voice making her rethink any objection to his macho attitude. "He's tied up."

"In her bed," Tag yelled.

"Do you want to die today?" she hissed at him.

"A day away, remember? He can't kill me until tomorrow. And he won't kill me anyway, he's a cop."

"He's not above beating the crap out of you. And I imagine there'd be something I had to do outside when he got here."

"You're a cold, mean woman."

"And proud of it."

"Alex?" Matt said. "I'm sorry. Over."

"No you're not." But at least he was calm enough to observe radio protocol.

"I'm sorry I got mad. But you should have called me before you went anywhere near that guy."

"If you're done criticizing, maybe you could check him out," she said to Matt. "He might not be the mass murderer you think he is."

"I'll do more than check him out. I'll take him off your hands."

"You won't be able to do that until tomorrow," Alex said. "In the meantime, run him and see what's what, okay? Over."

Matt asked for Tag's name again, and Alex repeated it.

"Spelled just like it sounds," Tag said, adding after she signed off, "he has a crush on you."

"Worried?"

"Grateful. I figure that means he'll get back to you right away, and once you learn I'm not a threat you can untie me."

"Let me know if he does," Alex said, and set to layering on snow gear, starting with wool socks, quilted pants, and a down vest.

"Where are you going?"

"Out."

"You're going to leave me here all alone? Trussed up like a Christmas turkey?"

"If the rope fits," she said with a half smile. "I have to go take care of Jackass before it gets full dark."

"I'm afraid to ask. But whatever Jackass is, I'm willing to bet it's male."

"Jackass is my horse."

Tag caught the affection that crossed her face, no more than a flicker, and realized he was learning to read her. It went a long way toward restoring his confidence.

"I put him in the stable, but he needs to be fed and rubbed down, and there's nobody else to do it."

"Why do you live all the way out here, anyway?" he asked. "Besides your complete disdain for other human beings."

"Now I'm supposed to get all defensive, right? Prove you wrong by untying you?"

"Not yet, but that was the ultimate goal."

"Well, gosh, I'd love to accommodate you, but my complete disdain for other human beings is too strong. Not to mention the fact that you're keeping secrets."

"You haven't exactly answered my questions. Why a cabin in the middle of nowhere?"

Alex took off the hiking boots she was wearing and tugged on a pair of heavier ones, then stood and went to the row of pegs by the door. "I'm out here on a grant to study mountain lions."

"Sounds dangerous."

"Only to the cats," she said, taking a shearling coat off one of the pegs and shrugging into it. "The farmers and ranchers will kill them off, given half a chance, because the lions go after their livestock."

She pulled a knit hat over her hair, winding the long ends scarflike around her neck. "See how I don't have any trouble telling you what I'm doing because it's the truth?"

That was the mistake most people made, Tag knew, thinking that telling the truth was the right thing to do when it was a hell of a lot smarter to keep your mouth shut. There were people out there who could twist the most harmless scrap of information into a weapon. He'd learned that the hard way.

Alex picked up her rifle, slung it over her shoulder, hesitated for a second, then clipped the satellite phone to her belt. "Rest up, Irish," she said. "When I get back I'll see if I can whip up something more appetizing than oatmeal. I'm leaving the dinner conversation to you. Make it interesting."

ALEX BUSTLED AROUND THE CORRAL, DOING HER EVEning chores the same way, in the same order she'd done them every night for the last four years. It felt good, comforting, considering the rest of her life had taken a sharp left turn from normal. Okay, more like she'd gone a whole planet away from normal. Things couldn't be weirder if she'd been beamed up by aliens.

Sad to say, the weirdest part of all was having a man in her bed. A man who was tied up and naked, except for his boxers, and leaving him those had been more of a struggle than she cared to admit. And, all right, she'd peeked. Once she'd gotten an eyeful of the muscles he'd been hiding under his preppy clothes it had been too tempting not to lift the waistband of his silk boxers and see if the rest him lived up to the advertising.

Her mouth went dry and her pulse spiked just remembering. Normally she would have felt a little slutty about that, but considering the circumstances she only felt stupid.

So what if Tag Donovan was movie-star handsome, action star buff, and porn star . . . Nope, not going there.

He'd fallen out of a plane, she reminded herself. He'd pointed a gun at her when she'd tried to rescue him, and withheld information that, at the very least, she probably needed to know in order to protect herself. He was too charming, too slick for her taste.

And yet she was smiling. She would have thunked her head against the wall—several times—but apparently her brains were already scrambled enough. What she'd been through would have turned Pollyanna into a pessimist, but not Alex Scott. No, she still wanted to see the best in people.

She had a feeling the best of Tag Donovan would be spectacular. As long as a woman didn't believe it was real. Or that it would last.

There was no chance of that in her case. The only thing she wanted was to see the last of him.

But suppose he was telling the truth? Suppose her ignorance was for her own protection? She found it hard to buy, but was that cynicism or a gut feeling? Either way it was a possibility she had to consider.

She needed to find out what he was up to before he left. Her life might depend on it—and yeah, she was curious, too. Who wouldn't wonder why some random guy fell out of a plane after being shot at? Who wouldn't want to know why the shooters had come back and tried to finish the job? And if they'd be looking for her after Donovan was long gone?

He hadn't told her anything, but that wouldn't matter to them. It mattered to her.

"I don't like being kept in the dark," she said to Jackass. "And look at what he put you through. Standing out here in the cold without being rubbed down. And after we rescued him. Some people have no sense of gratitude."

Jackass rolled his eyes and nickered, which could have meant anything from "we're both in the dark"—it being nighttime and horses being literal creatures—to "I'm hungry." She had to admit the latter was more plausible, since he fell on the oats she ladled out like he was starving to death.

She knew how he felt.

Her dinner, unfortunately, would have to wait because the minute she opened her front door an arm shot through and dragged her inside by the coat front. Her Winchester was pulled out of her hand and she was shoved, stumbling, into the cabin. Tag Donovan, dressed in his own rumpled and half-damp clothing, his pistol in his waistband, shut the door and stood between her and it.

"You always talk to your horse?"

She raised an eyebrow, which was easier than it should have been with a gun in her face and panic spiking through her bloodstream. Then again, the gun wasn't in her face, exactly. It wasn't even aimed at her.

Tag was actually using it to point at the back wall, the one the cabin shared with the stable. "Don't know what you were saying," he continued, "but I could hear your voice."

She looked around, saw the beer bottle by the bed, broken. That explained a lot. "I hope that was empty."

"You didn't leave me much choice. I couldn't get at the knots with my teeth, the way you tucked the ends between my wrists and tied them so tight."

The interchange—seeing as it didn't contain gunfire—steadied her nerves. "Guess I didn't think of everything," she said, edging to one side as she talked, trying not to be obvious.

"Don't bother," he said, pointing the gun at the radio. "I disabled it."

"Which means you don't want to shoot me."

"True, but I'm not so sure about you. And since the least you'll do is tie me up again, I think I'll hang on to the guns."

He was between her and the only exit, but Alex kept her snow gear on anyway. There wasn't much chance she'd be able to get one of the guns from him. That meant her most likely escape was going to put her outside.

She went to the haphazard stack of boxes in the corner, digging out some power bars and flipping him one, deliberately high. When he looked up to catch it she slipped a couple more in her pocket.

"What's this?" Tag asked.

"Dinner."

He studied it for a second then chucked it over his shoulder, pulled out a chocolate bar, and unwrapped it. "This," he took a huge bite and talked around it, "is dinner. Or at least a respectable dessert."

Alex went still, keeping her eyes off the chocolate and on Tag. "You went through my things." Pretty thoroughly if he'd found the stash of candy bars she kept in a place that was difficult for even her to get to.

"Yep. You were holding out on me." He brandished the candy bar by way of explanation. "And you have boring taste in lingerie."

"You didn't find that in my underwear drawer."

Tag just grinned.

"You try riding a horse and hiking all day in lace panties and you'll learn the true meaning of chafing."

"Gosh, that sounds fun, but I left all my lace panties at home." He took another bite of chocolate.

Alex's mouth watered, and her thigh muscles started quivering.

"You want one?" Tag asked her.

"I'll stick with this, thanks." She unwrapped her power bar and bit into it, trying to chew like it didn't bear a closer resemblance to Jackass's dinner than Tag's. "So now what?"

"How far is it to the nearest town?"

Alex wandered to the bed, leaned against the sturdy log footboard. "Why should I answer your questions?"

"You want me gone, I'm trying to leave."

"Not with my rifle, you're not."

"Fine, you can have it back," he said, although he didn't hand it over. "I'll take the horse."

"You can do that, but he's a horse, not a homing pigeon. He isn't trained to start at one place and end up at another. He goes where you tell him to go, or he stands still."

"I'll take my chances."

"Okay."

"You're not going to try to stop me?"

She shrugged. "I'll track you in the morning."

"I'll be long gone by then."

"You'll be dead by then. It'll drop well below freezing tonight, and it's dark out there—and not city dark, either. No ambient light, and a nice heavy cloud cover so no moon or stars. You won't be able to see your hand in front of your face.

"It's seventy-five miles to the nearest town," she continued between bites. "My coat won't fit you, so how are you going to stay warm? And even if you make it that far, the town consists of a half-dozen businesses, a few homes, and the sheriff's office. What do you think the chances are that A," she ticked off on her fingers, "they don't know Jackass on sight, B, they won't ask you how you came by him, and C, you won't end up in jail within thirty minutes of your arrival?"

Tag blew out a breath, leaning back against the door. "Got all the angles figured, don't you?"

"They're not angles, they're facts. That's the difference between you and me, Donovan. I deal with reality, you seem to think you can create your own."

"This is dealing with reality? Seems to me you're running away from reality."

"You don't know anything about my life."

"And you don't know anything about mine. If you want to stay here and bury your head in the sand, that's fine with me. I got dragged into this thing and I'm going to do every damn thing I can to get out of it in one piece. If you had any sense you'd do the same."

Alex opened her mouth to fire back at him, but he held up a hand.

"Shut up," he said, which would have fueled her temper if she hadn't heard what he'd heard. Another engine, but not a plane. Far, far worse than a plane.

Just like that her anger iced over. She exchanged a look with Tag, and suddenly they weren't opponents anymore. They weren't exactly friends, either, but they were in the same boat, and if they didn't want it to sink under them they were going to have to row together.

"Looks like you were wrong about the helicopter."

She stared at him, speechless, if only for a second before indignation kicked in. "So I was wrong. Why are you listening to me anyway? This is my first experience with . . . I don't even know what this is."

He slung the rifle over his shoulder by its strap. "Don't go near the window."

"I'm not stupid." But she was afraid, and she didn't like it. "The roof is made of logs at least twelve inches thick. Bullets aren't getting through."

Right on cue, something thumped on the roof. She didn't know how she managed to hear it around the distinctive whump-whump-whump of helicopter blades, Jackass whinnying and banging in his stable, and the roar of the fireplace from the constant change in air pressure outside, but she did. So did Tag. Both sets of eyes swiveled up then down to collide again, both brains coming to the same conclusion. They weren't shooting.

Tag voiced his suspicion first. "What about fire?"

"There's a foot of wet snow on top of the roof," Alex said.

Tag moved to the door, eased it open, and pointed his pistol up in the air, taking a couple of wild shots at the helicopter.

Alex heard the bullets ping off metal, then a couple more thuds, a muffled whoosh, and the sound of the helicopter beginning to fade.

Tag stepped all the way outside and took a cautious look around the corner of the cabin. "I think it's gone," he said, coming back inside, "but we have another problem. There was a pile of hay on this side of the cabin."

"Was?"

Right on cue smoke began to curl between the chinks in the logs.

"I wish I could create my own reality now," Tag said.

"You can't, so I guess you'll have to come with me." Alex headed for the door. "According to you I'm good at running away."

Tag gave her a look. "You're never going to let me forget that, are you?"

"We aren't going to know each other long enough for never."

"Maybe we could put out the fire before we part company," Tag deadpanned.

She shook her head and walked to the door, listening for

a second. No whump-whump, so she crooked her finger for Tag to follow her outside. They stood shoulder to shoulder a couple of seconds, watching the conflagration race up the haystack. Before a full minute had passed, the entire wall was ablaze and the flames were starting on the roof. The snowmelt dripping off the eaves did nothing but create steam to add to the smoke curling into the sky.

"This cabin is about a hundred and fifty years old," Alex said.

"That explains the lack of plumbing."

"Exactly. What are you going to put the fire out with? Snow? Or maybe you think we can open bottles of water fast enough to soak wood that's been drying out for a century and a half and was just hit with a gas bomb?"

He caught her around the waist and shoved her toward the cabin's front door. "You better get whatever you want out of there while you still can."

Alex dashed inside and grabbed her emergency pack—flashlight, flares, first aid kit—and the satchel that held her important papers. Tag was right behind her, but he wasn't doing anything useful. "I'd suggest you get the blankets off the bed," she said to him on her way out the door. "You're going to need them."

By the time she came around front with Jackass half saddled and dragging the supply sled, Tag was coming out of the cabin, one blanket over his head and another wadded up in his arms. "Supplies," he said, opening the blanket to show her about a dozen bottles of water and a case of power bars.

She took six bottles and shoved three into each of the saddlebags, then put some power bars in her pockets.

"What about the rest of it?" Tag wanted to know.

"This isn't Donner Pass," Alex said. "Trust me, I know how to pack for a trip. I've had all that experience, remember?"

"I take it back," Tag said. "I've only been with you for a few hours and it already feels like forever."

Alex opened her mouth, but the sound of the helicopter

stuffed the witticism back down her throat. Or maybe it was her heart she was choking on, because it was sure as hell trying to jump out of her chest. She spun around, saw the copter lifting into the air at the other end of her valley.

Tag grabbed her by the wrist, but before he could decide which direction to manhandle her in, the helicopter zoomed off, heading away from the cabin. Alex was relieved—until she heard the growling whine of snowmobile motors. Her mouth was still open, but Tag found his voice first.

"Apparently that thing was carrying more than fire-bombs."

chapter
4

"DAMN," ALEX SAID TO TAG, HER EYES ON THE snowmobiles. "What did you do to tick them off? Besides being you?"

"That seems to be enough in this part of the world."

"You really think geography is the problem?"

"I'd love to stand here and debate my downturn in luck since I crossed the Mississippi," Tag said, "but you'd have to have an open mind first."

"You blow into my life and ruin it, and you can stand there and accuse me of being overly suspicious?"

"What do you want, another apology?"

"Yes, but it would be insincere, so I'll settle for having my rifle back."

He handed it over, no argument. That seemed odd until Alex cracked it open and saw that the barrels were empty. She held her hand out, but no shells magically appeared on her palm. "Well?" she said to Tag.

He met her gaze, glanced in the general direction of the snowmobiles, then back at her, clearly debating. "How do I know you won't shoot me?" he wanted to know.

"You don't, but I can promise you won't be my first choice." Still no shells. "They're gonna be here in like two minutes. An immediate decision would be good."

Tag didn't come to one so she stiff-armed the Winchester, hitting him across the chest with it.

"Oomph," he said, rubbing his ribs. "That hurt."

The look on his face probably matched the irritation in his voice, but Alex didn't stick around to see it. She took a deep breath and held it, heading back into the cabin while it was only filled with smoke. "Bruised ribs you can live with," she said when she came back out, "it's the bullet holes that'll kill you."

She loaded the gun in her hand, sighted down the barrel at the guy on the nearest snowmobile, and shot. In the light from the growing fire she saw him jerk. Another ten seconds and he slumped over the controls. His snowmobile took a sharp left and the other sled crashed into it. Neither of the drivers got up.

"Jesus," Tag said, sounding a little shell-shocked.

"He's not dead." Alex held up her hand, showing him what she held. "Tranquilizer gun."

Tag blew out a breath, ran a hand through his hair.

"Why are you so relieved?" Alex demanded. "And why didn't you shoot at them?"

"I shot at the helicopter."

"But you didn't do it any damage, so you're either a really bad shot or you weren't trying very hard." She walked over to where Jackass had been waiting patiently and picked up his reins. "In light of recent developments, I'm leaning toward Door Number Two. What I don't know is why you're reluctant to shoot at the guys who tried to kill you. Three times."

"Maybe I didn't want to explain a couple of dead bodies."

She gave him a long, level look. "You seem to have an aversion to explaining things. It's irritating."

"You're driving me crazy, too," Tag muttered.

"Then my work here is done." But it wasn't. Alex looked

back at the cabin, at four years of her life going up in flames, and got good and ticked off.

"We should get moving," Tag said. "One of those guys is going to be out for . . ."

"At least four hours," Alex supplied.

"I don't know if the other guy is hurt. If he's not, we can only hope he's less interested in coming after us than he is in keeping his friend from freezing to death by bringing him to warm up at this nice, convenient fire."

She rounded on him. Even if she'd been able to express what she was feeling, words were unnecessary.

"We need to take advantage of the head start," Tag said. "I'm sorry, Alex."

"Yeah, that helps. If you want to make me feel better, tell me this is about world peace or . . . something equally critical," she finished when she couldn't come up with anything bigger than that.

"It's not world peace," Tag said, "but it's important enough to the guys in the plane to try to kill me."

She crossed her arms and waited.

"Ever hear of the Lost Spaniard?" he asked.

Her mouth dropped open and for a second she gaped at him. Then she did the one thing she never could have imagined under the circumstances. She threw her head back and laughed.

"IT'S COLD BACK HERE."

"We're outside," Alex said. "It's spring in the mountains. It's cold everywhere."

You'd never know it to look at her, swaying along with Jackass's ambling gait, not hunching into her collar or blowing on her hands. Of course, she was wearing sheepskin and she was mounted on a nice, warm horse. Tag was wrapped in a couple of thin blankets and huddled on the supply sled, which spent more time plowing through the snow than gliding over it. His ass was wet. And frozen.

"Isn't this one of those times we should be sharing body heat?"

Alex reached forward to give the horse a couple of fond pats. "Jackass and I have all the body heat we can handle, thanks."

"You're doing this because I pointed a gun at you, right?"

"I'm doing this because you burned my cabin down."

"I didn't burn it down."

She half turned in the saddle to look at him. Even in the darkness he knew that expression. It made him defensive in a way he couldn't ignore. "Fine," he said, "so I had the bad luck to fall on you."

"Bad luck for me," she muttered, turning back around.

"Then I guess you could say it was your bad luck that resulted in your cabin being burned down."

"You could say that 'til hell froze over and I'd still blame it on you."

"This is hell, and it has frozen over," Tag said, peering around and finding nothing but trees and snow. There'd been nothing but trees and snow since they'd left the cabin behind. And cold. You'd think the frigid air would numb some of the pain of falling out of a plane, but no, the cold made his bruises sting and his joints ache like an arthritic granny.

The only good thing about the journey was that it seemed to be all downhill.

"Trust me, this isn't hell," Alex said grimly. "Hell is a long way east of here."

No, Tag thought. Hell was being responsible for the death of the best friend you'd ever had. And if he kept thinking like that he'd have to roll off the sled and put himself out of his misery. If Alex Scott didn't do him that favor first. "I'll let you know when I get there," he said, "which will be right after I freeze to death."

She sighed dramatically and reined Jackass in, climbing down from the saddle and pulling out the flashlight she kept in her emergency pack. "Not exactly Indiana Jones, are you?"

Tag peered up at her, blinking in the sudden light. "I never said I was."

He didn't really look the part either. No fedora, no scarred bomber jacket. With his dark hair ruffled by the wind and a day's growth of stubble, he had the scruffy part down, but the physical resemblance ended there. It wasn't the physical that had made her think of Indiana Jones, though. It was the impression that the guy shivering and glaring at her from the sled like a sulky little boy was also a guy who could hold his own when things got rough. The kind of guy who could fall out of a plane, wake up a prisoner, and still proposition her.

The kind of guy she needed to be wary of.

"I'm on the verge of a hypothermic coma. How much farther is it?" he asked. "Where's the town?"

"We're not there yet."

"Then why are we stopping?"

"I'd never forgive myself if you sink into a hypothermic coma."

Tag gave her a look that made her grin. Probably not the reaction he was going for. "Jackass needs a break," she said, "we'll walk for a while."

"We?"

"Walking will get your blood pumping, warm you right up."

"Sure," Tag muttered, sounding even crankier, if possible. He tried to climb off the sled and promptly fell on his face in the snow.

Alex watched him flounder for a minute or so before she hauled him up by his armpit.

"Thanks," he said, scrubbing the snow off his face, "knees don't seem to want to unbend." He looked down, but the joints in question were well below the snow line. "My ankles aren't too great, either, but I'm sure the pain will go away when frostbite sets in."

Alex rolled her eyes, untied her snowshoes from Jackass's saddle and tossed them down in the snow. "Put these on."

He glanced over at the sled and then shrugged. "It'll be a change of scenery, anyway."

Jackass turned his head, baring his big, square yellow teeth in Tag's direction.

"I think you hurt Jackass's feelings."

"Aw, that just breaks my heart." Tag stepped toward the snowshoes—which took him closer to Alex. Which Jackass didn't like. Tag had to jump out of the way before the horse could take a chunk out of his ass. "I can see why you named him Jackass."

"That's not why."

He waited for her to elaborate, but he could have saved himself the trouble. She wasn't the average woman who felt the need to talk a man to death. But she was normal enough to get a kick out of him asking, and he wouldn't give her the satisfaction. "If I didn't know better, I'd say your horse is the jealous type."

"Horses don't have a lot of self-control," Alex told Tag. "If he was the jealous type, you'd probably be a lot less happy about being behind him the last couple of hours."

"Good point." But Tag kept an eye on Jackass while he strapped on the snowshoes. He flexed his knees a couple of times and, lulled into a false sense of confidence by the way he stayed pretty much on the surface of the snow, took a step. And fell on his face.

Alex laughed outright. So did Jackass—okay, he bared his teeth and whinnied, but Tag took it for the equivalent of equine laughter.

Alex helped him up, shaking her head and chuckling at the sight of him standing there, feet about a yard apart, arms outspread for balance. "You've never used snowshoes before?"

"Not a lot of treasure hunting goes on in the winter. The only time I had to do any winter work, it was on a snowmobile."

"Kind of hard to track anything wild on one of those," Alex pointed out unnecessarily, adding, "just keep it natural," as she took Jackass's lead and headed off.

Tag took a cautious step. The snowshoes tangled up and he sprawled on his face, Jerry Lewis without the laugh track.

"You have to keep your feet far enough apart so the shoes don't hit your legs midstride," Alex said, coming back to him. She knelt in front of him and tapped the inside of his right knee until his feet were where she wanted them. When she looked up he was grinning at her.

"In your dreams," she said.

"Maybe if you ever let me sleep again."

"You fell out of a plane and got my cabin firebombed, and then you didn't even shoot the guys who did it. If anybody is keeping anybody from sleeping around here, it's you."

She stood and set off again, leaving him to flounder along in her wake. When he got to the point where he was only falling down every five or six steps, he felt like he was making progress. Alex, however, finally felt the urge to assist him.

"When you get to a deep spot, lift your knees a bit higher and shorten your stride," she said without looking back at him.

"It's annoying how you know what I'm doing without looking at me."

"Who needs to look? You're making enough noise to single-handedly end hibernation. Every time you fall down you swear, and you puff like a steam engine when you're trying to get your feet under you again."

Tag righted himself, concentrating so hard on staying silent that he fell over with the first step.

Jackass laughed at him again.

"And try not to let the snowshoes hit in the middle," Alex said.

"Any other brilliant observations?"

"Falling down is bad." He could almost hear her smiling.

"Thanks," he said, struggling to his feet again.

He lost track of the number of times he fell after that. It felt like an eternity, but it was probably about an hour. He was soaked from head to toe, but he wasn't cold anymore. He was warm—steaming, as a matter of fact.

Alex was leading Jackass about fifty yards ahead of Tag. Her feet were sinking in to midcalf but she didn't seem to be laboring at all. That didn't improve his temper any. He chugged along in her wake, eyes glued to her back, resenting the hell out of her and her horse.

Bad enough being in the middle of nowhere, unarmed, and out of contact with people he trusted, he had to get dropped on a stubborn, irritating hellion of a woman who had no real appreciation for the predicament they were in. True, she'd saved his life, and sure, she had no idea she was in a predicament. But a helicopter had just lit up her cabin and sent two guys on snowmobiles after them, and did she get hysterical, or panicky, or whiny? No. Not that he wanted panic and whining, and hysteria never did anyone any good. But sarcasm and snottiness? Who in their right mind reacted that way in a dangerous situation? It just wasn't normal. And it definitely wasn't helpful. Hell, it was downright counterproductive. On top of which she seemed to take pride in being as antagonistic as possible.

Not that he blamed her, considering his grand entrance, and the subsequent violence. Then there was the fact that he was the proud owner of Y chromosomes, which in her book was probably the biggest infraction. No wonder she wanted to see the last of him.

Problem was, he had to convince her to stick around. For some reason she was a critical part of this fiasco. He didn't know why, but at least he understood what was at stake. Alex had no clue. The firebombing had proved that. If she'd been a willing participant, it wouldn't have been necessary to burn her out of her house to push her into helping him.

Which meant she was a pawn, and the guys in the plane weren't the only ones using her. Tag was, too. He even felt bad about it. Sort of.

She flashed the light in his direction, giving him a long, appraising look over her shoulder. "You're getting the hang of it," she said, and Tag realized that once he stopped over-thinking every footfall, walking on snowshoes wasn't such a big deal.

"Yeah, seems to be getting easier," he said, feeling daring enough to trot a bit so he could catch up and walk next to her.

Jackass reached around behind her and nipped at Tag again. Alex found that vastly amusing.

Tag didn't. "Stupid horse," he said.

"I think the feeling is mutual."

Since Tag knew where that kind of comment would lead, he decided it was time to change the subject. "Why aren't you grilling me about the Lost Spaniard?"

"Because it's a pipe dream."

"You don't believe it exists?"

"I didn't say that. All those old cowboy stories are based in fact."

"But you don't think we can find it."

"No," she said, flat absolute, no room for argument.

"Just no? That's all?"

"You want reasons? I'll give you reasons. It's been a hundred and fifty years since Juan Amparo supposedly hid a cache of gold. Do you have any idea how much the topography of this area has changed in that amount of time? Mudslides, rockfalls, erosion, and that's not including the man-made changes. And even if you managed to find it when everybody and their brother and their brother's maiden aunt has failed, it won't be the huge treasure you think it is. What people considered a fortune a century and a half ago isn't the same thing today."

"You're just a ray of sunshine."

"I'm sorry, did you want me to sugarcoat it?"

"I could do without the attitude in the future," he said.

"We don't have a future."

Famous last words, Tag thought. "Suppose I had new information?"

"I went through your pockets when I took your clothes off. There wasn't even a wallet."

"The guys on the plane took it."

"Well if it was in there—"

"It wasn't." Tag tapped his head. "It's in here."

"Great," Alex said, "I'm convinced now."

"You're not even curious?"

"Okay, fine. What's this new information?"

"Uh-uh. You come on board as my guide—my partner," he amended hastily when she shot him a look, "then I'll tell you."

"What makes you think I'd be any good as a guide?"

"You know the area."

She gave him a long stare, which he took as encouragement.

"You seemed to be pretty settled into the cabin," he said. "Your maps were dog-eared, so I figure you've lived here for a while. You've been walking for at least two miles through a foot of snow and you're not winded, so you must be used to physical exertion. You probably hiked the hills and canyons around here extensively, tracking mountain lions. And that means you have to be familiar with this area. You drew some pretty accurate conclusions about what went on in the plane, which means you're observant."

"And what do I get out of it, supposing I thought it was possible to find the Lost Spaniard?"

"You get half the treasure," he said. "You'll be able to rebuild your cabin and shun all human contact for as long as you want."

"Sounds good except for one thing. I don't trust you."

"I can live with that. And from your side of things, isn't that better? You don't trust me, so you'll keep your eyes open. If you're being vigilant there's less chance you'll get cheated once we find the treasure."

"You have an answer for everything, don't you?"

"You keep coming up with questions. I'm just trying to be helpful."

"You've been so helpful that I'm homeless."

And penniless, Tag thought, or close to it. "Then you

have nothing to lose," he said quietly, without the sarcasm that would have put her hackles up again. And sure, he felt bad that her cabin had burned down, even if it worked in his favor. If he could just get her to turn off that brain, he could tap into her emotions and get her to do whatever he wanted. "You can go to your family or whoever funded your research and ask for money," he said, appealing to her pride next, "or you can come with me and look for the treasure. If it doesn't pan out, all it's cost you is time."

There was a moment of silence, a moment when Tag could all but feel the hook settling into place.

"Sounds like you're pretty sure the treasure is around here," she said.

"The town we're going to is named Casteel."

"And you think it's named after the region in Spain."

He smiled. "Should have known you'd make that connection."

"A lot of people have made that connection. Why do you think the search around here has been so intense?" Alex stopped walking and turned to him. She'd clearly been thinking again. That always meant trouble.

"Don't try to overthink it, Alex. The map—"

"So you have a map that dates back to the Colorado gold rush. What I said before still goes. If whatever cave the treasure was in hasn't collapsed by now, it would've been found."

"Are you so sure of that?"

Alex didn't answer, but the silence spoke volumes. "What I'm not sure of," she said after a moment, "is what you're doing here. There's no airport close by—"

"Shhh."

They stood there for a minute, breath fogging on the night air, listening to the sound of the wind clattering through the bare tree branches.

"I don't hear anything," Alex said.

Tag held up a hand, cocking his head. "There," he whispered.

Alex met his gaze, her eyes wide and shining in the darkness. "Yeah, I hear it now," she said, managing to sound grim despite barely breathing the words.

It was the sound of yet another engine, and it was headed their way.

chapter
5

"IT'S A SNOWMOBILE," TAG SAID, NOT WHISPERING, but keeping his voice down.

Alex pulled Jackass into a thicket of trees and stood with one hand on the butt of her rifle, which was still tucked into the saddle holster.

The only cover they had was the darkness, but the clouds had thinned enough to let a sliver of moon and a few stars shine through, and the snow was like a night vision scope, picking up every scintilla of ambient light. And they'd left a trail a mile wide.

"If whoever it is crosses our path—"

"Yeah."

"Doesn't sound like our odds are very good."

"No." She sounded calm, but her breath was coming in hard little puffs that told him her adrenaline was surging just like his. And he knew just how to work it off.

"Since we're about to die anyway," he said as he closed the distance between them, putting her up against the nearest tree, and laying his mouth on hers.

He'd caught her completely by surprise, and when she

tried to protest, he took advantage of it, deepening the kiss. Her hands came flat against his chest, but she didn't push him away. So he sank into her, his mind going blank as he gave in to the lust that had simmered in him from the moment he'd seen her in the cabin.

His fingers fumbled at the closings of her coat, and he had one leg between hers. He felt her soften against him, one hand began to creep toward his shoulder—and Jackass head-butted them.

Alex shoved Tag away and stepped closer to her horse, ripping her glove off to rub at her mouth. "What the hell was that?"

It took a second before Tag's mental processes kicked back in so he could tell her, but he couldn't tell her because what had started out as taking advantage of the situation had ended up as something else. Something entirely too stupid to think about.

If not for that damned horse he'd have had her on the ground, half-naked in the snow and to hell with freezing to death. To hell with the snowmobile, too, and to hell with this case, and the next one.

To hell with him.

He'd forgotten his duty once and someone had died; he wasn't going that route again.

"I figured if we were about to die," he said, making his voice light, teasing.

"We're not going to die."

"How good are you with that rifle?"

"If you do that again you're going to find out."

"At this distance you could hardly miss me."

She made a rude sound in the back of her throat. "I'd have to use my fist, since you haven't given me any cartridges."

"Oh. Right." He'd given her the rifle back because she had a place to carry it. He'd retained ownership of the cartridges.

"They're in your pocket," she reminded him.

"Yeah."

"Doesn't say much for your faith in me."

"It has nothing to do with my faith in you."

"You can hide behind Jackass if you want," Alex said, clearly amused, "but watch out for his feet. And don't try to kiss him."

"Glad you're enjoying yourself," Tag said. "Just my luck I had to get dropped on somebody like you."

"Who were you expecting in the middle of nowhere?"

"Miss USA," he muttered, just to mess with her.

"You ought to be grateful you got me instead," Alex said. "Miss USA wouldn't be stupid enough to risk breaking a nail, let alone her life, to save yours."

"At least she wouldn't be stubborn and distrustful of everything and everybody. What the hell happened to make you so suspicious?"

"You really have to ask that?"

"I wasn't talking about today. I was talking about the past."

"You want to know about my past? For the last four years I've been right here, minding my own business, me and Jackass and the mountain lions. And then you fell on me and ruined my life."

He tried to reply but Alex came toe to toe with him, her voice carefully modulated, and very well aimed. "You think I'm stubborn and suspicious and distrustful? Those seem like pretty good qualities to have when a snake oil salesman like you shows up out of the blue, talking like fame and fortune can be had just like that," and she snapped her fingers under his nose. "Normal people—"

"Normal?" he scoffed. "A normal person doesn't live seventy-five miles from anywhere, talking to a horse."

"I'd rather talk to him than you any day of the week."

"Because he can't talk back and tell you what a wacko loner you are."

"I might be a wacko and a loner, but at least I'm not a gold-crazed mercenary who'd get mixed up with the kind of people who'd toss someone out of an airplane. With no parachute."

"I'm not in it for the money."

"Then you're an adrenaline junkie."

"And you're a horse lover."

"Con man."

"Pain in the ass."

They'd come to a verbal line neither of them wanted to cross, so they just stood there, inches apart, chests heaving hard enough to bump together. Their eyes met, Tag saw Alex's gaze drop to his mouth, and all his blood rushed south at the same time, leaving him light-headed. He stumbled backward, and once his eyes had uncrossed he noticed that Alex wasn't exactly unaffected.

It should have made the situation better, knowing he wasn't the only one feeling . . . attraction, but Tag was wondering how the hell it had happened.

Alex Scott was clearly the guide he needed, but she could read him like a book. That took away a measure of his control. And pissed him off. Throw lust into that mix and he might as well forget about hanging on to his focus long enough to stay alive, let alone find the treasure. He'd already proven that once tonight; he'd better get a handle on it or they'd both regret it.

"The snowmobile is coming this way," Alex said. "And it's close."

Close enough they could see the headlight cutting through the darkness, and although the person on it was helmeted and dressed for arctic conditions, Alex said, "It's Matt."

Tag hung back, but she led Jackass out of the trees and into the path of the headlights. The sound of the engine throttled back to a throaty rumble, then changed direction slightly, heading their way.

In a few minutes Matt pulled up beside Alex and turned off the sled. "Started out about four a.m.," he said. "Couldn't get you on the radio. Got worried. What are you doing out here?"

"The plane didn't come back," Alex said, "but a helicopter showed up and burned down my cabin."

Matt was off the snowmobile, ripping at his gloves, heading straight for Tag.

Alex stepped between them. "It's not his fault," she said to Matt.

"Like hell it's not. You could've been killed."

"So could he."

"My bet is he deserves it."

"Based on what?" Tag said.

Matt glared at Tag, but he spoke to Alex. "Got some information back on him. No record, but he gets around a lot for a guy who's on the up and up."

"Maybe I'm a salesman," Tag said, "maybe I'm a travel agent. Or maybe I just like to see new places."

"Are you finished?" Alex asked him.

"Yeah."

"Then tell him the truth."

"It's none of his business."

Alex smacked him on the arm, which stung since his skin was ice cold. "Fine," he snapped, "I'm looking for the Lost Spaniard."

Just like when he'd told Alex, there was a split second of stunned silence, then Matt threw his head back and laughed.

THE TOWN OF CASTEEL HAD SPREAD ITSELF HAPHAZardly along one side of a small valley with a shallow river running through it. The other side of the valley was public grazing land for the livestock owned by the town's residents. Once upon a time that had been a lot of animals. Nowadays not so much—not that the empty grassland had been converted to another use. Tradition was as much a part of the town as the mountains around it, and just as enduring. Being a resident of Casteel required a certain amount of resistance to change.

It also took a special kind of approach to life, eccentricity being a central theme. The place was filled with kooks, Alex thought fondly as they made their way down the final hill toward the bridge at the west end of town, and it didn't say much for her that some of those kooks thought she was strange for living alone up in the hills, communing with animals that could rip her to shreds. But they kept their opinions to themselves. At least when she was around. Discussing her with others, now that was another story. Literally.

Gossip was as much a part of daily activity in Casteel as breakfast, lunch, and dinner. These were simple people, with workdays that often outlasted the sun at both ends of the day. Except for television, there wasn't a whole lot in the way of entertainment to be had in such a small town. Who could blame them for having an overdeveloped interest in the lives of their friends and neighbors? And sure, the tale might be a little embellished by each subsequent narrator, but a person could live—or at least drink—off a choice tidbit of gossip for weeks.

So, when Matt, Alex, and Tag hit the edge of town, it was quite the event. Admittedly they were a strange procession, consisting, as they did, of a sheriff on a snowmobile, a zoologist on a horse, and a half-frozen, thoroughly pissed-off stranger on a sled.

Of course it was Tag who got the most attention, Alex noticed as they wended their way down the single main street, a small parade of Casteel residents queueing up behind them so they formed a little parade. Tag was back to sulking, when he wasn't shivering, although it was his own fault he'd ended up on the sled. He wouldn't ride behind Matt, and Matt wouldn't let him ride the snowmobile on his own. Tag couldn't get close enough to Jackass to climb into the saddle—not without losing a chunk of arm or leg—and he didn't last long on the snowshoes. He'd gotten the hang of them, but he didn't have the staying power after the day and night he'd been through. Neither would she, Alex had to admit, but Tag had only looked sour when she'd made that observation.

The sheriff's office was in the center of town, but it

didn't take long to get there, since the town wasn't much over two miles long from end to end.

"You want to lie down in one of the cells?" Matt asked her once they'd gone inside. He started to open the door to the small back room that was subdivided into two cells. "You must be exhausted."

"I'm pretty tired," Alex agreed, "but I intend to have a huge breakfast and then I'll get a room at the Casteeley Inn and sleep for a couple days."

Matt's face fell. "You could stay with me," he said.

"In this town?" she teased. "Word runs through this place faster than a starving mountain lion on the chase."

"I never thought gossip bothered you."

"Doesn't," Alex said, "but I think it would bother Annabelle."

Matt looked away, the tips of his ears turning red. "You kept turning me down," he muttered.

"Maybe you should rename this Melrose Place." Tag was over by the wood-burning stove, turning like a chicken on a spit. When he rotated to face her, Alex saw that he was smirking.

But there was a glint in his eyes she didn't like. That glint looked like it concerned her, and her relationship with Matt, and Tag forcing himself on her in the forest. Okay, so it hadn't exactly been force, more like she'd been surprised. It hadn't exactly been unwelcome, either, but it had been stupid, and she especially didn't like feeling as though Tag Donovan was staking his territory.

"Peyton Place more your speed?" he said to Matt, clearly intent on picking a fight.

The flush spread from Matt's ears, encompassing his whole face, except for a white ring around his mouth where his lips were pressed tight together. One of his hands fisted, but the other ran over the badge on his chest and that seemed to steady him. Lucky for Tag.

"Haul out your wallet," Matt growled at him, "and sit down."

"He's not carrying a wallet," Alex said. "Or any other identification. Just a wad of cash."

Both men turned to her.

"I checked while he was unconscious."

Matt gave her a long stare. She returned it. Tag, thankfully, kept silent.

"Doesn't matter anyway," Matt finally said. "Just about any form of ID can be faked these days." He sat back in his chair. "We're gonna get this treasure BS out of the way and then you can leave town."

"I don't want to leave town," Tag said.

"You aren't staying here," Matt informed him, calm but immoveable. "I can't find any wants or warrants on you. Or anyone matching your description. 'Bout the only thing I could arrest you for is stupidity, but that's what natural selection is for."

"It's a free country," Tag said. "I'm staying."

"So you can look for the Lost Spaniard?" Matt sneered.

"That's right."

"Smarter people than you have looked for that treasure, Donovan, people who know how to survive in the wilderness." Matt's gaze traveled over Tag's completely unsuitable clothing. "If none of them found the treasure, what makes you think you can?"

"He claims to have some new information," Alex said when Tag remained mulishly silent. "And he seems to think he can convince me to be his guide."

Matt's face went almost to scarlet, his fists clenched.

"You talking about the Lost Spaniard?"

Matt jerked the rest of the way to his feet, but he only gave Tag a last furious glare before he turned toward the door leading to the cells. A rail-thin man with a gray-shot beard and ratty clothes was standing there, looking like death warmed over.

"What're you doing here, Trankey?"

Joe Trankey, town lush, put one hand on the doorjamb and when that didn't completely steady him, grabbed the other side. "Got drunk last night. You wasn't around so I came over and slept it off. What're we paying taxes for anyway, when you're not around to do your job?"

Matt crossed the room and caught him by the collar, half dragging, half supporting him to the front door and depositing him on the boardwalk outside.

"You can't do this to me," Trankey yelled, kicking at the door and winding up on his butt for his efforts. "I'll call the capital," he said as he climbed unsteadily to his feet. "I'll call Homeland Security. I'll call your mother."

Matt just shook his head and sat back down.

"Maybe you shouldn't blow that off," Tag said, "him calling your mother."

"Unless he has a direct line to the afterlife he's not getting anywhere near my mother."

"He wouldn't waste the time anyway," Alex added. "By now he's down at the diner, telling anyone who will listen that there's a guy in town who claims to have some new information about the Spaniard."

Tag shrugged. "I don't care who he tells."

"You will." Matt crossed his arms and smiled. "Just wait and see."

chapter
6

"SO," TAG SAID TO ALEX AS THEY LEFT THE SHERIFF'S office, "breakfast?"

"No." She started off down the boardwalk to where she'd left Jackass tied up at an old-fashioned hitching post across the street.

Tag kept pace a couple of steps behind her, telling himself he was doing it to annoy her. But his eyes were on her backside. It was pretty cold, and he still wasn't wearing a coat, but he kept his eyes on her ass and didn't notice the frigid temperature. "I'm buying."

"It's the least you could do after I saved your life. Twice."

"You didn't have a choice. Someone like you doesn't leave a man in the snow to die."

"That doesn't change the fact that you're still alive because of me." She stopped at the corner, waited until his eyes lifted from her backside to her face, then shook her head and stepped off the curb.

Tag didn't miss the way one side of her mouth turned up before she caught herself. "You must be hungry after all that hard work," he called after her.

"I have to get Jackass settled."

"Is that a yes or a no?"

Halfway across the street she turned back to him, maybe not the smartest move, but there wasn't a lot of traffic in Casteel. Hell, there was no traffic in Casteel. Except for the pickup truck that roared around the corner on two wheels, engine racing, heading straight for Alex.

She froze, mouth open, eyes wide. Tag took a running leap and hit her broadside, his momentum carrying both of them out of the pickup's path to sprawl in a heap against the market on the opposite side of the street, arms and legs tangled, Alex mostly on top.

She lay there a few seconds, heart galloping so hard her chest and neck hurt, and little black dots dancing in front of her eyes. Eventually the cold of the slush soaking through her jeans worked its way around the terror. "That was close," she said to Tag, pushing up with the heels of her hands braced on his chest.

He didn't open his eyes.

"Tag?"

Nothing.

"You did it this time," she muttered, stripping off her gloves and trying not to notice that her hands were shaking when she ran them through his hair. No bumps, no blood.

And then she realized he was smiling—although he groaned as she untangled herself from him. The groaning might have had something to do with her knees and elbows. But he still wasn't getting up.

"Where does it hurt?" she asked, kneeling beside him, her hands on his chest again.

"Lower."

She followed his directions, but the only thing she moved were her eyes. Yeah, there was a distinct swelling south of his zipper. "I thought you were in pain."

"There are all kinds of pain."

She slugged him.

"Ouch," he said, holding his side. "Do you have to keep aiming for my ribs?"

Alex eyed his bulge. "I could think of another target."

"The ribs are fine," Tag said, climbing stiffly to his feet.

Alex got up, too, stepping to the edge of the curb and looking into the empty street. "What was that?"

"Why don't you ask him?"

The same pickup truck came around the corner, backward, slipping and sliding to a stop next to where they stood. It sat in the street, rusted fenders rattling along with the engine's rough idle. The passenger window cranked slowly down.

Tag stepped in front of Alex.

"Not in this century," she said, and stepped up next to him again.

"Is it true?" the man inside the cab wanted to know, craning his head to peer out in their direction.

"Unfortunately, yes," Alex replied.

"Yee haw," he shouted, gunning the truck and leaving them ankle deep in slush and awash in a cloud of noxious exhaust.

"I take it you know who that was?"

"Trankey's brother," Alex said.

"Shit. Was he drunk, too?"

"Gold fever. Same thing." She turned to look at Tag, hands on hips. "But you thought it was our friends from back at the cabin, right? And before you answer, it would be nice if you kept the bullshit content to a minimum."

Tag shrugged. "It wouldn't be the first time they've taken a shot at us."

"It would be the first time it was aimed specifically at me."

"It wasn't aimed at you. This time. What do you think is going to happen when everyone finds out you came to town with me?"

"You're the one with the new information," she reminded him. "I think they're going to drive you crazy and leave me alone."

"Isn't that a little optimistic for you?"

"It's realistic. The people around here know me, and

when I tell them I have no idea where the treasure is they'll believe me."

"It might be a good idea for us to stick together."

"That's what got me into this position in the first place," she said, untying Jackass and heading toward the stable at the other end of town.

Tag caught her arm, hauling her to a stop. "You have no idea what you're up against," he said.

"Then maybe you should fill me in."

He thought about that for a minute, but nothing had really changed. He still didn't know enough about her, or the situation, to safely weigh his options and pick a course of action.

"Well?"

Tag let go of her arm.

"I didn't think so," she said. "I'd tell you it's been a pleasure, but . . ." she spread her hands.

"Yeah," Tag said, catching her drift.

"Good-bye."

"I hope that's not a permanent sentiment," he called after her.

"NICE TO KNOW YOU'RE STILL ALIVE."

"Just barely," Tag said to Mike Kovaleski, his handler at the FBI, adding "pay phone," by way of warning. Not only was it an unsecured line, the pay phone was outside, no booth. Too big a risk that someone would overhear something they shouldn't. "I got dumped out of an airplane in the middle of nowhere, on a woman who stalks mountain lions and talks to horses. The guys on the plane gave me a wad of cash and took everything I had on me including my wallet and phone."

Not that there were a lot of cell towers around here anyway. There wasn't much of anything around here. One vet, one gas station, one feed store, one market—that sold coats, thankfully—and one too many sheriffs. An odd assortment of houses squatted on the narrow, rutted dirt lanes behind the main drag, and quite a few horses were tethered on the west side of the street.

The sheriff's office sat at one end of town, and a closed railroad station anchored the other; Tag suspected they'd driven it out of business so they could hunker in their little valley and not be tainted by the outside world. Good thing there were pickups and cars parked on the east side of the street or he'd be concerned about inbreeding.

"This is the first chance I've had to check in," he said to Mike.

There was silence from the other end of the phone, the kind of silence that came from disbelief warring with past history. Past history won out. "It's not the most outlandish thing you've ever told me," Mike finally said. "Hell, it's not the strangest report I've had this week. You should hear about Jack Mitchell's last mission. I'd tell you—if it wasn't classified."

"Mitchell? He still breathing? I figured some drug dealer would've gotten him by now."

"It's not the drug cartels, it's the women," Mike said, chuckling. "He ran into one who . . . Let's just say Pablo Corona was no match for her. Neither was Jack."

"Sounds entertaining, but can we focus on me for a minute?"

"Yeah, chucked out of an airplane on Dr. Doolittle," Mike said, all business despite the amusement still light in his voice. "How'd you live through that?"

"The plane wasn't very high when they pushed me out, there was a couple feet of snow, and Dr. Doolittle has a conscience." He told Mike the rest of the story, filling in some pieces he hadn't shared with Alex, carefully cleansed for public consumption, just in case. "About all I know is that Alex is in the middle of this thing and I need to stick close to her if I want to find out what's going on."

"If? You still hoping I'll pull you off this case?"

"I shouldn't be on this case."

"You're right, you should be taking time off like the psychs suggested."

"You're not going to start that garbage about how I shouldn't be in the field so soon?"

"Would it do me any good?" Mike didn't wait for an answer. "I gave you this case because I knew you'd go crazy sitting around, and then you'd go after Anthony Sappresi."

"He killed Zukey," Tag said. "He tried to kill me. You're damn right I'm going after him—"

"You know the rules, Donovan."

"Yeah." The bureau wouldn't put him on the investigation into his partner's murder. Tag chewed on that for a minute, but he already knew he was in for the duration. That didn't mean he had to be happy about it. "Okay, so now that this busywork case is going to shit, what do you suggest?"

"I suggest you get into Dr. Doolittle's brain, see what she knows."

"She doesn't know anything," Tag muttered sourly, then hissed out a breath. "That's my gut talking," he admitted, and he didn't trust his gut anymore.

"Yeah? Well, my gut's been talking, too," Mike said. "And this case may not be the open and shut busywork you think. Watch your back."

"Spill it," Tag said, grateful Mike hadn't questioned his instincts. Tag had been doing enough second-guessing for the entire bureau.

"Can't," Mike shot back, his gravelly voice dropping to what passed for a whisper. "You aren't the only one who can be overheard."

And the FBI offices were hotbeds of gossip, just like every other white collar beehive in every other city in the world. "You saying you didn't send me on this assignment just to keep me busy?"

"It may turn out that way," Mike said, "but there's been some rumblings coming out of Boston, from Sappresi's general direction. And before you ask I'm not getting into specifics."

"Fucking rules again," Tag said.

"Not just the fucking rules," Mike shot back. "I could be

jumping to conclusions, here, Donovan, or I could be flat-out wrong."

But he wasn't. Tag might have lost faith in his own gut, but he'd have staked his life on Mike's. There was more going on than simple fraud being perpetrated on a bunch of ignorant investors. Still, Mike was right about jumping. Kind of like being pushed; you never knew where you might land. Or on whom.

"I've done what I can," Mike continued. "I took the regular treasure hunter out of commission and made sure you'd get the gig. It's up to you to connect the dots. If there is a connection. Just be careful."

"You could've told me that before I got on the plane."

"Hindsight," Mike said. "Guess you still have to earn his trust, Donovan. He dropped you on the animal lady for a reason, maybe you should focus on that."

The rest went unsaid. This case was like all the others—nothing more than a game. Life or death might be the stakes, but there were still rules and players, and a game board. Sometimes the rules were written by a homicidal maniac or a terrorist, or, in this case, a money hungry hemorrhoid of a con man. Didn't matter. The rules still had to be followed, at least until all the players were identified and their motives understood. Until Tag figured out Alex's role, and uncovered her affiliations, he had to play along.

"Give me her name again," Mike said, "and I'll check her out."

"Alex Scott."

"Alex? That short for something?"

"Don't know," Tag said, smiling at a middle-aged woman and her daughter who were passing by.

The woman curled an arm around her daughter's shoulder and hustled her away. The daughter watched him over her shoulder, eyes wide, not sure what to make of him.

What was with these people? Tag wondered. And then he remembered he was an outsider, which would be synonymous with serial murderer in a little town like this one. He felt something hot on the back of his neck and glanced over his shoulder, thinking they should be more worried about their own citizens. A burly man with bloodshot eyes, a thirty-year growth of beard, and breath like a cesspool stood close enough for Tag to count his nose hairs. Grizzly Adams with an emphasis on grizzly.

"Phone," he said, his breath hitting Tag full in the face this time.

"I did a quick and dirty search," Mike was saying. "Alexandra Scott, Boston, blue blood and old money, University of Michigan, dual degrees in zoology and some sort of history. Here's an interesting bit of information—"

"Now," the guy behind him grunted.

"Gotta go," Tag said to Mike, trying his best not to inhale through his nose when he spoke. He didn't have any problem dealing with a local yokel, but he couldn't talk in front of the guy. And anyway, he'd heard enough to light a fire inside him. After being empty for so long it felt damn good. "I'll call you back when I can."

Tag relinquished the phone, headed to the diner, bought a thin local paper, and settled in to wait. It was the only restaurant in town, so he figured someone who'd missed a day's worth of meals would have to show up there sooner or later. His reasoning was sound, and lots of people came in, but none of them were Alex. And none of them left. Barely a half hour after he arrived, the place was full, a line of people stretched out the door and curved around the sidewalk in front, and faces were pressed to the big front windows, peering in. At him.

In a small-town diner like this, breakfast conversation ought to consist of work, the weather, whose cow had strayed into the wrong pasture, and the stranger in town. Those topics were pretty popular, but one by one every conversation eventually made its way around to the Lost Spaniard, and the talk gave Tag a pretty good idea what the sheriff had meant when he said "wait and see."

No one had the slightest notion where the treasure was, but everyone had a plan to find it. He wasn't shaping up to be the most popular guy in the room, either. It seemed the idea of an outsider finding their treasure made the Castillians a bit touchy. By the time Alex showed up at the door he was thinking of her as the only friendly face in the town, even if her expression when she spotted him was a few degrees south of polar.

Tag gestured to the seat across from him, but she looked around, took her time assuring herself there were no other empty places. Even then she remained reluctant, but he could see the moment when hunger got the better of her.

She made her way to his table, dropped her satchel on the bench seat opposite his, and slid in next to it without hesitation or complaint—or greeting for that matter. But he caught the way she scoped out the place again, taking the pulse of the crowd, much like he'd done when he first arrived. She might not be a pro, but she seemed to have an instinct for reading situations. And people.

"Deputy Dawg was right," Tag said to her, "I wouldn't't've believed the news would get around this fast if I hadn't seen it with my own eyes."

Her gaze circled the place again; when it got back to his face she didn't look encouraged. "A lot of these guys are unemployed, and every one of them wants to find the Lost Spaniard for himself. I'd watch my back if I were you."

"I'd rather watch yours."

"My back's not the one with the target on it," she said. "The treasure isn't the only part of the story they've heard."

"Then they know you came into town with me, and they're probably wondering what part you're playing in all this."

They'd kept their voices down, but it didn't do them much good because a man appeared at her shoulder, a man about a hundred years old. Faded blue eyes peered out of a seamed face with so many age spots they'd blended together into a natural suntan. He had a slight palsy, no teeth, and ears big enough to pick up a sneeze in Reykjavik. He stood there, looking at Alex, twisting an ancient hat around in his hands.

"It true you're looking for the Lost Spaniard, Miss

Alex?" he asked in a voice that sounded like it had come from someone half his age and twice his strength.

She looked up at him, her expression softening. But not her attitude. "No, Jess," she said.

"Because you'd tell us, right? I know you keep to yourself out there, and we understand when somebody wants to be let alone—"

"Not everybody understands that." She looked around the room, a familiar hard light in her eyes. More than one man fidgeted and looked away.

So that was why she carried a gun, Tag thought, and why she didn't trust strange men. It must have been a hell of a culture shock for a woman like her, educated, refined. *Blue blood and old money.*

Something had driven her out here, and not just studying mountain lions. Tag stuck with his first guess that it was a man. And then a couple of the bastards around here had finished the job by deciding to try their luck with a woman on her own seventy-five miles from anyone who gave a damn. And more than one of them looked like they wouldn't take no for an answer—if they even bothered to ask. That thought almost took him out of his chair, his hands clenching with the urge to beat somebody to a bloody pulp.

He stopped himself, regulated his breathing, and unknotted his muscles one by one. He didn't waste a minute deliberating over the emotion burning through him, either. He'd learned a long time ago that emotion was dangerous. All emotion. He wanted Alex, even bruised and groggy he'd wanted her. But that was lust and lust could be dealt with. What he felt when he looked at her now was respect. Respect was acceptable, and in this case it would also make his life a hell of a lot easier. She could take care of herself, so he wouldn't have to waste time watching out for her.

That would make up for the time he'd need to spend convincing her.

He checked back in to her conversation with Jess, figuring he hadn't missed anything since they were talking

about someone named Maudey, who needed braces and
wanted to be a zoologist, just like Alex.

"He thinks the treasure can help him put his grand-
daughter through college," Alex said after Jess shuffled off.
"The treasure could help a lot of people in this town. If it
was ever found."

"You still don't believe it will be."

"If it is, it probably won't be anybody from Casteel.
Matt's right about news traveling fast," she said. "Most of
the people in here are local, but the ones waiting in line
outside aren't. They're drifters, itinerant cowboys, oppor-
tunists. They won't waste the effort of looking for the treasure, but they're more than willing to take advantage of the
nutcases who will."

The nutcases, Tag decided, were the ones approaching
Alex. They came to the table in ones or twos, to ask her
about the Lost Spaniard.

Tag recovered his coffee and sat back, feeling pretty
smug until Alex stood up, raised her hands, and said into
the sudden hush, "I don't know anything about the Lost
Spaniard, and I don't want anything to do with it."

"C'mon, Alex," somebody called out, "Trankey said
you and that fella you're with was talking about some new
clue—"

She stood up again, meeting the speaker's eyes, then doing a slow visual survey of the room. "This fella is Tag
Donovan. Neither of us has eaten or slept in thirty-six hours.
We'd appreciate being left alone to have our breakfast—if
we can ever order it," she added, glancing at the counter
where the lone waitress stood glaring at her, arms crossed.
"After that, feel free to ask him your questions." More grum-
bling. "Or maybe you'd like him to announce what he knows
to the room at large."

That did it. The crowd went completely silent. Then the
whispering began, people huddled together over their tables, wanting to pick Tag's brain but not in front of everyone else. Alex knew it was only a matter of time before
someone worked up the gumption to approach him. The

waitress broke the ice by sashaying over, steaming coffeepot in one hand, order pad in the other.

"I'll have a ham and cheese omelet, hash browns, wheat toast, and orange juice," Alex said before she could ask Tag what he wanted, "and coffee."

The waitress gave her a dirty look, so Alex stood up and yelled her order to the cook. She looked at Tag, he shrugged, and she added, "make that two of everything," then sat down, pulling Tag's freshly refilled coffee over in front of her.

"Let me guess," he said as the waitress flounced off, "that's Annabelle, the sheriff's new girlfriend."

"You're smarter than you look."

"I generally like conversation with my meals, but if you're going to be nasty . . ."

Alex smiled and tipped her head toward the line that was forming. "I don't think you're going to lack for conversation."

Tag retrieved his coffee cup. "I don't know if you can call it a conversation when I'm expected to do all the talking."

"Don't worry, they'll be asking questions. Lots of questions."

"I have a feeling there's going to be a common theme."

Alex laughed. It was almost worth the ordeal ahead to see her guard drop. Almost.

"I don't suppose there's any chance they'll believe me if I deny it," Tag wondered. "It's just a rumor anyway."

"Rumors are gospel in this town," Alex said, waiting until Annabelle set their plates on the table with a cranky little snap and walked away before she continued.

"That leaves me with two choices, misdirection or silence."

"Lie," Alex said. "You're good at that."

"Thanks. What do you suggest I tell them?"

"You'll figure it out," she said around a bite of omelet. "You seem to be very resourceful."

Okay, she was challenging him to handle this without her running interference. It should have ticked him off, but he was still smiling. "I'm sure you understand why I'm keeping what I know to myself," he said loud enough for the whole room to hear.

Alex's gaze lifted from her plate, her eyes narrowing on his face.

"I will tell you that I'm hoping Alex will be my guide," Tag finished.

"Her?" one old man scoffed. "She's from Boston." Which might as well be Mars, judging by his tone. "Hell, Harp Santiago knows these valleys like the back of his hand."

"Really?" Tag said. "Where can I find Mr. Santiago?"

"In the cemetery," someone called out, and the whole restaurant erupted in laughter.

Tag joined in, but he was thinking, great, I finally found people who don't laugh about the treasure and they're all as crazy as a three-dollar bill. And apparently he was one of them. It didn't say much for his chances of success. "Anyone else who could help?"

Names were called out, but those who were present in the diner immediately supplied a reason they couldn't guide Tag. Some of the reasons were pretty lame, and as people realized they'd gotten all they were going to get out of him, they began to leave.

"I guess it's you as my guide or no one," Tag said to Alex.

She pushed her empty plate aside and drank some more of his coffee. "You know all those people who couldn't guide you?" she said. "They're going out to look for the treasure themselves. Within a week the hills and valleys around here will be so crowded they'll be tripping over each other. They'll all be carrying guns, and some of these people shouldn't have passed the three-day waiting period to own one. They're harmless most of the time, but I wouldn't want to be wandering around with armed men all over the place."

"You think they're going to shoot at me?"

"I think they're likely to hit you. Hunting accidents happen all the time."

Tag thought about that, and while he was mulling, Matt came in and stopped at their table.

"Is it as bad as we thought it would be?" he wanted to know.

"Worse," Alex said. "A lot of these guys are from out of town."

"I was kind of hoping the people around here would keep this to themselves."

"Word got out a lot sooner than you expected."

"Yeah." Matt gave Tag a hard, warning look, and wandered off to the counter. Annabelle was there almost before he got his butt on the stool, pouring him coffee and batting her eyes.

"Isn't he going to do anything about these lunatics?" Tag asked.

Alex shook her head. "From what I understand this happens about every ten years and blows over in a few months. Your best bet is to wait it out."

Except he didn't have a few months, Tag thought. He had to figure out what was going on. In order to do that he needed Alex's cooperation, and she was still refusing to come on board. Things could probably get worse, but he didn't see how.

"There's some sort of commotion outside." Alex stood up so she could see out the windows.

Tag retrieved his coffee and racked his brain for a way around the dead end.

"Looks like more newcomers," Alex said, "in black SUVs. And the guy in charge is really . . . short."

She headed for the door. Tag kept his seat. The dead end had just grown another wall. Shit.

chapter
7

BY THE TIME THEY GOT OUTSIDE, A HUMMER, A
Land Rover, and a Jeep were parked in the middle of the
street. All three of the vehicles were shiny, unadorned black,
and all were equipped with tire chains. The rear license
plate on the Hummer read "Eureka1." Alex figured the others were "2" and "3," since the overall theme was "private
army" and armies generally encouraged uniformity.

The Hummer was dragging the kind of trailer workers
used to transport a lot of tools, shiny black and completely
enclosed. Keeping its own secrets. The Land Rover and the
Jeep were keeping their secrets, too, the drivers staying inside, behind dark tinted windows.

The Hummer driver was standing on his running board,
one hand on the open door, the other on his hip, surveying
his surroundings like Bluebeard on the poop deck of his pi-
rate ship. Hilary atop Mount Everest. Pee Wee Herman in
his playhouse.

His head barely reached the top of the Hummer's window, and Alex caught herself craning her neck to see if he
used a booster seat. She was having a hard time taking him

seriously, but she was the only one holding back her merriment. The rest of the crowd was speechless—which was saying something in Casteel—huddled together like a herd of wildebeests sharing their water hole with a leopard.

Alex was puzzled about the fear until she looked into his hard black eyes, and then she understood. Cold was the word that came to mind, along with unfeeling, cruel. Ruthless.

He peeled off a pair of leather driving gloves, one finger at a time, and took off his Ray-Bans to look around the town, ending with a slow and disdainful perusal of the people crowded along the sidewalk. They recoiled like baseball fans doing a reverse wave. Since Alex and Tag had chosen to remain by the diner's door, the disdain passed them by. Alex still couldn't suppress the sudden urge for a shower.

"What's he compensating for?" she asked Tag from behind her hand.

"Nothing," Tag said, "the guy is good at what he does."

"What does he do?"

"He finds things for people."

"Sounds like you know him."

"Mercenary," Tag said grimly. "I ran across him a few years back." Tag had been undercover working for one side of a mob turf war, the Hummer driver, at his mercenary finest, on the other. Tag could have said a lot of things about the guy—all of them bad—but he had great instincts, great enough that somehow he'd smelled the end coming and had gotten out before it came down to handcuffs and mug shots. Good for Tag, since his FBI affiliation hadn't been discovered. Bad because a criminal was free to roam the world doing anything he wanted, for anyone. And apparently he held a grudge. "Name's Pierre Phillipe Francois Dussaud II."

"Nooooo," Alex said. "The second? As in junior?"

One corner of Tag's mouth quirked up but his eyes stayed on the Hummer driver. "I wouldn't say that within earshot."

"His name is bigger than he is."

"So's his ego. From what I hear, he lives up to all your expectations of men."

"He's not the only one."

Tag grinned at that. "I have some surprises left."

"I'll take your word for it." She would have walked away, but things had started to get interesting. Just because she enjoyed her own company so much didn't mean she couldn't appreciate what other people got up to.

"We are looking for the Lost Spaniard treasure," Junior announced in a pronounced French lisp. "We would be grateful for any help that can be provided, and then if you would kindly keep out of our way, we would be most appreciative."

"Does that usually work for him?" Alex wondered.

"I don't know, but I'm not impressed," Tag said.

He wasn't the only one. It started with one lone voice Alex didn't immediately recognize, probably Jess or one of his cronies. The voice sounded old, and the tone of it was senior-citizen-with-a-right-to-know. The effect on the crowd was the Little Dutch Boy pulling his finger out of the dike.

Junior was peppered with questions. The crowd surged forward in a mad panic to establish a pecking order, threatening to flatten him against the side of his vehicle. Death by Hummer. Hummercide.

"What are you grinning about?" Tag asked her.

"Nothing." But she kept grinning. It was the only entertainment she was likely to get, because the intended victim lifted a hand and crooked a finger.

The Land Rover and the Jeep vomited out a passel of black-clad knuckle-draggers who locked arms and shoved everyone back so there was an island of personal space big enough for the Hulk.

The crowd subsided verbally, too, relegated to threatening looks and angry mutterings, and subjected to some pretty fierce body odor, judging by the grimaces of the people in armpit proximity.

Junior looked down his nose at everyone, very French aristocrat. Then he caught sight of Tag. And he smiled.

"That's not a nice smile," Alex said, apparently too loudly.

Junior shifted his gaze to her, held her eyes long enough to give her the creeps, then went back to supervising crowd intimidation.

"Is that sulfur I'm smelling?" she asked.

"He's small, but potent," Tag said. "Not somebody you want to mess with."

"There's no love lost for you, either."

"He considers me competition."

"What do you consider him?"

"A loose cannon. And a pain in the ass." A dangerous one, but Tag could see she'd already figured that out. What she hadn't clued in to was the possibility she was in Dussaud's sights right along with him.

"A loose cannon and a pain in the ass. That sounds like something you'd say about me," Alex observed. "In fact, I'm pretty sure you have."

"Not yet. I was saving those for the next time you ticked me off."

"I wouldn't want you to overwork your vocabulary," she said. "I think you're going to need all the words you can come up with, and maybe a few weapons, to deal with Junior."

Tag didn't have a response for that. She was in the same boat, but telling her that wouldn't do him any good. She was more the actions-speak-louder-than-words kind of woman, a philosophy that, if she wasn't careful, might get her killed.

"I'm going to my room, and I intend to sleep for about a week," Alex said. "Hopefully when I wake up this will all be over," she pushed away from the wall where she'd been leaning next to Tag, adding for his benefit, "and you'll all be gone."

The crowd had begun to thin out, Junior apparently having grown tired of flexing his hired muscle for the benefit of the entire town. Unfortunately, he'd decided on a private showing. Alex's forward momentum ground to a halt behind what she thought was a pedestrian traffic jam. Turned out the obstruction was one of Junior's flunkies. The people in front of her went either way around him. Alex tried to do the same, but he shifted to block her. Not so much an obstruction as a brick wall with an IQ just high enough for him to follow orders. And the orders were to keep her from leaving.

"Mademoiselle Scott."

She turned, but not toward the voice. She knew who the voice belonged to, but she was looking for Tag. She found him standing where she'd left him, leaning a shoulder against the diner wall. Watching.

Alex squashed her irritation. She wanted him to leave her alone, and he was leaving her alone. Even when it wasn't convenient for her.

Three more of Junior's flunkies lined up with the first one, and she thought maybe it would be in her best interest to deal with Junior now and Tag later. If there was a later. *"C'est dommage,"* she said, shifting her attention sideways—and down—to Junior.

"What is a pity?" Junior asked.

She looked over her shoulder at the no-neck brigade.

"You mistake me, Miss Scott. I feared you would not want to talk with me, and I am right, *n'est-ce pas*? I wished only for a chance to . . . how do you say, talk my piece."

"You could have asked."

"You would not have listened." Dussaud looked over at Tag.

He straightened away from the building—he stayed where he was, but something dangerous came over his face, and it wasn't aimed at her. These two were definitely communicating, Alex thought; there was a whole subtext she wasn't clued in to. And didn't want to be, she assured herself. In fact, the subtext ticked her off. It was bad enough to be dragged halfway into some stupid treasure hunt, but add in a couple of alpha males intent on butting heads, and she couldn't get out of there fast enough.

This time, when she tried to walk away, Dussaud was the only one who stopped her, with a hand on her arm.

"I really do not mean you any harm, Miss Scott."

She brushed his hand off. "How do you know my name anyway?"

"I make it my business to know as much about a predicament as I can, before I go into it."

"I'm not a predicament."

"I have a feeling you will be. If you continue to keep company with Monsieur Donovan."

"Your feeling is wrong this time," Alex said. "I'm not going after the Lost Spaniard," her gaze swiveled to Tag, "no matter what you hear."

Dussaud gave Tag a long, disdainful look. "Mr. Donovan can be very persuasive, especially where the ladies are concerned."

"Then I guess it's a good thing I'm not a lady." She attempted to leave, but it was hard to make a classy exit when you couldn't actually exit. She tried to stare down the goon in front of her. His lip curled and he sort of growled at her—very junkyard dog, trained to mindlessly guard his territory, considered eye contact a challenge, possibly rabid.

"Do you really think you could leave if I preferred you to stay?" Junior asked her, the French accent making the question condescending. Even at his most irritating, Tag had never talked down to her. It would have been a point in his favor, if she'd ever intended to subject herself to his good points again, let alone the bad ones.

"Do you really think it's macho to turn three hundred pounds of muscle—three-ten with his head—loose on a woman less than half his size?" she said to Junior.

"I have a feeling you can take care of yourself, Miss Scott."

"Damn right she can," someone in the crowd called out. "Drive his gonads up into his armpits, Alex."

She was still staring at the flunky, so she raised an eye-brow. He hunched automatically, but she had to give him credit; he didn't budge. He looked at his boss, and after an-other minute of torture, Junior the control freak inclined his head and let his hireling step aside.

Alex started to walk past him, but there was something she really needed to know. "Tell me you're not the one who burned down my cabin," she said turning back to Junior.

"*Mais non*. Of course not." He even seemed genuinely surprised. "In fact, I had hoped I might convince you to work with me."

"No."

"I will pay you, of course. I will even give you some of the money up front. You will be able to rebuild your cabin and return to your studies."

"I have insurance."

"That will take time. With my help, you could order the things you require, and by the time our search is over everything will be in readiness." He spread his hands, all benevolence. "I will even leave one of my men here to put things in order for you."

Alex perused the choice of potential worker bees and concluded they didn't have one good brain between them. "Tempting, but I have a feeling traveling with you would be detrimental to my health."

Junior took a moment to digest that, not happy about be-ing refused but doing his best to play along. Clearly it wasn't an easy task for him, which made Alex wonder why he was making the effort. She might have asked if she'd thought it would ever matter.

"I am sorry you feel that way," he said after a moment. "If you change your mind . . ." He held out a card.

Alex shrugged and took it, tucking it in her pocket with-out looking at it. "We won't be crossing paths again," she said.

"In a town this small, Miss Scott, we can hardly avoid it."

* * *

THERE WERE SOME PEOPLE WHO WERE BETTER OFF alone. Alexandra Scott was one of them. It wasn't that she didn't like people as a rule, and it wasn't that they didn't like her. It was the disappointment.

Alex had grown up in Boston, where blood was blue, money was old, and those who had both stuck together like a big, inbred dysfunctional family. Alex had tried to fit in. She'd never quite managed it, swallowing her disappointment when she begged to go to science camp but instead was enrolled in finishing school in hopes she could be pressed into the vapid, mall-haunting, socialite-in-training mold. Breeding would tell, her mother insisted, then set out to prove it. No matter what it took.

It turned out her mother was right. Unfortunately the only thing Alex had inherited was the knack for disappointment, beginning with the four years she'd spent in a tiny sub–Ivy League dorm room with three red-blooded, nonmonied roommates, and ending with a bachelor's degree in the history of American settlement on the indigenous animal species of the West, then a PhD in zoology, and finally a grant to study mountain lions and a one-way ticket out of Boston.

Okay, so there'd been a detour, a major detour. She'd been young and she'd wanted to please her mother. One thing had led to another, and she'd actually wound up engaged. That had been a mistake, or rather he'd been a mistake. And a liar and a cheat and a minuscule excuse for a human being. But she'd fixed that, and come out the other end with a rock-solid determination to never again let other people's expectations dictate her life to her.

She hadn't regretted her decision once in six years. She might have been living in a log cabin only slightly larger than her dorm room, with no electricity and no indoor plumbing, but there were no other occupants, and solitude, Alex decided, made up for a lot.

She'd have that again. She'd rebuild the cabin and finish her survey of the mountain lions, then move on to another study. Just as soon as she found out what her insurance covered.

"Nothing," her agent said when she finally managed to get hold of him. "You didn't pay your last premium."

"I . . . don't recall getting the bill," she said after she racked her brain and came up empty. "Mail delivery is kind of spotty where I live." Her memory was at fault for the rest of it. She tended toward tunnel vision when she was working—which was most of the time. She counted on the mail to remind her of that sort of thing, and that brought her back to the beginning of the circle. Her agent was sympathetic, but sympathy wasn't going to buy her power bars and bottled water, let alone rebuild her cabin.

So she called the rest of her contacts, which took precious little time—the downside to being a loner—and netted her exactly what she'd gotten from her insurance company. The grant money had all been awarded for the year, and the few friends she had in the business weren't the kind of people who had spare cash lying around. Field zoology wasn't a profession you went into if you wanted to get rich. It wasn't a profession you went into if you wanted to have an actual savings account. Alex had just enough left in her checking account for some clean underwear and about a week of living out of a hotel room. Then she'd be truly homeless.

Except for Boston. But she was going to have to be a lot more desperate before she could bring herself to go that route. Besides, who would look after Jackass? He wouldn't fit in with the pedigreed mounts in Boston stables any more than she belonged in the drawing rooms.

It seemed like a good time to get some sleep, forget about her problems for a while. Thank god she'd gotten a room first thing, because in the two hours it had taken to exhaust her funding possibilities, Casteel's population seemed to have doubled, and not in a good way. A lot of the newcomers seemed to be looking for an easy buck, but greed wasn't unique to the newcomers. She'd have bet the prices at the diner and market had already gone up, and there wasn't a room left to rent within fifty miles.

Not that she could get to hers, situated as it was above the bar in the Casteeley Inn. The place was wall-to-wall people, all of them had questions, and as soon as she made her appearance, she was elected answer man. Her own, site-specific, fifteen minutes of fame.

If she'd been hungry or thirsty, she might have hung around. She could probably live off her insider status for a while. Hell, considering the way she was being pestered every other minute she ought to set up a booth and charge for what she knew. Not a bad idea. Except she didn't know anything.

So there she was, halfway between the front door and the stairs, completely surrounded by strangers, when a hand reached into the press of people, latched on to her arm, and dragged her out of the throng and face-to-face with Tag Donovan.

"You have a room in this dive?" he wanted to know.

Great, because of him she had nothing and he wanted half of it? "You're not sleeping with me."

"No offense, but I'm really tired. How about you let me into your room for now and we'll talk about your pants later."

"How about no to both?"

"You saved my life," he said, "twice. In some cultures that means you're responsible for me."

"This is America. Land of every-man-for-himself."

"The rest of these guys can find their own women to sponge off of."

Alex rolled her eyes and started to work her way toward the stairs, head down, not stopping for anyone. Tag was right behind her, taking advantage of the path she was cutting through the crowd. The next time somebody asked her a question, she pointed a thumb over her shoulder and said, "Tag Donovan." She didn't have to tell them who he was; his name was already better known than Bigfoot—and he had about the same amount of credibility as far as she was concerned.

Unfortunately her diversion backfired. News traveled around the room in about two seconds, everyone converged on Tag's position, and there went her hope of getting to the stairs. But there was a wide-open path to the front door.

Sighing, she went back out to the street and pointed her weary body toward the sheriff's office. A wafer-thin cot over wire mesh was a far cry from the soft mattress she'd been looking forward to, but she was at the point where anything horizontal would fit the bill.

She woke up an indeterminate time later, and after the second attempt at trying to stand up she decided it might be best to lie there for a few minutes. Vertical was still a bit much to ask for. Her head was buzzing and her muscles were stiff. If not for her rumbling stomach she probably would have slept the night through.

Matt hadn't been there when she arrived earlier that afternoon, and he wasn't there now. Probably somewhere in town breaking up . . . something. Or arresting somebody.

That got her on her feet. She didn't want to be around when the occupancy rose in these particular sleeping quarters.

The clock on the wall said it was past midnight by the time she began the eight-block walk to the bar. The clouds of the day before had cleared off completely, but Casteel didn't count streetlights among its modern conveniences.

From the look of things a tent city had sprung up in the grazing land across the river. There were a lot of lights that appeared to be campfires over there, anyway. The street seemed to be pretty deserted, but Alex felt like somebody had painted a target on her back. All those warnings from Tag and her run-in with Junior were getting to her, she decided.

Or maybe it was the two guys who grabbed her from behind and shoved her into the alley between the sheriff's office and the bakery next door while she was in that first breathless moment of disbelief and shock.

She got a handle on herself pretty fast and put her back to the wall, heart pounding, eyes straining to make out anything in the absolute blackness of the alley.

"What did Donovan tell you about the treasure?" one of them said, his face close enough to bathe her in garlic breath.

Disgusting, but she had more to worry about than a few singed nose hairs. Like how to get herself out of this alley in one piece. Amped on adrenaline, she could probably handle herself against one ruffian, but not two, especially if they were armed. She didn't have her Winchester because Matt didn't allow guns to be carried in town. She thought it was a bit too optimistic to hope her assailants were obeying that particular ordinance.

"He didn't tell me anything," she said, thankful to hear her voice steady after the first couple of words. Dealing with men was like dealing with any other animal. If you showed them fear you could kiss your ass good-bye.

"What do you take us for, idiots?"

No, dangerous idiots. She kept that to herself, though. "Do you really think he would tell me his secrets and take a chance I'd head out on my own?"

Okay, maybe not complete idiots, since the logic of that appeared to be working its way past the steroids and testosterone to somehow find the few operating brain cells they possessed. They conducted a short, whispered conversation that Alex didn't try to overhear since she was busy attempting to slip away while they weren't paying strict attention to her.

"Hey!" Garlic-breath finally clued in and slammed a hand against the brick wall next to her head. "You'll have to come with us," he said. "Donovan wants you to guide him for a reason."

"So you're going to force me to guide you instead? Without Donovan's alleged information? And what happens if we don't find the treasure?"

"You better hope we find it."

"We're not going to actually hurt her, are we?" the other guy wanted to know.

"She wouldn't be much good as a guide if she was hurt."

Alex was happy to hear that, but there was no way she'd let these two morons drag her out of town. She ducked under the arm and aimed a kick at its owner's kneecap. He shifted aside, trying to block the blow, and instead took it right in the crotch.

He went down, wheezing every molecule of air out of his lungs, leaving the alley smelling like an Italian restaurant, and flattening his partner underneath him. Some of the businesses along the main drag were still open, pandering to the population boom. There was enough light from the window of the shop across the street for Alex to see the two of them rolling around in a tangle of arms and legs, Garlic-breath on top, trying to curl into the fetal position and completely pinning his partner down.

"Jeez, Mick," he moaned, "you said nobody was gonna get hurt. And by nobody I mean me."

"Shit, Franky, can't you keep your mouth shut?"

"I kinda forgot when she *kicked me in the balls*."

"Get off me, dammit, she's gonna get away."

Alex knew she should do exactly that, but really, watching the two of them was like comic relief. Definitely made it difficult to take them as a serious threat. There was the chance she'd learn something, too, but entertainment was her primary goal.

"I'm in agony here," Franky groaned. "I think she permanently ruined my chances of fatherhood."

"I'm sure the female half of the human race will thank me," Alex said.

"There's no reason to get mean about it," Franky said. He tried to lift himself off his smaller partner and wound up collapsing on top of him again.

All the air whooshed out of Mick's lungs, and Alex decided to leave while they were both still incapacitated. She set off toward the bar, not taking her time, but careful to keep watch in case they recovered and came after her again.

She was so busy looking over her shoulder, she didn't realize they'd circled around and come at her from the front until they grabbed her again and shoved her into another alley. "Jesus, Franky, give it up. I'm not guiding you."

"You're not guiding anybody," a voice said—a voice that was all wrong. No garlic, for one thing. It didn't sound like Mick or Franky, either, and whoever it was meant exactly what he said. The knife blade glinting in his hand made that perfectly clear.

chapter
8

ALEX WASN'T NORMALLY A SCREAMER, BUT THIS seemed like a good time to give it a try. She opened her mouth, but before she could work up a really excellent shriek there was a muffled thud and a lot of grunting that hadn't come out of her mouth. Somebody slammed her into the wall, and she felt a burning pain in her leg. That got a verbal reaction from her, and it was a word no Miss USA ever would have uttered.

She clutched at her thigh and found a ragged tear in her jeans. There was something wet on her hand, obviously blood, but not a lot, and from what she could tell the wound wasn't too drastic. It still hurt like hell.

Meanwhile, a scuffle was going on in the dirt at her feet. She couldn't see much of anything, but she was hearing a lot, heavy breathing, more grunting, and some pretty inventive swearing. Almost as good as hers.

Something flew by her face and fell at the mouth of the alley, what little light there was glinting off the blade of a knife. Alex limped over and retrieved it, then didn't have a clue what to do next. Even if one of the scufflers had come to her rescue—

Okay, the guy who'd come to her rescue was almost definitely Tag—there was no getting around it, although his intentions seemed to be better than his follow-through. And since he'd intervened so she could get away, she should probably beat a hasty retreat. Unfortunately hasty wasn't one of her gears at the moment. Slow and steady was even stretching it.

She'd barely made it to the mouth of the alley when a hand fell heavy on her shoulder, spinning her around. Reflex kicked in, the knife came up, and another hand clamped around her wrist.

"Jesus," Tag said, "you trying to gut me like a fish?"

She'd been accosted, wounded, and threatened with death, and it wasn't until she heard his voice that her heart pounded so hard she had to fight the urge to throw herself into his arms. And then the aftermath of the adrenaline started to kick in.

"You okay?"

"No," she said, grateful it was only her body shaking and not her voice. "I've been stabbed."

Tag took the knife out of her hand and towed her out to the street, where there was marginally more light. "It's only a scratch," he said with his face about an inch away from her thigh. The top of her thigh. "Thanks to me."

"Thanks to you?!"

"You're not going to start that if-not-for-you crap again. I saved your life. That ought to make up for some of the other stuff."

"You saved—" Alex threw her hands up and stomped off—or tried to. Hard to stomp really well when your leg is on fire. "He said he was going to kill me so I didn't guide you."

"Oh. Shit. That's not good."

Alex halted, swung around, and got in his face. "Does he work for Junior, or did your friends in the plane send him?"

"Does it matter?"

"Not really. Either way it's your fault." She whipped back around and took off for her room again, anger getting her to at least second gear. "If they don't want you looking for the treasure, why aren't they coming after you?"

"Because you're the easier target."

"And if they succeed and take me out of the picture you'll just find another guide, so again, what does that gain anyone?"

"I don't know," Tag shot back, pissed off and not bothering to hide it. "It doesn't matter why they keep coming after you. As long as you're a target, I'm your only hope."

Alex racked her brain but she didn't have a comeback for that. There was something wrong with his argument, but she couldn't put her finger on what it was.

Tag might be responsible for a lot of the mayhem and violence that had been directed at her lately, but he hadn't personally perpetrated any of it. He'd shown up when she needed him most, too, and he hadn't hesitated to jump in front of her. Sort of. She still didn't know why he was so hell-bent on her cooperation, and that bothered her. A lot. But she couldn't exactly call him an enemy. She wasn't ready to call him a friend yet, either, or a partner. Not until she understood what was driving him.

At the moment it was probably a place to sleep. Tag dogged her steps all the way to the inn, waited for her while she stopped and got the first aid kit and a couple of beers from behind the bar, then took the stairs after her. "Maybe you should see a doctor," he said.

"Sure, I'll start out on Jackass in the morning. It'll only take me two days to get to the nearest clinic."

Tag rolled his eyes. "Borrow the cop car."

"It's not that bad." She plopped down on the bed, swatting at his hand when he tried to peel back the ragged edges of denim around her wound. "I don't need any help."

"What's that, your personal motto?"

"It is when you're around."

"You'd let that sheriff help you, right? I'll bet he's seen all there is to see."

"He's done more than see." She stood and peeled off her jeans, holding his gaze the whole while. She'd gotten used to walking around in her underwear—and sometimes less—a long time ago. "What's the big deal about seeing?"

A lot, Tag thought. Seeing, especially before you'd done anything, was pretty damn powerful. And judging by the way she was watching him, she knew that. And she was using it.

If he'd had any self-control he'd have kept his gaze level with hers, but the temptation was too much. And his imagination more than lived up to reality. Funny, he'd always considered himself a silk and lace man, but one look at her white cotton bikini panties and he was a goner. Breath shortening, pulse spiking, brains dropping into his crotch.

It took a Herculean effort, but he managed to control his lust. The long, bloody gash in her leg might have had somewhat of a sobering effect if he hadn't made the mistake of kneeling on the floor beside her to take a closer look. Having his head six inches from her denim-clad thigh, on a pitch black public street, was a hell of a lot different than putting his face six inches away from a whole lot of smooth bare skin, only meagerly covered by all that pure white cotton.

Tag glanced up at her. Her cheeks were pink, and her upper lip was sweating. Maybe it was pain, maybe not, but he figured the pulse fluttering in the hollow of her throat had something to do with him. "You're not as cold as you want everyone to think," he said quietly.

"I don't want everyone to think I'm cold. Just you."

"We're stuck with each other, Alex." And for a moment he regretted that, regretted putting her in a position where armed men were coming after her. But neither of them had a choice. "We might as well get used to it."

She chewed on that for a minute. "Tell me about your new clue."

Tag tried to hide his satisfaction. Judging by the way her expression went sour, he wasn't all that successful.

"I'm not agreeing to anything until I see what you have."

"You don't have a choice. Somebody tried to kill you. You need me."

"You're smirking again," she said, but without any real heat. "I can leave Casteel. I can leave North America if that's what it takes."

Tag lifted a shoulder. "You could, but you're not the kind of woman who runs away."

"That's not what you said at my cabin."

"I was wrong."

Alex snorted.

"What? I can admit when I'm wrong."

"You're an opportunist. You don't believe in right and wrong. The only important thing to you is the treasure, and you'll say whatever it takes to get it."

She was right about him being an opportunist, but she was wrong about his value system. Right and wrong were the ultimate motivations for him. Kind of hard to convince her of that when he couldn't tell her the entire truth.

Alex got up and limped across the room to retrieve her satchel. She opened it and pulled out her maps, spreading them out on the small table under the window.

Tag joined her, having to squint to read the tiny, meticulously printed notations. "Even your handwriting is anal," he muttered.

"This really isn't about my handwriting."

"True." Tag settled in to hover over her shoulder. She was almost as uncomfortable as she'd been with his face practically in her crotch.

"This map is a lot more complete than the one I saw, obviously, but I think the treasure is somewhere in this area," he said, reaching around her to point at the spot he meant.

Alex concentrated almost fanatically on the map so she wouldn't notice the way his body curved around hers, a big, solid hunk of man who smelled faintly of cologne instead of beer and sweat and horses. He felt comforting and safe—if she didn't notice the warmth of his chest against her back and the way his hips nestled up against her bottom. Her all but naked bottom.

Walking around in her panties had been something along the lines of a dare—to herself and to Tag. See how little you affect me? she was saying to him. Now prove you can keep your eye on the goal, and not the panties. He was doing pretty good ignoring them, but she was having major trouble thinking about anything else.

"The map I saw had a lot of old writing on it," Tag said, his voice edged with something that rasped along her nerve endings, "and it had a little drawstring bag attached, so old it was practically falling apart. The bag was empty but it tested positive for gold dust."

Alex slipped out from between him and the table, aiming for nonchalant and figuring she got the speed right if not the attitude. "The map you saw?" She picked up a beer and twisted the cap off, enjoying the way her question wiped the smirk off Tag's face.

His eyes dropped to her panties and she forgot that he wasn't answering. Escape seemed so much more important suddenly, and her wound provided the perfect solution to that problem. She went into the bathroom and wet a cloth so she could clean the knife slash. It hurt like hell, and that was good because a certain clarity of mind came along with pain—not to mention it crowded the other things she was feeling right out of her. "You told me you had the map."

"Um . . . I may have exaggerated on that point."

"Exaggerated? They call that something different in this part of the world."

"You mean the land of the tall tales?" Tag came to the bathroom door, leaning against the jamb. "I don't think they should be passing judgment on me."

Alex met his eyes in the mirror. "You don't think anyone should be passing judgment on you, which is why you keep lying to me."

Tag clapped his hands to his head, like he was afraid it would explode. "Is it necessary to keep track?"

"Yes. It helps to know what's the truth and what you've only told me—which isn't the same thing."

"Okay, so I lied to you about the map. There's an upside."

Alex crossed her arms and waited.

"If you know I'm not being strictly honest," he explained, "you won't trust what I tell you, and if you don't trust what I tell you, you'll check everything out for yourself. And while you're checking my facts, maybe somewhere along the line you'll pick up on something I missed."

"It's possible," Alex said, "but it seems like a stupid way to operate."

Tag agreed with her, at least privately. This assignment, not to mention his life, would be so much easier if he could just tell her the truth—the entire truth. But until he could pin down her role in this whole fiasco, he couldn't take that chance. And it wasn't just her. She didn't trust a lot of people, but she wouldn't hesitate to confide in those she did trust. If she told the wrong person and the truth got out, Tag could end up keeping his partner company in the hereafter. That didn't hold a lot of appeal—although he could use the rest.

"You can get your hands on this map, right?" she said.

"Sure. Probably."

"Not very reassuring, Donovan. At least tell me you memorized it."

"No."

"The area you pointed out is about six square inches on the map, but it's a lot of real estate to cover in three dimensions. What you're telling me is useless, so unless you can get your hands on the map, you might as well give up now."

"Getting my hands on it will be kind of . . . problematic."

"The way you say that gives me a bad feeling."

Tag could see her racking her brain, and the a-ha

moment was written on her face, followed by disbelief. "Junior has it."

"Yeah." At least that would be his guess.

"He didn't strike me as the type who'd share."

"I don't know him personally, but I don't think 'playing well with others' is part of his repertoire. Dussaud will work for anyone as long as they pay him enough money."

"And you're in it for what? The adventure?"

"Among other things."

Alex limped back into the main room, sat on the bed, and pulled the first aid kit over. "You're sure the bag wasn't a fake? Somebody salted it to get investors?"

"I didn't invest anything. The guy who owns it isn't hurting for cash, so if it was salted somebody did a hell of a job. And all the testing checks out. The paper is authentic, so's the cloth of the bag, and it's impregnated with gold dust that assays in line with the early Colorado strikes. Even the Spanish is authentic for the time period. The expert I consulted verified that much, but he had no way to match the names to the landmarks."

"That's where I come in," Alex finished, putting the last bit of tape over her bandage. She retrieved her beer and sat back, taking a half-hearted sip.

She looked exhausted, like a woman who'd run out of options. Tag would have bet the call to her insurance agent hadn't gone well. He already knew she was short of money and friends, and she was curious about the treasure—which added up to good news for him. Or maybe not, since he wasn't the only game in town anymore.

"Junior doesn't seem like the type of guy who chases wild geese," she said after a moment.

"And I am?" Tag wanted to know.

She shrugged. "He has the equipment, he has the manpower. If one of you is going to find the Lost Spaniard, it seems to me he has the edge."

Tag shoved away from the wall where he'd been leaning and picked up the second beer. "You're easily convinced," he said, taking a long drink that didn't do much to clear the sour taste from his throat. "A couple of nice vehicles and a few muscle-bound goons and you're ready to put your life in his hands."

"It's not the vehicles, it's the cost. Equipment like that takes a lot of capital to keep up. Nobody is going to put all those resources behind a project they don't think is going to pay off. And on that scale they're expecting a big one."

Tag stuffed his hands in his pockets and swallowed his anger. If Junior's sideshow was what it took to convince her, so be it. "Now all we have to do is get hold of the map."

"We?" Alex said. "Why do I need you?"

"I think I answered that question about an hour ago. In the alley."

ALEX WOKE UP, BLEARY-EYED, FUZZY-BRAINED, TAKING a while to comprehend that something was different than it had been when she'd hit the sheets—she raised her head and looked at the clock—a scant two hours before. And then it came to her, right about the time she dropped her head and it didn't hit the pillow. Instead there was something firm, and warm, and slightly hairy under her cheek. She was lying on her left side, and there was something bony and warm and hairy under her left arm and leg, too.

She tried to ease away, and that was when she noticed something hard and warm—and slightly hairy—around her waist, because it tightened, rasping across the bare skin between her T-shirt and panties.

"Stop moving around, I'm trying to sleep," Tag grumbled, his breath warm on her forehead, his body heat wrapping around her like a blanket—no, Tag was more like a cashmere sweater, warm, extravagant, and very, very sensuous against the skin. Except she'd never gotten this kind of a rush from a sweater.

"You were supposed to be sleeping in the chair," she reminded him—and herself.

"Too uncomfortable."

"Too bad."

He opened one eye, peered down at her. "Everything was fine until you decided you liked my side of the bed better than yours."

"Did not," Alex protested, and then she realized he was right. She was plastered against him, and they were definitely not on the half of the bed she'd started the night out on. "If you'd stayed put, it wouldn't be an issue."

"Right, it has nothing to do with your lack of self-control."

"I can control myself just fine." She tried to roll away, but his arm tightened again.

His hand splayed low across her belly, shooting heat into parts of her that had no business being hot. And then the warmth turned to need, and the need to something that wound inside her, tighter and tighter until it was nearly impossible to resist. She closed her eyes and allowed herself to imagine, just for a moment, how it would be if she gave in and let herself sample all that hardness she felt against her, to have his mouth on hers and his hands on her body. She shifted and stretched, restless, trying to ease the tightness and at the same time savoring it.

"If you don't stop that neither one of us is getting any more sleep tonight."

"You started it."

"And I'm more than willing to finish it. You're the one who's afraid."

"Afraid!" She reared up, braced her hands on his chest, and knew immediately that she'd played right into his hands—among other body parts.

He slipped a knee between her thighs and up, until his leg was pressed against her. The pressure felt so good her eyes fluttered closed and her breath sighed out, and all she could think was *more*. So she kissed him, and she liked that so much she let her body get into the act. Tag seemed to be enjoying it, too, right up to the moment he jerked away from her, rolling onto his back and letting out a huge breath.

For a minute she was simply stunned, then she said, "Who's afraid?"

"Not me." And he was obviously still willing, but he wasn't doing anything about it.

Neither could she, after he'd rejected her. If one of them was going to initiate the action again, it was going to have to be him.

"The chair is over there," she said.

Tag lifted up and looked in the corner. "Yep," he said, "there's the chair."

"We agreed you were going to sleep in it."

"True. Problem is, I wasn't sleeping. I didn't get any sleep last night, either, and that's no good. Not if I want to get through tomorrow in one piece. Exhaustion causes mistakes, and there isn't any room for error in this."

"Fine. You need the bed, it's yours." She threw the covers back and got out of bed before her body could change her mind. Tag reached for her but she slipped away and went into the bathroom to cool off. And get over her embarrassment.

Before this he'd been the one making all the advances, and she'd been the one fending him off. She didn't like having the tables turned, especially the part where he put on the brakes. Sure, if he hadn't put on the brakes they'd have had sex, and she *really* wouldn't have liked that—okay she'd have liked it during, but after, there would have been regrets. Major regrets.

She probably should have thanked Tag for saving her from the regrets, but she was still stinging from the rejection.

"Alex?" Tag said through the door.

"Yeah."

"You staying in there the rest of the night?"

"I might. It's nice to have indoor plumbing. I think I should take my time and really appreciate it while I can."

He laughed, sounding relaxed and sexy. The jerk.

"I think you should go," she said.

And while she was fighting the urge to call him back she

heard the window open and close and she knew he'd snuck out. It was part of the agreement they'd made before they'd turned in; an agreement that didn't involve the exchange of bodily fluids. She'd violated that arrangement, not to mention him, by sticking her tongue in his mouth. But she was blaming it on Tag; he'd agreed to sleep in the chair, so he'd broken the agreement first.

But she was too honest with herself to ignore the truth. The two things didn't equate—his climbing into her bed and her kissing him. The difference was, sleeping in the chair was an inconvenience, sneaking out got him closer to the Lost Spaniard, and having sex with her might be more trouble than it was worth.

The only important question was, would he live up to the rest of the pact they'd made?

chapter
9

ALEX TRIED TO GET BACK TO SLEEP AFTER TAG LEFT.
By six a.m. she decided it was a lost cause, so she dragged
herself upright, stumbled into the shower, and came out to
find a pale, hollow-eyed woman staring back at her from
the mirror. Her leg was sore, her ego was bruised, and she
was exhausted. And she was blaming all of it on Tag.

The night had started off okay—after the attempted kidnapping, and the attempted murder. She'd floated off to
sleep on a haze of beer and aspirin, and okay, having Tag
close by had contributed to her peace of mind. As long as
he'd stayed on his side of the room. Climbing into bed with
her, that was crossing boundaries. Getting her all worked
up, then leaving her with an itch there was no way to cure?
That was cruel, and the only remedy she had was to take
her mind off it and hope her body would follow suit.

She went to see Jackass, and the quiet of the stable was
soothing—if she ignored the way he looked at her. Reproachful was how she'd describe it, like he knew she'd
been an idiot last night and he was disappointed.

"I didn't go through with it," she said to him, choosing not to mention that Tag had been the rational one.

Jackass didn't look completely mollified, but he let her take him out for a long walk in the prairie across the river. Her thigh hurt, but by the time they got back to town she felt better, almost back to her pre-Tag self.

It didn't last long. Part of it was reality sinking in. She had a mission to accomplish that morning, an unpleasant mission. Casteel was the other downer.

The town was wall-to-wall people, all four square miles of it. People asking questions, people staring and whispering, people acting loony. Not that loony was all that unusual for Casteel, it was just that the craziness had always been on the periphery of her life. Now it was hitting her right in the face. Full frontal craziness.

She worked her way from one end of town to the other, fending people off with a glare when she could, a brusque "I don't know" when a visual put-down didn't cut it.

She'd have given her left arm to see one normal human being—and she didn't mean Tag, she thought, rolling her eyes when she realized his was the face she'd been searching the crowd for. Normal was the last adjective she'd use to describe Tag Donovan. Irritating. There was a word for him. Untrustworthy, confusing. Fraud.

She didn't really know who Tag was, but she knew he was using her. So what the hell had she been thinking, jumping him like that? Sure she'd wanted him, but that had been more along the lines of . . . repayment than personal interaction. She was entitled to some instant gratification. After everything she'd lost because of him, he owed her that much. And she ought to have her head examined.

If she had any sense she'd get out of town, but that would be running away, and dammit if she couldn't hear Tag saying "I told you so" with that stupid smirk on his face because she was thinking of bolting, just like she'd done the last time her life got a little rough.

She was a target, and if she wasn't going to run away she needed to pick a side. Between Tag and Junior, there really wasn't a choice. Of course, she could always go off and find the treasure on her own.

"Hey, Alex." Rusty Hale halted directly in front of her so she had no choice but to stop. She blamed Tag for that, too. If she'd been paying attention to something besides the way he'd felt wrapped around her in bed—

"That's some limp you got there," Rusty said.

—her idiot radar would have gone off in time.

"I seen you take that city feller up to your room last night," the idiot said. "Boy howdy, you must have put a smile on his face."

Then again . . . "You were at the inn last night?"

"Me and half the town."

"Any of the guys from the SUVs in there?"

"Nope, they pretty much stay to themselves. I heard old man Winston moved in with his daughter and rented his place out to that French guy and his crew."

She already knew that. Tag had told her last night. "You're sure one of Dussaud's men wasn't sitting in a corner somewhere?"

"Positive. The whole town is jacked up because they're being so standoffish."

Alex let her breath out, rolling her shoulders to work out some of the tension. "I guess they think they're too good for us."

"Some folks say that about you," Rusty said, "but I ain't one of 'em." He smiled and sidled a step closer. He probably thought he was being charming. Alex was fighting her gag reflex. "A woman as pretty as you can afford to be choosy, that's all."

"Choosy, as in I don't date married men."

"What if I told you I was separated?"

That made her laugh. "Last time you tried to pick me up you said you were divorced."

"I was probably drunk when I told you that. Guess I should keep better track of my stories."

The look Alex gave him said it all. Unfortunately, he didn't get the message.

"Maybe we could have a friendly drink later. If you're still gonna be in town."

"Sure, bring your wife along. I imagine Verna would like to get out of the house."

"That ain't funny."

No, it wasn't funny, but she needed the comic relief or she might pop Rusty in the mouth.

"I heard you were burned out of your cabin," he said. "Where you gonna go?"

She shrugged. "I can't stay at the hotel indefinitely, so I guess I'll have to camp out this season."

"The weather is finally warming up, but it's still pretty unpredictable," Rusty reminded her.

"That'll give me time to pick up the gear I'll need."

Rusty slid his hands into his back pockets, which was apparently his thinking position. "Be awfully convenient to look for the treasure while you're camping out."

"It sure would be. If I had any idea where to look."

Rusty snorted. "If you didn't know before, I'll bet that Donovan character told you last night."

Now she really wanted to pop him one. In fact her fist was already clenched and moving before she stopped herself. Nothing said "you're right" quite like a violent denial. "What I do and who I do it with is none of your concern," she said, injecting ice into the words.

"Now Alex, don't go getting all indignant on me. I was only hoping you'd cut me in. For old times' sake."

"We don't have any 'old times.'" He was just trying to ferret out her plans, although rat would have been a more appropriate rodent. "I'll tell you what. I'll ask Tag if he wants to cut you in, and if he says it's all right—"

"Now, there's no need for that. He's liable to get the wrong impression."

"What impression? That you think I'm trying to screw him out of the Spaniard's location? Or that you're trying to screw us both?"

Rusty had the good grace to flush. "I, uh, oughtta get home for lunch," he muttered, brushing by her and hotfooting it down the sidewalk.

Probably afraid she'd beat him home and tell his wife. Tempting, but if Verna didn't know she was married to a philandering idiot, Alex wasn't going to break the news. And anyway, she had shorter fish to fry.

She headed in the opposite direction and hung a left at the last crossroad before the end of town. Willow Street ran parallel to the main drag and one block north. She made a right, and another block brought her to old man Winston's small frame house.

The place across the street boasted a gated arbor covered with winter-browned ivy and clematis. It provided precious little camouflage, but standing inside it made Alex feel marginally less exposed. At least physically. In every other respect she might as well be bare-assed in the wind.

She couldn't trust Tag Donovan, and she couldn't trust Junior. She was broke, homeless, and people were trying to kill her because they thought she was after the Lost Spaniard. Solution? She needed that treasure map. She wasn't sure what she'd do if she actually managed to get her hands on it, but adapting to circumstances seemed to have worked so far.

Present circumstances, however, weren't all that flexible. The way she saw it there were two options. Option One involved knocking on the front door of old man Winston's house and having personal interaction with Junior—translation, ego stroking. Not one of her better developed skills. Option Two would entail black clothing and a total disregard for law and order.

Faced with those choices, Alex thought she could psych herself up for armed robbery. She'd gotten pretty good at stealth working with mountain lions. But there was a guy stationed at the front of the house and she'd caught a glimpse of another pacing along the back, and it wasn't a very big place. She'd never get away with it, and knowing the local cop wouldn't be any help whatsoever. If she got caught she probably wouldn't have to worry about currying favor or cooling her heels—unless it was in an actual cooler. And she was wearing a toe tag . . .

Okay, so there was really only one choice. She took a deep breath and walked across the street before she could change her mind. The goon out front tracked her with his eyes, but otherwise he could have been a gargoyle standing in the shadows at the corner of the house. A particularly ugly gargoyle.

The front door was opened before she could knock—which explained why the gargoyle hadn't tried to intercept her.

"Mademoiselle Scott," Junior said, the epitome of Frenchness, smooth, charming, more than a little creepy. Marquis de Sade in miniature, with some Casanova thrown in just to make things even more uncomfortable. Okay, Casanova was Italian, but it was the best she could come up with.

"I am so happy you have come to call." Junior stood back, smiling wide, inviting her in with a sweep of his arm.

Alex accepted his invitation, trying to ignore the tingle between her shoulder blades when the door shut behind her. It took some doing, but her knees didn't knock, and as long as she kept breathing she wouldn't pass out. The thought of being unconscious and helpless in enemy territory scared her enough to make her gulp in some air.

"This is an unexpected pleasure," Junior said. "I was delighted to see you at my front door, but at the risk of being unforgivably rude, I must ask what brings you here after you so decidedly refused me in the street yesterday?"

And embarrassed him. She didn't miss the accusation in his voice, or delude herself that he wanted to make her suffer for it. "Call me Alex," she said, deciding to dispense with the groveling right off the bat; the sooner it was behind her, the sooner she could do what she'd come to do and get the hell out of there. "I guess I owe you an apology, Mr. Dussaud. It seems I forgot to pay my last insurance premium."

"So you are, how do you say, up a creek? And you are wondering if my offer is still open."

And this is where it got really tricky. "I'm just . . . exploring my options."

"Let us be honest with each other, Alex. You would not be here if you had other options."

"Not true," she shot back, tired of everyone telling her she was helpless without some big strong man at her side. Or a really short one who had big strong men on his payroll. "I have other resources. Professional associates, professors and advisors from college."

"You have not mentioned family."

She looked down, going for pathetic, but she was watching him through her lashes to see if he bought it. When she saw him smile she knew she had him. Tag wasn't the only one who could manipulate.

"You pretend to be rough around the edges," Junior said, "but you have failed to completely rub off the polish of your upbringing. And you would rather not go home a failure, I think."

She gave him a level stare so he could have a moment to congratulate himself on his insight. Not that he was wrong, but she'd never tried to rub anything off. She was who she was, and she didn't apologize for it. "You wanted plain? Here's plain. I didn't lose everything. I still have a responsibility to fulfill the terms of my grant. If I don't, my reputation will be ruined and I'll never work in my field again. I need to make some money. Fast."

Another self-satisfied smile, one he didn't try to hide. "My offer still stands. I will pay you for your services as a guide."

"Tag Donovan made the same offer."

"Last night, in your room?"

"He followed me to my room last night, and he left last night. Or didn't your spy report that to you?"

Junior didn't respond.

"Fine." Alex pushed away from the wall and headed for the front door.

Junior laid a hand on her arm. "Donovan was seen in town this morning. I understand he looked very . . . cranky was the word I believe was used. I doubt he would appear so unhappy if he'd spent the night in your bed."

Alex resisted the urge to brush his hand off. And wash her arm. It was harder to ignore the way he looked at her. The way he looked at her was icky. Suggestive icky. She was perfectly willing to manipulate him to get what she wanted, but she wasn't using sex. Not even the hint of sex. "If we come to an agreement, it'll be a business arrangement only."

He nodded, removing his hand from her arm. "Suppose I offered you a percentage of the treasure."

"And if the treasure isn't found?"

"Then you prefer a lump sum payment."

"Up front," she qualified, "and I can't afford to waste my summer looking for a fairy tale."

"Ah." He fingered the half dozen hairs on his upper lip masquerading as a mustache. "You want to know if I can offer you some assurance of success."

"Donovan can't," she said simply.

He pursed his lips and held her eyes for a moment. "If I say I have a map?"

"Then I'd want to see it," she said, hiding her relief. Tag hadn't been a hundred percent sure Junior had the thing.

"To reveal the map, it would be *tres stupide, non?*"

She let her mouth twist in a derisive smile. "Stupid how? We're in your house, surrounded by your men. And you're not going to let me see it long enough to memorize anything."

"But you are asking me to trust you."

Alex shook her head. "I haven't given you any reason to trust me."

"And I have given you no reason to doubt my word. Yet you do."

He took another of his long pauses, trying to unnerve her with a cold stare. Obviously he'd never come face-to-face with a hungry mountain lion.

Interestingly enough, not getting a reaction seemed to please him. He turned and left the room; Alex, puzzled, followed him. Maybe she'd underestimated him. He seemed to like her strength, so maybe he wasn't just a short guy with a Napoleon complex. That made him a whole lot more dangerous. Which didn't change her predicament at all.

She followed Junior into a small bedroom, the single bed and chest of drawers shoved aside to make room for a makeshift desk, complete with a laptop.

Alex skirted the desk and dropped into the chair behind it.

Junior seemed to be having cold feet. He certainly wasn't producing the map.

"No offense, but you're not the first stranger to show up in town claiming he has a map to the Lost Spaniard."

He smiled slightly and came around the desk, waiting politely while she moved out of his way—which she was only too happy to do.

Behind the desk was a portable safe. Junior hesitated, hand on the dial. Alex turned her back while he worked the combination, heard the door open, then close again, followed by some rustling.

"Well, Alex, here it is."

She turned back around and had to fight to keep her mouth from dropping open. There on the desk was a large swatch of natural linen, centered on which was a piece of yellowed parchment with some faded markings on it. It was about eight inches by twelve, weighted down at either end, but curled at the corners, as if it had been rolled for a long time. There was a small, ragged hole in one corner, through which had been threaded a piece of braided horsehair. The other ends of the makeshift string were around the neck of a small drawstring bag so old the weaving was coming apart in places. In the worn spots Alex could see something glittering. Gold dust, she assumed. Just like Tag had said.

She traded a look with Junior, and at his nod she bent

closer. She didn't touch it. It was obviously old and no doubt delicate, and she wasn't taking any chances—not that she cared about the age or historical value of the document, but there was no telling what would happen to her if she damaged it, even by accident.

It didn't take long to discover that Tag had been right about a lot of things. It was obviously a map, and it did appear to represent the area she worked in. One portion of it looked so much like the valley where her cabin stood—had stood—that she felt an almost overwhelming need to wrap her hands around the pip-squeak's throat and choke him to death. Junior may not have been the one who burned her out, but he worked for the guy who had.

And the big, mean men who worked for Junior would be on her in a heartbeat if she so much as called him a nasty name.

So she concentrated on the map instead. There were notations on the parchment, the writing faint and spidery. At least one was in Spanish, and the only landmark she recognized before Junior flipped the linen over it and whisked it back into the safe was Denver.

But she'd seen enough. "I'll give you six weeks of my time. You pay me up front. Twenty thousand dollars. I can order equipment, and while I'm waiting for it to arrive, I'll help you look for the Spaniard."

"Twenty—"

"That's my price. If you don't pay it, Donovan will."

"Done," he said, no more hesitating. "Shall we drink a toast to our partnership?"

Alex bumped up a shoulder. "I assume you want to start tomorrow," she said, taking the glass of Cognac he poured her but not drinking it. "If we get the details settled, I can use the rest of the afternoon to get my equipment lined up and buy the supplies I'll need."

"Of course," he said, "you lost all your belongings in the fire. You would not be here otherwise," he added, "so forgive me for seeming to enjoy that."

"No problem," she said, thinking he really was a sawed-off little fathead. "I have a checking account at the bank."

"I shall do my part, Alex. See that you do the same."

"WHAT'S THE PLAN AGAIN?"

Tag shushed her, barely a whisper of sound that blended with the wind blowing cold down off the snowcaps.

They were crouched across the street from the Winston place, behind a rusted-out hulk of a pickup that had been there so long it was half-melted into the landscape. Crocus shoots speared up around the tire rims, amid the bones of last year's mums. The weather had taken a sharp turn toward spring. It was almost balmy during the day; at one a.m. it made her joints ache.

She was tired of squatting in the cold and dark, and he was feeling kind of silly, like a kid playing at cops and robbers. "How long—"

"Shhhhh."

"They can't hear us," Alex said.

"How do you know?"

"They're not coming over here and shooting. What are we waiting for? I'm an icicle."

"I want to make sure we know where everyone is before we go in. You're new at this."

"And you're a pro?"

He didn't say anything, but she could tell he was grinding his teeth.

"There were five men total with Junior when he arrived in town yesterday," Alex whispered, her mouth close to Tag's ear. "There's a guy at the back door of the house, like there was this afternoon. You can see the one at the front, and there are two more at the hotel, waiting for me to come out."

"You're sure they didn't see you."

"Positive." And she was pretty proud of herself. She'd snuck out the window of her hotel room, along the roof of the covered boardwalk, shimmying down one of the roof supports and hopping to the ground once she'd she made it to the side street. Then she'd crept along in the shadows, going between buildings and through backyards until she'd caught up with Tag. "We've been here an hour and counting. If they knew I was gone, they'd be here by now."

"That leaves one guy inside with Pierre," Tag said, his face a pale blur in the darkness.

"And them." Alex took his chin in her hand and turned his face toward the house next door to Junior's rental just as a man materialized out of the shadows.

There was a brief scuffle, and one of the men dropped to the ground and didn't get up. The muffled sounds of a second set-to floated across the street to them, coming from the back of the house. No sooner had it gone quiet again than another man joined the first at the front.

"They took out the guards," Tag said, which she'd already concluded. If it had been the other way around an alarm would have been raised.

"Dammit," Alex hissed, smacking Tag on the arm.

"Ouch." He caught her wrist before she could smack him again. "This is good. When they come out with the map we'll just take it away from them. Less risk for us since they won't be expecting it."

Alex jerked her arm free, but she had to admit his new plan sounded good since it also meant less potential they'd be used for target practice. And less waiting as it turned out.

The two men went in. Within a half minute lights blinked on inside the house, Alex saw shadows wavering wildly against the lit windows, and then there were a couple of gunshots.

"Shit."

"Do you think they're dead?" Alex wondered.

"If they are half the town is about to be witness to murder."

Sure enough lights came on up and down the street, front doors opened, and people in an assortment of sleepwear accessorized with cold weather gear appeared on their front doorsteps. Within minutes, Matt's white Blazer cruised up the street, stopping in front of Junior's house. Behind him came a crowd of people on foot, mostly men and probably coming from the Casteeley Inn, the only business that would still be open and packed at this time of night.

Matt got out of the Blazer and stood looking at the sea of faces, both hands on his police belt. He didn't try to disperse the crowd, though; it would have been wasted effort.

He didn't have to investigate a potential homicide, either, as it turned out. The front door of Junior's rental opened and two men were ejected onto the front lawn, very much alive. And completely naked, hands cupped over their crotches, bare feet dancing on the cold ground.

Alex hissed a breath in through her teeth. "That's not a good look for them."

"Not a good look for any man," Tag said, sounding sympathetic. And resigned. "We'll have to wait to go in."

"We're going in anyway? Tonight?"

"We have to. If you're still around tomorrow Junior will expect you to head out with him. And they won't be prepared for another invasion tonight. They'll figure sending two guys out wearing nothing but goose bumps will put everyone else off."

"It put me off, that's for sure."

Junior and his one remaining conscious gargoyle came out.

"The two guys at the hotel must've stayed put, despite the commotion," Tag continued. "Junior must really want you if he gave that kind of order."

"As a guide, just like everyone else. Thanks to you."

Probably just as well she couldn't see his expression, Alex thought, easing up to peer through the empty truck windows as Tag was doing.

They were only catching about every other word over the crowd noise, but the tone was unmistakable.

"Junior is pretty mad," Tag said.

"Matt doesn't look very happy, either."

"Come on." Tag took her by the wrist and towed her out to the back of the crowd, nonchalantly working his way around the outer perimeter of people toward Junior's house.

Alex's heart was hammering so hard she still couldn't make out more than the fact that Junior and Matt were arguing. She followed Tag through the dark yard of the house next to Junior's and behind, stepping over the still unconscious goon and sneaking in through the unlocked back door.

"Where's the safe?" Tag asked her, and when she didn't answer he took her by the shoulders and gave her a little shake. "Now you have trouble talking?"

Her mouth snapped shut and her nerves steadied. "Sorry, it's my first B and E," she said, pointing to the back bedroom Junior had turned into his office. "Under the desk."

Without so much as a dirty look, Tag slipped into the bedroom, knelt by the safe, and put his ear against the door. He had the thing open inside of fifteen seconds. For a guy who claimed to be honest and aboveboard, Donovan knew an awful lot about underhanded behavior.

"Where did you find your treasures before this?" Alex asked him. "Behind the vault door at your local bank?"

"I read a book on safecracking once," Tag said.

"No, seriously."

"Can we discuss this later?"

"You say that a lot, and then the subject never comes up again."

"Excuse me for wanting to get out of here in one piece before I give you my life story." Tag unbuttoned his shirt and laid the map against his chest, buttoning back up.

Alex couldn't really fault that logic, so she waited while he eased the bedroom door open and peeked out. "Is the coast clear, Indiana?"

He heaved a sigh and let his head fall forward.

"You dragged me into this."

"Don't remind me."

"Any time you want to call it off, Donovan, just let me know."

"Tempting, but I'm not the only one you have to worry about."

"Don't remind me." Alex slipped by him, into the hallway and out through the back door, Tag on her heels. They half-jogged through town, sticking to back streets and coming up behind the stable.

"I brought your things while you were at Junior's earlier," Tag said once they were inside, "but that beast wouldn't let me anywhere near him."

"Men," she muttered in disgust. She took her satchel from Tag and dropped it next to the small duffel of new clothes and personal supplies she'd bought with the last of her own funds and dropped off earlier. Junior's money was still in her bank account and that's where it would stay until this thing was over and she could decide what to do with it. If she was still alive.

It only took a few seconds to saddle Jackass and secure her things, but when she tried to lead him out of the stall he wouldn't budge.

"Come on," Tag said. "As soon as Junior gets done reading the riot act to Barney Fife and making his point to the rest of the town, he's going to check on the map."

"If he's familiar with your skills, he'll know it was you."

"He'll know you told me where to find the map, Alex. He'll go straight to the hotel, and when he discovers you checked out, he's going to come here next."

Quite the incentive. She took hold of Jackass's bridle and pulled with all her might, finally managing to get him moving. Sort of. He took a couple of steps and went down on his front knees before struggling to his feet again.

"Jesus, what's taking so long?"

"There's something wrong with Jackass."

"Leave him."

"Absolutely not."

"Junior is going to be really pissed off, and when he's pissed off he doesn't have much self-control."

"And he has big, nasty men to do his dirty work. I remember," Alex said. "Jackass is sick. If I leave him, the people in this town will put a bullet in his head rather than pay to have him treated."

Tag blew out a breath, but she had to give him credit; he stuck. "What's wrong with him?"

"I don't know. I'm not a vet."

"Maybe he's been drugged."

She held it together long enough to look in his eyes. And then she got a whiff of his breath. "Son of a . . ." She met Tag's eyes. "He's not drugged, and he's not sick. He's drunk."

chapter 10

"DRUNK?"

Alex took another whiff of his breath, which was pretty easy since he was lipping at her chin. "Shit-faced."

"Your horse is drunk," Tag repeated, incredulous, disgusted. And a little smug.

"What can I say? He likes beer. And whiskey. Everyone in town knows it."

"Great. The only way we can get out of here is on horse-back, and Jackass is drunk." Tag stomped off a few feet, came back. "There's no way you can ride him like that. You'll have to take another horse."

"Then I'll have Matt after me, too," Alex pointed out, "and there are pretty stiff penalties for horse thieves, even these days."

"You ride that horse, you're going to die. I'd call that a stiff penalty."

"Ha. Ha."

"I wasn't making a joke. Stop being so damn stubborn—"

"I'm not being stubborn. Jackass won't let me down."

She took him by the cheekstraps, one hand on either side of his face, and looked him in the bleary eyes. "Tag thinks you're going to get me killed," she said right in his face. "Let's prove him wrong."

She climbed into the saddle and waited for Tag to do the same with his horse. He stood there a minute, staring at her in disbelief.

"Come on," she said. Jackass nipped at Tag; he only missed because he was tipsy.

"It's your ass," Tag said, mounting the horse he'd bought earlier that day, a mare named Angel. He'd paid twice what she was worth, but that was the way with women. There was always a price, and it rose steeply when you really needed them. "And speaking of asses, what was with that cowboy in town today?"

Alex laughed, nudging Jackass in the sides so he'd follow Tag's horse out the door. Jackass wasn't entirely sure-footed, but Alex had faith in him.

"You didn't answer my question about the cowboy."

"Are you jealous?"

He didn't say anything, but she could feel him sulking.

"For crying out loud, he was only flirting with me so he could find out what I—what we were up to."

"That's not the only reason," Tag grumbled.

"Fine," she huffed, trying to ignore the jazzy little flip-flop her heart did at the notion of Tag being jealous over her. Hearts were stupid organs that ought to stick to pumping blood and stop inflating the hopes of women everywhere. Men couldn't be trusted; Rusty Hale was a perfectly despicable example. "I'd bet real money he's the one who got Jackass drunk."

"And the only reason he wanted to keep you in town was the treasure."

Alex rolled her eyes. "He's married. Can we concentrate on escaping the real bad guy?"

"Why? All you need to do is come on to Junior and he'll let you go—well, not let you go, but he won't hurt you."

"No, but he'll hurt you."

"I didn't know you cared."

"You've got the map."

"Fuck the map," Tag said.

"You're the one who wanted it," she reminded him. "You needed me to find out where he was keeping it, and that's what I did. Why are you getting pissy about the way I did it?"

"We need to concentrate on getting out of town."

"Typical man," she said. "The minute the conversation becomes uncomfortable for you, you change the subject."

"Escape?" he said, sticking with the typical man thing.

And since he had a point, Alex let him get away with it. "Turn left when you hit the street," she said to him, "and head for the river."

"I don't remember seeing a bridge on that end of town."

"That's because there isn't one. The snow in the mountains hasn't begun to melt yet. The river is shallow enough for us to cross."

"Nothing you've said so far is insurmountable to SUVs."

"It's the best chance we have," Alex said. "If we can get to the trees, we'll be all right."

"Great," Tag muttered in disgust. "It's still not too late for you to trade sex for safety."

"A fate worse than death? If I thought it would work, you'd still be knocking around town trying to figure out a way to get your hands on the map, and I'd be sleeping in a feather bed right now."

Tag snorted. "You're not the kind of woman who sleeps around."

"Then apparently you think I'm just a tease."

Before Tag could answer she stung his mount with the end of her reins. The mare took off, Jackass weaving along at her heels. They didn't get far before they heard the roar of an engine behind them, followed by another and another. And then headlights appeared at the other end of the street.

Apparently that was all it took to sober Jackass right up. He took off, no urging. Even drunk he gave the mare a run for her money. They hit the end of town, splashed through the river where it was shallow, ice and water foaming up around them, three SUVs closing in.

By the time they reached the opposite bank they'd lost the Hummer, Junior choosing not to take up the chase. Probably he thought the Jeep and the Land Rover were more than capable of catching two map thieves on horses. Why get the expensive Hummer tires wet, let alone risk scratching the paint job?

What he hadn't counted on was the tent city. The noise and lights brought men pouring out of the tents, most of them dressed in nothing but long underwear and cold steel.

Alex turned Jackass, heading right for them. Tag yelled something, wondering if she'd lost her mind probably. She didn't bother to yell back. The men in the tent city didn't know what was going on, but they would recognize the black vehicles and realize the hoity-toity foreigner who'd come to town that morning was involved. And they would take the other side.

Tag must've come to the same conclusion, because his mare fell in behind Jackass, following the path he wound between the tents. Some of them were barely far enough apart for one horse, let alone anything with four wheels. The Land Rover skirted the settlement. The Jeep, being smaller, followed them in, staying as close as possible without causing too much damage, property or physical. And it wasn't shooting at them, either. Too many witnesses, Alex decided. Armed witnesses, who might shoot back.

But the tents didn't go on forever. And the Land Rover was waiting for them. Still no shooting, still too many witnesses. But there were a lot of accidents that could befall a couple of horses on rugged land at night.

The pasture was flat, open country, but very rough, riddled with natural ditches where runoff from the mountains eroded its way down into the river. They couldn't push the horses too hard. One of them could trip and throw the rider, or get a foot stuck in some hole and break a leg.

The SUVs didn't have that problem. Tag and Alex split

up, Tag cutting behind Alex so she was lost to the head-lights just long enough for both vehicles to go after him when he veered sharply to the right. Alex didn't know if that was his intention, and there wasn't time for her to do anything about it because in the split second it took her heart to slam against her rib cage a couple of times Tag was past her and the SUVs had left her in their dust.

In the wildly bouncing glare of the headlights she could see Tag bent low over the mare's neck, John Wayne, dust-ing his horse's hindquarters with the ends of the reins so it would run flat out, no caution whatsoever. The Jeep was behind the Land Rover, and the Land Rover was behind the mare, her flying heels seeming so close to its headlights Alex cringed, waiting for one of her hooves to catch on the Land Rover's bumper and take her down.

And then the Jeep driver seemed to realize there was only one horse in front of them. The Jeep fell back and cut left, coming after Jackass. Out of the corner of her eye Alex saw the Land Rover fly up over a little rise and then go nose down into a ditch. Water fountained into the air, and she heard the engine revving at about a million rpm. She got one last impression, like a camera flash, of the Land Rover's wheels spinning wildly, and then the Jeep's headlights found her.

She bent forward, her mouth next to Jackass's ear, and said, "I'm sorry," clapping her heels against his sides and pointing him for the trees. Jackass came through as best he could with ninety-proof blood, but her heart was in her throat, and with every hesitation, every tiny stumble, she was certain they were dead.

Fifty yards from the forest and she had to resort to zig-zagging, Jackass managing to change directions just barely faster than the Jeep. Thirty yards and the Jeep was right on their heels, illumination from the headlights bouncing wildly on either side of their shadows in front of them. And then she spotted the deadfall off to her left, about grille high.

She aimed Jackass right for it, sent up a prayer, and dug

her heels into his sides. There was a little "oh-shit" hitch in his gait and then she could feel him gather beneath her, muscles bunching as his front legs came off the ground and his powerful hindquarters sent them soaring over the tree.

There was a crash behind her and the Jeep's headlights were snuffed out. Jackass dropped back to a trot but Alex kept him moving in case the driver had a gun and decided to use it. No shots rang out, but she saw movement coming in from her right and started to freak out because she knew Jackass had nothing left in him. And then she realized it was Tag and his mare coming up next to her.

Tag said something that didn't register because she was still a little shell-shocked from the close call. And now that she wasn't about to die, she noticed her leg was throbbing, and probably bleeding in a couple of places. Jackass wasn't in great shape either. He'd done amazingly well running across country, but now he could barely walk a straight line.

"What's wrong with Jackass?" Tag wanted to know the third time he stumbled into Angel.

"He's still drunk," Alex said.

"He didn't have any problem running full out across the prairie back there. I think he's doing it on purpose."

Jackass bumped the mare again.

"Cut it out," Alex said.

Jackass whinnied and flattened his ears, sidling over casually to snort in Angel's ear.

She went wonky, bucking a little, starting and stopping abruptly, and catching Tag by surprise, enough surprise that he fell off.

Alex laughed. So did Jackass. The mare seemed pretty amused, too, tossing her head and nickering.

Tag picked himself up off the ground and went eye to eye with his horse. "That won't be happening again," he said to her.

"You're talking to a horse," Alex pointed out.

"She's the one I thought I could reason with," Tag said.

"You didn't reason with her, you threatened."

"Whatever works."

* * *

THEY TRAVELED FOR A COUPLE MORE HOURS, RIDERS
and horses moving mechanically through an exhausted stupor. Most of the snow had melted on the slopes with a
southerly exposure. Alex was doing a damn good job of
avoiding clear ground. The horses had to pick their way
over obstacles hidden by the snow, their hooves slipping
often enough to keep Tag in a constant state of uneasiness.

He didn't notice Alex fidgeting in the saddle, didn't
think about the fact that her thigh must hurt like hell. But he
perked up a little bit when she dismounted, and he would've
had to be in his grave to miss the limp.

If he'd learned one thing about Alex Scott, it was that
she detested weakness, especially her own. At the moment
he didn't give a crap.

He climbed down from the mare and let her struggle
along for half an hour, only because he knew the horses
needed a break. And then he put his foot down. "Get on the
horse, Alex."

"No."

"Don't be an idiot. You can barely walk."

"You're not doing all that well, either."

"It's been a while since I've been on a horse, but I'm
just stiff. You're in pain."

"Jackass needs a rest. He's not all that steady on his feet
yet."

"Then ride Angel."

"We don't have that much farther to go."

Tag wasn't wasting any more time trying to reason with
her. He picked her up and dumped her on the mare, feeling
barely a second of regret that he was rough enough to have
her hissing in a breath and clutching at the saddle horn.

"This isn't a whole lot better," she said, but she swung
her uninjured leg over the saddle.

Tag reached into his saddlebag, handed her a bottle of
water and a handful of painkillers from the bar's first aid

kit, which he'd . . . borrowed. She peered at the pills, tossed a couple over her shoulder, and downed the rest of them.

"You should have taken them all."

"Only if I want to fall off and break my neck."

"Why would I go to all the trouble to save your ass back there if I was going to let you break your neck now?"

"You cut across behind me on purpose? To draw them off?"

"Yeah."

"I thought you were a bad rider."

"It's been a while since I spent any time in the saddle. Doesn't mean I don't know what I'm doing."

She snorted softly, her breath steaming in the dark. "Is that a metaphor, or are we both talking about horses?"

"At least I'm in a position to use it as a metaphor."

"Oh, ouch. I'll bet there are notches on your bedpost back home."

"At least I never had to tie any woman in it to keep her there."

"I imagine a woman never introduced herself to you by way of Smith and Wesson."

"That was a Ruger, nine millimeter."

"Sure, that makes all the difference. And you know the really stupid part of this?"

"That we're arguing about the size of my gun?"

"That I saved your life to begin with." She braced her hands on the saddle and twisted to look at him. It was too dark to see her expression, but the tone of her voice made "pissed off " a safe bet. "You stuck a gun in my face, and I saved your life," she said. "Your friends in the plane came back and shot at you, and I saved your life. Then they brought in a helicopter and burned my cabin down, and I *saved your life*."

"Hold on, that third time is stretching it."

"Then I guess you're the one who shot the snowmobile driver with a tranquilizer gun."

"Okay, I'll give you that."

"And you were up to walking seventy-five miles in damp preppy clothes?"

"I repaid the favor—two of the favors," Tag amended. "I'm not counting the third one, so that makes us even."

"This isn't about keeping score. This is about stupidity. And stubbornness. I've been blaming you for being in this mess, but it's my own fault. You can't help how you are, being manipulative and dishonest and—"

"Breaking your neck doesn't sound so bad anymore. At least you'd be quiet."

"And you'd have no hope of finding the treasure before Junior does."

"We have the map, remember? I don't think that'll be a problem anymore."

"Unless he made a copy."

"If there'd been a copy it would've been in the safe."

Alex huffed out a breath. "That wouldn't be very smart. Jeez, you need to stop thinking like a treasure hunter and start thinking like a cop or something."

Damn. Tag rubbed at the back of his neck, hating it that she was right. And that he hadn't thought of it first. She kept making him crazy, and he kept losing sight of what was important. If Junior had a copy . . . If Junior had a copy . . . "If he had a copy, he would have shown that to you instead."

"Not if he wanted me to believe it was authentic. I wouldn't go out in the field with him for a copy. And even if there weren't any copies, he could've memorized the original well enough to make a useful re-creation."

"You're a regular ray of sunshine, aren't you?" Tag grumbled.

"Just being realistic," she said around a yawn. "I've had enough surprises over the past few days to last me a lifetime. The last thing I want is to get out in the field and have Junior and his merry men waiting for us."

"Let's just take this a day at a time." Or night, he thought, since most of their interaction seemed to come during the hours between sundown and sunup. "Where are we going?"

"A friend of mine owns a ranch not far from here. Her place will be safe."

Her. That buoyed him up a bit. He was getting tired of Alex's men. He was tired, period. "How far is it exactly?"

She pointed off ahead of them. "See that break in the trees?"

Tag squinted, making out the place where the treeline met the slightly lighter sky. "Do you mean that opening in the trees on the next ridge?"

"Yes."

"The one across the really deep valley?"

"That's the one."

"That's your definition of not far? It would be not far if we could fly."

"I've seen you fly," she said with a slight giggle. The painkillers were definitely kicking in.

"I didn't fly, I landed."

"Sounds like fun." She made a "wheeee" sound, listing to one side then the other, well on her way to breaking her neck.

When she swung back around in his direction, Tag braced a hand on her shoulder and shoved her upright, then had to fist his hand in her coat to keep her from going off the other side.

Good thing she'd only taken half the pills. Even at that there was no way he could stay on the ground and keep her from falling off the mare. He contemplated the possibility of riding Jackass, for all of two seconds before he gave up the idea.

Jackass wasn't in much better shape than his owner, plodding along, head down, barely able to drag his own carcass forward a step at a time. He probably wouldn't put up a fuss, but Tag didn't want to be the proverbial straw. Not that the mental picture of Jackass on his belly with all his legs splayed out hurt Tag's feelings, but Alex wouldn't be too happy about it, and he needed to keep her happy. To whatever degree that was possible.

Falling onto her head in a drugged stupor would probably be contrary to that ambition.

Tag picked up Jackass's reins, careful to keep as far away as possible, and climbed up behind Alex on Angel. He was braced for the inevitable insults and objections—or at least a feeble attempt to shove him off. Instead she sighed and snuggled back against him. Instant hard-on. Another reason he disliked riding. Not that he'd spent a lot of his time on horseback in this condition, but anything that put a man's package in close proximity to a hard surface that was under the control of something with the IQ of a five-year-old was just wrong in his book.

Alex let her head drop back against his shoulder and said, "Ummmmmmm," and things got measurably worse. And there wasn't a whole lot he could do about it.

He wrapped an arm around her waist, tucked her head into a more comfortable position, and fought like hell to remember her whining and obnoxious instead of warm and sleepy and soft. He accomplished the first, but it didn't come close to outweighing the second.

And for the first time since he'd crashed into Alexandra Scott's life, Tag began to wonder exactly what he'd gotten himself into.

chapter
11

TAG FOLLOWED ALEX'S VAGUE DIRECTIONS, WISH-
ing the painkillers would solve his problem. In the interest
of distraction—and necessity—he concentrated on keeping Alex's break in the trees in sight. Kind of difficult,
since they were traveling through heavy forest most of the
time. He resorted to picking out a landmark and aiming for
it. When he thought he'd arrived he repeated the process,
always keeping the tallest mountain peak at the same general place on the horizon. Finally he topped a hill, and
there spread out about a half mile below them was a flat,
treeless plain, in the center of which were a ranch house,
outbuildings, and corrals. Herds of animals he assumed
were beef cattle dotted the pastures.

Even at that early morning hour there seemed to be a lot
of activity. Jackass whinnied, seeming to perk up. Alex
even stirred, pulled partially back to consciousness by the
noise and the brightening light.

She stretched her arms above her head and dragged in a
deep breath. And then froze. Ever so slowly she looked
over her shoulder.

Tag tried to smile. He suspected he ended up with something closer to a grimace. He hadn't ridden in years, and having Alex in his lap all night had only compounded his problems. What wasn't numb was on fire, and not in a good way. He had a mean case of blue balls, and a killer chafing problem. But he'd be damned if he let her know it. "Morning," he said. "Sleep well?"

She slid off the mare, stopping dead when her injured leg hit the ground. She limped a couple of steps and either got a handle on the pain or just butched her way through it. Tag would have put money on the latter.

"How's the leg?" he asked.

She yanked Jackass's reins out of his hand and put some distance between them. He didn't think she was going to answer him but she bit off the word "fine."

"You seem to be walking better."

"It's still a bit stiff, but not too sore," she said grudgingly.

"You're welcome."

That earned him a look, and a criticism. "We shouldn't have ridden double all night."

"It was only a few hours." But he dismounted, wincing when he hit the ground.

The mare whuffled out a breath, sounding suspiciously like she was sighing in relief. Tag had a bad feeling Jackass was rubbing off on her.

"Females," he muttered, thankful he was following Alex so she couldn't see that he was doing some limping of his own and ask him why. And then he noticed the way her ass swayed when she walked, and his problems increased . . . exponentially. He really should have paid attention to the scenery, but the mountains and the sunrise just didn't hold the same attractions.

Even wounded Alex had a strong, ground-eating walk and a sort of defiant, athletic grace that offset all the drama she created just by being a woman. And a know-it-all, and way too smart for her own good. Not to mention her annoying ability to read his mind—or in this case his libido.

She looked over her shoulder at him, lips pressed together, one eyebrow raised, doing her disapproving-matron bit. She'd probably learned it in her mother's drawing room, but Tag had been on the receiving end of that look a million times in his own mother's kitchen. It was a weapon that defied class, and it still made him feel guilty.

It didn't stop him from looking at her ass, though. Some things were stronger than guilt.

Thankfully, it didn't take them long, even walking, to get to the buildings spread in the valley below. Most of the people he'd seen moving around from a distance seemed to be gone, with the exception of a woman with short salt-and-pepper hair who appeared to be somewhere in her midforties. Either that or she spent a lot of time outdoors, because she was well on her way to getting wrinkles on top of her wrinkles.

The smile she greeted Alex with dimmed when she caught sight of Tag behind her.

"Dee Redfern," Alex said to Tag. She took Angel's reins from him and looped both sets around a hitching post. "She owns the Bar D."

Tag held out his hand. "Any woman who names her place after a bar can't be all bad."

Dee gave a bark of laughter, punching him in the shoulder. She was barely over five feet, but there was enough power in it to knock him back a step.

"Does the *D* stand for dangerous?"

Another laugh. "'Bout time you brought 'round someone with a sense of humor, Alex."

"Yeah, he's a real laugh riot."

Alex stepped out from between the horses, and Dee's eyes dropped to her thigh, and the blood staining her jeans.

Every shred of amusement dropped out of her expression. "What happened?"

"It's a long story," Alex said wearily. "The kind I won't get through without coffee."

"He ain't coming into my house until you tell me he ain't responsible for that."

Alex gave Tag a long, level stare, long enough that he started to wonder what she'd say. And how Dee would react.

"He's not," Alex finally said.

Dee didn't seem all that convinced, but she was willing to take things at face value.

"Well, c'mon inside, then, and I'll get you that coffee. Probably rustle you up some breakfast, too."

"The horses need to be dealt with."

"They'll be all right for a while longer."

Alex shook her head, already loosening the belly straps on Jackass's saddle. "Some joker in town got Jackass drunk. Then we had to race a Jeep and a Land Rover and ride all night."

"This is getting better and better," Dee said.

"He needs water, he needs some oats, and he needs to rest for a while." Alex looked over at Tag. "So does Angel."

Jackass swung his rear end around and knocked Tag into Dee. They had to grab on to each other or go down in a heap in the dirt.

Dee laughed, but she didn't appear to be in too much of a hurry to disentangle herself. "I always knew that horse was too smart for his own good."

"You're responsible for creating that freak of nature?"

"He was born here," Dee said to Tag. "A mare and a stallion created him. Alex came by here four years ago asking if she could use that old line cabin on the edge of my property. Truth be told, I didn't pay much attention because one of my men was trying to break him at the time—"

"You don't know what his name used to be, do you?"

Dee thought about it a couple of seconds then waved her hand. "Old age. All I remember is her renaming him because he reminded her of her ex-fiancé. Jackass didn't seem to care what she called him, and it allowed Alex to avoid thinking of The Jerk and insult him at the same time. And she got to keep the horse, so it worked out for everyone."

Ex-fiancé. That explained a few things, Tag thought, looking over at Alex. She wasn't the kind of woman to commit herself lightly, and deep feelings led to deep hurt. Maybe it was best if he didn't know The Jerk's name, because he had a powerful urge to look him up and teach him a lesson. Right after he found the treasure. And dealt with the man who'd killed his partner. Okay, so dealing with Alex's ex wasn't actually his top priority. It still said something that he was on the list, and that something was dangerous, since it hinted at emotional involvement. Any sort of emotional involvement was dangerous to a man in his line of work.

"Nobody could break him," Dee was saying, "but he took one look at Alex and that was it."

"Love at first sight?" Tag interpreted.

"And don't you doubt it. Horses get attached to their owners, just like cats or dogs. Not that I've ever seen one take to somebody out of the blue like that. Dangdest thing." She shrugged. "I was so glad I didn't have to put Jackass down that I tried to give him to her outright. He's got a pedigree, you know. Would have cost me more than hurt feelings to destroy him.

"Anyway, Alex insisted on paying fair price for him, and to top it off, she studs him back to me in the season. She won't take payment." Dee paused to shake her head. "Says he gets depressed if she doesn't bring him to the ranch, so I deeded her that worthless cabin and five acres."

Even more worthless now that the cabin was history, but Tag decided to let Alex break that news. "Don't his neuroses breed true?"

Dee bumped up a shoulder. "So far it hasn't been a problem. The colts have a tendency to bond with their owners, but nothing as fanatical as Jackass."

"Fanatical isn't the word for it. Unnatural is. She talks to him, and I swear he talks back."

Dee's reaction was a full, rollicking belly laugh. "It does look that way, doesn't it? Does it make you jealous?"

"No. Absolutely not."

"Funny, you sound jealous to me." She ignored his attempt to sputter out another denial, turning to yell at Alex instead. "Let the horses be. I'll have one of the hands see to them."

Alex didn't disagree verbally, but she continued to unsaddle Jackass.

Dee shrugged and headed for the house. "It's best to let her have some space when she gets in that mood," she said by way of explanation.

Tag fell into step with her. "Are you saying she has another mood?"

Dee chuckled. "How'd you meet her?"

"If I told you that, you'd just ask me a bunch of questions. I'd wind up telling you the whole story, and Alex would be pissed." He paused before he went through the door and looked back at her, catching the death look Alex was sending his way. "Correction, she'd be more pissed."

"She's not usually all that talkative."

"She never seems to run out of things to say to me. Most of them aren't that nice."

"Imagine that," Dee said, not sounding very sympathetic.

Grinning, Tag followed her inside and found himself in a big country kitchen with a long pine table that seated about a dozen and held the remnants of a huge meal. Dee cleared off one end of the table, and Tag took the chair she indicated.

She set a steaming cup of coffee in front of him. He inhaled deeply, his eyes all but crossing at the aroma, but he didn't drink. "This isn't Rocky Mountain espresso, is it?"

Dee laughed, taking a seat across the table with her own cup. "That's generally a trick reserved for outsiders."

"You mean Alex has a sense of humor?"

"You must not've been around her very long if you have to ask me that."

"Three days," Tag said, taking a sip of coffee and savoring the slam of heat and caffeine for a few seconds before he continued. "There's been a lot of sarcasm. I haven't seen any actual humor."

Dee looked at him for a minute, then shook her head.

"So how'd you meet Alex?" he asked, mostly because it seemed like a good time to change the subject.

"Over the end of a rifle." Dee offered him the cream and sugar, and when he declined both she added a couple of heaping spoons of sugar to her coffee. "Alex got in between me and a mountain lion that was killing calves. I almost shot her."

"She has that effect on people."

"She does provoke strong emotion in everyone who meets her. Question is, what kind of strong emotion does she provoke in you?"

"She makes me want to . . ." yell, punch a wall, hurt something or somebody. The thoughts were accompanied by a variety of expressions and aborted motions, ending with his hands spread wide.

"Frustration," Dee supplied.

"That about sums it up."

"That's a shame. For me," Dee added with a wink. She got up and went to the stove, which was a good thing for Tag since he didn't have any comeback for her come on.

"I think those yahoos might've left some food, and it could still be hot."

Tag went to the door, intending to call Alex in, but she was leading the horses away.

"She'll be along when she's done."

He hesitated, watching even after she'd disappeared into the dark beyond the big, open barn door. He had his hand on the doorknob when Dee spoke again.

"Don't go feeling sorry for her. That girl knows her limits."

"I'm not feeling sorry for her." What he was feeling was guilt. He hated the thought of her out there alone, hurting and tired but seeing to the welfare of their horses before she sought her own comfort. He hated knowing that she didn't want him around. And he hated that he was sitting there examining his feelings. There was only one feeling he should be concentrating on, and that was gut feeling.

"Maybe I should rename you Jackass."

Tag could hear the humor in Dee's tone, but her comment stung all the same. Or maybe it was the insight behind the comment. He went back to the table and sat down, refusing to acknowledge her meaning or his feelings—which was easy since there was a plate of food next to his coffee cup.

Alex came in as he was packing it away.

"Did you leave me some?" she asked, going to the sink to wash her hands.

Dee took a second plate out of the warming oven and set it across from Tag, along with a cup of coffee. Alex sat down and dug in. Except for a brief pause to turn down the strawberry jam Dee offered her, she didn't lift her head until her plate was empty, eating with a single-minded focus and a lack of self-consciousness that was astounding.

"Well," she said to Tag when she was finished, "let's take a look at it."

Tag slid a glance in Dee's direction.

"She's okay," Alex said impatiently.

"What's this all about?" Dee asked.

"The Lost Spaniard."

Dee rolled her eyes. "That old chestnut."

"At least you didn't laugh at me," Tag said.

"Why would I laugh? The Lost Spaniard is serious business. Every few years some greenhorn thinks he can come out here with no experience and no common sense and stumble across a treasure smarter men have died trying to find. And when that greenhorn goes missing, I have to send all my men out looking for him. Waste of our time, waste of his life."

"Tag is this year's greenhorn," Alex said helpfully.

"And he thinks you can help him find it?"

"Fate thinks so," Tag said, and then he told Dee how they'd met. Alex filled in the rest of the story, including a detail or two that were new to Tag, namely Mick and Franky.

"Mick and Franky?" Tag said. "Mick and Franky tried

to kidnap you before the guy with the knife? You never told me that."

"It was no big deal," Alex said. "They weren't from Casteel—Mick's accent was almost East Coast, now that I think about it. Probably a couple of gold-fever newcomers who wanted me to guide them. I handled it."

"You—" Tag slammed out of his chair and loomed across the table, brandishing his finger in her face. "I—" But none of the accusations that came to mind were valid. He hadn't been there, and she'd had no choice but to handle it. "Mick and Franky?"

"Frick and Frack," Dee put in.

Alex smiled but Tag wasn't amused.

"You're pretty cavalier about it," he said.

Alex shrugged. "They said they wouldn't hurt me."

"Right, they introduced themselves, asked you a question or two, and when you refused to answer they just let you go?"

"Not exactly." She bit back a smile. "They asked me what you'd told me, and when I refused to answer Franky got a little . . . testy. So I kicked him. In the balls."

"Jesus." Tag hunched, strictly in reflex.

"I was aiming for his knee, and he moved," Alex said, sounding defensive—and obviously resenting Tag for making her feel that way. "It was his own fault. Franky sort of let Mick's name slip—"

"While he was writhing on the ground in agony?"

"What the hell did you expect me to do? Let them kidnap me without putting up a fight?"

"Why didn't you run or scream? It's not against the law to ask for help."

"When you helped me I got stabbed."

"It's just a scratch."

"This is entertaining and all," Dee said to Tag, "but what makes you think you can do what hundreds have failed at—and I might point out most of those people were familiar with this country. A hell of a lot more familiar than you'd be."

"Tag has a map," Alex volunteered.

"*The* map."

"Well, haul it out here and let's have a gander at it."

There was no reason to hold back, and considering Dee's probable—and very flattering—reaction to him unbuttoning his shirt, he untucked it instead, retrieving the linen-wrapped map from the bottom.

They all bent over it, holding their breaths while he unwrapped it, then letting them out when they'd stared at the map for a bit and no light bulbs popped on over their heads.

"Not much to go on," Dee said.

There were six sites marked on the face of the map: Denver, Casteel, and four others, at least two of which were in Spanish. There was a notation at the far right and one at the top, again both in Spanish, but it didn't make sense that either of those would lead directly to the treasure.

"I can see where some of the geography resembles this area," Dee continued after a moment, "but nothing's jumping out at me."

"It's not a very good representation of the terrain," Alex agreed, "but look at this." She pointed to a section just to the right and below center. "If you assume that's my valley and work your way out from there, it makes more sense."

Dee nodded, but she didn't say anything, just straightened and walked away. When she came back she was unfolding a current map. She laid it next to the old one and the similarities were even more apparent. "You make any sense of these Spanish words yet?"

"We, uh, just acquired the map," Alex said. "This is the first chance we've had to study it."

"I speak a little Spanish," Tag said. "Not enough to decipher something written a hundred and fifty years ago by a man trying to misdirect anyone who might get their hands on this without his permission." His Spanish ran more toward the modern, barrio version. He could curse like a gang leader, and he could threaten to kill somebody, but he couldn't order breakfast. "I can pick out a word here and there. That's east," he said, pointing at the right side of the map.

Dee stuck her hands on her hips, shook her head. "You plan to head out with nothing more than this to go on?"

"Nope." Alex sat back in her chair, her gaze settling on Tag. "There's no point in searching when we know so little. We'll have to go to Denver."

"Yeah."

"Maybe Junior will get tired of waiting and give up."

They locked gazes, both of them shaking their heads at the same time.

"Who's Junior?" Dee wondered into the silence.

"Trust me," Alex said, "you don't want to know."

THE SHEETS WERE CLEAN, SO WAS ALEX, AND SO WERE her clothes. She'd eaten three square meals—all in the one day—luxuriated in a hot bath, dosed herself up with painkillers, and somebody owed her a couple nights' worth of sleep.

She'd been in bed long enough to recoup a decent chunk of those lost hours—and she knew exactly how many pine boards made up the ceiling. She'd sung "99 Bottles of Beer" all the way through, counted sheep, and done a lot of pillow rolling to find the cool side. What she really needed to do was shut off her brain—or at least banish Tag Donovan from it.

Okay, to be completely fair and honest, it was waking up cradled in his arms that she couldn't forget. Nestled against him, with his arm warm around her waist and his chest hard under her cheek. And not just his chest had been hard, either. And all right, it wasn't only her brain she couldn't seem to turn off. But at least her brain was making more noise than her body. Maybe it had to yell to be heard, but it only had to shout one word and she got the message.

Fool.

He only wanted one thing from her—okay, two things. But his main goal was the Lost Spaniard. If he could get some side benefits along the way he'd go for it. Problem was, to him it would only be sex. She'd adopted a lot of the male approach to life, mostly out of self-defense, but she'd never mastered the art of disconnecting her libido from her emotions.

She'd used the time she'd spent tending the horses to get her priorities straight again. Fate and circumstances—and Tag Donovan—had contrived to sucker her into a treasure hunt. If she let herself get involved emotionally that would be her own fault.

A board creaked in the hall and she went still, except that her heart jumped so high in her throat it felt like it was bouncing between her eardrums. It was probably just the house settling, she told herself. The fact that it came from the direction of Tag's room next door didn't mean anything.

The scuff of a booted foot outside her door was a lot less open to interpretation. The creep was coming to her room. And she had two choices.

There was her body, screaming at her to just stay put and see what he wanted. As if she didn't know what he wanted. And there was her mind, telling her to get up and show him what happened to a man who tried to sneak into her bed in the middle of the night. Both choices could be so satisfying, but she had a feeling sleeping with Tag wouldn't result in any actual sleeping. Before or after. It would only lead to more confusion.

So she went with her head.

All she had on was a pair of panties and one of Dee's T-shirts—and Dee was a good six inches shorter than her. But then Tag had already seen her panties; it was the possibility she'd tear them off herself to spare him the trouble that was worrisome.

She made a mad dash for the door, ending up behind it just as it began to open. Dee didn't believe in night-lights, so it was pretty dark, but Alex saw a head poke in, and there was something odd about that head . . .

Because it wasn't Tag's head.

Any other time it might have been a blow to her ego, or at least she'd have felt silly for thinking Tag was so desperate for her that he'd give up sleep. What she was thinking about was the bedclothes—not losing the opportunity to burn them up.

The white sheets were pretty visible, and it was obvious the bed wasn't occupied. About the time her unknown visitor was coming to the same conclusion, Alex slammed the door on his head. Okay, so she was imagining it being Tag's head, but that was going to be her little secret, and anyway the result was the same.

The guy dropped like, well, like Tag falling out of that plane. Only he didn't have as far to go and there wasn't a foot of snow to cushion the blow. Or anything to muffle the thud.

By then she could already hear the sounds of a scuffle coming from Tag's room. She raced next door and found two men locked in hand-to-hand combat. One was wearing jeans and a T-shirt, one nothing but boxers—familiar boxers. She plucked an antique, long-handled warming pan from the wall, waited long enough to get her bearings, chose her moment, and swung for the fences, clocking the fully-clothed guy upside the head.

Tag was in midswing. He went down on top of the other guy, yelling, "Shit, Alex, I had it under control."

She held out a hand and braced herself to help him up. "It's not against the law to ask for help."

"What's going on?" Dee asked from the doorway. She flipped on a light and had them both squinting.

Tag clambered to his feet, glaring at her the entire way to upright. "Alex rescued me again," he said.

"And look," she said, "nobody got stabbed."

He opened his mouth, and the look on his face was pretty comical, but he didn't seem to be getting any words out.

"That's one of my men," Dee said, toeing the guy out cold on the floor.

"There's another one next door," Alex said.

"What?" That came from Tag, who was already out the door, Dee hot on his heels.

"Couple of itinerant cowboys I took on for the spring roundup," Dee said when Alex joined them.

"They must've been trying to steal the map."

"And kidnap you," Tag told Alex. "What is it with you and men?"

Alex went toe to toe with him. "Everyone thinks I can find the stupid treasure because of you."

"That's not the only reason they tried to grab you," Tag snapped.

"I'm sorry to break up this tender moment," Dee interjected, "but you two have to leave. I've been working these guys from sunup to sundown, and they haven't been to town since last week, so I didn't figure they'd heard about the treasure. But if these two know, chances are the rest of the bunkhouse is talking about it. I trust some of those guys, others . . ." She did a hands up and disappeared through the door.

Tag stared at Alex for a minute, then his eyes dropped to her breasts, peaked nipples clearly visible through the white cotton T-shirt. His gaze passed over the strip of bare skin below the hem of the shirt and settled on the black lace bikini panties Dee had loaned her.

"If we had time . . ." he said.

"What makes you think time is the only obstacle you have?"

Dee saved him from coming up with a response by stepping back into the room and flipping a set of keys to Tag.

"I was going to lend you my old Lincoln," she said, "but I think it's better if you take the extra pickup."

"Why is that?" Alex wanted to know.

"It's got a bed."

Tag's gaze lifted to clash with hers again, and Alex knew he could see that she was . . . attracted to him. She held his eyes, let him see that she knew that he knew, and then she shook her head. "Not going to happen."

"I talked you into looking for the treasure, didn't I?"

"This would require a lot more than talking."

He grinned. "That's the idea."

"It would require a lot more than that, too. Like a personality transplant."

"From?"

"Somebody I like."

"I guess that would mean Jackass, then, because so far he's the only male you like."

"You know why? He doesn't talk."

chapter
12

DENVER WAS ONE OF ALEX'S FAVORITE PLACES.
Clean air, lots of space, and the kind of in-your-face attitude she could relate to. It had its touristy areas and its big
buildings, and streets that were sometimes jammed with
traffic, but despite a population numbering in the millions,
it didn't seem crowded. Maybe it was the sky that seemed to
go on forever, or the way the suburbs didn't crowd up
against the city limits. Whatever it was, she felt good there.
Even if she was forced to share it with Tag Donovan.

She had to admit he came in handy, though. He'd done
most of the driving between the Bar D and Denver, which
meant Alex managed to get in some sleep. And within an
hour of their arrival they had a room at a midrange hotel,
compliments of another one of Tag's shady acquaintances.
She would've expected something seedier, but she wasn't
complaining. She was wondering how he'd managed it.
Blackmail, threats, bribery? She hadn't seen any cash
change hands, and it definitely wasn't charm, judging by
the manager's face. Tag had made her stay on the other
side of the lobby while he talked to the guy. When he came

back he had key cards in his hand and a smug expression on his face.

"We can only stay two nights," he said, handing her one of the cards. "The Colorado Gold Rush starts this weekend. It's being held at another hotel, but they always get some of the overflow here, and they expect to start filling up tonight."

"The Gold Rush?"

"Must be some sort of historical thing," Tag said.

"Good, if we can't find what we need, someone here might be able to help us. Maybe our luck is changing. The hotel could be worse, anyway."

"You're welcome."

"It's your turn," Alex said, going proactive for a change. She felt pretty decent for the first time in four days. Rested. If she kept him from talking too much, she might not get pissed off and ruin her mood. "I handled the accommodations last night."

"And they were spectacular. I especially liked the attempted robbery and kidnapping."

"You're blaming that on me?"

Tag's smugness toned down a couple of notches, and he turned for the elevator. "Let's go up to our room," he said, "the room I got for us because you're broke and unconnected in this town."

"Sure," Alex said. "Let's go up to your room and unpack— Oh, wait, I don't have anything to unpack. Everything I own is in this duffel. Two changes of clothing and what's left of my research."

Tag halted midstride, spent a minute going through some sort of internal distress, then tossed up his hands. "I'm sorry, all right? I got you burned out of your cabin. I got you stabbed. I ruined your life. There, are you happy?"

"Huh," Alex said, "what's wrong with you? That almost sounded sincere." Sincerely deranged, but she kept that to herself. She had to share a room with him, so maybe it was time to stop pushing him before he went over the edge and throttled her in her sleep.

"I'm tired," Tag said, resuming his trek to the elevator, shoulders down, hands stuffed in his pockets. The black field bag he'd borrowed from Dee was over his shoulder. "Can we just go up to the room and get some rest?"

"Do whatever you want. I'm going to get started on the research."

He stopped again. This time he looked at her, and the edge of dementia in his eyes matched the one in his voice. "Not without me, you're not. We do the research together."

"Meaning you aren't going to give me the map." Alex brushed past him, her decent mood ruined. "You think I'm going to run off with it?"

No answer.

"Fine, you and the map have a nice rest."

"Where are you going?"

"Out."

He sighed, doing an about-face and heading for the front door of the hotel.

"I thought you were tired," she said, slipping the strap to her case over her shoulder and falling into step with him, reluctantly.

"I am."

"But you don't trust me. That's rich, Donovan. After all the garbage you've dumped on me, you think I'd double-cross you?"

"I don't think you'd see it as double-crossing," he said. "I think you'd consider it more along the lines of poetic justice."

Alex gave him a long, level stare but she didn't deny it. She'd always had her own self-interest firmly in the fore-front, but she'd allowed room for company. If Tag wasn't harboring any loyalty for her, though, she'd be damned if she had any for him. Besides, he was right. This whole thing stunk of every-man-for-himself—and she didn't see any reason a woman couldn't come out on top. In fact she was betting her life on it.

"Where are we going?"

She didn't feel like answering that question, either.

She'd really been looking forward to ditching him. Her nerves needed a break. So did her hormones.

Tag got the message but it didn't shut him up. "What I'm getting at is do we need to drive?"

"The Colorado State Archives is only a mile or so from here," Alex said, because it wouldn't do her any good to ignore him. He had the persistence of a bulldog. "We can walk."

"Are you serious? I fell out of a plane, spent eight hours on a horse for the first time in a decade, got into a fistfight, and then drove all night."

"I was there, remember? It's only a mile. If I can—"

"Yeah, yeah, yeah, you were stabbed, and if you can walk with a sore leg, so can I." And he stomped off.

Longer legs and a good head of steam had him setting a pace Alex would've had to trot to keep up with. If she'd wanted to keep up with him.

She stayed where she was, watched him go out through the revolving door and then come back in when he realized she wasn't behind him.

"Are you coming?"

"I was letting you have your moment."

He fought it for a minute, then he grinned. "I don't know where I'm going."

"That too." But she met him halfway and walked down the sidewalk beside him. She was careful to leave enough dead air space between them to neutralize that moment of camaraderie. It was a slippery slope, friendship with Tag Donovan, and she had no intention of sliding into anything with him that might create ties, especially the invisible kind. Those hurt the most when they were broken.

Best to stick with the very real treasure map. Chances were good they'd end up with nothing, but at least it would only be her hands that were empty.

When they got to the archives, they were referred to the Colorado State Library. Getting there wasn't a problem, either, since it wasn't even a quarter of a mile away. And the walk actually helped her nerves because it took them through

Civic Center Park. Very restful, especially since she managed to pretend she was alone until they got to their destination. And then she was forced to focus on Tag—and it was hard not to, considering the fact he was going out of his way to be accommodating.

Alex hit the computerized card catalog right off, Tag hovering over her shoulder like a big, sexually stimulating shadow. She flashed back to the previous morning, waking up in his lap, the pommel hard in front of her, Tag hard behind her. More of her throbbing than just her leg. And that made her think of the inn in Casteel. Kissing him. She'd have given him just about anything he wanted then. But he'd turned her down.

Some of the heat from her body moved up into her face. At least the attraction was only physical, she told herself, just a matter of him catching her with her defenses down. Thank god she was awake now and immune to his charms.

Thank god it didn't take her long to find what she wanted. The maps and reference materials they needed were kept in a climate-controlled, locked room, which nonmembers weren't allowed to access unless they had special dispensation. The only exception was for students of the local universities. She told Tag as much—from a few feet away.

"They won't mistake either of us for students," Tag observed, missing the look Alex shot him because he was already sizing up the librarian. Midforties, mousy brown hair, mousy expression, mousy . . . everything. No wedding ring.

He stretched his arms and ran his fingers through his hair a couple of times, checking his reflection in the nearest computer screen.

Alex crossed her arms and stood back. Con man, she reminded herself. "I think you should let me handle this," she said. "I've dealt with a lot of librarians in the past ten years."

"I've dealt with a lot of women. And it's been more than ten years."

"Maybe you should read up on Don Juan or Casanova first."

He shot her a look over his shoulder, but before he faced forward again he made sure he was sending out just the right combination of sincerity and confusion.

"The biographies are upstairs," the librarian said without so much as looking at him.

"My friend was only joking," Tag said. "Actually I'm doing some research on the gold rush, and it would be a big help if I could look at your maps."

That got her attention. She glanced up briefly, then did a double take. Tag didn't need to look over his shoulder and see if Alex was tuned in. He could feel her scorn.

He leaned on the counter, lowering his voice so the librarian had to lean in as well. He knew he had her when she blushed and looked down. "Jane Newstead," he read off her nametag. "Mrs.?"

"It's Ms., Jane, actually."

"Jane," he repeated, dropping the timbre as well as the volume of his voice.

Her blush deepened and she picked up a book from the counter, running her hands over the cover. It seemed to have a calming effect on her.

"My name is Tag Donovan, and I work for the FBI," he said, keeping his voice low so Alex wouldn't overhear him. The librarian looked up at him, her eyes wide. Oh, yeah, this was definitely a woman who longed for a little excitement. "I can't carry my ID with me." He started to glance over his shoulder, then checked the motion. "I'm on a case, so I'm sure you understand why."

Her gaze flicked up to Alex then quickly back down again. "Of course. If you got caught with it . . ."

"Exactly. I really need access to the map room."

"Oh, that's out of the question."

"But—"

"Every agent has a handler, right? Someone they can contact for assistance. Perhaps if you gave me his or her name, I could verify your identity."

Tag caught himself actually considering it until he realized that he couldn't let anyone discover he'd pulled out the old FBI card to impress a woman. Even if it was the truth, and necessary to the case. He already had enough to live down with the bureau.

He didn't like the alternative, either, but retreat was the only avenue left open to him, so he took it. He thought he pulled it off with a lot of class.

It didn't stop Alex from being amused. "Never underestimate a librarian," she said.

Tag snorted.

"It takes a special person to work in a place where you can't talk over a whisper and eye strain is a major job hazard," Alex said.

"It takes a person without dust allergies," Tag muttered, "and with an overdeveloped fondness for books."

"A lot of people throw themselves into their work. Maybe you should treat her with respect instead of trying to play her."

"You think you can do better?"

"I know I can," Alex said. She marched up to the desk and flopped her leather satchel on the counter. "Ms. Newstead?"

"Yes. Can I help you?"

"Absolutely. I need access to your research room. Specifically the older maps." While she was talking she pulled out her driver's license and her college ID.

Ms. Newstead didn't do more than glance at it long enough to note that it was dated four years before. She was on the verge of handing down another refusal until Alex pulled a *National Geographic* magazine out of her satchel. She made sure she kept the cover turned away from Tag.

Ms. Newstead looked from the picture to Alex's face, and when Alex flipped it open to the credits page, the librarian unconsciously straightened in instant respect for anyone represented by the printed word.

"Dr. Scott," she said, "what can I do for you?"

"My . . . assistant and I are doing some work for an article on the Colorado gold rush, and we need access to your research materials. Of course I'll include an acknowledgment for you and the library," she added, squelching the little voice of outrage in her brain—not because she was lying, but because she was using the woman's own personality quirks against her. It was a tactic Tag would have employed. If he'd come up with it.

Ms. Newstead bit her lip, glancing over Alex's shoulder, then leaning in to ask, "So he is with you?" with her eyes still on Tag.

"Yes."

"Is he really an FBI agent?"

"Did he tell you that? No, sorry, stupid question." Alex half turned to look at him, shaking her head. "Of course he told you he was with the FBI."

Tag had the good sense to keep quiet. He didn't, however, look apologetic. The rat.

"Mr. Donovan is a real practical joker," Alex said, and then realized she needed to explain away her apparent complicity in the lie. "And once in a while I indulge him. I'm sorry if you were offended."

"Not at all." Ms. Newstead pulled out a key card, similar to the ones used by hotels. "The card will give you access to the restricted room, and I assume you know how to handle delicate historical documents?"

Alex took the card. "There are gloves available in the room?"

"Of course," Ms. Newstead said. "Normally a librarian would accompany you, but we're short-staffed today. And since you're . . . well, I'm sure I can trust you, except I'll have to ask you to leave your bags here. You understand."

Alex slipped the magazine back into her satchel, extracted a pad and pen from it, and handed it over.

The librarian looked expectantly at Tag.

"Mr. Donovan is carrying our research materials," Alex explained hastily.

"That's not a problem," Ms. Newstead said, "but I'll

have to see what you're taking in so I can verify what you're bringing out."

Tag slipped the pack off his shoulder, but he obviously wasn't keen on sharing its contents.

"Go on," Alex said, then to the librarian, "Mr. Donovan is a graphic artist—"

"And an expert on antiques," Tag added. As if Alex needed to be convinced he could lie like a trouper. That was the nicest thing she thought about him. This lie was strictly for fun. If it irritated her, too, that was just a bonus.

"He's doing the visual aids for the article," Alex said, her poker face in place, "but he doesn't like anyone to see his work until it's finished. No self-confidence whatsoever."

Ms. Newstead seemed to warm up to Tag, his neuroses apparently striking a chord with her. "I completely understand," she said, smiling at Alex but blushing for Tag's sake, "but I'm afraid he won't be able to access these particular reference materials unless he follows the rules."

Tag joined them at the desk, still not a hundred percent happy about the situation, but coming to the conclusion that he had no choice. He set the backpack down, making sure his Ruger was hidden beneath the clothing inside before he slipped the map out and handed the bag over to the librarian. He laid the map on the counter and carefully unfolded the linen wrapping.

"Ooooooh." Ms. Newstead reached out, just touching the corner of the map. "It's wonderful, so authentic-looking."

He slid it away from her fingers. "The secret to a good reproduction is in the materials," he said, sending Alex a sidelong glance. "The right color ink, old paper—that's why this is wrapped in cloth."

"It's truly a work of art, Mr. Donovan. However, some of the markings—"

"The markings are what I need to authenticate," he said, rewrapping the map. It was one thing to let her see it; he didn't want her remembering any details.

He followed Alex down the stairs, leaning against the wall while she worked the door lock to the records room. "You could have a real career as a grifter," he said.

"I've spent the last few days around an expert, and I'm a fast learner."

"Ouch," he deadpanned. "You should learn to keep your lies simple, though. The more complicated they are, the less believable."

"We needed to get into the room. Your way wasn't working."

"Smart women," he muttered, hearing the bite to his own words and not liking it. "Using your brain too much crowds out the—"

"Gullibility?" Alex supplied before he could say something insulting. She went to the map section and started reading the labels. "Used to dating stupid women? And I'm using the term 'dating' very loosely."

"Not stupid, just the ones who know how to let go and have fun. You definitely need more fun in your life."

"And you're going to help me out with that? If the last few days are any indication, I'll pass."

"It's all in your outlook. If you focus on the negative in every situation, that's what your life will be about."

"Right now my life is about this map, and since I managed to get us in here . . ."

Tag slapped the map down on a high, wide table, choosing to ignore her reminder in the interest of his own sanity. "I'd have gotten in here if you gave me half a chance."

"So that's what you're really cranky about," she said. "You forced me into this to help you find the treasure, and when I help, you get angry."

"I'm not mad. I'm just tired of the scorekeeping. This is about the treasure. Finding it is the only point that counts."

"Getting my life back is what matters to me."

"I don't know why, it didn't seem like it was all that great."

"Like you care. All you want is to find the Lost Spaniard.

Beyond that you don't know anything about me and you don't want to."

"I asked, and I got two-word sentences and delusions of grandeur. If you're not willing to share—"

"It's none of your business."

"You can't have it both ways," he shot back, getting more and more frustrated, until he remembered she was a woman. Okay, he hadn't exactly forgotten she was a woman. How could he when his body reminded him on an hourly basis? But she had such a male approach to life, clinical, detached, pragmatic, that when he was dealing with her on an intellectual level it surprised him when he caught a glimpse of emotionally charged illogic in what she said or did. "I don't care if you want to wallow in the past, just don't judge me by it."

"Maybe I have some things to wallow about. Not everyone can go through life skipping over the unpleasant parts."

"You don't know anything about me," Tag said, going nose to nose with her over the table. He was already tired, his nerves raw, and she'd struck the wrong chord. "I didn't grow up rich and pampered. I had to work my way through college and even after I got the job I always wanted . . ." It had gone to crap, but he stopped himself from saying that, refused to tell her he'd gotten his partner—his best friend—killed. How he'd almost lost his own life. He didn't want her pity and he didn't deserve her sympathy. He was still alive. He was the lucky one.

"Money doesn't guarantee happiness," Alex said. "I've been rich, and I've been poor. Either way there are more important things." She stepped back from the table, from him, but the distance she put between them was more than physical. "I imagine you'd like to find that out for yourself, so why don't we do what we came here to do?"

She went to the end of the row and started reading map labels. Tag stayed where he was so she could have the space she wanted, but he was still hearing her voice. Not the words, but the tone. Whatever she'd been through had left her hurting and sad, and somehow it had brought her into this treasure hunt long before he'd gotten involved. The question was how? He had a feeling he wasn't going to like the answer.

And neither was Alex.

chapter
13

THEY WORKED SILENTLY FOR A WHILE, MULLING over what they'd learned about each other. And what they'd revealed about themselves.

Tag pulled out map after map, Alex deep-sixed them, one by one. The hand-drawn maps were subject to the personal distortions of whoever had drawn them a century ago. The ones created by the cartographers of the time were too precise to bear a lot of resemblance to Juan Amparo's efforts.

They finally found one that seemed to fit the bill, with enough physical characteristics in common with Juan's map to give them hope. Until they realized that the only landmarks the two maps had in common were Denver and Casteel. Not surprising for a time when a person could wander for months without ever seeing another human being, and when they did, the first choice of conversation wasn't geography. The only topographical features that had well-known names were the big ones: mountains, oceans. Saloons.

They put Alex's modern map, Tag's treasure map, and

the single hopeful map from the library side by side. At some point Tag had fetched a Spanish-English dictionary. They'd managed to decipher most of the words, but there was no a-ha moment for either of them. The place names were just names; except for Denver and Casteel—for which Juan had used the original Spanish spelling—they didn't coincide with any of the towns, cities, or other features listed on the more modern maps. Even the one that should have made sense, *Monte Rosalie*, didn't have a contemporary counterpart. There was no Mount Rosalie, or Rosalie Mountain, on the current map.

"The writing is faded, but Juan didn't take any pains to make this illegible," she finally said. "No landmarks are coming to mind, either."

"You sure we're looking at the right area?"

"It's the right area, but I don't see anything here that points to the treasure."

"Maybe if we find out where his original claim was, it might help."

"We'll have to go to the National Archives for that."

"Does that involve more walking?"

Alex met his eyes for the first time since their confrontation, her expression back to inscrutable. "It's about ten miles. If you want to walk some more, we can go to the hotel and get the truck. Otherwise I'd suggest a cab."

She started refolding her map and putting away all the things they'd taken off the shelves. Tag watched her, not liking where they'd gone. For four days he'd been trying to get her to open up, and in the space of five minutes he'd managed to take them back to square one. Not only was it counterproductive to his ultimate goal, it was damned boring being stuck with somebody who believed yes and no were complete answers. And mostly what she said to him was no.

Apparently she didn't give off that vibe, because the moment they stepped out of the library, she seemed to be attracting a lot of attention, and all of it was male.

They'd gotten to the library not long after it opened; it

was well past lunchtime when they hit the street again, and since there was a concentration of museums and government buildings in the area, the streets were hopping. Alex was wearing jeans and a T-shirt, both of which fit her well, but it wasn't like she was advertising for companionship.

"What is it with you and men?" he asked her.

She didn't say anything for a second, taking the time to shift her internal focus. And then she looked around, netting herself a suggestive smile whenever she made eye contact. She didn't smile back, which only seemed to egg them on.

"You have some sort of secret weapon?"

"Confidence. I don't need a man, and I don't want a man. They know I'm not interested, and men always want what they can't have."

That was probably part of it; Alex definitely came off like she'd be a challenge, and most men liked the chase. But there was something else about her that drew the eye and put the imagination into overdrive. Unfortunately, spending quality time together hadn't counteracted her effect on him. Or maybe he was a glutton for punishment.

They caught a taxi, mostly because Tag got tired of watching men fall over their feet when Alex walked by. It didn't take any time at all at the National Archives to find out that either Juan Amparo had failed to file a claim with the Federal Land Patent Office, or it had been lost. Neither was out of the realm of possibility.

"The only thing left to do is go back and start looking," Alex said once they'd stepped out of the cab at their hotel.

"Can we have dinner first?"

She sent him a look. "You're the one in a hurry to find the treasure."

Alex headed for the bank of elevators, fighting her way through the lobby, which was packed with women. Tall women, short women, all shapes and sizes, and all impeccably made up. Tag wondered if there was any mascara left in Denver. He wondered if some of them charged by the hour.

Alex was apparently on the same wavelength. "Are these women here for the Gold Rush?" she wondered out loud.

"They don't look like historians," Tag said.

"Maybe they're, you know, here to entertain the conference attendees."

"Then they're in the wrong place," Tag said. "I don't see anybody who looks like a conference attendee."

Alex stopped and took a better look around. "Y'know, you're right," she said, and collared a bellman coming out of the hallway leading to the bank of elevators. "What is the Gold Rush?" she asked him.

"Transgenders," the bellman said, looking slightly green, one hand creeping down to hover protectively over his crotch before he took off. He ducked behind the bellstand, relaxing visibly when he had full frontal protection.

"I was wondering why some of them had Adam's apples and five o'clock shadows," Tag said.

"Trust you to notice."

"What's that supposed to mean?"

"You were probably looking for cleavage."

"Nothing wrong with looking."

She grinned. "Nothing wrong at all. In fact, feel free to find yourself a date."

"I don't think it's me they're interested in."

Alex followed his line of sight and saw three really tall women huddled together, staring at her and whispering. Without another word she headed for the elevator.

The three women headed off in pursuit, taking advantage of the path Alex was forging through the crowd. Whatever was going on, Tag didn't intend to miss it. And it was going be good, he decided when the three began shouting "Miss USA!" and begging for autographs.

They caught up with Alex just as she got to the elevator. Her shoulders slumped, and Tag took pity on her.

"Sorry ladies, you're mistaken—"

One of them elbowed Tag out of the way. They closed ranks and surrounded Alex, all of them clamoring for her autograph and talking a mile a minute. Other Gold Rush attendees, attracted by the commotion, rushed over to see what it was about.

"Oh, honey," one of them said to Alex, "what have you been doing since you gave up your title? Living on a farm in Siberia?"

Tag couldn't hear her answer, but he heard the catty comments from the back of the group.

"Look at her nails," a tall woman with a manicure by Dracula sniped.

"And that hair," her companion said. "It looks like she cut it herself with pruning shears."

"Have you looked in the mirror lately?" Tag asked from directly behind the second woman.

She swung around and glared at him, eye to eye, more than the five o'clock shadow reminding Tag she was really a man, despite the window dressing.

"Oooo, snap. He's got a point, sweetie," the other woman said, adding for Tag's enlightenment, "Cris is early in the process so the hormones haven't totally kicked in yet. But you're yummy." She hip-checked her friend out of the way, running those bloodred nails through the two-day growth of beard on Tag's cheek.

"I'm with her," Tag said, pointing toward the front of the crowd.

"Miss USA? Lucky boy."

"She's really . . ."

"Well, she was. Before the scandal."

"Scandal?" Tag said faintly, still trying to wrap his brain around the fact that Alex had told him she was a former Miss USA. And he'd mocked her.

"Boyfriend, that girl walked away from her title halfway through her reign. Something to do with a man."

"Honey," the other person said, "it's always about a man."

The crowd around Alex began to thin, women peeling off in ones and twos. Tag finally caught sight of Alex. Signing autographs. "Oh. Shit."

The elevator pinged, the rest of the crowd backed off, and Alex said, "You coming?"

"Is that a royal decree?"

Alex gave him the same wave she'd used in the cabin.

Tag wasn't amused. He stepped into the elevator car, watched the numbers on the display count up to three, then stepped off. He didn't talk, but he was doing a hell of a lot of thinking, and he was taking a lot of sidelong looks at Alex—seeing her in a new light and feeling like a fool.

Alex shouldered her satchel and followed him down the hall, waiting patiently while he swiped the door key. It took him three tries. And he could feel her smirking behind him.

He tossed his pack into the overstuffed chair and turned a slow circle. The room's other furnishings consisted of a double bed, a dresser and television, and a table.

Even if Tag had had the faintest idea how to address the Miss USA issue, she didn't give him a chance, picking up his field pack and tossing it back to him. "I'd appreciate it if you keep your stuff off my bed." She dropped her satchel on the table. "It's only fair, since you got us the room."

Conversationally, Tag let the Miss USA thing drop, but he couldn't help imagining how she'd look in nothing but a sash and high heels. The visual took him a long way back to normal. Which, considering the circumstances, was half aroused. "I don't suppose there's a chance you'll sneak under the covers with me in the middle of the night."

"No, and I'm betting you won't try to cram yourself into the chair with me."

"Maybe if you wore your crown."

That got a reluctant smile out of her. "If you're a good boy, maybe I'll tuck you in. I can probably scare up a night-light and a teddy bear, too."

"I generally like something larger and a lot more energetic to wrap my arms around."

"If you go back down to the lobby, I think you can fill that order."

He grinned, gave her a suggestive once-over. "Nothing compares to original equipment."

"Not very politically correct, Donovan."

"It's not my job to be politically correct."

"You don't have an actual job."

"Then it wouldn't be fair to lead a woman on, me not being able to support her."

Not to mention that earning potential was a long-term consideration, and he struck her as a strictly short-term kind of guy. But she bet it was a hell of a roller coaster ride while it lasted. "I don't think they're looking for happily ever after." She collapsed into the chair, tipped her head back, and closed her eyes. "Yeah, this'll do."

Tag fetched a pillow and a blanket from the closet and dropped them in her lap. "What do you want for dinner?"

"Room service."

"Rather stay in here and avoid your fan club downstairs?"

She opened one eye and peered at him. "I take it you're over your remorse since you're teasing me about it."

"You want an apology?"

The chagrin on his face had her smiling. "All I want is a shower, a meal, and eight hours of sleep. In that order."

He opened the room service menu and leaned over her shoulder, making sure there wasn't an ounce of interest in his voice, expression, or body language. She wanted to sleep in the chair, that was fine with him. He wasn't about to give her the satisfaction of making a big deal about it.

"Order me anything," Alex said, stripping the top sheet from the bed and heading for the bathroom.

Tag ordered, and pretty soon he heard the water running. Not ten minutes before he'd been all but wrapped around her, and now she was naked not twenty feet away. Sure, there was a closed, and probably locked, door between them, and he wasn't Superman; he didn't have X-ray vision. But he had an imagination, and despite the workout it had been getting lately, it still managed to rise to the challenge. And it wasn't just his imagination doing calisthenics.

Every muffled splash of the water was torture, and when

the water shut off he could almost see her, nothing but
smooth, wet skin and sleek female muscles. Miss USA or
not, it was a killer combination when his interaction was
limited to aural and mental.

He needed to divert himself, so he pulled out the map
he'd stolen from Junior, retrieved Alex's satchel, and reached
in for her map, coming out with something that made him
smile, then laugh.

Yet again, she'd caught him off guard, Tag realized, not
a particularly comfortable thought. Whenever he believed
he'd sketched her personality completely, there was another facet to her. And it served to remind him that he kept
taking her at face value, kept forgetting she was a key part
of this treasure hunt. And that if he forgot that at the wrong
moment it might cost them both.

She came out of the bathroom just then, and all he could
do was thank god they weren't in danger at the moment because she made it pretty hard to maintain his focus on
the case. The top sheet was folded a couple of times and
wrapped around her toga-style, and she had her hair
slicked back, making the bone structure of her face even
more striking. If she looked athletic with her clothes on,
she was amazing half naked. And there was nothing as attractive as a woman who felt absolutely comfortable in her
own skin.

Apparently that hadn't always been the case.

He held up the item he'd found in her satchel, a photo of
Alex decked out in full Miss USA regalia, a stalking mountain lion by her side. " 'Beauty Queen Crusades for Beasts,'
National Geographic, October 2004," he read off the cover.
"No wonder you went to such trouble to hide it from me
when you showed it to the librarian—not that I realized you
were hiding it."

She stopped in the act of pawing through her duffel, just
her head turning. Her gaze shifted from the magazine to his
face, and her temper went from zero to fuming. "You went
through my things? Never mind, stupid question. You've in-
vaded every other part of my life, why not my privacy?"

"I was going to look at the maps and I pulled this out of your satchel by accident." He gave her a once-over. "Is this woman in there somewhere? Or have you killed her off entirely?"

"You should be glad it's me. You couldn't even get close to that woman." Alex plucked the magazine out of his hand and stuffed it away. "I'm not ashamed of my pageant days," she said, and if her voice was tightly controlled, he thought he'd seen her shoulders relax at least a little. "I kept it to myself because it was hard enough to get respect from the people in Casteel. A woman with a career, living alone in the woods, is strange enough to them. Add in beauty queen and it would've been hell."

Tag didn't say anything. He didn't have to.

"See? You're thinking about it, aren't you?"

"Trust me, I have no illusions about who you are and who I'm going to bed with."

"Just the going to bed part is an illusion," she said.

More along the lines of a fantasy, Tag thought. One that kept getting better and better. He hated to admit it, but she was right about the Miss USA thing—beauty, a killer body, and purity, the kind of combination that made every straight man want to do her, and every other man want to be her. Tag might've tried the former if he'd thought there was any chance she'd say yes. And if it wouldn't have proven her right.

"When is the food going to get here?" she asked. "I'm starving."

Tag shrugged, contemplating gravity, his eyes on the top of her sheet.

"You're still thinking about it," she accused.

"I'm sorry, all right? I can't help it. The whole Miss USA thing caught me off guard."

"You don't sound sorry. You sound angry. And I told you at the cabin," she reminded him. "It's your own fault you didn't believe me."

"You said it like it was a joke."

"Because it was a joke. Not the pageant. Me being Miss

USA. I did it for all the wrong reasons, and when I figured that out, I stepped down. Unfortunately that was after I got engaged to the biggest ass on this continent or any other. I dumped him right after I dumped the title. I thought I was doing him a favor, since it was the title he wanted to marry in the first place, that and . . ." She ran both hands through her choppy hair, flashed him a look, dismayed and slightly embarrassed to have said more than she'd intended. "I went back to college where I belonged, got my PhD, and came out here, and that's all I'm going to say about it."

Perfect timing, since a knock signaled the arrival of their meal. Tag was doing a pretty good job of behaving himself, but the waiter wasn't quite as immune to Alex's bedsheet, so Tag hustled him out of the room, shuttling the food to the table himself.

Alex took the silver dome off her dinner, barely paying attention when Tag did likewise. She dug in, eating with the same kind of disinterest she'd show tossing logs into her fireplace. And when she was full, she stopped. She didn't toy with the food, didn't pick at the remnants. She shoved her plate away and sat back.

To Tag, eating was like sex. Both were sensual experiences not to be rushed through.

He'd been attracted to Alex from the moment he set eyes on her—or at least since the moment he remembered setting eyes on her. She was a striking, physically appealing, and self-confident woman, and he'd never doubted that sex with her would be an intense experience. But he was beginning to wonder if the reality would live up to the advertising. She kept herself so tightly controlled, he wasn't sure she'd be able to let go.

And then he took the cover off the dessert tray and something came over her face he'd never seen before. Desire. Pure, intense, unadulterated longing.

"What's that?" she asked.

"Chocolate mousse." He poured her a glass of wine, and she picked it up and chugged it without taking her eyes off the two little glass dishes in the center of the table.

Tag chose one, spooned some up and put it in his mouth, watching her eyes follow the spoon. "Not having dessert?" he asked, taking another bite. "Or would you rather just watch?"

She looked away, but when he deliberately clinked the spoon against the glass she flinched. And Tag smiled. It had been impulse, really, an afterthought that had him ordering dessert. "You told me to order whatever I wanted."

Alex shrugged.

"You had a stash of candy bars at your cabin."

More shrugging, still no looking.

"You must like chocolate, so why are you turning your nose up?"

Her head turned, and she started to say something bitchy. Tag shoved a spoonful of mousse in her mouth.

Her eyes closed, her head fell back, her breath came out on a long, moaning sigh, and Tag didn't wonder anymore if having sex with her would be amazing.

She took her time, savoring that single mouthful of chocolate like it was all the pleasure she'd ever need. It was Tag who wanted more.

If she looked like that, and he felt like this, after just one spoonful, he didn't know if he could survive watching her take another taste, especially sitting all the way across the table from her. But he'd never been very good at self-denial. He slid the other bowl across the table; Alex met him halfway, clamping a hand around his wrist.

"I don't think this is a good idea," she said. Her voice was even smokier than usual; her eyes, when she lifted them to his, were dark, sexually hazed, and slightly crazed. Quite the turn-on.

"I'm going to take a shower," he said, almost as surprised to hear those words come out of his mouth as she was. He didn't mind shocking her, but that wasn't why he'd said it.

He took his turn in the bathroom, and okay, he had to run the water cold. But he knew he'd been right to hold off when he came out and found Alex pacing, keyed up, needing to work off some energy and looking for a handy way to do it. He didn't want to be handy. They were going to hook up sooner or later. He'd be damned if he gave her a built-in excuse to blow it off the morning after, and it was clear as glass that to Alex chocolate was the same thing as getting drunk.

"I'm turning in," he said, getting into bed before she could notice that the cold shower was wearing off.

"I'm not tired."

"No problem. Just keep it down, if you don't mind."

"Sure," Alex said, and then she added cracking her knuckles to her pacing routine. She turned on the television, shut it off, and continued to prowl the room, opening drawers and checking the closets.

"What are you doing?"

"Looking for something to read."

"I thought you were going to be quiet."

"That was quiet."

He gave her an oh-right look.

"I'm doing my best."

"Your best sucks," Tag said. "It wouldn't have anything to do with the chocolate, would it?"

"You know it does," she said. "You knew it when you shoved that dish over in front of me, and now I'm all . . ." She waved her hands, "Nervy."

"Nervy?"

"Worked up."

"And nowhere to go with it?"

She was still wearing the sheet, pacing back and forth again, her bottom lip caught between her teeth.

Tag nearly jumped out of bed and took over for her.

"Does this hotel have an exercise room?"

He looked at the clock, trying to hold on to the ragged ends of his self-control. "Probably closed by now."

"I don't suppose you have any other suggestions?"

"You could go for a walk."

"Hmmmm. I hear chocolate is an aphrodisiac," she said.

His gaze tangled with hers. "I've heard that too."

"I could be convinced—"

Tag was out of bed, his mouth on hers before she could finish the sentence. She kissed him back wildly, her teeth nipping at his bottom lip before she gave him the heat and softness of her mouth. Her hands rushed over him, tearing his shirt from him pants and burrowing underneath.

He bore her back to the bed, rolled her underneath him, and staked her wrists to the mattress. He wanted some skin left on his back when they were through.

"You have a condom?" she asked, her breath coming in hot little pants, her eyes frantic on his.

"We won't have to worry about it if I can't get through this sheet," Tag said.

Alex shoved him away, whipped the sheet off, and tugged him back down before he could get a really good look at her.

"Condom?"

"Don't have any."

She shoved him off again.

"The guys on the plane took my wallet. You're not on the pill?"

"I live in the middle of nowhere. Alone."

And she was armed, Tag thought. He sat up on the edge of the bed and reached for the phone.

"What are you doing?"

"Calling the concierge."

She slammed her hand down on the phone.

"No, you're not."

"Somebody in this hotel has to have a condom."

"And what? You're going to go door to door and ask all the Gold Rush conventioneers? Not happening."

"I could get dressed and hit the nearest drug store."

Alex sighed. "Don't bother."

Tag reached for her.

She pulled the sheet back around her. "That's not happening, either."

"Then how are you going to work off all that energy?"

Alex reached over and opened the drawer in the bedside table. Out came the Bible.

"Do you really think that'll stop me?"

"Let's see, your name is Donovan . . . Yeah, I think this will work."

chapter
14

ALEX WAS UP HALF THE NIGHT. SO WAS TAG. TOO
bad it was for different reasons. And in different ways.
Alex spent some time pacing, some more time poring over
the maps and muttering to herself. She finally collapsed
facedown on the bed, forgetting she'd intended to sleep in
the chair.

Tag never got to sleep.

About the time dawn began to show through the cur-
tains he pulled on his clothes and skulked out of the room,
staying quiet more to keep in practice than anything else.
He could have ridden an elephant around the place and not
roused Alex.

He exited the hotel and made a beeline for the nearest
drug store. He wasn't spending another night like the last
one; if Alex got within a foot of chocolate again, he intended to be prepared.

He should have brought his Ruger instead. Condoms
weren't a whole lot of protection against the occupants of
the long black car that pulled up to the curb just as he was
getting back to the hotel. The rear door of the car opened

from the inside; the man in the backseat was hired muscle, from the shoulder holster under his cheap suit coat to the clutch piece strapped to his ankle.

"Hey, Mick," Tag said, showing the small of his back and both ankles to save himself the public pat-down. He didn't want to give the Gold Rush attendees the wrong idea about his personal preferences. Not getting shot by Mick was a pretty strong inducement, too.

When Mick nodded, Tag ducked into the back and closed the door behind him. "Where's Franky?"

"Franky still ain't walking too good."

Alex didn't do anything halfway, even by accident. Tag would have been amused, if they'd left it at that. "That why you pulled a knife on her? Getting even?"

"Knife?" Mick looked over at him, expression flat. "Nobody pulled a knife. We just threatened her, like we was told. So you could save her."

"I got held up by some old man with a thousand questions about the treasure. Lost sight of her."

Mick snorted, turned forward again. "She did a pretty good job of saving herself."

"She has a habit of doing that," Tag muttered, mostly because his mind was racing, trying to make sense of this new information. Since there wasn't a lot to go on, he came up woefully short.

Somebody had attacked Alex; he'd been expecting that, which was why he'd been following her. But apparently he'd missed the fake attack and stumbled onto a real one. "You don't know who the other guy was?" he asked Mick.

"Nope."

"Any guesses?"

"Nope."

Shit. This just got better and better. The logical culprit was Junior. When Alex had refused to throw in with him that first morning in town, he must've decided to take her out. But how far out, Tag wondered? Would he have been satisfied with Alex hurt and out of commission so she couldn't guide anyone else? Or had he wanted her dead?

Tag unclenched his fists, fought to think through the need to feel Junior's scrawny little throat between his hands. There were holes in the theory, he told himself. The scent of buried treasure did strange things to otherwise normal people. Not that the people in Casteel were all that normal, and the strangers flocking the town ran the gamut from the mildly opportunistic to the downright criminal-minded. Any one of them could have gone after Alex. Or Tag might be about to come face-to-face with the culprit.

The car pulled up in front of the Brown Palace, no surprise since it was arguably the best hotel in Denver. The place had been built in the nineteenth century, and it was everything a shallow, appearance-conscious, greedy son-of-a-bitch could want. Old, exclusive, and expensive.

Still fuming, Tag got out of the car, following Mick inside and through the lobby. Mick would have made a satisfying target, too, but he was no more than a loaded gun, and Tag already knew whose finger was on that trigger. He wanted the fist around the knife handle.

"You coming?" Mick was holding the elevator when Tag looked up. "He don't like to be kept waiting."

Tag hopped on, no choice but to care what "he" liked. If he wanted to clear this case, he had to stop focusing on what might have happened to Alex. She was alive, and if he was going to stay that way long enough to see what kind of hangover chocolate left behind, he needed to pull back into the moment, to focus on what would face him when he got off the elevator.

There were three Presidential Suites in the Brown Palace. Mick led Tag to one of them, knocked politely, then opened the door. For a snake's den, it looked pretty harmless. Including the man seated at the table, having breakfast.

He was decked out in what he probably thought was a rich man's morning attire—if the rich man was Tony Curtis forty years ago. A crisp white ascot was tucked between the lapels of his dark blue paisley silk robe, which was belted over silk pajamas and fleece-lined leather slippers. A square jaw, blue eyes, and thick blond hair, swept dramatically back from a high forehead, completed the Hollywood looks.

Women would find him attractive, at least any woman who didn't look close enough to see his perpetual sneer of superiority. Anyone who wasted the time getting to know him would find him vain, self-indulgent, self-aggrandizing, petty, and vindictive. For starters.

Tag had known Bennet Harper all of five minutes before he'd pegged him as the kind of man it would be easy to write off as all talk. That would be a mistake, because Harper was just smart enough to cause real trouble. Tag was barely-living proof of that.

Harper sat at a table set with fine china, silver-domed dishes, and a single red rosebud in a crystal vase. He didn't offer Tag a seat or a cup of coffee; he barely flicked him a glance, just shifted his gaze long enough to let Tag know he'd been noticed so he'd understand that he was being kept standing there like the hireling Harper thought he was.

After a few moments Harper folded his paper and laid it precisely next to his coffee cup. He smoothed the lapels of his robe and took a sip of coffee, making a face. He held the cup out in Mick's direction, but he looked at Tag.

Mick jumped to refill the cup. Tag just stared back.

Harper gave it another thirty seconds, tried a scowl that still didn't produce instantaneous groveling, and finally said, "I'm waiting for a progress report."

It might be the wrong approach to take, and it was definitely petty, but Tag wasn't going to be toady. "What makes you think I'm still working for you after you threw me out of that plane?"

"It was necessary to create an . . . illusion. For Alexandra's sake."

"You almost created a corpse," Tag pointed out, not missing the way he called Alex by her full name.

Harper waved the notion off, his diamond pinkie ring—

yet another affectation—sparkling in the sunlight streaming in the window. "You were perfectly safe, and I imagine she felt a great deal of sympathy toward you."

"She felt a great deal of suspicion," Tag said, careful to keep his tone just on the respectful side of mockery. Not wise to forget he needed Harper, at least until he found out what this treasure hunt was really all about. "She still doesn't entirely trust me. Even after the plane came back and shot at me a second time. And the firebombing, and the snowmobile attack."

"As you said, Alexandra takes a lot of convincing."

She took a hell of a toll, too, Tag thought, glancing over at Mick. "Who took the tranquilizer dart, you or Franky?"

Mick didn't have anything to say—until Harper looked at him. "Franky," Mick said, adding for his boss's benefit, "when we came at her on the snowmobiles she shot at us with a tranq gun."

"And you chose not to tell me."

"You didn't want us getting too close anyway, and it gave us an excuse to let them go, so I thought—"

"I don't pay you to think."

Mick snapped his mouth shut, jaw knotted, not liking his boss very much.

"Then there was the kidnap attempt in Casteel," Tag said, deliberately inflaming the situation.

"My spies told me she was still refusing to guide you," Harper said.

"She was, and being shoved into an alley and threatened by two men helped change her mind, but I think the knife attack was overkill."

Harper whipped around, pinned Mick with another look.

"That wasn't us, Mr. Harper. We threatened to kidnap her, just like you wanted, and then we let her go. It must've been that little French twerp. I told Donovan that in the car."

And Tag had believed Mick. What he'd really wanted to see was Harper's reaction to the news, and it was pretty telling.

"She's all right?" he asked, sitting forward, hands clenched around the arms of his chair. He wasn't a good enough actor to convincingly simulate breathing, let alone this kind of shock and anger. And the concern was definitely genuine.

"Yeah," Tag bit off, not as immune to the memory as he would've liked to be. "I tackled him and Alex wound up with a gash on her leg. Not serious though."

Harper straightened his robe, his eyes going cold again. "That was clumsy of you, Mr. Donovan," he said.

"It could've been a whole lot worse if the person holding the knife was serious." It still didn't follow that it was one of Junior's men, but the assumption fit Tag's purposes. "It was stupid of Dussaud, and since you hired him you need to call him off. It'll be hard enough to find the treasure as it is. You keep throwing roadblocks up in front of me and you can kiss it good-bye."

"That sounds like a threat."

"I've got the map."

Harper sat back in his chair, hands steepled, the picture of calm and deliberation—if you didn't know there was a spoiled little boy underneath the slick exterior. A spoiled, game-playing little boy. "I heard Dussaud had managed to lose the map in that sorry little town . . . what was it called?"

"Casteel," Tag said. "Alex and I stole it, right after your two geniuses failed."

Harper sent Mick a look, clearly not happy.

"What I don't get," Tag continued, "is why you gave it to him in the first place if you were going to have your men steal it back."

"I have my reasons, just as you had your reasons for robbing Dussaud."

"I told Alex there was a map," Tag said slowly, trying to figure out what he was missing. Why, he asked himself, would Harper go to such lengths to bring Alex into this idiocy and then make it more difficult for her to find the treasure? "She wouldn't hook up with me without it."

"And no doubt she insisted you come to Denver to research it. I expected as much—just as I expected you to give in to her."

"You made it clear she's a necessary participant, and she won't do this unless we do it her way. She's pretty stubborn."

"Stubborn doesn't begin to cover it," Harper said. But there was indulgence layered under the exasperation. Tag knew exactly how Harper felt, and he didn't like having that particular common ground.

"She's necessary. The map isn't."

"Okay, what's going on?"

Harper looked at his yes man, grinning. "Shall I tell him, Mick?"

"You're in charge, Mr. Harper."

"Yes, I am in charge, aren't I? And you're just a tool, Donovan, and tools don't get to ask questions. Your job is to get Alexandra out in the field looking for that treasure, and so far I've had to do most of the work. She has no choice but to help you, so get your ass, and hers, out of Denver and do what I hired you to do."

"Call off Dussaud. I contracted to find the treasure and I'll find it."

Harper smiled his I-know-something-you-don't-know smile again.

"Dussaud and his goons don't have a clue what they're doing in this kind of territory," Tag said, "and now they don't have the map. He's only going to get in my way, and there are enough people wandering around out there already."

"That's your fault," Harper said. "You let the cat out of the bag."

"A guy with three SUVs and five men wouldn't have done that?"

"Dussaud has his purpose."

"What's that?"

"My concern. He's already been paid, and I understand he doesn't give up. Even if I called him off, and he went, what guarantee do I have that you'll turn the treasure over to me if you find it?"

"Besides the ten percent finder's fee? I don't double-cross my employers," Tag said. Of course, the U.S. government had first dibs on his loyalty.

"It's best for us both if you don't," Harper said. "My investors are getting impatient, and I'm . . . eager to keep them happy. And so should you be, Mr. Donovan. I dislike violence, and I would never stoop to murder."

"But at least one of your investors would," Tag interpreted.

"Let's just say I've heard stories more than one law enforcement agency—including the highest in the land—would be very interested to hear."

BENNET HARPER WAS NOT A MAN WHO LIKED TO wait for things, and when it came to getting rich, impatience was an understatement. If the world had worked the way it was supposed to, he'd have been born into money. But fate had a sick sense of humor, dropping him into the lap of a poor, if affectionate, single mother who'd never had two nickels to rub together. True, she'd spent every spare penny on her only son, but she'd never had a real appreciation for nuance.

Community college had been in her budget; Ivy League had been in Bennet's sights. He'd won that battle, but even if Jean Harper had owned anything worth mortgaging, her credit status would have failed them, so he'd been saddled with loans. He'd long since paid them off, but he'd never forgiven her. He hadn't, in fact, seen her in years. But then he wouldn't have anyway. A bargain basement childhood didn't fit into his hand-tailored life.

Neither did working for a living. He'd tried the Wall Street route, started at the bottom of the heap, spent endless days with a phone glued to his ear, and come off the cold call desk with an investor list anyone in his field would envy. He could read people better than any broker Wall Street had ever turned loose on the unsuspecting public. Problem was he couldn't read the market. And rich men didn't give second chances to brokers who lost their money. Or to ones who'd run afoul of their own class.

To be truthful, it was a toss-up as to what had done him in, bad investments or being dumped by Alex Scott. He'd decided to blame it on Alex, for breaking off their engagement just when he was at his lowest. And all because he'd used her connections. Wasn't that a wife's duty, he asked himself? To put aside her own selfish opinions and family affiliations, to support her husband. Fine, they hadn't actually been married, but she'd had his ring on her finger, hadn't she? And yet at the first sign of trouble she'd taken it off with barely a second thought for him. The others had pulled their money and made sure his inadequacy was well known, but that had been business. Alex was personal. She'd pay for doubting him, Bennet had promised himself. For hurting and humiliating him. When the time was right, she'd pay. Just as soon as he was back in a position where he could make her suffer.

For a while he'd limped along with the two or three investors too old or too stupid to dump him. Until he'd lost their money as well. That final disaster had goaded him into one last desperate investment. And that investment had been a stroke of luck, a lottery win.

He'd bought a share of a shipwreck, one that was supposed to pay off big. He'd known going in it was nothing more than a gamble, no different that placing his last dollar on the spin of a roulette wheel. And yet, investors had begged and pleaded for a stake in that treasure, smiling and patting each other on the back just to be allowed a single share. They'd been blinded by the glory of it, the tiny hope of success shining so bright they couldn't see the bottomless pit they were throwing their money into.

It still amazed him that the shipwreck had paid off. Of course, the owners of the diving company had been stupid enough to declare every last doubloon they'd found—for which Bennet was eternally grateful, since he'd used that stake to fund his own treasure hunt.

He might not have been handy with the stock market, but he could sell water to a drowning man. What he sold now was excitement, adventure, the chance for men and women with more money than God to buy something money couldn't buy. Something priceless.

It was laughingly easy. All it took was a convincing artifact—an ancient map or a historical journal—and an equally convincing Indiana Jones type to follow said map or journal to the amazing treasure at its end. Not so simple, Bennet had soon discovered. But since failure on his first treasure hunt would have provided a poor track record, he'd "found" a small hoard, compliments of the Internet and anonymous auction purchases.

The investors weren't entirely happy about the small return, but as they'd been guaranteed nothing, what could they do? And anyway, it hadn't stopped most of them from investing in his next venture. The total failure of that second treasure hunt had cost him one or two of the choosier investors, but he'd had no trouble replacing them, and in replacing them Bennet had learned a very valuable lesson. It paid to know whose money he took. He hadn't been careful there, and this third game had changed on him. The time had come to change it back, to put himself in control again.

His regular treasure hunter had gone off and gotten himself a broken leg, and he'd found another, hadn't he? He'd hired Tag Donovan to look for the treasure, figuring when Donovan didn't find anything he'd put together a nice, tidy, convincing report to placate the losers. Well, a report wasn't going to be enough anymore. That's where Alex came into the picture.

And since Donovan was going to be squeamish where she was concerned, Bennet had no choice but to adapt again. "There's a change of plans, Mick," he said, knowing he could trust Mick and Franky to follow his instructions to the letter. No matter what the instructions were.

"Just tell me what you want me to do, Mr. Harper."

Bennet never got tired of hearing those words. It was amazing what you could get people to do for you. When you had enough money.

chapter
15

THE ROOM WAS EMPTY WHEN ALEX WOKE UP.
Thank god. The bad part about getting buzzed on chocolate
and sugar, aside from being completely out of control and
making a fool of herself, was that she remembered every
second of it. Including the part where she'd jumped Tag
Donovan.

What she'd needed, after a shower and a pot of coffee,
was fresh air. She left the hotel, picked a direction at random, and walked aimlessly. It wasn't all she could have
asked for, seeing the sky around stone and steel and glass,
but at least the sky was blue, the air cool, and the sun warm
on her face.

And Tag Donovan was nowhere in sight.

So why did she feel like she was being watched? Probably she was just paranoid, but after being accosted twice in
Casteel, she wasn't taking any chances.

She stopped at the next corner, trapped with a handful
of city dwellers at the mercy of the little red Do Not Walk
man. She casually turned her head to see who was behind
her. A couple of women window shopping, a family, a man

walking along, comparing the slip of paper in his hand with the building addresses. Various other pedestrians crowded the sidewalks, no one in the least alarming. But she didn't relax.

The light changed, she crossed the street, and the pesky tingle between her shoulder blades started up again. So she ducked into a lingerie boutique and picked up the first thing that came to hand. She lifted the thong and push-up bra high enough so she could look between the swatches of red lace and out the front window. At the guy looking back in at her.

His eyes widened, then he gave her a smile and a thumbs-up and sauntered off, looking for all the world like he was on his way someplace else. She might even have blown off the chance encounter, except for one thing. The guy getting his jollies by leering at lingerie was the same guy who'd been trying to match addresses on the last street.

Alex hung the panty set back up, then really looked at it. Tasteful but sexy. Once upon a time she'd worn lingerie like that on a regular basis. Thongs weren't very practical for horseback, and lace chafed when you hiked a few dozen miles and got sweaty. She'd left all that behind when she quit the circuit a decade before, and she was surprised to find that she kind of missed it—not the circuit. She missed wearing pretty things and feeling feminine. There was strength in bringing a man to his knees with just a look. But it wasn't the kind of strength she needed at the moment.

She took a deep breath and left the store, turning back toward the hotel because it was the only course of action that made sense. The cops wouldn't believe she was being followed, so Tag was her only hope. And Tag, damn him, would probably tell her she was just imagining things. They'd argue about it for a few minutes and then he might admit it, by which time they'd both be in trouble. Okay, so maybe it was better that Tag wasn't around.

She looked over her shoulder a couple of times, trying to be casual but getting more and more pissed off when she saw the same guy keeping pace behind her. By the time she

sighted the hotel at the end of the next block she'd had
enough.

She stopped dead in the middle of the sidewalk and
turned around. The stalker's eyes widened. Alex recognized the split-second hesitation for a frantic attempt to
consider his options and decide he had no choice but
to keep walking. He veered to the right, but Alex sidestepped
so she was right in front of him again. Confrontation might
not be the smartest thing, but what could he do on a busy
street?

"Why are you following me?" she asked him.

"I don't know what you're talking about," he mumbled,
head down, angling to go around her.

Alex caught his sleeve. He jerked to a stop and looked
at her, half panicked, half pissed off. They stood there staring at each other until the screech of tires broke the standoff.

Alex whipped around and saw a long, black car at the
curb behind her, the driver leaning over to yell, "Get in,
Franky."

"Franky?" she echoed. "Franky from Casteel?" She
shifted her grip to his shirt front, although she had no idea
what she was going to do with him. Give him another shot
to the balls?

He broke her grip with one arm, cupped his crotch with
the other, and made a break for the car. Alex was one step
behind him until an arm wrapped around her waist, holding her back long enough for Franky to jump in the car.
Mick sent it shooting away from the curb and into traffic,
tires squealing, horns blaring, pedestrians gawking.

Alex slapped Tag's hands off her and spun around,
drilling a finger into his chest. "What the hell did you do
that for?"

"Protective custody." He caught her finger so she couldn't
poke him again. "What the hell were you thinking?"

"Those guys are the ones who tried to kidnap me in
Casteel."

"And what, you were going to jump in the car and make

it easy for them? How can you be so sure they were the same men anyway? They give you their names again?"

"Well, yeah."

Tag threw his hands up in the air, walked away, then back. "They have to be the stupidest kidnappers ever."

"Why are you so disgusted? And why did the second guy show up at the same time you did?"

"They must've split up," Tag said. "One of them was following you, and one of them was following me."

"Not so stupid." Alex searched his face, but if he was lying she couldn't see it. "Where did you go this morning?"

"I had breakfast with the guy who comped the room for us."

"Why didn't you invite me? I'm hungry in the morning, just like normal people."

"Need another chocolate fix?"

"You're changing the subject," she said, refusing to be embarrassed. Or amused.

"He's a hound, okay?"

"It's not like I haven't dealt with the type before."

"True, but I know how you hate it, so I thought I'd spare you the trouble of fending him off."

"It sounds more like you wanted to keep my presence a secret."

"If you don't trust me, there's no point in taking this any further."

"Easy to say when you know I'm a target and I don't have a choice."

"There's always a choice," Tag said, going inside and across the lobby, bypassing the elevator to stiff-arm his way through the door to the stairs. "You can still take off, disappear until this all blows over. In fact that's the best idea I've had in at least a week."

Alex double-timed after him. "How did they know we would come to Denver?"

"It was the logical next step, after we stole the map."

He had her there, but Alex couldn't shake the feeling she was missing something. "What aren't you telling me?"

Tag pushed through the door two floors above and headed for their room. "You're like a dog with a bone," he said, "a pesky, annoying dog that won't stop yapping."

She smiled, far from being insulted. She'd rather be compared to an animal than a person any day of the year. "Your point is?"

"Whether I lie or tell the truth is moot."

"No, it's not."

"It is when you don't believe anything I tell you. I don't know what happened to you, but I'm sick of being punished for it."

She knew he was turning the tables on her, changing the subject, but he'd pushed a button she couldn't ignore. "I'm not punishing you."

"You can stand there and tell me that with a straight face but don't lie to yourself." He keyed the door lock, stalked into the room, and began to throw things in his duffel.

Alex stood in the middle of the room, watching him, at a loss. Tag had been irritated, exasperated, aggravated, and downright mad at her so many times she'd gotten used to it. This time, though, she could see he was on the ragged edge of control. What she didn't know was why. "Tag," she said, laying a hand his arm, "I'm sorry."

"No, you're not."

"Why are you so angry?"

He grabbed her and plastered his mouth to hers. She should have felt violated, or at the very least insulted. But he broke the kiss first. "That's why," he said.

Alex stared at him, shocked, disappointed, *turned on*. And then she was on him. No way was she letting him kiss her like that, like he wanted to get back at her for something. If anybody needed to get back at anybody, it was her. He'd dragged her into this . . . this stupidity. Now he thought he could kiss her, get her all stirred up, and then just walk away?

Tag fell back on the bed, Alex on top of him, disaster on his mind. He couldn't think of anything he wanted more

than Alex's hands on him, but he knew it could only compli-
cate things. And things were already complicated enough.

"Wait," he said, "we shouldn't do this."

"Nope." She ran her hands down his chest to the snap on
his jeans and the complications faded to insignificance.
Once she learned he was an FBI agent and he was using
her to accomplish his mission, she'd hate him anyway.
Adding sex into the mix wouldn't make it any worse. Probably.

He had two choices. Do it right, or do it right now. She
reared up and stuck her tongue in his ear at the same time
her hand snaked down into his pants. His eyes rolled back
in his head, his temperature shot up so fast it felt like his
skull was going to explode, and right now was the only option left. Especially since somehow his clothes were disappearing. So were Alex's, and if he hadn't completely lost
the ability to think he'd have taken a couple of minutes to
appreciate the long, lean lines of her.

There was a brief power struggle, which Tag won by
flipping her onto her back, staking her arms to the mattress, and dropping his head to her breast. Instead of taking
the fight out of her, it felt like he'd found her "on" switch.

She wrapped those hiker's legs of hers around his waist
and practically crushed his spine. Okay, he thought with
his one remaining operative brain cell. They weren't going to waste any time, so he'd give her what she wanted.
Since it was what he wanted, too, it worked out for everyone.

He searched for his pants, fumbling in the pocket for
one of the condoms he'd picked up that morning. Alex
plucked it out of his hands, ripped it open with her teeth,
and rolled it on. Her eyes were on his the whole time, her
hands slipping down and back—

Tag lost it, fisting his hand in her hair and dragging her
head back, plundering her mouth while he buried himself
inside her. And even though he'd have bet every last nugget
of the Lost Spaniard that she couldn't make him any more

desperate, he'd have lost. And his control shredded in direct proportion to his level of desperation.

He'd known she was a strong woman, but she was also an elemental one, a woman in tune with her body, and almost scarily intuitive about his. She did things he couldn't describe except in terms of how they made him feel, and how they made him feel was criminally, intensely, erotically fantastic.

Her hands moved over him, lingering at places he'd never thought were so sensitive. Her body met the rhythm his set, seeming to tighten around him more with each thrust. Her eyes held his the whole time, stormy gray and intense, until he all but lost himself in them, in her. And just when he thought that sex with Alex couldn't possibly get any better, it did. She rose up and used her mouth on him. Her teeth scraped along the straining ridge of muscle on his chest, his shoulder, finally reaching his mouth, her tongue tangling with his. At the same time she reached down between their bodies and touched him in a way that dragged a soul-deep groan out of him, and when she came he'd barely begun to enjoy the way her body clenched around him before the agony and ecstasy of it yanked him over the edge.

By the time she was through with him he was flat on his back, weak as a limp rag and dragging in air like he hadn't drawn breath for an hour. She, on the other hand, had barely broken a sweat.

"I'm not sure you're human," Tag managed to mumble.

"You did most of the work," she pointed out. "I tried to help, but you were pretty insistent about being on top."

"If you'd been on top I think you'd have killed me."

"Not until I was done with you," she said, stretching her hands high overhead and then running them down her sides all the way to her hips, which did a little shimmy like she was enjoying an aftershock of the orgasm they'd just shared.

Tag nearly swallowed his tongue.

He shifted to his side with his head supported on one bent arm, and slid the back of his fingers down from her collarbone, between her breasts to her belly. His eyes were on her the whole time.

She didn't like the look in them. There was intensity and mischief, both shadowed with something calculating, something dark and dangerous—

He rolled the rest of the way suddenly, kneeling over her. Before she could scoot away, he'd wound her wrists tightly with his shirt, pulled them over her head and tied the arms of the shirt to the headboard. The binding didn't hurt, but she couldn't get free.

"What's this all about," she asked, hearing the breathless sound of her own voice. She twisted her wrists, feeling a small flutter deep in the pit of her belly. It wasn't entirely fear.

"You're a strong woman." Tag lay on his side next to her again, weighing her legs down with one of his. "You like to be in control," he said, easing one hand up her rib cage, "but there's strength in being vulnerable, and more pleasure than you can imagine."

"What are you doing?"

"I didn't get to use my hands last time," he said, sliding a palm over her nipple.

He barely touched it, but the sensation speared through her, again and again until it was all she could do not to scream.

"Or my mouth."

His tongue flicked out, teasing her nipple, drawing it deep into his mouth. She clenched every muscle in her body against it, fighting the pleasure for all she was worth.

"Let go," he whispered against her breast, his hands stroking over her, between her legs, finding the exact spot begging to be touched.

She did cry out then, his breath was so hot against her skin, the pleasure so intense that she heard herself whimper, "Stop."

And he did, instantly easing away. "Say that again," he said, "and I will."

His breathing was as ragged as hers, his voice sounded like it had been dragged from the depths of hell. Alex opened her eyes and realized that for each second he pleasured her he was torturing himself.

No, was her immediate reaction, *don't stop*. But it went so deeply against everything she'd become in the last four years that she couldn't bring herself to utter that one syllable and surrender.

"Alex?"

Her eyes shifted to Tag's face and she understood that no matter how much safer she felt in her isolation, she couldn't do that to him. That didn't mean she couldn't put the game back on a more comfortable footing. "Untie my hands."

He shook his head. "Drop your armor, Alex. I won't hurt you." He nuzzled her breasts. "And I'll let you tie me up later."

She heard the smile in his voice along with the strain of holding back. It was the same strain inside of her, and in that one instant, she understood that there was protection in shutting out the rest of the world, but there was also pain and loneliness.

She closed her eyes and let her muscles go lax, her breath sighing out at the feel of two-day-old stubble rasping across skin already sensitized. "Yes," she said. There was an endless second of stillness, and then her world narrowed down to sensation, to the touch of Tag's hands and mouth on her skin, hot and gentle at first, burning and urgent as his control began to shred.

His breath was coming in harsh bursts by the time he slipped his knees between her legs, lifted her hips in his hands and joined their bodies in one long, slow thrust. She cried out, he groaned, and then they both began to move. Tag dropped his mouth to her neck, and Alex begged. She heard herself begging. A part of her was appalled by it, but she'd come too far to turn back now. And it felt too damn good, which was her last thought before the world exploded. Tag went rigid, she locked her legs around him, and they stayed that way for what seemed like forever, wringing the last ounce of pleasure out of each other before he collapsed next to her.

He wasn't so gone that he didn't untie her first, though. Alex was too spent to do more than pull her arms down in front of her. Her wrists still wound in his shirt, she turned onto her side and curled herself within the pleasure. Tag spooned himself around her, slipped his arm over her, and snugged her back against him, his breath, easier now, warm against her ear.

One of his fingers tickled lazily over her skin. She squirmed, and when that didn't stop him, she opened one eye and found him grinning down at her. He cupped her breast, sliding a thumb across her nipple, so sensitive now that she hissed in a breath and dragged his hand down—which he then tried to slip between her legs.

"Keep that up and I'll be using this shirt on you," she said.

He groaned and flopped back down. "If I let you use that shirt on me in the next hour, you will kill me," he said, adding philosophically, "but at least I'll enjoy it more than the last time you tied me up."

chapter
16

"IS THIS STILL BOTHERING YOU?" TAG RAN A FINGER
lightly along the healing scratch on Alex's thigh.

She pulled his hand away. "You're bothering me," she
said. "That tickles."

"You weren't complaining a minute ago."

"True." But now that the pleasant hum of the orgasm
was fading away she was able to count the damage to the
rest of her. She was exhausted, for one thing, her thigh still
hurt, and her face and neck were raw from Tag's beard.
"When's the last time you shaved?" she asked him.

"Huh?" he mumbled, sounding half-asleep.

"We're quite a pair," she said, propping herself up and
taking a good long look at him, not including his most potent weapon. She knew firsthand—and secondhand—what
he was packing there.

He was spotted with yellow and purple bruises, especially along his ribs, from falling out of the plane, and the
insides of his thighs and knees looked like they'd been
rubbed raw from Angel's saddle. She ran the tips of her fingers over a particularly large bruise blooming along his

side and came across a rough patch of skin just under his arm. "What's this?"

"Nothing." He rolled over and got out of bed, wobbling a bit before he found his feet.

She would have smiled over that if she hadn't caught a good look at the scar, that nice round little scar, when he reached for his pants. "That looks like a bullet wound." And depending on the direction of the bullet, it could have killed him. "Somebody shot you?"

"Treasure hunting can be a dangerous game." He gave her one of his disarming grins. "And not all the danger comes from armed opponents. I think you damaged me for life."

"It's been a while," she said with a slight laugh.

"I'm not complaining. What puzzles me is how someone so passionate can just cut herself off from the human race for months at a time."

"It's not that difficult." She hesitated for a second, but it felt so good to let go with Tag that she decided to get it all off her chest. "All you need is the right incentive, and trust me, I ran into a doozy named Bennet Harper."

Bennet Harper. Shit. Tag sat down in the chair—collapsed would be a better way to put it, crushed under the weight of his own stupidity.

"We were engaged," Alex said, thankfully not looking at him. If she looked at him she wouldn't finish the story because she'd be asking him who he wanted to kill, and he wouldn't know whether to say Bennet Harper or himself.

"I grew up in Boston," she continued. "My parents—"

"Alex."

That one quiet word made her jump. "Too much intimacy?" She got up and drew on her clothes, not bothering with underwear. "You've been asking about my past since the day you fell on me, and now you don't want to hear about it?"

No. Suddenly he didn't have the stomach for it. "Only if you want to tell me."

She must've realized she was wringing her hands because

she stuffed them in her pockets. And paced instead. "I grew up in Boston," she said again. "My parents were an interesting couple. From what I hear. My mother was—is wealthy. Old money, *Mayflower* old. My father didn't have any money, and the marriage didn't last very long. My dad left before I could crawl, and he died not long after that. But that's not really the point of this story. My mother is.

"I don't know what brought her and my father together, and since it's my parents I don't think I want to know anyway, but somewhere along the line she grew afraid that my . . . lowlier genes would rear their ugly heads someday, so she decided I was going to be the perfect little debutante. It worked." Her mouth curved in a half smile. "For a while.

"And it sounds like I'm complaining." She drew both hands through her hair, stopping to look out the window. Tag didn't think she'd say any more, but the view must have steadied her. "I had all the advantages, and oddly enough a lot of what my mother insisted I learn has come in handy out here. Horseback riding lessons, skeet shooting, even the pageant." She glanced over her shoulder, still with that slight smile curving her mouth. "There's nothing as cutthroat as a beauty queen on a quest for a crown. Some of the girls I competed with make that guy in the alley look like a playground bully."

"You never got stabbed by a beauty queen."

"Not with a real knife." She turned away, started pacing again. "That wasn't the biggest problem with the pageant circuit. The biggest problem was the men. Sometimes escorts were provided, but there were men hanging around at all the pageants. That's how I met Bennet."

Fuck, Tag thought, the name hitting him like a solid right to the gut, even though she'd said it once already. He still had trouble believing Alex would have anything personal to do with a man like Harper. Sure, it had been six or seven years ago; she wouldn't have been the suspicious soul she was now . . . Until Bennet Harper got through with her. And Tag would have bet his right nut that whatever Harper had done to her, she'd paid him back, at least in part. Why else would he be so hell-bent on dragging her into this mess that he'd burn her out of her home?

The really tragic part was that that should have been his first clue, and looking back now there'd been plenty of other opportunities to figure out the connection. Not to mention Mike Kovaleski. Mike had been trying to tell him something about Alex that first morning in Casteel. Giving the phone up to a bad-tempered hick with sewer-breath might have been the right decision; not calling Mike back, that was sheer stupidity.

But hindsight was twenty-twenty, and if he kept looking over his shoulder he wasn't going to see what was about to hit him in the face. That would be the biggest mistake of all.

"Tag?"

"I'm listening," he said, focusing on her face but tuning her out almost immediately. Nobody was dead, he reminded himself. Alex was going to be pissed off. He caught sight of the rumpled bed behind her. Okay, she was going to be really pissed off, but he could get around that. He'd just have to find the right time to tell her the truth. And the right time, he decided, would be when they were out in the middle of nowhere and she wasn't anywhere near her horse. Or her gun.

"—after my money," Alex was saying when he checked back into the narrative, "or rather my mother's and stepfather's money. Bennet started his career off as an investment banker, and when he failed at that, he decided to become a financial planner."

And now that he'd failed at that, Tag thought, he was selling fantasies.

"He was building a client list when I met him," Alex continued. "About five seconds after we began dating he started filling that list with friends of my parents'."

"And then he lost their money."

"Sounds like you know him."

"I know the type," Tag said. "He's a user. He wants—no

he deserves certain things in life and he'll use anyone he
has to to get them. It probably wasn't personal, Alex."

She winced a little at that.

"I'm sorry, I didn't mean—"

"No, you're right, it definitely wasn't personal. I was
just another of those things he wanted to acquire, a wife
with a pedigree who opened the door to a class of people
with nice, plump portfolios he could hijack. It took me a
little too long to figure that out, but once I did I called off
the wedding. My mother didn't want to go public with the
reason, but it was enough for her friends and my stepfather's business associates to know we broke up. He'd
already made so many bad investments, lost so much
money . . . Once we were through, nobody wanted anything
more to do with him."

Nobody in Alex's social class, Tag thought. Harper had
found investors somewhere.

"I went back to college after that," she continued, "took
classes year round until I finished my PhD. Then I won the
grant to study mountain lions and came out here."

"He wasn't just marrying you for your money," Tag
said, taking that for the end of the story.

"No, he was getting social standing, too."

Alex might choose to believe that, but Tag had seen
Bennet Harper's face when he talked about her. And a man,
even one like Harper, didn't go to such lengths to get revenge on a woman if there weren't any feelings involved.
"If all he wanted was social standing and exposure to people with money, he would've found someone less intelligent to marry."

Alex stared at him blankly for a few seconds, and then
she smiled. "You're good for my ego, Donovan."

"You're entitled to your ego, Scott. Colorado couldn't
have been easy, compared to Boston."

She bumped up a shoulder. "It was a big transition, but
I fought my way through it and I'm glad I did. Bennet
Harper may be a large part of the reason I came out here,
but he's not the reason I stayed. And on that embarrassing

note, I think I'll take a shower." She started for the bathroom, then thought better of it and came back, resting one hand on his bare chest and leaning in to kiss him.

It was a hell of a kiss, too; it would have incinerated his thoughts, if his thoughts hadn't already been on fire, burning with questions. He finally understood why Alex was in this mess, and it wasn't good news for anyone on her side. Revenge was definitely part of Harper's game plan; the question was, what could he do to her that was worse than what he'd already done? And what part did he expect Tag to play in getting even?

As soon as he heard the shower running, he got Mike Kovaleski on the phone. He filled Mike in on what had happened since their last conversation just three days ago—omitting the hour he and Alex had spent in bed—and gave him the high points of the story Alex had just told him.

"She was engaged to Bennet Harper," Mike confirmed, "which I tried to tell you the last time you called."

"I don't have time for a lecture," Tag said. "Harper doesn't trust me anymore. I handled the meeting with him all wrong. The fact that he ended the conversation with a threat proves that."

"You think he knows you're . . ."

"No. If he knew who I was, I'd be dead. He said as much, said he has an investor who knows how to deal with cops—he's heard stories the law enforcement agencies would be interested in, is how he put it. Including the FBI."

"Zukey?"

"The thought crossed my mind."

"Maybe it's time to pull Sappresi in for questioning."

Tag almost said yes. It lodged in his throat, that single word, and it went perfectly with the picture in his brain. Tony Sappresi in an interrogation room, spilling his guts, was the one thing he'd wanted for months, right before Tony went to trial and then to jail for the rest of his life. And if they brought him in, what would happen to Alex? For the first time since Zukey's murder, something, or rather, someone, was more important.

"Nothing I'd like more than watching Sappresi sweat," he said to Mike. "Problem is, we don't know if Harper is talking about Sappresi, and if he is, Sappresi is just an investor. A victim."

"We could bring Harper in. How long do you think he'd hold up in interrogation?"

"Forever. We don't have any proof yet that he's done anything wrong. No proof, no leverage, so how do we get him to roll on Sappresi?"

"I think you're overestimating his ability to withstand questioning," Mike said.

"I think you're underestimating Harper's fear. He was real careful not to name names, and trust me, he was trying to scare me because he's scared himself. He knows exactly what will happen to him if he rolls on somebody nasty enough to take out an FBI agent. And what about Alex?"

"What about her?" Mike asked in his usual terse style. "Taking Harper out might solve her problem—"

"Or it might not. Harper is after more than treasure here. He wants something from Alex, but he doesn't want to hurt her," at least not physically, "as long as she's of use to him."

"Okay." Mike went silent, thinking.

Tag heard the water cut off. "Can't talk much longer," he said. "Put somebody on Harper's investment list. We need to find out if Sappresi is on there, and there's no way I can do it myself right now—not with Alex around anyway. She won't agree to stay in Denver while I wait for an opportunity to search Harper's room unless I give her a good reason." Which meant he'd have to tell her the truth, and if he did that the whole fiasco was going to blow up in his face.

"Jesus, Donovan, you really have got your nuts in the wringer on this one."

"Brilliant observation," Tag said.

"I'll put Jack Mitchell and Aubrey Sullivan on digging out Harper's investor list," Mike said.

"Wait, Aubrey Sullivan? She's an agent?"

"Yep."

"Jack Mitchell took a partner. Never thought I'd live long enough to see that. Or he'd live long enough to do it."

"It's quite a story. I'll tell you about it someday when you're not in mortal danger from Miss USA and her boy toy."

"Funny," Tag said. "Just get Mitchell started on that end. I'll take care of things in Colorado."

"How?"

"Play the game. What else can I do?"

The only response he got was a dial tone, none too soon, it turned out.

Alex poked her head out the bathroom door just as Tag put the phone down. There was a question in her eyes.

"I was going to order room service for lunch, but I thought maybe you'd rather get out of here for a while."

"I was kind of expecting you to join me in here."

"I'm still recovering," Tag said, but he couldn't help grinning.

She smiled faintly in return, but she obviously had something else on her mind. "I— I've had pretty bad luck with men," she said, and when she lifted her eyes to his the gray was clouded with uncertainty. It was a powerful emotion to see in a woman who was nothing if not confident. "I hope you understand that this . . ." her eyes cut to the bed and quickly away, "what happened earlier, that was just . . ."

"Sex?"

"I'd like to think there was some friendship involved."

"There is."

She nodded, easing the bathroom door closed. In a minute Tag heard the blow dryer whine to life.

He laid his head against the back of the chair and called himself every kind of fool there was.

He'd walked into this case thinking it was just busy-work, something to keep him out of trouble while he dealt with losing a partner. All he needed to do, he'd thought, was hang Bennet Harper out to dry for running a con.

And then he'd been dumped out of an airplane on an

innocent and unsuspecting woman, who'd saved his life and wormed her way into his affections. There, he'd admitted it. This wasn't a game anymore; it was personal. And he and Alex were in a whole lot of trouble if he didn't start figuring some things out.

Like where did the treasure fit in? In the beginning, Tag had believed the treasure was nothing more than a white elephant, a shill for the investors and a wild goose chase for him. It seemed, however, that Harper actually believed there was a treasure. Why else hire two teams to search for it, and why else shanghai Alex into guiding him? And if Harper believed there was a treasure, and he didn't trust Tag, why was he letting them go after it? Why take the chance he and Alex would find it and double-cross him?

He was pretty sure Harper would have answered some or all of those questions this morning, if Tag had kept his head in the game. All he'd had to do was play along, find out exactly what Harper hoped to gain by bringing Alex into this mess, and deal with it. Instead, he'd let it slip that Alex was more to him than just the pawn Harper intended her to be. As a result, he'd become a pawn himself, and the odds sucked for pawns surviving the chess game.

If Alex found out he was working for Bennet Harper, those odds would drop sharply. It would have been bad enough when she only thought he was lying to her. Now they'd slept together; there weren't any excuses good enough to get him off the hook for taking advantage of her that way. It wouldn't matter that he was an FBI agent, or that he was trying to put Harper in jail. It would matter that he was using her. He wouldn't just lose her trust, she'd hate him.

If he had an ounce of decency he'd yank her out of that bathroom and tell her everything—and she'd run. History told him that much. She'd take off and tell herself she could deal with whatever Harper threw at her. She was a capable woman, but she had no idea what she was up against, and Tag wasn't about to let her out of his sight until he knew she was safe.

She'd find out the truth at some point, but with any luck that wouldn't happen until they were out in the back of beyond, and she didn't have anywhere to run. Of course he'd have to take her gun away from her first. And make sure they were nowhere near Jackass. And tie her up.

He looked over at the bed, hot at the thought of tying her up and completely forgetting about the moment of truth to come. He'd cross that bridge when he got to it. And hope to hell Alex didn't throw him off it. Yeah, the truth could definitely wait.

If that made him a coward, then he was a coward.

And Alex really did have bad luck with men.

chapter 17

TAG AND ALEX HAD LUNCH ON THE ROAD, HALF-
way back to the Bar D. He drove again. Alex stayed on her
side of the bench seat, gaze confined to the scenery outside
the passenger window. Sleeping with Tag had seemed right
at the time; so had telling him about Bennet Harper. Now it
was just uncomfortable.

"Wishing you hadn't told me about your ex?" Tag said.

"I'm struggling to come to terms with it, hence the
silent contemplation."

"Hence?"

She didn't take the bait. Not that it discouraged Tag.

"So what platitudes are you using?" he wanted to know.
"Water under the bridge? What's done is done? One day at
a time?"

"Actually, I was going for out of sight, out of mind, but
it's kind of hard to forget you when you keep talking."

"That's not a platitude, that's an insult." He grinned
over at her. "I'm unforgettable."

He had her there, but she thought it was best to keep that

to herself. Tag wouldn't be around any longer than he had to be. That was a reality she had no trouble facing.

At the moment he'd disappeared into his own thoughts, so Alex went back to looking out the window. After the noise and commotion of the city, the endless blue sky and wide-open spaces were soothing. Although the temperature was still crisp in the mornings and evenings, the weather had turned for good. She cracked the window and took a deep breath, the air gliding like silk into her lungs, without the aftertaste of exhaust to catch at the back of her throat.

An eagle was riding the thermals off in the distance. She watched it for a while and felt like she'd been gone a million years instead of two days. She wasn't really free, not yet, but out here, with the mountains around her, she felt like she would be again, soon.

When they pulled into the Bar D ranch yard Alex went directly to the barn to check on Jackass and found Dee in there with him. Dee greeted her with a hug. Jackass greeted her with a long, reproachful look over the top of the stall. After that he turned his head to the wall and refused to acknowledge her presence.

"He dogged the mares for a while," Dee said, "then he got bored with that and tried to bash his way out of the corral, so I put him back in here. Now he's just depressed."

"She's only been gone for two days."

Jackass didn't appreciate Tag's observation. Jackass enjoyed being the center of attention. Alex opened the stall door, prepared to give him what he wanted, but he nearly flattened her in his rush to exit the barn. They followed him out and found him at the corral just outside, Angel standing on the other side of the rail. The two horses nuzzled each other, Jackass not so depressed anymore. In fact, Jackass looked downright happy. For a horse.

"Huh," Dee said. "Will you look at that."

Alex just rolled her eyes and went back inside, returning with Jackass's saddle.

Tag wasn't quite so eager to be on horseback again, but after a long, level stare from Alex he retrieved his own personal torture device.

"Maybe you should spend the night here," Dee said to Alex, "for his sake if nothing else."

"We have to get back to Casteel," Tag and Alex said almost in unison.

Tag dropped the saddle.

Alex jammed her hands on her hips. "I thought you wanted to get out in the field right away."

"Why do you want to go back there?" he demanded at the same time. "Because the sheriff of Mayberry asked you to?" She'd called him from the room before they left Denver. The side of the conversation Tag could hear had consisted of one-word responses. At least one of them had been "yes."

"If you mean Matt, then you're right," Alex said, "and don't change the subject. Why do you want to go back?"

"Does it really matter? Your mind is made up and you won't back off until you get your way."

"And you're the soul of compromise?"

"What the hell are you arguing about when you both want to do the same thing?" Dee put in, then held up her hands when both Tag and Alex turned on her. "Fine, you two hash this out." And she walked away. Not out of earshot, though; that wouldn't have been any fun at all.

"There's nothing to hash out. Alex has a date." Tag hefted Angel's saddle and headed for the corral.

Let Alex think he was pissed off because she was running back to Matt at a moment's notice. He didn't want to add another lie to the list he was already going to have to explain, and he couldn't tell her the truth. They had to go back to Casteel because the only way to figure this thing out was to play Bennet Harper's game. That would be kind of hard to do if the rest of the players didn't know where they were, and the rest of the players were in Casteel.

And he wasn't jealous.

"Knowing Matt, he has a good reason to drag you back

there," Dee said when she came over to help him saddle Angel.

"I don't like it," Tag said, even though it worked in his favor. Maybe Matt just wanted to see her because he was infatuated. Maybe Harper had bought him off—that might be a stretch, but from this point on Tag was putting everyone under a microscope. Starting with Matt Harrison.

Several hours later he wasn't as sanguine about the decision. The insides of his legs, from the knees up, felt like raw meat, and he'd begun to look forward to the times they got off and walked to give the horses a rest. His back hurt, his feet hurt, his head hurt, and the weather had warmed up enough for the bugs to start hatching. Yeah, the scenery was spectacular, but he was really beginning to hate springtime in the mountains.

It was nightfall—dinnertime for the mosquitoes—by the time Casteel appeared in the next valley. Tag was actually glad to see the place, even though he could already tell it was worse than it had been when they'd left. Campers were parked everywhere, tents were pitched on front lawns, and people were getting themselves arrested just so they'd have a place to sleep for the night.

"Prices are ten times what they were when you left town," Matt told them when they got to his office. "George down at the diner tried to charge me twenty-five dollars for breakfast the other day. I had to threaten to arrest him before he'd be reasonable."

"Sounds like an abuse of authority to me," Tag observed.

"Just ignore him," Alex suggested, which was enough to make a lapdog like Matt Harrison toe the line.

"It's a damn gold rush around here," he said. "National news crews were here yester—"

There was a clatter at the front door. They all looked around and saw a face peering in at them through the little window.

"It's her," the face said, the words muffled by the closed door but still depressingly clear. "She's back in town."

Matt got up and checked out the situation.

Alex joined him. "You've got to be kidding," she said, adding for Tag's benefit, "there's already a crowd gathering."

Matt stated the obvious. "They're convinced you know where the Lost Spaniard is."

"Well, they're wrong. We narrowed it down, but we still can't pinpoint the treasure."

"So you changed your mind?" Matt wanted to know. "You're going out there to look for it?"

"Yeah." Alex sent Tag a warning look—as if he'd had any intention of launching into a spontaneous rundown of her reasons for going treasure hunting.

They were already dealing with Frick and Frack, Pierre's handful of wannabe thugs, and a knife-wielder who might not be a member of either group. The last thing Tag needed was Barney Fife bumbling around in his business.

Matt poured two cups of coffee and handed one to Alex, offering the other to Tag.

He shook his head and stayed put, leaning against the wall where he could see out the front windows and still keep track of the conversation.

"I've been to your cabin," Matt said to Alex, settling behind his desk again while she took the chair in front of it.

Alex went still, but Tag knew her well enough to see the anger iced beneath the calm. "Is it a total loss?" she asked.

"Only two walls burned, but the roof caved in and the animals got to what wasn't destroyed in the fire. I managed to dig out your steel fire safe, which was halfway through the floor."

"I thought there was dirt under the floor."

Matt shrugged. "Dirt's had a century to settle. I brought the safe back. There wasn't anything else worth saving, but I figured the important stuff would be in the safe anyway."

"Like the deed to five useless acres of woods." Alex took a long sip of the bitter coffee, looked up at Matt's face, and smiled faintly. "I'm sorry, Matt. The rest of my research was in the safe, too. Thanks for going out there, especially with everything going on around here."

"I deputized Tom Mackey," Matt said, but a pleased flush was creeping up from underneath his collar.

"That's why you dragged us back here?" Tag said. "So you could be the big, strong sheriff who rescued her paperwork?"

Matt jumped to his feet, but Alex was faster, putting herself between them, a hand planted on each chest.

"I don't want Alex out there wandering around with all the crazies," Matt said. His tone included Tag in that category. He held Tag's gaze for another fun-filled moment, then looked down at Alex. "I thought if you saw firsthand what's going on around here . . . I mean, it would be great if you found the treasure—"

"So you could rebuild your cabin and stay," Tag muttered.

Alex glared at him, jerked her head toward the door, and watched long enough to make sure he went before she turned back to Matt. "Thank you," she said, "for everything. I don't know what I would have done without you. You're like the big brother I never had—well, not at first, of course, but you've been the best friend . . ." Across the room she saw Tag's shoulders hunch and realized it was about the worst thing she could have said to Matt. But she was so hopeless with her feelings. "You know what I mean, Matt."

"Yeah." He gave her hands a squeeze. "If I don't think of you as a sister, you won't mind."

She laughed softly. "That's the most flattering thing any man has ever said to me. If I had half a brain," or heart, "well, anyway, thanks for everything."

She didn't get a whole lot of time to feel bad. The minute she and Tag opened the door there was a mad rush from the crowd outside.

Matt came to stand behind Alex, looking over her shoulder at the eager faces, and the curious faces, and the calculating faces. And the ones who looked like they were contemplating violence. "You sure you don't want to stay here?"

"No way am I sleeping in a jail cell."

"At least you'd be safe."

"With this crowd following me around, what could happen?" She'd be safer than she'd been since Tag Donovan had landed in her life. What she wouldn't be able to do was look for the Lost Spaniard and get rid of the threat once and for all. "I'm not leaving Jackass alone to get sabotaged again," she said.

Alex gave Matt a peck on the cheek that Tag chose not to notice—easy since she was leaving with him. "Any idea how we can get out of town without an entourage?" Tag asked.

Alex slid him a sidelong look. "Why are you asking me?"

"These are your people."

"My people are uptight, East Coast, tea-drinking snobs." She glanced over her shoulder. "These people are one step away from a circus sideshow."

"The bearded lady isn't usually armed to the teeth," he pointed out. "I'd rather they didn't follow me around until their patience wears out."

"That's it."

"What's it?"

"If we don't want them to follow us, maybe we should give them a head start." Alex stopped, scowling at the front rank of the crowd, pressing close to hear what they were saying. They took a collective step back. "I think you should let it slip that we're leaving tonight," she continued, setting off again and keeping her voice down. "In the opposite direction we're actually going."

"Why me? Why don't you let it slip?"

"Because these are my people. They won't believe it if it comes from me."

Tag gave it some thought, seeing the possibilities. "Okay,

Charlie McCarthy, how do you suggest I let the cat out of the bag?"

"Charlie McCarthy was the dummy," Alex said.

Tag grinned. "I know. C'mon, genius, put some words into my mouth."

"I've only known you for four days, but I haven't noticed you having a particular problem coming up with words. Sometimes they even sound believable." Alex patted his arm. "This should be one of those times."

"Ouch," Tag said, but he was smiling.

"It might help to pretend you're drunk. And you should probably tell a woman."

"A woman?"

"That way you can romance her," Alex said, "make it seem like secrets just pour out of you because she's so beautiful. You know, con her."

"I should probably be insulted, but I'm feeling like I have to prove I can rise to the challenge," Tag said.

"And I feel like I should apologize to the female population of Casteel."

"Now that's insulting."

Alex rolled her eyes. "Pick the right woman, get her to believe she knows where we're going, and it'll be around town inside of an hour. A bunch of these people will try to get a head start."

"But not all of them."

"Do you have any other suggestions?"

Tag looked over his shoulder and sighed. "I'll go off and plant misdirection. What are you going to do?"

"I'll get the supplies."

"I have the money," Tag reminded her.

"You heard Matt, the merchants around here are scalping."

"But they won't overcharge you?"

"When this thing is over, we all have to live in this town together. I have a better chance of getting them down to reasonable prices than you do. Besides, I know what to buy and how much we'll need." Alex held out her hand. "And I don't have much time before the stores close."

Tag reached into his front pocket and pulled out the wad of cash Harper's goons had given him when they took his wallet on the plane. He was careful to keep his back to the crowd so no one got the idea of making a fast killing. Literally.

He handed about half to Alex; she stuffed it in her pocket and held her hand out again. Tag gave her about half of what he had left, shaking his head and muttering, "Women."

"You should say that with a little more gratitude," Alex said. "Without women you wouldn't get away with half the stuff you pull."

"Present company excepted."

"Unfortunately," Alex muttered as she walked away, "that remains to be seen."

"YOU'RE LATE."

Pierre Dussaud plucked a paper napkin from the tabletop dispenser and fastidiously wiped the chair across from Tag before taking a seat. "In Europe, we understand the importance of making a fashionable entrance. We also consider it unforgivable to go where one is not invited."

Tag rolled his right shoulder, reassured to feel his pack slung over the back of his chair. He'd chosen a corner table in the diner, and taken the side that put his back to the wall, but there was something about Dussaud that made him wish he had eyes in the back of his head.

It might be seen as a less than intelligent decision to bring the map to a meeting with the man he'd liberated it from, but there really hadn't been any other choice. Alex was already a target, and the only other potential safe harbor in town was the sheriff, hardly the best person to entrust with stolen property. "I hear you go where you're not wanted plenty."

Pierre waved that off. "Rumor, innuendo. If there was at any time proof that I had done as I was accused, I would be in prison."

"I could say the same." Tag kept his voice down. He'd needed some place neutral to meet with Junior, a public place where it wouldn't matter if he had backup because Junior and his goons couldn't pull anything in front of witnesses. The downside? Word of the summit between the two top treasure hunters was bound to get out in no time flat; everyone in town would flock there, including Alex. What Tag had to say to Junior, however, wasn't going to take that long. "Why didn't you go to the sheriff?"

"I do not need a . . . a country *gendarme* to handle my problems."

"That sounds like a threat."

"It was intended as such."

"I guess that means there's no hope we can find some common ground—other than the fact that we're both working for Bennet Harper."

"*Pour quoi?* Who is this man . . . Harper?"

Tag didn't move a muscle, but his mind was racing, and the headline was Pierre, telling the truth. Dussaud might delude himself that he played his cards close to his chest, but a man who traveled with five enforcers really didn't need to cultivate a poker face.

So who was he working for?

"Clearly, this is a surprise for you."

"I'll get over it," Tag said.

"Will you?" Pierre looked around the diner.

Tag didn't need to do the same to catch his meaning; he already knew two of Pierre's goons were in there with them, and two more were outside. The fifth was awol, probably lying in wait for him. Or Alex. Tag hoped to hell she was staying in plain sight, that she hadn't found a way to ditch the crowd following her around, and that Matt was anal enough to keep an eye on her, like Tag had counted on him to do.

"The map," Pierre said. "I want it back."

Tag's gaze swiveled back to him. "Tell me who hired you."

"I think not. I was instructed to keep that information private."

"I never took you for a bootlicker."

He could all but hear Junior's teeth grinding, but he didn't take the bait.

"So this guy who hired you," Tag said, "is he going to understand that you kept his name a secret at the cost of finding the Lost Spaniard?"

Pierre shrugged, very continental, totally unconvincing.

"I guess you could use that line about how it's fashionable to be late in Europe."

"The map for information?" Pierre fired back. "You must want this man's name very badly."

"About as much as you hate coming in second."

Pierre made a purely Gallic, purely derisive sound in the back of this throat. "Do not offer a bribe you are not prepared to pay, Donovan. And do not make the mistake of counting me out so quickly. I had the map in my possession for some time. I have already managed to re-create a good portion of it from memory. And let us not forget that ownership can change hands with very little notice."

"You don't think I'd be stupid enough to carry it on me."

"I think you would be stupid enough to care about your partner."

"Alex is perfectly safe."

"For the moment."

"I think we're done with each other," Tag said.

"No, Monsieur Donovan, we are not." But Pierre pushed away from the table and walked out, his goons following along behind him like the trained apes they were.

Tag stayed put and finished his coffee. On the surface it might seem he hadn't learned very much. Truth was, the only hard fact he'd come away with was that Junior hadn't been hired by Bennet Harper.

Junior was afraid of whoever had hired him, though,

afraid enough to keep the man's identity a secret, even after he'd been insulted. It didn't follow that it was one of Harper's investors, or that it was the same investor who "knew how to deal with law enforcement." But it was a hell of a coincidence otherwise, and Tag didn't believe in coincidences.

Besides, why else would Harper make it look like he'd hired Junior, unless he was scared of whoever had?

Tag stood, dragged a bill out of his pocket, and dropped it on the table, angry and frustrated. This case was supposed to be child's play, but he was tired of taking baby steps.

He fought his way across town to the Casteeley Inn and went straight to the bar. Alex had suggested he find a woman and slip in some bogus treasure hunting tips among the flirting and flattering. That was too risky; he might stumble on a woman who wasn't prone to gossip, probably a long shot in this town—or the solar system for that matter. The way his luck was running, it was more likely he'd choose a woman who wanted to keep her inside information to herself. Not only would that be a waste of his talents, it wouldn't get them anywhere.

If he was going to sow the seeds of misdirection, he needed the most fertile ground possible. For his money, that spelled bartender. Since the bartender also owned the inn, he was likely one of the few people in Casteel who wouldn't be going after the treasure personally. Why would he when he was making a fortune selling cheap booze and basic rooms at five star prices?

From what little Tag gathered in the few minutes he had to observe before the man took his order, Hooker—that was his name—wasn't very discriminating about what he repeated, or to whom. Tag ordered Bushmills, straight up, double, putting enough of a slur in his voice so it would appear he'd gotten a head start before he walked into the inn. And he pretended not to notice when Hooker substituted something that only resembled Irish whiskey because it was brown and wet.

It was no surprise when Hooker started asking questions, or when the nearest barflies inched closer so they could hear the answers. And it was pathetically easy to pretend he thought his answers were clever while at the same time appearing to be confused about what lies he'd told. After about a half hour he wobbled his way to the door, betting himself that the word would make it up one side of the street and down the other before he'd walked the four blocks to the stable.

Unfortunately that meant he had to continue pretending to be drunk. He stumbled through the big stable doorway, laughing his ass off at all the hicks who'd bought his act—and then he was grabbed from behind. There were two men. One ripped the pack off his shoulder, and both of them dragged his arms back. He fought to get free, knowing it was hopeless. But before darkness closed in, he had a split second to congratulate himself on one more accomplishment; coming back to Casteel had been about smoking the cockroaches out of the woodwork.

It looked like he'd been successful.

chapter
18

ALEX PICKED UP MOST OF WHAT SHE AND TAG
would need in the way of nonperishables. A tarp for tent-
ing if the weather turned bad, bedrolls—two—a coffeepot,
a fire grate, a couple of pans, water purification tablets. Picks
and shovels. Each time she made a purchase a few more
people would be convinced she was actually leaving town
and her entourage would shrink, competitors going off to
make their preparations. That was a nice side benefit, but
she was pretty proud of the fact that she hadn't overpaid—
much—for anything.

She'd already dumped her supplies at the stable, and she
was at the market waiting for her order to be filled when she
decided to call her mother. It wasn't exactly a sudden decision. There'd been moments of guilt over the past five days,
and moments of dread. She'd been pretty abrupt to her
mother on the phone; Cassandra hadn't called back, but even
a thousand miles away Alex could feel her stewing, and that
was never good.

She stepped outside, looking for privacy and spotting
Matt instead, for the third time. Keeping an eye on her, she

figured, and waved to him. He waved back and turned away, pretending it was just a coincidence that he hadn't been more than a half block away from her since she'd left his office. Good old dependable Matt. Why couldn't she fall for someone like him, she wondered? Someone sweet and steady and predictable, who'd be home for dinner every night, never forget her birthday. Someone who thought of her before he thought of himself?

Because she was an idiot, the kind of idiot who went for jerks like Bennet Harper. And Tag Donovan. Okay, she didn't want to label Tag a jerk, but she couldn't deny there were similarities between the two men. They both lied, for one thing, and that was a pretty big thing. But there was also a major difference; she'd stepped into this relationship with Tag Donovan eyes wide open. He wasn't feeding her any garbage about commitments, and he wasn't going after her family. But he wasn't telling her everything, either, and she knew firsthand that ignorance might be bliss, but it also added a layer of foolishness to the hurt and betrayal that would come along with the truth.

Yet here she stood making excuses for him, trying to put him in the best light. If that didn't spell trouble, she needed a new dictionary. With a sigh she dug the satellite phone out of her satchel and dialed her mother, the queen of giving men the benefit of the doubt.

One of the household staff answered, of course, and went to fetch her mother—apparently in Antarctica since it took a while for Cassandra to answer, and when she came on the line the temperature seemed to drop fifteen degrees.

"Alexandra, how lovely of you to call."

Alex rolled her eyes. "If I apologize now, will you stop talking to me like that?"

"I'm sure I don't know what you mean."

"The battery on the phone isn't going to last long enough for you to get a guilt fix, Mother."

"Oh, all right then," Cassandra said. "I can never stay angry with you anyway, darling, but I must say it was cruel of you not to call me back and tell me your cabin burned down. I was positively sick with worry."

"How do you know my cabin burned down?"

Silence.

"Battery, Mom."

Cassandra heaved a windy sigh. "Bennet called me."

Alex didn't say anything for a full thirty seconds. Her mouth was open, but nothing came out.

"Battery, darling."

"How does Bennet know my cabin burned down?"

"He calls every now and then to find out how you're doing," Cassandra said in her fiddle-de-dee voice, like she'd admitted to cheating on her diet. "I told him about our conversation the other day, and he knew how worried I was so he made some calls. It was very sweet of him."

"He calls every now and then?" Alex repeated slowly. "And you talk to him?"

"Alexandra . . ."

"After what he did?"

"Oh, well now, that was just business, darling. And he's really very sorry about it, you know. He apologizes to me each time we speak."

"Mother!"

"He thinks it's his fault you ran off to that godforsaken place," Cassandra plowed on.

"I didn't run anywhere, I went to college," Alex said through clenched teeth, "and I have a feeling if God was to forsake any place it would be wherever Bennet Harper was."

"You wouldn't say that if you didn't still care."

"You're right, Mom. I care that he's still butting into my life. All I want is to be left alone, and you should feel the same way. He tried to rob you and Preston blind."

"Nonsense. Your stepfather lost very little money, what with the tax deduction. And you ruined Bennet for it."

"I didn't ruin him. I broke our engagement—"

"You know how class-conscious people are, Alexandra. Bennet was cut from our social circle—"

"Not because of me. You swept the reasons for our breakup so far under the carpet the dust mites had trouble finding them."

"I saw no point in making a spectacle of ourselves . . ."

Alex tuned her out. She could recite the rest of the argument from memory—not airing dirty laundry, putting on a brave face, keeping up appearances—Cassandra had enough platitudes to keep even Tag Donovan happy, and there was nothing worse in her book than giving her friends fodder for gossip.

Beep.

"What, darling?"

Alex checked the readout. "The phone is going dead."

"If talking to me is such a trial, I suggest you hang up," Cassandra said irritably.

"The phone is really going dead."

"Oh."

"I don't want to argue, Mom. I just called to let you know I'm all right."

The grocer poked his head out the door and said, "Your order's ready, Alex."

She nodded and looked around for Matt. If he was going to follow her around anyway, he might as well play pack mule. But he was busting up a fight between two of her faithful followers. She watched him grab the combatants by the back of their shirt collars and quick-step them off in the direction of the sheriff's office. So she covered the mouthpiece of the phone and said to the grocer, "Can you pack it for horseback and send it to the stable?"

He nodded and ducked back inside.

Alex checked back into the phone conversation and discovered that her mother was relaying the latest about Muffy Van Amstettler's face-lift. And the phone beeped at her again.

"Mom," she said, "I have to go. I'll call you again when I can."

"All right, then. Good-bye, Alexan—"

The phone died. Alex made a mental note to charge it at

the stable and went inside to pay for her supplies, coming out the front door just as they went out the back. She was only a few steps behind the delivery boy, and for once she was alone, her small entourage having been lured away by the prospect of a fistfight.

"Leave the packs there." She pointed to a spot just inside the stable door, handed the delivery boy a five, and waved off his thanks. It was Tag's money, and Jackass was making a ruckus inside.

Somebody was messing with him, was her first thought. Trying to get him drunk again. Or worse. She didn't think twice, picking up a shovel and heading back to his stall.

She didn't get ten feet before the shovel was torn from her hands, her arms were pinned from behind, and something that felt like burlap and smelled like manure was tied over her eyes.

Jackass was still kicking at his stall. Now that her eyes were out of commission her ears were all she had left, and in between blows she thought she heard someone groaning. And she was helpless. She hated helpless. But at least her brain was still working, and if she could convince her attackers not to knock her out maybe she could find a way out of whatever she was being dragged into now.

Jackass let out an equine scream, rage or pain, and there went any hope of staying calm and using her brain. Her feet were so much more satisfying. She lashed out, twisting and fighting to free her arms.

"No you don't," her captor said. "I ain't getting kicked again."

Alex went still. "Franky?"

"Christ, Franky, can't you ever keep your mouth shut?"

"And Mick." Absurdly that made her feel better. They hadn't wanted to hurt her before; she doubted they would this time, especially since she hadn't kicked anyone in the balls. Yet. "I should have known."

"We're real happy to see you, too."

Alex's voice had quieted Jackass for a few seconds; as soon as Mick spoke he started to make noise again.

"He'll have the whole town in here if we don't shut him up," Mick said.

Alex didn't like the tone of his voice. "If you let me go to him, he'll be okay."

"No."

"Are you going to kill me?"

"We're taking you for a guide."

"Then I'll need a horse."

There was a whispered exchange, one of them swore, and she heard the cock of a gun.

"You shoot him and I won't cooperate."

"Fine," Mick said. "You cooperate or we shoot him."

She clenched her jaw, but she nodded. The blindfold came off, and she saw Franky jump back. That would have been pretty satisfying, not to mention amusing, if she hadn't seen Tag slumped against Jackass's stall. He wasn't blindfolded, but his hands were tied and he didn't look too good. Nobody was holding a gun on him, so Alex figured he'd come out the worse in whatever confrontation had occurred before she arrived. Knowing Mick and Franky's affection for surprise attacks, probably they'd hit him over the head. "Are you all right, Tag?" she asked, clamping down on another surge of violent tendencies.

"Yeah," he said, sounding a bit groggy and definitely in pain. He still had to be a smart ass. "I tried to tell them you're nothing but trouble, but their minds are made up."

"What minds?"

Franky took a step forward, but Mick stuck his arm out and stopped him. "The boss wants you two looking for the treasure."

"The boss?" Alex asked.

"You just do what we tell you and everything will be fine."

"You're going to ride horses?" Alex looked them over, shaking her head. "It takes more than a pair of cowboy boots and some brand new Levi's to get along in this country."

"We aren't doing nothing but following the two of you around until you find the treasure."

"Right." Like she was going to lead them anywhere near the Lost Spaniard—not that she knew where it was, but she wasn't taking Frick and Frack out to the middle of nowhere, digging a bunch of nice, convenient holes, and ending up in one of them when they got tired of the search. "What are you going to eat and drink?" she asked them. "Where are you sleeping?"

"We'll use your stuff," Franky said.

"No you won't," Alex told him. "There's only enough for two, and we're not sharing."

"We've got guns."

"If you shoot us, your boss will probably be unhappy."

"She's got us there, Mick."

"Stop thinking," Mick said to Franky. "We got some stuff. We'll make do."

Alex crossed her arms. "You can force me to be out here, but I won't look for the treasure."

"Then—"

"Then what? You'll kill me?"

They traded a look.

"We do this my way or not at all," she said.

"If I were you, I'd listen to her," Tag put in.

"Nobody asked you," Franky said.

"Fine, but she can out-stubborn a mule, and if you have any patience left when she's through with you that animal of hers will use it up. If you want to get out of here some time this week, and without the entire town on your ass, you'll do what she wants."

"Thanks," Alex said to Tag.

"Just trying to help."

"I can see that."

"What? They hit me over the head, and all this arguing is making my headache worse."

"So you're taking their side?"

"They have the guns. I was trying to save time."

"Nice to know what your priorities are."

* * *

IN THE END IT WAS A COMPROMISE. ALEX AND TAG retained ownership of their supplies. Mick and Franky kept the guns, including Alex's Winchester and Tag's Ruger.

Tag's misdirection seemed to have worked, or maybe anyone watching for him and Alex wouldn't expect a party of four leaving in the middle of the night. Franky made a point of telling them how many people had cleared out of Tent City while they were waiting for Alex to show up at the stable, and then he went over and stole as much as he could carry. He was sadly misguided when it came to what would be useful where they were going. Alex didn't see how it would help her to set him straight.

And the fun didn't end there. Mick wasn't happy about being on horseback. Neither was Tag.

Franky *really* wasn't happy. "The only good horse is under the hood of a gas-guzzling American car," he grumbled. "Preferably one made in the eighties."

"The kind that gets about six miles to the gallon?" Alex scoffed.

"The kind with a nice big trunk to carry around mouthy, obnoxious broads."

"Jackass has never complained, and he travels on grass and water. Those are free."

"Cars don't usually bite," Tag pointed out.

"They do where I come from," Franky said.

"What is it with you people, talking all the time?" Mick wanted to know. "Let's hit the road."

"There aren't a lot of roads where we're going."

"Or streetlights," Tag put in. "That's why it's always so much fun to travel at night."

"At least you're still alive," Mick said.

"You don't want us dead," Tag said. "You want us to find the treasure."

"What I want right now is for you to shut up."

They all sat there for a couple of minutes, nothing but the slight sigh of the wind and the occasional creak of leather to break the stillness, and then Mick asked, "Which way do we go?"

Alex didn't say anything; neither did Tag.

"Mick asked you which way," Franky said.

"Oh, we can talk now?"

Franky pulled on his reins, and his horse sidled over next to Alex.

"I wouldn't do that if I were you," Tag said, "you might end up—"

Jackass nipped at Franky's horse, Franky's horse went wonky and launched Franky into the air.

"—on your ass in the dirt," Tag finished.

Franky climbed stiffly to his feet, hissed in a breath and cupped his balls, then limped in Alex's direction, dragging his gun out of his shoulder holster. Tag got there before him, but Franky didn't point the gun at Alex, he pointed it at Jackass. The horse rolled his eyes, but he didn't move.

"You want to go look for the treasure or do you want to shoot Alex's horse?" Tag asked Franky.

"Both."

"Which is more important to you?"

"Get back on your horse, Franky."

"But Mick—"

"Now."

"Not so fast," Alex said before he could heave his bulk into the saddle. "You aren't treating that animal like that again."

"Like what?"

"Sawing on the reins hurts her mouth. She's not stupid. A little nudge goes a long way."

"Oh." Franky walked around to look in his horse's face. "I didn't know she was a girl," he said, looking up at Alex. "Maybe I'm too heavy for her."

Mick gave him a shove with his foot. "Just get on the damn thing. We ain't got all night."

Franky took a deep breath, huffed it out, and put his foot in the stirrup, dragging himself upright and standing there until Jackass nipped at his backside, at which point he vaulted into the saddle and groaned in pain.

Jackass nickered out a laugh, nudging Tag with his head as if he wanted to share the joke.

"I think he likes you," Alex said to Tag.

"I'm touched." And stupidly, he actually was. Next to Alex, Jackass was the . . . creature whose respect it had taken him the longest to earn.

"The minute this thing is over, I'm shooting that bastard," Franky grumbled.

Jackass snorted and rolled his eyes in a take-your-best-shot kind of way.

"Men," Alex said, then leaned forward and patted Jackass on the neck. "Take the high road," she said in his ear.

"Jesus, she's talking to the horse," Franky announced.

"She does that a lot," Tag said.

Alex looked over at him. "He's the one I thought would listen."

chapter 19

THEY RODE ALL NIGHT. AGAIN. DAWN WAS BREAK-
ing when Alex stopped Jackass. Tag would have stayed
where he was until some of his muscles unknotted, but she
looked over at him. It wasn't like she challenged him or
anything, but she swung down from Jackass so effortlessly
he felt compelled to do the same. He hoped it looked a hell
of a lot better than it felt.

"What do you think?" she asked.

Tag shrugged. That hurt, too. "You're the expert," he
said when there was a fair chance he could manage actual
words instead of just groaning.

"Why don't you look at the map?" Mick suggested.

"How do you know we have the map?" Alex asked him.

His gaze flipped to Tag. So did hers. Tag didn't so much
as breathe for fear he'd give something away, and he didn't
mean his personal agony.

"We followed you in Denver," Mick finally said. "Talked
to the, uh, chick in the library."

"The librarian?" Alex asked.

"Yeah, sure, the librarian."

Alex narrowed her eyes, but nobody contradicted Mick because, Tag thought, it was a perfectly plausible explanation. Mick and Franky had been following them in Denver; they could have pumped Ms. Newstead for information, and the woman probably wouldn't have thought twice about telling them. Alex didn't look entirely convinced, though, and when Tag saw her turning his way he got real busy unloading Angel.

But he could feel her watching him. And wondering.

"We are camping here, right?" he asked.

"This is as good a place as any," Alex said. "We can't be far from the first landmark on the map." She glanced over at Mick, but he was currently ignoring her to wander off and answer nature's call. He didn't go far enough for her taste. She made a face and turned back to Tag. "This little valley will allow us to have a fire that can't be seen for miles around. We can stay here for a few days, search the surrounding area, then move on if necessary."

"A few days?" Franky asked, switching his focus to Mick when he strolled back to join them. "How long we gonna be out here?"

"Until we find the treasure," Tag said. "There's no telling how long that will take."

"Then I guess we better get moving," Mick said. "I ain't sleeping on the ground forever."

"I am." Alex pulled the packs off Jackass and dropped them. "Sleeping on the ground, that is. Just as soon as I take care of my horse. I was up all night. I'm not hiking this kind of terrain while I'm exhausted, and even if I did, I wouldn't be any good."

Tag had to admit she had a point. They'd ridden pretty much due north from Casteel, bypassing her valley and leaving the pine forest behind. The terrain had gradually morphed from low, leafy plants and wood debris into an area of rocky outcroppings and low, scrubby underbrush.

But it wasn't just the landscape they needed to worry about. "There's no telling who might be wandering around out there," he said, "and since you won't return our guns we have no way to protect ourselves."

"You don't need a gun," Mick said, "we'll watch out for you."

Right, Tag thought, if it came to armed conflict Franky was likely to shoot them in the back and blame it on the other guys so he could get back to civilization.

Tag looked over at Alex and knew she was thinking the same thing. They had to figure out a way to get rid of these bozos, or get away from them. But there was no way they could come up with a plan with Harper's hirelings listening in, and it wasn't just them overhearing the discussion that concerned Tag.

He was walking a fine line. He couldn't appear too friendly with Alex in front of guys, who would report it back to Harper, but he couldn't let her think he was done with her, either. Because he wasn't. Not even close. And if she thought he was done with her, she'd treat him like the enemy. He couldn't afford to have her working against him, not if they were both going to get through this thing in one piece.

He had to find a way to make it look like they were only putting up with each other for the sake of the treasure, nothing personal.

He said as much to her when she laid their bedrolls out side by side, tipping his head toward Harper's bad guys.

"Nothing personal," she repeated, looking at Mick, then Franky. Realization dawned, and she nudged the bedrolls apart a couple of feet.

She didn't look upset while she did it, so Tag figured they were on the same wavelength. Consciously.

Subconsciously there seemed to be a different agenda altogether, and while a two-foot separation might be enough to fool Mick and Franky into thinking there was nothing personal between them, it wasn't nearly enough distance for their libidos to overcome.

Somehow during the course of the morning they wound

up spooned around each other. At least Alex couldn't blame him for it, Tag thought, since they seemed to have met in the middle, a compromise they couldn't always manage during their waking hours. And there was nothing he could do about it. Except simmer.

He wasn't the only one, either. Alex was in one of her moods, pulled back into herself, completely uncommunicative—unless it was to hand out orders.

They'd camped at the mouth of the valley where they should find the first site named on Juan's map. *La Cruz de Piedra*, which translated to "Cross of Stone." It sounded obvious, but if it was really obvious, Tag figured somebody would have found it before now. Bottom line? They had no clue what they were looking for. But Alex seemed reasonably confident they were looking in the right general area.

It was a lot of territory, though. Alex led Mick, Franky, and Tag down one side of the valley, searching every nook and cranny big enough to hide a poker chip, leaving no stone unturned, literally. She enlisted the three men to move any boulders that might be hiding the mouth of a cave or small opening until Tag pointed out that Juan Amparo would likely have been alone when he hid the treasure. After that she let them take turns.

It couldn't have been much over sixty-five degrees, but the sky was cloudless, the air was breezeless, and the landscape was treeless. The sun had been beating down on the rocks all day, and the rocks were currently reflecting heat back in shimmering waves. They were sweaty, tired, and thirsty, and Alex had gone from grumpy to genial, her temperament brightening the longer she watched them toil, although Tag wasn't sure why she included him in the punishing work. Until he remembered how they'd met.

"Getting a little retribution?" he asked a couple hours after they'd started their trek up the valley.

"As a matter of fact," she said, grinning.

"Retribution," Franky repeated. "Does that mean she's only doing this to get back at us?"

"I'm doing this because somebody has to look behind the rocks, and since you insist on tagging along, you might as well make yourself useful."

Franky plopped down on a handy boulder. "I ain't moving no more rocks. I'm tired and I'm hot and I'm sitting right here for a while."

"Okay, you sit right there, but if I were you I'd watch out for the wildlife."

"Wildlife?" Franky shifted his ass from one cheek to the other, checking underneath it and finding nothing but rock.

"She's just talking about rattlesnakes," Mick said, "and you'd hear one of them before it got close enough to bite you."

"Sure, rattlers make noise to scare you off, but bears don't, or mountain lions."

"Wouldn't we see something that big coming?" Tag asked, although he was clearly amused.

Alex shrugged. "Maybe, but there are lizards everywhere."

Franky's gaze skittered to hers.

"And spiders. Yellow sacs, hobos, black widows. But those are just the poisonous ones. And they especially like rocks. Nice warm rocks."

Franky yelped and jumped up.

Mick rolled his eyes. "She's just screwing with you, dumbass."

Franky didn't sit back down. "What did I ever do to you?" he demanded.

"You're kidding, right?"

"Hey, lady." He stabbed a beefy finger in her direction. "You ain't the only one suffering. You think I want to be out here walking around in these fucking boots? Who invented them anyway? Why are the toes pointed and why do they hurt like hell?"

"Aw, are your feet sore?" Alex asked. "I'm all broken up for you."

Franky lunged for her, but Mick held him back.

"If we finish this site before dark," Alex taunted, "we can ride to the next one in the morning."

"She's asking for it, Mick."

"What? I'm only trying to get you off your feet."

"And on that damn horse again." He cupped his balls and grimaced.

"You know an ice pack would probably help that— Oh, we don't have any ice out here, do we?"

This time it took Mick and Tag to hold him back until he got his temper under control and shoved away from them.

"You have a real mean streak," Tag said, taking Alex by the arm and towing her off a little ways. "It's fun to watch Franky's face turn purple, but maybe you should try to remember they have the guns."

"They won't shoot us."

"Mick won't," Tag corrected. "Franky is standing on the psycho ledge and you keep trying to push him off."

"I'm the one who's being pushed around. I'm just pushing back. Why are you so worried about toeing the line?"

"I'm waiting for the right moment. The longer we're out here, the more tired they'll get. In the meantime we're doing what we wanted to do anyway, and that's look for the treasure. Jesus, Alex, try to see the big picture."

"That's what I've been trying to do since you fell in my valley." She tore her arm out of his grip. "I know where they fit in," she said, tipping her head toward Mick and Franky, "and I know where I stand. You're the only shadow, Tag."

"If they know how . . . close we are, they'll play us off against each other." She didn't look convinced. "I'm trying to buy some time until we can figure out how to get away from them."

"Maybe if I had the first clue what you were up to, I could be a real partner instead of always playing catch-up." She walked away and left him standing there with an odd feeling in the pit of his stomach. Probably impending doom.

"Let's get moving," she said for everyone's benefit.

"What's your hurry?" Franky wanted to know. "Why don't we just call it a day?"

"We ain't had very much sleep," Mick chimed in. "You two got a solid six."

"Yeah," Franky added, "and you looked pretty cozy, too."

"It was cold," Alex said.

"And I'm not above taking what's offered," Tag added. He could see, even though she knew what he was doing and why, that she was pissed off. But there were more important considerations.

Mick and Franky had been in a hell of a hurry to get out in the field, but now they didn't seem the least anxious to look for the treasure. Letting them sleep the morning away, for starters, proved they weren't overeager. Sure, Alex hadn't given them much choice, but they hadn't even argued with her. And now they wanted to take the rest of the day off? True, they had to be tired, but Harper wasn't a patient man. Mick should be pushing them, not holding them back.

"This is stupid," Alex said. "If you want to go back to camp, go ahead. I'm going to finish up here."

She headed off, not giving a damn if anyone came with her. Including him, Tag decided. Or maybe she'd taken his tongue lashing to heart, and she was putting on a show for the kidnappers. But did she have to be so damn good at it?

He'd started the trek thinking this hostage thing wasn't so bad. And sure, if Mick and Franky hadn't been around he'd have been able to sleep a whole lot closer to Alex and there wouldn't be this urge percolating constantly under his skin. But at least they got to sleep. Mick and Franky had to take turns standing guard. These guys weren't rocket scientists to begin with; as the nights added up and they got more and more tired, sooner or later one of them would let something slip. Tag was betting on Franky, and he was betting on sooner. Of course, he'd have to make damn sure it wasn't Harper's name. That would be a huge mess. But he thought he could control that. He just had to keep Alex from provoking Franky into strangling her with his bare hands.

Not a bad game plan. Now all he had to do was remember it. Alex wasn't making it easy, striding along about ten yards ahead, arms swinging, ass swinging, well-toned muscles flexing in a way that made him think of sex. Hot, sweaty, any-flat-surface-handy sex. If she'd been trying to torture him, she couldn't have chosen a better way. And then she notched the torture up to excruciating by stripping her T-shirt over her head, stuffing it in her back pocket so it flapped behind her like a flag, and walking off in nothing but her sports bra and jeans that had faded and shrunk to fit her like a second skin.

He'd cooled off once they stopped moving; he reheated so fast he felt like a baked potato in a microwave. And somebody had forgotten the little fork holes. He caught up with her and ripped the shirt out of her pocket, holding it out before the top of his skull blew off from the pressure. "Put this back on," he said, holding it out.

She glanced at the shirt, then lifted her eyes to his face, giving him a look that would have singed his eyebrows, if he hadn't already been at thermostatic overload. "No."

"This isn't a game, Alex."

"Isn't it?"

"Put. This. On."

"I'm perfectly covered," she said.

"And leaving nothing to the imagination."

From behind them, Franky made a wolf whistle.

Alex laughed, but when she spoke again her voice had an edge to it. "The imagination is highly overrated. I prefer the straightforward approach."

"What you see is what you get?"

"More like what you see is what there is."

"But keep your hands off? That's a game, too, one of the oldest."

Alex plucked her shirt out of his hand and replaced it in her back pocket. "I took my shirt off because I'm hot. You're the one who's making this into something else."

"You ought to be a damn politician," Tag muttered.

"I spent my childhood in Boston society, followed by eighteen months on the pageant circuit. I am a politician."

She clambered onto a pile of rocks and stood there, one hand on her hip, the other shading her eyes. If she was trying to piss him off it was working. Then she dropped her arms, and something about the tension in her body spelled excitement. Not the kind of excitement he'd been feeling since she took off her shirt. But the look on her face when she turned around made him forget about sex—okay, not entirely, but at the least the boil cooled back to a simmer.

She beckoned him, and he climbed up behind her. There wasn't much room; he had to plaster himself against her in order not to fall, looking over her shoulder so he could follow the direction of her pointing finger. The fact that she didn't object, that she'd completely forgotten their argument, was pretty compelling.

"There, do you see it?" she asked him.

"What is it?" Mick wanted to know.

"That rock formation at the head of the valley," Alex said.

"It looks like—"

"*La Cruz de Piedra*. Cross of Stone." She scrambled down, covering the last five hundred yards at a near-run.

Tag was about a second behind, the two of them stopping at the end of a cross with three short arms and one long one, each about two feet wide, measuring about twenty-five feet in total length. It was made up of all different types and textures of rock, some smooth from being carried out of the mountains in a long, dried-up stream, others rough.

"This has to be man-made," Tag said.

Alex was already moving rocks. "Definitely," she said, adding when Mick and Franky arrived, "don't just stand there and watch. Either the treasure is under these rocks or we can rule out this site."

The possibility of downtime, one way or another, was all the incentive Franky needed. He and Mick began to heave rocks, forgetting they were supposed to be adversaries. Once they got about half the cross dismantled, Tag and Mick set to work digging. It only took a couple more hours to decide there was nothing there—and work off the gold fever. They stood there in silence a moment, night falling, dejection setting in.

"This doesn't make any sense," Alex said, slapping at a mosquito. "Why would Juan make this cross for no reason?"

"He had a reason," Tag said. "But it doesn't necessarily follow that he buried gold here. The Spanish were rampantly Catholic. This could be nothing more than a profession of faith."

Alex swung around and stared at him. Mick joined her in her consternation.

Franky had a one-track mind. "Does that mean we can go back to town?"

"We can go back to camp, at least."

They headed back down the valley, Mick and Franky lagging behind, not caring if they were in on the conversation.

"There are four more sites marked on the map," Tag said quietly.

"It's not Denver," Alex said. "Even if Juan would have hidden the treasure that close to a settlement, we'd never find it after all the growth around the city since 1859. Same goes for Casteel."

"Was the town that big then?"

"Probably not, but it was a big enough settlement to make it dicey for him to hide anything there without someone stumbling across him. And it would have been found by now anyway. Nobody knows where Juan lived, exactly, but he spent a lot of time in Casteel. There have been more holes dug around that town than there are in Franky's head."

She said that loud enough to carry back.

"Hey," Franky yelled, "why you gotta say things like that?"

"Gosh, I don't know, you kidnapped me?"

"You ain't the only one been inconvenienced, you know."

"Inconvenienced?" She stopped and turned around, planting her hands on her hips. "That's what you call this?"

"Everybody's tired," Mick said. "Let's get back to camp, have something to eat, get some sleep."

"I don't get to sleep," Franky grumbled, "that's a inconvenience."

"Listening to you whine is an inconvenience," Alex said. "You not getting to sleep is poetic justice."

Franky opened his mouth, but the next sound they heard was a gunshot.

chapter
20

ANOTHER SHOT RIPPED THROUGH THE STILLNESS, rolling through the hills like thunder. Tag and Alex ducked behind a handy rock. Mick and Franky hit the ground about thirty feet away, behind a rock of their own.

"Which way did it come from?" Mick asked.

"No telling, the way it echoed," Tag said.

It was big country, big enough to lose the entire population of Denver. Tag hadn't realized that until they got out there, the landscape rolling off into the distance like a rumpled cloth, no matter which way you looked. A whole army could be hiding in the hills around them and they'd never know.

Even if he hadn't known that most of the other treasure hunters had stuck closer to Casteel or gone in a different direction, it seemed impossible that someone had stumbled upon them by chance. But not improbable that someone would have tracked them on purpose.

Another shot rang out. The sound bounced around like before, but it was easier to pinpoint now that they were ready for it.

"I think it came from up ahead," Alex said.

"Between us and camp."

"Yeah. I didn't hear the bullet hit anywhere nearby, and I'd imagine whoever's out there is a pretty good shot. Probably a signal."

Probably for Dussaud, Tag thought. Alex proved to be right about their aim. Tag was wrong about their identity.

"Hallo," a man called out.

Alex's expression changed, starting with an eye roll and ending with a heavy sigh.

"You know who that is?"

"Yeah. So do you. Rusty Hale."

Tag thought about it a minute, then repeated her eye roll. "Your cowboy in town? The one you think got Jackass drunk?"

"Sounds like him. And knowing Rusty, he's not alone." Alex waved an arm. "Rusty?" she called out.

"Alex. Hoo-eeee," he yelled back, "I told you boys it was Alex Scott, alive and well and looking for the Lost Spaniard."

She gave Tag one last I-told-you-so look and got to her feet. Tag joined her.

Mick and Franky stayed behind their rock, but Tag heard the distinctive sound of a gun cocking, coming from that general direction. He and Alex shouldn't have been the ones in those particular crosshairs, but the spot between Tag's shoulder blades started to tingle. You never could tell with Franky.

He glanced at Alex. "Damned if we do, damned if we don't."

"You do love those pithy sayings, don't you?"

"It seems to sum up the situation pretty well."

"But it doesn't make me feel any better."

"Friends of yours?" Mick asked, still behind his rock.

"Not really," Alex said.

"Then I suggest you move it or lose it."

"Now there's a saying I can get behind." Alex edged off to one side, giving Mick and Franky a clear shot.

That wasn't enough for Tag. He hooked a finger in the

waistband of her jeans and towed her backward, so they were behind their kidnappers—who were suddenly their protectors, much as he hated to admit it.

"Say something to him," Mick told Alex.

"No."

"Say something, dammit."

"Promise you won't shoot him."

Mick didn't make any promises, he didn't look at her, but his shoulders slumped for a second before he squared them. Tag knew just how he felt.

"I'm not gonna shoot him. I just want him to know he's got some competition."

"Competition for him is a guy who can stay on a really mean bull longer than he can."

"Fine, so I want him to know I have a gun. I'm not planning on using it on him." *Unless he makes me.* Mick didn't finish the sentence, but they all knew how it ended. Including Rusty.

Alex called out to him. He walked toward her, rifle carefully held out to one side. When Mick and Franky stood up from behind their rock, his step faltered, but only for a moment.

"Hired muscle?"

"Something like that," Alex said.

Rusty's smile lost a bit of its charm. "Sorry about the noise," he said. "I was just taking potshots at lizards, y'know, keeping in practice."

"You were signaling to your buddies," Tag said.

Rusty made to spread his hands in an "aw-shucks" manner. Mick and Franky didn't like the fact that he was still holding a rifle when he did it.

"Whoa," he said when two pistols were leveled at him. "I'm not here to cause any trouble."

"What about your friends?" Mick asked.

Rusty tried a smile, gave it up when it didn't work on the "hired muscle." "Come on out, fellas," he said.

Three men appeared out of the rocks behind Rusty, who wasn't the least embarrassed by his own scheming. " 'Course now that we stumbled across you folks," he said, "you won't mind if we tag along."

"I mind," Franky said.

"Seems to me Alex is in charge here," Rusty said.

"We're in charge," Tag corrected. "I mind if you tag along. Alex?"

She hesitated.

"I know what you're thinking," Tag said under his breath, "but do you really want these guys having a shoot-out with us in the middle, unarmed?"

She flashed him a resentful look, but she made the only decision she could. "I thought I made myself clear in town a few days ago," she said to Rusty.

"You sure about that, Alex? You might be thankful for our help some of these days. We ain't the only ones shadowing you."

"How many?" Tag asked.

"Don't know. At least four."

"How long?"

Rusty lifted a shoulder. "They were here when we got here, just sitting out there in the middle of nowhere. We figured they were waiting on something, and that something was probably you."

Tag exchanged a look with Mick.

Rusty didn't miss it. "We'd be glad to hook up with you, provide a little additional . . . insurance."

"We've got all the insurance we need," Mick said. "It would be in your best interest to move along."

"Well, now, it's a free country—"

"Not always," Mick said. "Think about how high a price you want to pay before you get too close next time."

"JESUS, IT'S A FREAKING PARADE," FRANKY SAID.

They'd broken camp that morning at daybreak and set off for the next site marked on Juan's map. Every now and then Rusty and his pals appeared at the top of a hill at the same time Alex, Tag, Mick, and Franky topped a hill. Ground distance–wise they were about a mile ahead. As the crow flies they were within rifle range. It was making them all edgy, but Franky had proven himself particularly susceptible to edgy. And when he was edgy he talked. A lot.

That gave Alex ideas.

"By tomorrow this place will be crawling with hicks like that."

"Let 'em come," Mick said. "What do we care?"

He had a point, Alex thought. Rusty and his friends weren't so bad as shadows went. If it had been Junior and his goons trailing them, the gunfire probably wouldn't have been a wake-up call so much as a get-dead call.

If they found the treasure it might come down to that anyway. Rusty and company were only hanging back to see if the Lost Spaniard got found. If they found the Lost Spaniard Mick and Franky weren't going to let them keep it. The smart thing would be to run like hell and let the guys with the guns shoot it out, winner take all. But it was her sweat, and Tag's, that would have made it possible; the idea of having it stolen out from under them ticked her off. There had to be a way to prevent it.

She would have loved to discuss the problem with Tag, but they couldn't exactly make plans with their kidnappers listening in. Even if he hadn't made that clear, she'd have figured out that much for herself. What puzzled her was the way he was acting. And if she was completely honest with herself, it was the "nothing personal" that stuck in her craw.

What did Tag care if Mick and Franky knew they were closer than partners? Hell, what would Mick and Franky care if they knew she'd slept with Tag? It wouldn't make a difference in their search for the Lost Spaniard, right?

She was missing something. Something important. And it wasn't just the strange and troubling symbiosis between Tag and Mick, the way they seemed to silently concur when there was a decision to be made. There was a subtext riding below the surface of every happenstance and every conversation that had taken place since she'd met Tag Donovan.

And now he was watching his words and guarding his expressions, and she wasn't quite sure how to get through to him.

Mick and Franky were another story, or at least Franky was. They were definitely keeping secrets, and she hadn't missed the way Mick stepped in every time Franky started to lose it. Or Tag did—another mystery that kept her mind spinning and her stomach churning.

What she felt for Tag . . . She'd fought it, but there was no getting around the fact that she had feelings for him. And she'd taken enough college psychology to know she was using sarcasm and bitchiness to try to push him away because she was afraid. He'd destroyed her defenses so quickly, wormed his way into her heart so deeply that she didn't know what she would do if she discovered he'd been lying to her. And considering how their relationship had started, and how it had progressed so far, she figured there was a better than even chance that he was.

If she had any sense she'd cooperate and keep her eyes and ears closed. But she couldn't allow fear to blind her to the truth. She'd lived through Bennet Harper, she could live through Tag Donovan if she had to. Letting a man, any man, destroy her again wasn't an option. Neither was passivity.

The sooner they searched the last two sites the sooner this thing would be over, she told herself. She could get back to her life without having lost more than a couple of weeks. And there, she thought, was a lie worthy of Tag Donovan. There was no going back to her old life after this. With or without him.

They'd moved due east this time. The Rockies were still a beautiful, very dominant backdrop to the scenery, but they were moving farther into the foothills. There were fewer patches of bare rock and more wild grasses and spring flowers. And there were fewer obvious landmarks.

The area was far from flat, the land stretching away like a big wrinkled carpet as far as the eye could see. They reined in at the top of a hill and stared out at the landscape,

all having the same thought—or at least three of them were.
Franky was gazing at the sky, looking like he was contemplating the meaning of life. Or sleeping with his eyes open.
The rest of them were coming down from the previous
day's high and realizing just how daunting and impossible
the search really was.

"So what now?" Tag asked.

"This is going to be a challenge," Alex said dryly.

"And the last one was a piece of cake?" Mick said.

It was on the tip of her tongue to ask him if he'd rather
abandon the search, but she had a feeling he'd say yes, and
she wanted to give this a fair shot before they up and quit.
Otherwise she'd wonder for the rest of her life if they were
inches from the treasure and had allowed themselves to be
intimidated by poor odds.

"I guess we spread out and see what we can find."

"Don't spread out permanently," Mick warned, his hand
on his shoulder holster.

Alex didn't entirely buy the threat, but when bullets were
involved there wasn't a lot of margin for error. Besides
which, Franky had a gun, too, and Franky wasn't what
you'd call a stable personality. That was enough to keep her
on the obedient side of the line. As long as it suited her
purposes.

They spread out a little and rode forward, watching the
ground for anything likely. This time it was Franky who
stumbled across the place, literally. His mare caught a hoof
and went down to her front knees, pitching Franky over her
head. He started cussing and yelling; they all went racing
over and found him on his ass in the dirt, his mare grazing
serenely about fifteen yards away.

"Stupid horse tripped," he said, giving his mare a look
that had Jackass sidling over to stand in front of her.

"Anything broken?" Alex asked hopefully.

"No, but my ass hurts." Franky gingerly got to his feet
and patted himself down, hissing in a breath and bringing
his right palm about an inch from his face. "And I got a
sliver."

Mick rolled his eyes, but Alex jumped off Jackass and hunkered down a couple of feet from Franky.

"I think this is something," she said, brushing carefully at the dirt with her fingers.

"This decayed log?" Tag asked, squatting down beside her.

She met his gaze, nodded. He flashed that easy grin of his, and her heart lurched. But it was more than her heart, it went deeper. Just for a second she felt like they were together, a couple, on the same wavelength. And then the stupid filter fell off, the picture snapped back into focus, and he was just a guy who was in her life until . . . until he wasn't anymore. She could either obsess about it or take it as it came.

"I don't think it's just a decayed log," Alex said, getting to her feet and pacing the length of it, half stooped over so that when another decayed log intersected it at a right angle she saw it. By the time she was done, she'd paced a square roughly fifty feet on a side that brought her back to where Tag was standing.

"Maybe it's the remains of a wooden structure," he suggested.

"It's definitely man-made."

Franky was still sitting in the dirt, digging one grubby nail into the palm of his hand. Mick had wandered back to the top of the hill behind them and stood so he could just see over the top of it. Watching for Rusty, Alex figured, then she put them all out of her mind.

"I don't think it was a building," she said to Tag. "Look at the ground inside, it's pretty rough."

"If this site was about gold, they wouldn't have bothered with wood floors."

"They wouldn't have bothered with wood buildings. If they had, the floor would have been dirt, but it would have been level, at least. This follows the slope of the hill."

"And?"

"I think this was a corral. There were dozens of temporary settlements peppered throughout the area around the gold fields. Juan labeled this *riachuelo de Smith*. The Smith part is obvious; *riachuelo* translates as 'stream' or 'creek,' which makes sense. Back then there was water running through here that would have washed some gold down out of the mountains. Mr. Smith and whoever was with him would have needed a place to keep the horses, but they wouldn't have built permanent housing just to pan for gold. They would have lived in tents."

"You think Juan might have been one of them?" Tag asked.

"Possibly. We couldn't find a claim filed for him at the National Archives, and the sack attached to the map contained gold dust, which would indicate panning instead of placer or lode mining. Maybe we should dig some exploratory holes, just to see what we find." She didn't honestly think anything was there. Even if there was, the chance of them stumbling across it was practically zero because there was nothing to indicate a possible hiding place, on the map or at the site. But there was still an opportunity there. "There're four corners," she said, "let's each take one."

"I ain't digging no holes," Franky said. "My hand hurts."

"It's just a sliver," Alex said. "Jeez, my little sister is more of a man than you are."

Franky jumped to his feet, both hands fisting.

Tag grabbed Alex by the arm and pulled her aside. "This is the first I've heard of a sister."

"That's because I don't have one."

"What are you up to?"

"It's pretty obvious," she said, pulling her arm out of his grip. "And you're not a man who can't figure things out for himself. I seem to always be one step behind. I'm just trying to catch up."

She turned away. Tag's hand slid down her arm to close around her wrist. She didn't turn back, but she stopped.

"There are some things going on here that I don't understand yet," he said.

"But you know more than I do."

"You're right," he said quietly. "I'm keeping things from you, but I have good reasons. If you do something stupid—"

"It's too late for that," she said and walked away.

Falling in love with him wasn't the smartest thing she'd ever done, but that was involuntary. Compounding her lunacy with blind trust would be the supreme act of stupidity, and that she wasn't prepared to commit.

chapter
21

TAG COULD FEEL THE WHOLE CASE SPINNING INTO
the toilet. Everything appeared normal, but it was going
down the crapper, sure as shit. They made camp and opened
a couple of cans for dinner. The three men were having pork
and beans. Alex was having Franky.

She had a plan, Tag concluded, and it consisted of gnaw-
ing holes in Franky's patience and self-control, in the hope
that information would come spewing out of him volcano
fashion. There wasn't a whole lot of patience and self-control
there to begin with; she'd be damn lucky if he didn't explode
all over her in the process. Or maybe she was counting on
Tag and Mick to run interference.

They'd been trying like hell to. Tag had attempted to
take her aside but she wasn't having any of it, and it was
kind of hard to talk sense into her if she wouldn't talk to
him at all. He'd thought about gagging her, but it was to the
point where just the way she looked at Franky was enough
to make him mutter and squirm.

Mick wasn't having much luck either, but Tag had to give
him credit for his persistence. And optimism. "So where do

we stand?" Mick asked Alex the next time she drew a bead on Franky.

"We'll go to the third site tomorrow," she said. "It's south of here, back into the rockier terrain like we searched yesterday." Her gaze shifted to Franky. "Not great on horseback, but it shouldn't take us more than two days to work our way through it."

"Two days! Aw, Mick . . ."

"Shut up, Franky."

"Why we gotta do this anymore? We already been out here two days, ain't that enough?"

"Enough for what?" Tag asked.

"What's the matter?" Alex said in a tone of voice that was all the more infuriating for its casual matter-of-factness. "Can't handle a little physical exertion, Franky? You've got kind of a low pain threshold for a guy in your line of work."

"I ain't usually the one in pain."

"And when you are you turn into a whiny, sniveling baby."

Franky spiked his plate onto the ground and took to his feet, looming over Alex. Mick jumped up and planted both hands in his chest, shoving him back a couple of steps. "Back off," he said, then he whipped around to loom over Alex himself. "And you shut your trap."

If she was afraid she kept it to herself, right down to the slight, derisive smile on her face. "Or?"

"Or I'll shoot you."

She laughed, her gaze going to the guns. Mick usually kept them out of sight, but tonight Alex's rifle was propped on a handy rock next to his blanket—in honor of Rusty and his friends, Tag figured.

"That threat might work coming from Franky," Alex said. "If I thought he had the guts to do it."

Franky's response was an inarticulate roar. He shoved Mick aside, hands out, going for Alex's throat when Tag threw himself in the way. Thankfully, Mick took a side and between the two of them they were able to drag Franky away from her.

Alex followed, as that didn't suit her purposes. "You think you're sick of this after two days?" she asked, getting back in Franky's face. "I've been manipulated and lied to and pushed around for nearly a week now."

"You kicked me in the balls," Franky countered. "Do you have any idea what it's like to ride a horse when your balls are sore?"

I do, Tag thought, but Alex was on a roll, and he was beginning to think she might actually get something out of Franky besides whining and sniveling—to use her terms.

"I don't have balls," she said, "which I've always considered a huge advantage. But I know what it's like to ride a horse with a knife wound. And I know how it feels to be abducted, held at gunpoint, and forced to search for treasure."

"You think I'm having a picnic here? I had to ride a horse—"

"Trust me, your horse isn't enjoying it either."

"—and move rocks all day and now you're planning to walk me to death."

"Shut up, Franky," Mick said, but Tag could tell his heart wasn't in it anymore.

Tag knew how he felt. Trying to stop Alex was like attempting to bail out the *Titanic* with a teaspoon. Franky would be the iceberg in that scenario, big and brainless, an accident waiting to happen.

"And let's not forget I was nearly frozen to death. Twice," he said. "Top that."

"I was . . . wait," Alex said, "what do you mean you were nearly frozen to death?"

"They tried to steal the map," Tag reminded her, mentally bailing like hell.

"That was them?"

"You mean you didn't recognize me?" Franky said.

"I wasn't looking at your face. Maybe if you take your pants off."

He dropped his hands to his fly.

"She's kidding, jackass," Mick said.

From outside the circle of firelight, Jackass neighed.

"I don't think he appreciates the comparison," Alex said to Mick, then went right back at Franky. "When was the other time?"

Instead of answering her question he said, "Ow," because Mick gave him a shot to the head. "I musta been mistaken."

"You can't count, either? You can't ride a horse, it took you two tries to kidnap me, you're afraid of spiders and snakes, and you've spent the last two days complaining about everything. Is there anything you're good at?"

"Yeah," he growled right in her face, "lighting fires and shooting people. Too bad we didn't cap you and that damn horse when we smoked you out of that stupid cabin."

Tag closed his eyes, but he could see the wheels spinning in her head.

"That was you on the snowmobiles," she said.

"You shot me with a tranquilizer dart. I ain't paid you back for that yet, either."

Tag opened his eyes. Alex was staring at him. The look on her face was . . . bad. In so many ways. And it only got worse.

"That's why you almost froze to death," she said, her eyes on Tag, the hurt and betrayal in them growing deeper. Darker.

"Yeah, Mick dragged me over to your fire and kept me warm until I woke up," Franky said. "I guess it was lucky we firebombed your cabin."

"You were on the plane." Her words were for Franky, but the disgust in her voice was for herself, for being such a fool. "You pushed Tag off, and then you came back in a helicopter and burned my cabin down."

"Don't feel so good to be the only one who don't know what's going on, does it?"

"And you weren't supposed to tell her," Mick reminded Franky.

"Screw that. Mr. Harper wouldn't have brought her into this if he didn't want her to know it was him behind everything."

She went still, so still and pale. Almost lifeless. Except for her eyes.

"Alex—"

Her hands came up, both fisted. "Bennet Harper?"

"That would be him," Franky said, sounding pretty cheerful about it.

She stepped back until she had some distance from the three men. Putting herself on the other side. Her against them, and "them" included Tag. "You're working for Bennet Harper," she said in a voice that sounded like the breath had been knocked out of her.

Tag knew how she felt. He wasn't out of breath, but he was definitely out of ideas. He couldn't deny working for Harper, not in front of Mick and Franky, but he couldn't bring himself to admit it, either. Unfortunately, there was an expiration date on the question, and silence was as good as an admission.

He saw Alex's gaze flick to the guns a split second before she moved. She ducked around Mick and elbowed Franky in the gut on the way by. Tag made a grab for her; she made a grab for the rifle. She won, spinning and racking a shell into the chamber, all in one slick move fueled by fury more than self-preservation. All three of the men ended up on the business end of the Winchester. Tag couldn't help but notice it was pointed directly at him.

Time drew out like a razor. He'd faced down Uzis in the hands of drug-dealing gang members, but the look in her eyes tied his colon in greasy, cramping knots. Under normal circumstances he'd have bet his life she wouldn't shoot him. The circumstances, however, weren't normal, and he felt like more than his life was at stake. How much more didn't bear tabulating.

Before he could get his mind functioning beyond the impossibility of the situation, she whipped around and ran out of the circle of firelight, hooking Jackass's saddle on the way. Franky made to chase after her. Tag stopped him.

"Let her go," Mick said, "we done what we came to do."

"And what's that?" Tag asked, well aware of the fact that Alex was getting ready to take off. Without him.

There was no answer, and Tag didn't have time to play nice. He caught Franky by the front of his shirt, and pulled the gun from his shoulder holster. "You guys were in a big hurry to get us out here, but you've been complaining and slowing us down ever since. You don't give a shit if we find the treasure."

Franky grinned. "You found it, and you ran off with it. We tried to stop you, but . . ." He spread his hands and looked down at his gun in Tag's hand. "Harper is already telling his investors how you made off with their gold."

Suddenly Tag could understand exactly how Alex felt. Maybe the same depth of betrayal wasn't there, but the world was crashing around him—around them. "There never was a treasure. Alex and I are the scapegoats to get Harper off the hook with his investors."

"Sorry man," Mick said. "Under other circumstances I think we coulda been friends."

Under other circumstances Mick and Franky wouldn't even be there. If Harper hadn't lost faith in him at the meeting in Denver, hadn't figured out that Tag had feelings for Alex, he would have revealed that he was trying to set her up. He would have enlisted Tag's aid, and his hired muscle wouldn't have been necessary. Knowing the score would have put Tag in the driver's seat. Instead, he'd lost focus and given too much away. And probably gotten them both killed. Just like Zukey.

"It would've been nice to partner with somebody who uses his brain instead of his mouth," Mick said.

"Hey, what's this, bash Franky day?"

Mick shook his head and handed Tag back his Ruger. "You could shoot us," he said when Tag looked like he was considering just that, "but it would only make Harper's story more convincing."

"We found the treasure and took off with it—after killing the witnesses." Yep, they were well and truly screwed. "Mind telling me who the investor is?"

"What investor?"

"The one Harper's so afraid of that he had to concoct this fiasco."

Mick shrugged. "Don't know. But you're right, Harper is afraid of him."

"Is Dussaud working for him?"

"Yeah."

"You wasn't supposed to tell him that," Franky said.

"You shoot your mouth off to Harper and I'll cap your ass myself." Mick turned to Tag. "You oughta go after her. Maybe the two of you can disappear and stay alive."

Tag had no intention of disappearing, but he was determined to stay alive. Unless Alex killed him.

ALEX COULD HEAR TAG TALKING WHILE SHE SADDLED Jackass. The part of her brain still functioning past the fury was yelling at her to nurse her broken heart later and save her life now by listening to their conversation. But she couldn't even stand the sound of his voice. Realizing that she wanted him to come after her didn't help matters.

She dragged herself into the saddle, feeling like she weighed a ton, then clapped her heels to Jackass's sides and took off. She didn't look back.

Jackass was the one who balked, his gait lagging so often she swore at him. He stopped altogether then, stamping and blowing, swinging his head around and looking wounded.

"It better be Angel you don't want to leave," Alex told him. But she knew Jackass had accepted Tag. Just like she had in Denver. Right after he got back from his secret meeting with Bennet Harper.

God, she hated that thought, hated feeling like a fool, because truth was, she blamed herself as much as Tag. She'd thrown herself at him, and then she'd unloaded all over him. She couldn't fault him for taking what she'd willingly offered. The minute she mentioned Harper's name it was a wonder he hadn't disappeared for good . . .

Why hadn't he disappeared? For that matter, why would Bennet Harper toss Tag out of a plane if Tag was working for him? Not that it wasn't just like the bastard. Bennet loved games, loved to screw with other people's lives, and he hated it when someone went against him. Maybe that was what Tag had done. Maybe he'd gone against Bennet and gotten himself thrown out of that plane. Or maybe Bennet had done it so she'd take pity on Tag. It was hard to feel threatened by someone you pitied.

It made sense. Now that she looked back, none of the threats were actually . . . life threatening. Tag landing in her valley, her cabin being firebombed. Mick and Franky certainly weren't a threat. No, Bennet had been playing games with her all along, but that was going to stop because the first thing on her agenda was to find him and end this thing once and for all. And not with a gun. Much as she liked the finality of that solution, she'd be damned if she went to jail on account of his sorry ass.

She'd ruin him this time. And she knew just how to do it. If she lived long enough.

Hands grabbed her out of the darkness. The reins were torn out of her grip, and Jackass began to kick and fight, nearly ejecting her from the saddle. There was a lot of yelling and swearing, some hers, some in a male voice. Alex went for her rifle and ended up in a wicked fight for it. Somebody was pulling on it from the barrel end. Alex struggled to keep a grip on the stock with her sweat-slick hand, without pulling the trigger. Kicking Franky in the balls by mistake was one thing; accidentally blowing somebody's head off wasn't on her list of mistakes she wanted to make.

The gun popped free so fast she nearly set it off again, and suddenly Jackass was free, too. And he made the most of it. Someone yelped. Alex looked frantically around, spotting two men, black outlines in the weak starshine. One seemed to be cradling his arm. She did another quick check, bringing her eyes front in time to see the uninjured man moving toward Jackass again. She pointed the rifle at him and said, "If my horse doesn't take your arm off, I will."

He took her seriously. And then he became a minor problem.

"How many of my men do you think you can shoot before they triumph?"

She'd really thought she'd run into Rusty and his pals. Junior was so much worse. "Do you really want to find out?"

"You have but two bullets in your weapon."

"At this range it'll take them both out."

"Which will leave you defenseless."

Jackass snorted.

"My horse disagrees with you." And he'd reminded her she had a problem if she was hoping to escape any time soon.

She dismounted, careful to keep the gun leveled on Dussaud's men as she retrieved Jackass's reins and climbed back into the saddle. Not that she was concerned about controlling him, but if they had to make a run for it she didn't want to have to worry about him stepping on the reins and her winding up with a broken neck.

"What is it you expect will happen here, Alex?"

"I expect you to let me leave."

"You stole from me."

"Even if you had the authority to detain me, you have no proof. I don't have the map."

A flashlight popped on. Junior didn't try to blind her with it, but he played it over her saddle, completely devoid of any packs or saddlebags. And she clearly wasn't carrying the map on her since she wasn't even wearing a jacket.

More importantly, she gained some vital information from that flashlight, namely that three of Junior's goons were flanking him and the other two were standing about twenty feet from her. With everyone accounted for, she could relax, at least a little, and maybe think her way out of this standoff.

"Donovan has the map," she said. "We didn't find the

treasure—but you already know that since you've been following us all along."

Junior chuckled. "Bravo."

Yeah, it had only taken her a week to get up to speed. "You were planning to steal the treasure. If we found it."

"And why should I not? The map was mine. If you had not robbed me the treasure would have been mine. *Et voila*, justice is served."

"And you don't have to do any of the work."

"Even better."

"Well, be my guest. Donovan and his friends are that way." She pointed over her shoulder. "You don't need me."

"On the contrary. You are . . . leverage." He gave it the French pronunciation, but it was still an ugly word, a word that would drag her back into proximity with Tag Donovan. The lying weasel.

"Trust me, you don't want me around if you expect to get anything useful from Donovan. I'm as likely to shoot him as you are."

"Trouble in paradise?" Junior asked, clearly amused.

"Purgatory's more like it." Alex thought she caught movement out of the corner of her eye. Just a jackrabbit scared up by all the commotion, she figured. "You have an argument, it's with Tag Donovan and his boss, Bennet Harper. He's the brains behind this operation. I was just stupid enough to let Donovan sucker me into helping him, and for that I apologize."

"A very pretty speech, but I'm afraid I cannot allow you to remove yourself from the game so soon."

"And I'm afraid you don't have a choice," came a voice from out of the darkness. Tag's voice. "Ease back toward me, Alex," he said, "and let's get out of here."

"Get lost."

Junior laughed. "Miss Scott doesn't seem very eager to renew her . . . friendship with you, Mr. Donovan. Perhaps she would rather take her chances with me."

"Alex—"

"Go to hell."

"We're all going to be there if you don't . . . *duck*!"

He shouted the last word. Alex dropped low over Jack-ass's neck, strictly on reflex. Tag and Angel appeared out of the darkness, just as a bunch of horses came racing by her, the riders whooping like the Indians in a John Ford Western, guns blazing. Junior and his men dove out of the way, which was all they had time for.

Angel and Jackass touched noses, whuffling in each other's breath. It might have been a poignant scene if she hadn't been busy wrestling Tag for control of her mount.

"This is supposed to be a rescue, dammit."

She tore the reins out of his hands and held them out of his reach. "Feels more like out of the frying pan into the fire." But she had no choice other than to follow his lead. "It wasn't Mick and Franky who rode roughshod through Junior's camp. Care to tell me where you found the rein-forcements?"

"I heard your gunshot," Tag said. "I knew you hadn't run into anybody friendly, and since Rusty told us we were being shadowed I thought it might be Junior. And then I came across Rusty and his pals."

It wasn't a big surprise when she saw the silhouettes of four horses and riders, dark against the starry night sky. One of the riders walked his horse forward. Tag met him halfway and said, "You scattered their horses?"

"Yep, and they won't be able to look for 'em until day-break, so I'd say we bought you a good six hours."

"This bought me six hours," Tag said. It was pretty dark, but Alex thought she saw Tag flip him something. "That's all the cash I have," he said.

Rusty didn't say anything, but his body language spoke volumes. The way his friends spread out to back him up was pretty telling, too.

"Don't do it," Tag said. "I'm not prepared to give you anything else without a fight."

Alex nudged Jackass up beside Tag and pulled her rifle from the saddle scabbard, making sure Rusty and his pals heard the distinctive sound of steel sliding out of leather.

There was another quarter minute of tense silence, then Rusty wheeled his horse and took off, his friends getting lost in the darkness behind him.

"I appreciate the help," Tag said.

"I didn't want to get caught by a stray bullet." Alex holstered her Winchester, turned Jackass, and headed off at a right angle to Rusty.

"Everything was under control. Rusty just needed to know he wasn't going to get anything but the money I promised him."

"And yet again someone saves your ass and you get off scot-free."

"You're forgetting that I saved yours," Tag said, guiding Angel in beside Jackass.

"Rusty saved mine."

"Rusty didn't put himself between you and the guns."

"Rusty didn't drag me into this in the first place."

"Shit. Are we back to that again?"

"I know how you dislike the truth," Alex said, "so let's go our separate ways and you can twist the truth around to suit yourself without anyone calling you on it." She clapped her heels to Jackass's sides, nudging him into a ground-eating trot.

"Can I borrow the satellite phone before you take off?" Tag called after her.

"The battery is dead."

"Shit." There was a half minute of silence, then, "Don't you want to know what's going on?"

Absolutely. She couldn't think of anything she wanted more than an answer to that question. Except to be away from Tag Donovan.

Unfortunately, Jackass didn't feel the same way about Angel. He kept looking back, and Angel apparently didn't need any urging to catch up. The problem was she brought Tag along with her.

"Aren't you wondering why Mick and Franky just let us go after they went to so much trouble to drag us out here?" he asked.

"If I wanted to know, I could ask them," she said. "Their word is as trustworthy as yours."

"I had good reasons for lying to you."

"I'll bet."

"But you don't want to hear them," he continued. "You don't want to know the truth because then you might have to face some things you'd rather not face."

"Yep, that's it," Alex said, "so go away and take your fairy tales—I mean your truths—with you, and leave me to my blissful ignorance."

"I could do that," Tag said, "but believe it or not I do have a conscience, and as you've pointed out I dragged you into this. I feel kind of responsible for you."

"I'm touched."

"You're a smart-ass. But that's still better than being dead—which is a distinct possibility without me. I can keep you safe, Alex."

"If that was your goal, you should have left me out of this to begin with."

"That was an option, but if I'd walked away from you, Bennet Harper would only have sent someone else."

"Are you trying to scare me?"

"Would it do me any good?"

chapter
22

IF HE'D BEEN TRYING TO SCARE ALEX, TAG HAD
failed miserably. Jackass ambled along at a steady pace
throughout the remainder of the night. Alex dismounted
periodically to give him a break, but walking or riding, the
two of them moved along as tirelessly as the Energizer
Bunny, without the annoying enthusiasm.

Angel kept pace a bit behind and to the right of Jackass.
Tag walked when Alex walked and rode when she rode, his
thighs chafing and his gut stewing. Of the two he was more
concerned about his gut for once. He knew it was only a
matter of time before curiosity got the better of her, but
while she was wallowing the clock was running out on them.

Sure, the truth must have been devastating for her. He'd
expected that, and she was entitled to some time to come to
terms with it. Right after they figured out how much danger
they were in and took steps to get out of it.

"Harper isn't wasting any time putting the rest of his
scheme into action," Tag finally said, about the time another day was dragging its feet into the world.

Alex stopped at the top of the hill and sat there watching

dawn break, which, Tag thought, ranked right up there with watching grass grow for sheer excitement value. The sun crept over the eastern horizon, shining on the crest of the mountains and crawling with agonizing slowness down the rocky slopes. Tag waited about six inches worth.

"I'm an FBI agent," he said. No preliminaries, no easing into it. No giving her a chance to tell him to shut up. "My partner, Tom Zukey, was killed six months ago."

He thought he saw a flicker of sympathy. Or maybe he'd imagined it. Either way Alex was determined not to dignify his commentary. But she wasn't the only one who knew how to push buttons, and it wouldn't be long before the sarcasm built up in her like gas behind a champagne cork.

"All I wanted was to find the guy responsible and make him pay," Tag continued, "and I'm not talking about a jail sentence. Mike Kovaleski, my handler, sent me on this assignment to keep me from doing something stupid."

Tag took the derogatory sound she made as a sign that at least she was listening—and she thought that everything he'd done had been stupid. He had no choice but to agree with her, but since her criticism had been nonverbal, so was his acknowledgment.

"The bureau received a couple of complaints out of Boston, from a couple of big names. Or maybe I should say they were big political contributors. I'm sure you know what I'm talking about; nobody can bitch quite like the entitled wealthy when something doesn't go their way. A friend—it's always a friend—invested some money with a guy named Bennet Harper who was promising big returns. What they got back was nothing, and I was tasked to find out why.

"It was a fluff job, a nothing assignment meant to keep the money men happy. And then I got dropped out of an airplane in your valley, and things began to get complicated."

"Why didn't you just tell me the truth?" Alex said, her voice busting out of her, loaded with resentment and temper that had gotten the better of her.

"I should have," Tag said, "but it's protocol. When I'm

on a case I can't blow my cover for any . . . No, that's a cop out. Zukey didn't follow the rules and now he's dead."

"And you're blaming yourself."

"It was my fault. I should have known what he was up to, but my gut—my famous intuition—failed me." Tag ran a hand through his hair, swallowed the bitter taste in the back of his throat. "He was the senior partner, more experience, more time on the job, so I did what he told me to do. By the time I found out he was taking a meeting with Tony Sappresi—he's the mob guy we were investigating— it was too late. Sappresi had him killed. I didn't get there in time to stop it."

Alex looked over at him, her eyes level on his. "You got there in time to take a bullet of your own," she said. "The scar on your side."

Tag shrugged that off, along with the collapsed lung, the endless days lying in a hospital bed, and the weeks of physical therapy, haunted by the need for vengeance.

"And now you don't trust your instincts," she said when he remained silent. She was still furious, but she understood what he was going through. Because he had Zukey on his conscience. She'd lived with the fallout of being responsible for hurting someone she loved.

"Mike sent me on this assignment because he knew I was going after Sappresi," Tag said, "and he wanted me to hold off. When Harper dropped me on you, I knew I should trust you, but I played it by the rules, figuring it would get me out of here sooner."

"So you could go after your revenge."

"Yes."

"And you'll use anyone to get it."

"You're damn right I will," he flared up. "And I'm not apologizing for it. I should be tracking down the scum who killed Zukey, but I'm stuck on this dumbshit case instead."

"And I'm not?" she shot back. "You dragged me into this, and now I'm just as stuck as you are."

"Fine. Do whatever the hell you want, Alex, go back to your cabin—"

"You burned it down."

"That's not really the point, is it? I'm sure you can find another place to hide away from the world, so you don't have to take a personal risk ever again."

She stared at him for a minute, her hands fisted on the Winchester. Then she spun around and reached for Jackass's reins.

Tag caught her wrist.

She brought the rifle up with her other hand. "I'm done being manhandled and pushed around."

"How about taking your life back? How about not moping about Bennet Harper for another decade while your life passes you by?"

"I'm not moping about Harper."

"You're not over him, either."

She pulled her wrist out of his grip, but she didn't try to take off again. "It's not him."

"No, it's the damage he did," Tag said. "You don't trust yourself any more than I trust myself. The difference is I'm doing something about it."

And she'd gone into hiding. The realization of what she'd lost made Alex sick to her stomach. She had run away. True, she'd needed the distance, but somewhere along the line she'd deluded herself that she'd put the whole mess behind her—willful ignorance, and that was the worst kind of lie. She'd gotten over the man, but not what he'd done to her life. He'd stolen her trust, and she'd let him get away with it.

"You're right, Tag, I'm a fool," she said carefully, because the cold, hard anger that had kept her upright and moving through the night had been replaced with a big, hot ball comprised of self-pity, hurt, and a stew of other emotions that had all boiled themselves down to tears. And she'd be damned if she let him see her cry. "Thanks for waking me up, although I have to say destroying everything I've worked for over the last four years was a bit extreme."

"I'm not the enemy, Alex. I can help you—"

"You're asking me to trust you?" She jammed the Winchester back in its holster, knowing it would be a mistake to face him again with a gun in her hands. "Like you trusted me right from the beginning."

"I didn't know what was going on, and by the time I was sure you weren't involved—"

"You mean when Bennet Harper had my house burned to the ground?"

"Okay, I knew pretty early, but I'm a federal agent. There are rules, and one of them is need to know."

"And you didn't think I needed to know any of this?"

"You already knew you were in danger."

She hissed out a breath, anger mixing back into the stew. "And it never occurred to you that I might be able to help you figure out what was going on?"

"You were doing that anyway."

"Because you lied and manipulated me into it."

Tag met her gaze, but she wasn't ready to take the bleakness in his eyes as regret.

"When we were in Denver and you told me about Harper," he said carefully, "that was when I began to realize there was a lot more going on than I understood."

"So why didn't you tell me then?"

"I was afraid you'd do something we'd both be sorry for."

"Like sleep with you? Because I'm sorry for that." She knew it was a low blow, but she wanted him to be angry, wanted him to yell and say terrible things back to her. She wanted a reason to walk away and write him out of her life. Because she was beginning to believe him.

"I didn't want you to take off before I had a chance to tell you the truth," Tag said. "The other . . . just happened."

Because yet again she'd been a fool. "Don't count on it happening again." She reached for the pommel and lifted her foot, but Jackass sidled away so she couldn't mount. Another attempt left her hopping on one foot, feeling like an idiot.

"It's pretty bad when a jackass has more sense than its rider."

"Ha, ha, very clever."

"Look, Alex." He laid a hand on her arm but not to re-
strain. "It wasn't easy for you to leave everything you knew
and come out here. You fought, a hell of a lot harder than I
can imagine, to make a life for yourself. But you haven't
dealt with Harper, and until you do you aren't really free."

"You have no room to talk."

"I'll deal with Sappresi when the time comes. And it
will, Mike was right about that. Now's the time for you to
deal with that son of a bitch Harper once and for all."

"I don't need you to tell me that."

"Good. Then let's—"

"And I don't need your help." She shrugged his hand off
and looked over her shoulder at him. "I'll deal with Bennet
Harper. I know what makes him tick."

"Then you know exactly how to hurt him."

"Without leaving a mark, or going to jail."

Tag had once called her a cold, mean woman, but he'd
been wrong. There was a fire burning inside her. Maybe it
had been banked for a while, but he could see it now, and
he didn't want to be in the way when she unleashed it. Not
that he had much of a choice. "That's admirable, Alex, and
I'd be happy to step aside, except for one thing. Harper
isn't the only one you have to worry about. He had investors."

"Oh, no, you're not dragging me back into that stupidity. You deal with his investors, I'll deal with him."

"Yeah, I wish that was possible, but Franky wasn't done
spilling his guts when you left."

"And of course you knew the right questions to ask."
But she stopped trying to climb on Jackass.

"Harper's been running a new con since you left Boston,"
Tag said unapologetically. "He gets his hands on a completely authentic artifact that's supposed to lead to a treasure
of some sort."

"Like Juan Amparo's map."

Tag nodded. "He assembles a list of investors, lets them
test the map, and when they discover it's real, they can't

wait to plunk down money for a chance at a hoard of buried gold. This isn't his first con since you left Boston. There were some complaints on the last one from a couple of guys with Washington connections. The complaints got to the bureau, and here I am, pretending to work for Harper."

"You knew there was no treasure."

"I had no idea the treasure didn't exist until today."

"But it was all part of an assignment—"

"Not everything."

Alex knew what he was getting at, but she wasn't going there.

"I had to play the game—I know you don't like that word, but that's the way it is. The bad guy sets the parameters and decides the rules."

"And the rest of us are rats running a maze."

"If you want to see it that way. Harper dropped me on you. I didn't know who you were, or whose side you were on, so I had to take careful steps. Yeah, I realized pretty quickly that you were in the dark. I also knew you didn't trust many people, but when you did you trusted completely. I couldn't risk who you might tell, and who they might tell."

Especially in a town like Casteel where word of mouth was as good as the evening news. She had to grant Tag that one—at least privately. "Keep talking," she said.

"I knew Junior had the Lost Spaniard map because Harper gave it to him," Tag said. "You know the rest, except for my meeting with Harper in Denver."

Alex thought her heart couldn't sink any lower, but it dropped all the way to her toes with that revelation.

"I didn't tell him we were going to be there. Mick and Franky let him know the map had been stolen. Harper assumed I'd done it and figured Denver would be our next logical step, so he flew into town and had us followed, waiting for an opportunity to hijack me."

And that pissed her off more than anything else, the fact that Bennet Harper had known what her reaction was going to be, right down the line, and then he'd used it against her.

"I, ah, went out to find a drugstore that morning," Tag was saying. "Mick picked me up and took me to meet with Harper. I'm pretty sure he was intending to tell me what he wanted me to do next, but I blew it. He realized you and I—"

Alex popped up an eyebrow and crossed her arms.

Tag chose to rephrase. "He must have figured out that I wouldn't betray you, so he sent Mick and Franky to take my place."

"That's why they didn't care if we actually found it or not."

"All they had to do was put on a good show," Tag said by way of agreement. "By now they're halfway to Denver, and they're telling everyone they run across that we found the Lost Spaniard and took off with it."

"To get Harper off the hook."

"Exactly."

She spent a moment digesting that, but it was pretty straightforward and disgustingly clear, except for one thing. "So who's the investor and why is Bennet afraid of him?"

Tag smiled. "You're thinking, not reacting emotionally. That's good."

"That's logic," she corrected him, refusing to let his praise mean anything. "And you haven't answered my question."

"I don't know who the investor is. Mike has a couple of agents working on it from his end. It won't be easy, since Harper is probably the only one who knows the entire list."

"Well, have fun with that," Alex said. "I'd tell you to give me a call sometime and let me know how it turns out, but I don't know where I'll be."

"You'll be dead," Tag said. "Whoever this guy is, he's a shark, and Harper is tossing you to him like raw meat."

"It's my life and my choice. What do you care?"

"I care, Alex." He looked away. "It's my job to care."

For a second there she'd thought . . . But that would be stupid. He'd been using her all along. Maybe his motives were altruistic but that didn't change how it felt. "Don't want another Zukey on your hands?"

His gaze flashed to hers and she knew she'd scored, again, but it didn't feel any better than it had the last time. "So if I'm gullible enough to believe everything you've told me—"

"Call Mike. He'll confirm everything."

"Right. Some slimy friend of yours who's willing to say whatever you tell him."

Tag walked over to Angel and retrieved Alex's satchel and packs, and handed them to her. "Go ahead, take off and waste another decade telling yourself whatever you need to believe about me."

Alex clutched her satchel, amazed, and confused. All she wanted was to get away from Tag, and now that he was letting her go, she didn't want to. And it got worse. She actually believed him. Except the part where he talked about his feelings.

"You just don't want to admit I might be everything I say I am," he said.

She wasn't afraid to admit it, she was afraid to believe it. And she was tired of being afraid, of making choices in her life because of fear. The time had come to do something about it, and if Tag was the conduit, then she'd just have to accept it.

She crossed her arms, huffed out a breath. "What do you suggest we do about it? Because I'm not spending the rest of my life wondering if I'm going to wake up dead."

Jackass bumped her with his nose, pushing her in Tag's direction.

"Looks like Jackass has an idea," Tag said.

"Then I guess it's a good thing he doesn't get a vote."

He nudged her again.

Tag's grin turned wolfish. "Us guys gotta stick together."

"Disgustingly macho," she said. "And you haven't answered my question."

"We need to get to a phone."

"The closest phone will be in Casteel. We can leave the horses there, too." She took a deep breath, met his eyes. "And then I'm going to Boston."

Jackass snorted and stamped a hoof. Jackass didn't like that idea. Neither did Tag. Harper was in Boston, but so was Sappresi. He hadn't told Alex about Sappresi on purpose. He couldn't risk her running into him by accident.

"*We're* going to Boston," he said.

She shrugged. "It's a free country, do whatever you want."

"As long as I don't get in your way? Dammit, Alex, the last thing I need is you going off on your own. I can keep you safe, but we have to do this my way."

"Nope. I said I was going to deal with Harper. That's exactly what I intend to do." She swung up into the saddle and nudged Jackass into a walk.

"That's really annoying," he called after her, "you leaving in the middle of the conversation."

"The conversation was over."

Like hell it was. Tag jammed himself into the saddle, wincing when he had to urge Angel into a trot. "You might know what you're doing out here, but you can't carry your Winchester in the city."

"What I have in mind for Bennet Harper calls for an entirely different kind of weapon."

chapter
23

"I DON'T KNOW ABOUT YOU," ALEX SAID, "BUT I need some rest."

"You're the one who got back on the horse."

"I thought it would be best to find somewhere protected before we camp."

Tag wanted to continue their argument, she could see it in his eyes, the cranky set to his mouth. She turned her back on him and nudged Jackass into a walk. Let him stew for a while, she thought, and sure, she was getting some petty satisfaction out of it. But she wasn't changing her mind, either. Bennet Harper had messed with her life for the last time.

She led them back toward Casteel, traveling until they'd worked their way into the heavier tree cover. They made camp not far from where the wreckage of her cabin stood. She didn't have the heart to see it yet, but it got her started thinking about the entire fiasco, examining every conversation she'd had with Tag, trying hard not to filter it through anger and hurt. She'd let those emotions dictate her actions for too long.

He'd lied to her, there was no getting around that. But now she knew why, and she was having a hard time holding it against him. Sure, he'd kept things from her in the interest of closing the case, but would she have done anything differently in his shoes? He hadn't known her any better than she'd known him in the beginning, and the circumstances of the game had been designed by Bennet Harper to make them distrust one another.

Then there was the game itself. Tag's explanation was logical and followed the series of events too intricately to be anything but the truth. Not to mention she knew the scumbag behind it all too well to doubt he was capable of setting them both up.

It would have been nice to know, going in, what she was up against, and there was a point at which Tag could have come clean. But there again he was reacting to a history she understood all too well, one that had crippled his judgment and his ability to trust his own instincts. And he at least had the excuse of timing. His loss was recent, not to mention his partner had died; she'd only been betrayed and used.

They made a cold camp, not wanting to risk a fire. Tag had gotten their personal belongings from Mick and Franky, but he hadn't wasted his time with amenities, and that included food and water. And blankets.

The sun was high in the sky when they went to sleep. Sometime during the day, however, they ended up in the shade. Alex woke up first, wrapped in Tag's arms, hip to hip with him. And face to face.

She'd seen him like this once before, when she'd studied his face while he was unconscious after falling out of the airplane. He'd been pale and drawn then, but she could see the toll the last week had taken on him. He looked exhausted, and even in sleep she could tell he was restless. Worried. His mind seemed to be moving a mile a minute, wrestling with their predicament and looking for a solution.

She lifted a hand, tracing the lines around his mouth. She'd barely touched him, but his hand came up and latched on to her wrist, his eyes flying open. She could see the shadows in the usually laughing blue depths before the cobwebs cleared and he came fully awake.

"It's all true, isn't it?" she said.

"Yeah." He released her hand and rolled onto his back, looking up at the sky.

"And you've told me everything?"

"I'm in love with you," he said, exhaling heavily. "I haven't told you that."

Alex rolled onto her back next to him, closing her eyes while she fought to tame her pounding heart and overcome the foolish need to cry. "You have a hell of a way of showing it," she said when she thought she could trust her voice.

"You play by the rules, you miss all the fun."

"This isn't exactly what I'd call fun."

"Sure it is," Tag said like the adrenaline junkie he was. "Maybe there've been some lows, but doesn't that make the highs so much better?"

"I'm still waiting for the highs."

He rolled onto his side. "Let me see if I can help you with that."

She laughed softly—not the reaction he was going for, judging by his expression. "You said that with an absolutely straight face," she explained.

"Yeah, and?"

"You don't think it's a little arrogant to describe yourself as a high?"

"How about I give you a demonstration and let you be the judge?" And he kissed her, not the kind of kiss that assaulted her senses and caused hormonal oblivion. This kiss was slow and thorough, so tender it all but broke her heart. So did the uncertainty in his eyes when he pulled away.

He was giving her a chance to tell him no.

She took his face in her hands and kissed him back. But when she would have deepened it, he kept it soft and light, a seduction of her mouth, her senses, her defenses. He pulled her to her feet, kissing the palms of her hands, her forehead, all with the kind of gentle deliberation that made it impossible to refuse him. Or protect herself.

He peeled off his shirt, keeping his eyes on hers as he laid it on the ground so that when he slipped her shirt and jeans off she had more than the cold ground at her back. She had his body heat.

He surrounded her, his hands sliding up to cup her breasts as he laid his mouth on hers again. She breathed him in, felt the heat of his skin against hers, swore she could hear his heart pounding as frantically as hers.

She didn't feel the cool air, or hear the wind sighing through the trees. The world fell away and there was only the touch of his hands, his mouth, the pleasure that spread through her, robbing her of breath and thought and pushing her toward a place she wanted desperately to go. But not on a wave of tenderness.

Sex with Tag Donovan was one thing. Physical pleasure, she could handle. It was the emotional assault that scared the hell out of her. With each gentle kiss, each touch of his fingertips, Tag was working his way over and around and through the walls she'd built to protect herself. With each passing moment it became harder to shut him out. And then he made it impossible.

"Look at me, Alex," he said, waiting until she opened her eyes before he joined his body to hers in one long, slow slide. "Let go. Don't fight what you're feeling."

She didn't want to open up to him, but he didn't give her a choice. Need swamped her, pleasure stripped her raw, and the depth of feeling in Tag's eyes stole what little resistance she had left. She gave him everything she had to give, physically, emotionally, let him take her over the edge of reason, felt him fall with her. And when he gathered her into his arms and simply held her, she turned an emotional corner there was no walking away from.

So she tried to hide from it. "I think you could call that a high," she said, going for a light, teasing tone. The tears probably kept her from hitting the mark, not to mention the sobs that seemed to come all the way from her toes.

Tag just wrapped his arms around her tighter. Her capability was sometimes annoying, her sarcasm frustrating, but her tears were devastating. There was nothing quite as disarming as a strong woman's tears, and nothing was more difficult for a woman as strong as Alex than to bare her sorrow in front of anyone, let alone a man.

She turned onto her side, but he refused to let her run away. He went with her, holding her while she cried herself back to sleep. He should have done the same—not the crying part, although he felt pretty raw after all the upheaval of the last twenty-four hours. What he needed was more sleep. Unfortunately he couldn't seem to turn off his brain.

As horrible as the last week had been, Alex didn't really understand that it might be infinitely worse when they got back east. Tag didn't know for sure who they might be up against. If it was Sappresi, he was more than ready to face him. The problem was, Alex refused to let him handle it, and taking her into danger scared him spitless. The possibility that he'd make another mistake, that she'd get hurt, or worse, was unbearable.

For the first time in his career he wanted to walk away from a case. He might have if he hadn't known the case would follow him—follow them—for the rest of their lives. And that the rest of their lives might not be a very long time unless he did his job, and did it right.

THEY RODE INTO CASTEEL THE NEXT MORNING, WELL rested if not exactly easy in each other's company. Tag had opened himself up, but Alex hadn't done the same. At least not verbally. She was holding back, and the silence between them was deafening.

Alex stepped through the front door of the sheriff's office and went right into Matt's arms. Tag felt the hot breath of the green-eyed monster, another first for him. She needed comfort and she hadn't turned to him. That stung more than he would have expected and had him reevaluating some decisions he'd made.

Matt sent him a what-have-you-done-to-her-now glare over the top of Alex's head, which had Tag rolling his eyes and getting back to what was important, namely, keeping them both alive.

"We need food and water," he said.

Alex stepped back, shoved both her hands through her short hair so it stood on end. "We'll have to leave Jackass and Angel at the stable, but we don't have any money."

"I'll take care of that," Matt said. "You two can't be seen in town."

"What's going on?" they said, almost in unison.

"A couple guys hit town last night, said you found the Lost Spaniard."

"Shit," Tag said.

"Mick and Franky," Alex supplied, with the same kind of disgust in her voice. "We didn't find the treasure," she told Matt. "It's a long story, but the bottom line is we're being set up. Tag is an FBI agent—"

"Figures," Matt said, his turn to be disgusted. "He dragged you into one of his operations, and now you're in danger."

"I really appreciate the support, Matt, but if we don't have time to explain, we really don't have time for you to be pissed off before you help us," Alex said.

Matt ran a hand back through his sandy hair and down to knead at the back of his neck. "I'll take the horses around back and get you something from the diner, and then . . .?"

"We need to get to an airport," Tag supplied.

"Then I guess I'll have to drive you to Denver." Matt pulled open the door, then shut it again. The look on his face was enough but he gave them the bad news anyway. "Jackass has been recognized."

"There'll be a mob out front inside of ten minutes," Tag said, needlessly, as they were all thinking the same thing. "It's a good thing there aren't lynchings anymore."

"Don't count on it," Matt said. "Tension in this town is thick enough to shovel up with the horse manure. There're fist fights practically on the hour, and the other day Mort Hackett pulled a gun down at the market because they tried to charge him fifteen dollars for a package of Oreos."

Alex gave a little half smile. "If somebody messed with my chocolate, I might try to shoot him, too."

"This is all fascinating," Tag cut in, and the fact that Alex had actually smiled felt like something to get excited about, "but we need to hit the road."

Alex squared her shoulders, and when she looked at him, Tag knew there was going to be trouble. "I can't remember the last time I showered, I've been wearing these clothes for a week, and I probably smell worse than Jackass. I'm sick of this whole stupid fiasco, and I'll be damned if I let the hicks in this town scare me off without food and water."

Tag and Matt shared a look, both of them thinking some variation of *don't mess with Miss USA*.

"What do you suggest we do about it?" Tag asked her.

"I suggest we pay a visit to the diner."

Tag and Matt both started to object, but she was already out the door, marching down the steps. She was surrounded before she could get to the hitching rail. Jackass took care of that; a fondness for alcohol wasn't his only well-known personality quirk. He'd made his dislike of being separated from Alex painfully clear, and apparently he'd decided to extend his protection to Angel.

A hand—likely belonging to an out-of-towner—reached for the mare's bridle. Jackass bared his teeth and went for the hand, which disappeared back into the press of bodies. The look Alex sent around the crowd was even scarier. When it came to nonverbal threats, Junior had nothing on Alex. Hell, Medusa couldn't really compare. Nobody was turned to stone, but they were careful not to make eye contact with her, either.

Alex set off, leading Jackass. People scurried out of her path, but they didn't go away. And they didn't curb their curiosity for long.

"Word is you found the Spaniard," someone called out before they'd made it to the end of the block. The questions came hard and fast after that, people shouting each other down and breaking into side arguments over who got to be heard.

Alex wasn't dignifying any of the commentary. She was focused on her empty stomach. But she was getting more pissed off with every remark shouted at her. By the time they got to the diner, Tag decided it would be a good idea to remove her Winchester from temptation range. Jackass didn't bite his hand off, which was a good thing since the look Alex sent him suggested he go off and do something that would be anatomically impossible without two operational hands.

He probably should have gone into the diner with her, but he figured crowd control would be a better idea. And there was the way Alex stared in the wide front window before she went in, crazy still shadowing the exhaustion in her eyes. Annabelle had treated Alex like crap, and if Tag knew his girl, she was about to get a little of her own back. At least he hoped she stopped at a little.

The few occupants of the diner all turned to stare when she burst in. She started off by pulling four bottles of water from the cooler by the register and stuffing them into the saddlebag she'd slung over her shoulder. Then she slammed a hand on the counter and made a couple of gestures. Annabelle folded her arms and gave back as good as she got. Alex headed around the counter, probably intending to exchange more than words with Annabelle when Matt arrived.

"You let her go in there alone?" he asked Tag.

"Did you see the look in her eyes?"

"Yeah." Matt sighed, and pulled out his wallet. "Any idea how much grief this is going to cost me?"

Tag took it for a rhetorical question. Compared to what he and Alex were going to face, Matt catching hell for buying his ex-girlfriend a meal was nothing.

A picture was worth a thousand words, Tag thought, and in Annabelle's case they all spelled pissed off, but after a few words from Matt she dumped the plated food waiting to be served into foam takeout boxes. Tag's mouth began to water, his empty stomach knotting, but he laughed out loud when Alex demanded another container and cleaned out the donut case. He saw, with some regret, that she'd left anything with chocolate behind, but he had to admire her style.

She came out with two plastic bags, gave one to Tag, and took her Winchester back, keeping her eyes on his while she slid it into the saddle holster.

"Let's go," Tag said, gathering up Angel's reins.

"At least show us the treasure," someone called out.

Alex turned to look at the small crowd. "If we found the treasure, don't you think we would have paid for breakfast?"

"Not if you hid it again."

She rolled her eyes, looked at Tag.

He lifted a shoulder and said, "You're right, we hid it again, next to a big rock that looks like a finger pointing straight at the sky."

"A raised middle finger," Alex added, then to Tag, "you need to be a little more specific around here."

Most of them got the point, but to his amusement there were a few whispered consultations resulting in belated comprehension. The knot of men standing halfway down the block didn't seem amused.

"I don't think they got the joke," Alex said, following his line of sight.

"Yeah, and they're coming this way."

She watched them spread themselves across the road and start toward the diner, then she met Tag's eyes.

"What do you think?" he asked her.

"I think I've had it with this town."

Before Tag could stop her she strode out into the middle of the street. Her hands were empty, but she wasn't completely without weapons. "We're in Casteel, not Dodge City," she said, unleashing her face, in all its crazed, pissed-off glory, on them. "This isn't *High Noon*."

The men looked at one another, kind of drawing together, unsure suddenly.

"Jeez, Alex," somebody behind her said, "you got PMS or something?"

She whipped around, and everyone recoiled. Even Tag had the urge to cross himself.

"It's this damn town," she said. "You're all nuts."

The place fell so silent they could hear the wind sighing through the trees, then someone said, "Well hell, Alex, you're one of us. If we're nuts, so are you."

She snorted, turning back to the men ranged across the street. She took Jackass's reins and walked straight at them. "I've been shot at, burned out of my house, kidnapped, and I haven't eaten in two days. Crazy doesn't begin to cover it."

The line of men parted like the Red Sea, all of them lifting their hands in the air and eyeing the Winchester within the crazy lady's reach.

Alex swung up on Jackass, Tag following suit on Angel, and the two of them rode out of town, unhindered.

"We're heading west," Tag observed. "Too bad the sun isn't setting."

She looked over at him, the corners of her mouth lifting. "By the time you get out of that saddle again, it will be."

"Is it too late to go back and let them shoot me?"

chapter
24

DEE WAS READY FOR THEM WHEN THEY GOT TO the Bar D, thanks to Matt. She'd sent all her men out on the range in case any of them had already heard the rumor about the Lost Spaniard being found, and she'd managed to round up some clean clothes.

A shower and a stationary meal did wonders for Alex, but she didn't want to stay there any longer than Tag did. Matt wasn't the only one who knew Dee was her best friend; if he could figure out she'd gone there, so could others, and Dee's men had to return some time.

Tag made a single phone call that produced a federal arrest warrant on Mick and Franky for kidnapping, a couple of first class tickets for him and Alex, and his ID waiting for him at the Denver airport.

Alex made a single phone call, too. When they walked out of the airport in Boston a car and driver were waiting for them.

"You okay?" Tag asked when her steps faltered.

"Not really."

For the first time since Tag had met her, Alex looked

like she might actually back away from something. "What's going on?"

She took a deep breath, met his eyes. "Just shouldering my emotional baggage," she said, walking over to the limo and leaning inside without actually getting in. Clearly she didn't want him to see who was in the car just yet.

So Tag looked over her shoulder.

A man and a woman occupied the limo, both in their late fifties to early sixties, both impeccably dressed and reeking of money. The man wore a thousand-dollar suit and an air of quiet authority. The woman looked like an older version of Alex—if Alex was still Miss USA. Pink suit, matching shoes, pearls at her ears and throat, not a hair out of place. Her expression was set to "benevolence-for-the-little-people." Alex's could best be described as deer-in-the-headlights.

"Hello, Alexandra," she said, her gaze shifting to Tag. "Aren't you going to introduce me to your friend?"

Alex straightened, and Tag yanked her out of the limo before she could bang her head on the door frame.

She leaned into him, just long enough so he knew he hadn't imagined it, then took him by the hand and pulled him a few feet away. Distance apparently made breathing easier, but she wasn't talking.

"I take it that's your mother," Tag said. "Who's the man with her?"

"My stepfather, Preston Hobbs. They were married not long before Harper . . . happened. I went on the Miss USA tour, which I cut short, thanks to my fiancé's attempt to rob everyone I knew. After that I went back and finished my PhD, pretty much year-round, then I went to Colorado. I've never really lived with Preston, and the most recent interaction we had was the apology I made when Bennet Harper conned him."

And yet she had a hell of a lot easier time talking about him than her own mother. "When's the last time you were back in Boston?"

"Almost two years."

"You wouldn't be trying to put off the reunion, would you?"

"I spent the entire flight dreading it. Putting it off seemed like the next logical step."

"Alexandra," Cassandra trilled.

"Or a last-ditch effort." But she pasted a smile on her face and turned back toward the limo. She didn't let go of his hand until he was imprisoned inside with her. "Tag Donovan, my mother, Cassandra Hobbs, and my stepfather, Preston Hobbs."

Tag shook Preston's hand, squeezed Cassandra's fingers, and kept his thoughts and opinions to himself. He didn't know what was going on, but it was Alex's show.

"He's very handsome," Cassandra said, dimpling at Tag but talking to Alex. "Should I be assuming anything from the fact that you brought him home to meet us?"

"I didn't bring him home to meet you, not specifically. More like he tagged along."

"Cute," he murmured. "What Alex isn't telling you is that I've gotten her in some trouble—"

Cassandra shrieked, pressed a hand to her bosom. "I'm too young to be a . . . a . . . grandmother," she said with high drama—but she perked up almost immediately. "Who are your people, Mr. Donovan? When is the wedding?"

"There's no wedding, Mom."

Cassandra reached out blindly. Preston took his wife's hand, winking at Alex.

She worked up a faint smile for him, then shifted her gaze, met Tag's. He was beginning to suspect that her decision to move a thousand miles away from Boston wasn't all about Bennet Harper.

Alex clearly resembled her mother—same finely drawn features, same gray eyes—but where Alex's were sharp and almost frighteningly intelligent, Cassandra's eyes were softer. And appearances seemed to be high on her list of priorities.

"Maybe if you were properly clothed, Tag would marry you and give my grandchild a father." Cassandra held out a

Chanel bag, saying when Alex hesitated, "You'll be staying at the Colonnade, of course. You simply can't check in
without luggage."

Alex took the bag, setting it on the seat beside her. "Thank
you, but it really wasn't necessary."

"Of course it was necessary. I knew you would be wearing your outback raggedy things, and you can't check into
the Colonnade dressed like that. You might run into someone I know."

"I was in Colorado, not Australia. And everyone wears
jeans."

Cassandra waved that off. "It doesn't matter if it's the
moon, there's no excuse for being poorly dressed."

"I'm not pregnant, nobody's getting married, and it
doesn't matter what I'm wearing. And you're looking at
me like I'm speaking Mandarin," Alex finished, her impatience leaking out on a sigh. "I need you to focus here,
Mom."

Preston put his arm around his wife's shoulders. "I believe Alex and her friend may be in need of assistance,
Cassie. Perhaps we should worry about their wardrobe
later."

Alex shot him a grateful smile, but now that she had the
floor, she didn't know exactly how to begin.

Tag came to her rescue. "The trouble started when I fell
out of an airplane near Alex's cabin in Colorado," he said.

Preston sat forward, and Cassandra was already ramp-
ing up for another performance when Alex stepped in.

"It all started with Bennet Harper," she corrected. "He
decided to pay me back for what happened six years ago—"

"But that wasn't your fault," Preston said.

"When Bennet is involved it's always someone else's
fault. He decided it was time to get back at me."

Between the two of them, Tag and Alex sketched in the
story, omitting a few pertinent details—like the possibility
of death, and the possibility of pregnancy—and ending with
being set up by Bennet Harper.

Preston's eyes were hard by the time they finished. So

were Cassandra's. Tag took one look at her and revised his earlier opinion; the resemblance between mother and daughter wasn't only skin deep. Now he could see where Alex got her strength and determination. And he began to suspect what her secret weapon might be. Or rather who.

"We don't know who the investor is," Tag said. "That's why we're headed to the Colonnade, to meet up with the agents who were putting Harper's investment list together."

Cassandra sniffed. "You can be sure it's no one we associate with."

"No," Alex agreed, "but you'll know a lot of the other names on the list, and you know the people Bennet will be recruiting for his next scheme."

"And you want us to put out the word," Preston said.

"I want you to destroy him." Alex scooted forward, took her mother's hands. "I know you thought it was just poor business sense on Bennet's part before, and I know how you hate other people gossiping about us. But he has to be stopped, Mom, and I can't think of anyone better equipped than you to hit him where it hurts."

Tag fought back a smile, but he allowed himself to appreciate the sheer genius of Alex's revenge. Cassandra might give the impression of being flighty, but her position in Boston society meant she was on a first-name basis with everyone who was anyone—or at least their wives. And the wives would tell their husbands. It was only a matter of time before every powerful man in Boston would be scrutinizing Bennet Harper's business dealings. And this time they were putting the word out to everyone.

"He'll hate being ruined by a woman," Tag said.

Alex smiled. "The thought had crossed my mind."

THE COLONNADE WAS ONE OF BOSTON'S FINEST, AND most expensive, hotels. Alex had insisted they stay there, and Tag figured they owed her that much after what she'd been put through. Knowing Mike would be strangling on the requisition was just gravy.

As they completed their check-in, they were approached by a bellman who seemed to be channeling Cassandra, looking down his nose at their rumpled jeans and shirts, sneering over their lack of luggage. Alex waited until the man lifted his gaze to hers, then froze him with a look.

Tag nearly laughed when she handed the man the Chanel bag her mother had packed for her, one eyebrow inching up to her messy hairline. The man all but fell over himself leading them to the elevator and up to the suite.

Alex walked through the door, not sparing him another glance. "Adequate," she said, flicking a hand over her shoulder.

Tag played along, pulling a fat money clip out of his pocket, glancing at the single bag on the bed and tipping the prescribed amount.

Alex turned, still wearing her Boston diva expression. But her eyes were sparkling as she watched the bellman bow himself out of the room.

"You're a diabolical woman," Tag said, "but you have good taste. Expensive anyway."

"He deserved it," she said. "So did your boss."

"I'm not complaining."

The suite was done in rich, dark wood and fabrics, gleaming chrome and glass. A baby grand sat off to one side of the main room, and wide, floor-to-ceiling windows overlooked the city behind it. If he'd had to make a comparison, he would have said it resembled the drawing room of a Beacon Hill mansion.

Alex walked over and picked out a tune, one-handed, on the piano.

"Chopsticks?"

She smiled faintly. "Chopin. It was my talent. Miss USA."

"You have a lot of talents," Tag said. Including, he thought when she turned her back, the talent for ignoring what made her uncomfortable. She wasn't used to taking compliments; meeting her mother pretty much explained that. Sarcasm was more her thing. Or silence.

She retrieved the Chanel bag the bellman had left at the edge of the sitting area and disappeared behind the bedroom door. When she returned forty-five minutes later, she'd showered, tamed her hair, swiped on some mascara, and changed into slim black slacks, a plain white blouse, and strappy, spike-heeled sandals that put her almost eye to eye with him. Understated and casual, if you saw the clothing hanging on a rack. On Alex it might as well have been satin and diamonds.

"I don't know about you," she said, "but I'm in the mood for a big, juicy steak."

Tag lifted his gaze, very slowly, from her toes up to her face. "That would be Number Two on my list."

Alex lifted a brow.

"We could get room service."

"We could." But her attitude said it wasn't likely.

"They won't let me in the restaurant like this," Tag said, indicating his jeans and shirt, which gave every evidence of having been worn continuously for a good portion of the last week.

"They'll loan you a jacket."

"Nope."

Alex shrugged. "There's always room service."

Tag caught her arm as she tried to sweep by him. "Why the sudden urge to dine with people you've been avoiding since you broke up with . . .

"Shit, Alex. You *want* Harper to know you're in town."

"It's me he's after. Not you, and not my mother."

"You don't need to stand in front of your mother," Tag said, heading for the phone. "She'll be protected, and so will you. He's not getting within a mile of either of you."

"What are you going to do, have him arrested? You can't. He hasn't done anything wrong. Not that you can prove, anyway."

Tag swore under his breath, but he put the phone back in the cradle. They hadn't found Mick and Franky yet; Tag needed one of them, Mick preferably, to verify for the U.S. attorney what he'd told Tag in the field. The treasure was a

wild goose. Alex had been lured into the chase so Harper
would have a fall guy to toss to his investors—one in particular, although without the investor list they didn't know
who she was being set up for. All they had was a web of
assumptions—pretty accurate assumptions, Tag figured, but
personal opinion wouldn't hold up in court.

He'd be damned, though, if he let Alex dangle herself
under Harper's nose like live bait. It would have been nice
if she cooperated by keeping a low profile, but there was no
point in saying as much. She already knew how he felt, and
she was still walking out the door. And he wasn't letting
her out of his sight.

That didn't mean he couldn't look good while he did
guard duty. They hit the gift shop before the restaurant.
The FBI sprung for a new jacket for Tag, and when the
maitre d' eyed his rumpled jeans, Alex dropped names unapologetically. The fact that several of the men in the place
raised hands in greeting to her probably helped. The women
weren't as welcoming. There was a lot of whispering, and it
spiked every time Alex left the table.

"You want people telling Harper you have a bladder problem?" Tag asked her the fourth time she came back from the
ladies room in the space of an hour and a half.

She smiled, but it didn't reach her eyes. "As long as he
knows I'm using a Boston bathroom."

"Harper's a coward, Alex. He won't come after you. He
doesn't have to. That's why he set you up, so he can walk
away free and clear while you pay for his lies."

"I'm not the only target."

No, Tag thought, and if he had his way she wouldn't be
a target at all. "There's nothing we can do about that tonight."

"Then let's not worry about it."

Tag stood when she did and followed her from the
restaurant. When they got on the elevator, she didn't push
the button for their floor. "What are you up to now?"

"Something I've been dying to do for four years."

The elevator hit the top floor, and she began to unbutton her blouse. Tag's mouth went dry. He watched her walk to a door with words on it, but he couldn't have dragged his gaze off her bare back to save his life. And when her slacks began to slide down, revealing the top of a lace thong, he tried to go after her and almost fell on his face because his legs had gone completely numb. There wasn't much sensation in the upper part of his body either.

All feeling seemed to be concentrated . . . centrally, contracting to a point of almost unbearable heat and need before it burst out to every extremity and threatened to blow off the top of his skull.

"This door is locked," Alex said, turning to him.

Tag opened his mouth, but since he'd stopped breathing he had to suck in a lungful of air, and then he had to get his brain to kick back in so he could locate his vocabulary and put together a coherent sentence. The word "pool" on the door behind her helped. "It's after ten o'clock," he wheezed. "The pool is probably closed."

"Don't tell me you can't get it open."

Tag closed his eyes. That helped. When he opened them again he kept his gaze above her Wonderbra. "I don't have any lock-picking tools."

Alex slipped off her slacks and stood there in a lot of bare skin and not very much lace, staring expectantly at him.

Tag spun around to face the door. Turning his back on her might have made him feel slightly more in control if the sight of her hadn't been burned on his retinas. He fumbled a credit card out of his wallet and tried to slip it between the door and the jamb. It didn't work, and since that had been his only idea, he settled for pure brute force, backing up far enough to plant his foot on the door next to the lock. He bounced off. It might have had something to do with the fact that he was in no condition to lift his leg and there was very little blood flow to his muscles.

Alex rolled her eyes, handed him her clothes, and eased

him aside with the back of her hand. She took hold of the
doorknob, put her shoulder against the door, and did something with her hip that made his breath wheeze out and the
door pop open.

She sent him a smile then walked through the door and
straight to the pool, pausing only to kick off her shoes before she dove in. She swam a length and back, folding her
arms on the edge. "You have no idea how much I missed
this," she said, looking up at him. "There was a stream not
far from my cabin, but even in the spring it was only a couple of feet deep." She gave herself a little shove away from
the side and rolled onto her back, lazily sculling with her
hand to keep herself afloat. "It's like being in Colorado
with all the stars, only better."

Tag looked around. The pool was only eleven stories up,
and they were almost completely ringed in by office buildings. Only a few lights were on in the high-rise windows,
enough to dim the stars to mere specks. But he could attest
to the fact that imagination counted for something.

"Are you coming in?" Alex asked.

Tag stripped down to his boxers, sat and dangled his
feet in the water.

"I thought you were the kind of man who jumped into
things head first."

"Only life-threatening situations," he said. This was danger of another kind entirely. He'd told Alex he loved her, but
until that moment he hadn't really thought about what that
meant. The case was almost over and he was going to have
to make a decision that would affect the rest of his life. He
looked into Alex's eyes and couldn't imagine spending that
life without her—any more than he could imagine giving up
the career that defined who he was.

"Is something wrong?"

"Yes," he said, slipping into the water, and into her
arms, adding because he knew she was waiting for an explanation, "what else is new for us?"

She laughed softly, but her eyes were serious. "How
about I take your mind off it?"

"You already did that."

"It doesn't look that way." She smoothed a finger over the frown line between his eyes, flicked off the water that dripped from her hand to the end of his nose, then laid her mouth on his. Her lips were cold from the water, her tongue hot, and at some point during the kiss her bra and panties disappeared.

She did a little shimmy and pressed her body against his, bare, water-slicked skin from head to toe. Her hands slipped down his sides, tickling over his ribs before her fingers hooked in the waistband of his boxers, easing them down. Or trying to.

She started to say something, but Tag cupped her bottom, lifted her half out of the water, and dropped his mouth to her breasts. Her words trailed off into a moan, her legs wrapping around him. He barely had time to get his boxers off the rest of the way before she took him in and began to move.

The water was cool, but sweat popped out on his upper lip. What Alex was doing felt so good his eyes rolled back in his head, his knees went weak, and his mind went blank. Involuntary activities like breathing were suspended, and all he could do was stand there and take it. Her body wrapped around his, every breath she took and every movement pushing him closer to the edge. But he'd be damned if he went over alone.

He took her mouth with his, let the water buoy her up, and put his hands to good use. In the space of a few frantic heartbeats he felt her tighten around him and swallowed her cry as she came. He exploded a split second later, his breath trickling out on a satisfied groan.

Alex let her legs slide down, slumping against him. "A perfect ending to a mediocre day."

Tag laughed. "As long as it wasn't a mediocre ending to a perfect day."

"It could be an embarrassing end if I can't find my underwear," Alex said, casting around in the water.

Tag hooked her bra, which was floating not far away.

Alex found her panties, but decided not to put either of them on in favor of toweling off and wearing her outer clothes commando—so she didn't end up with embarrassing wet spots in case they ran into anyone in the hallway. Not to mention it came in handy when they got back to the room.

The bed was turned down and waiting, they were both too keyed up to sleep, and fortunately for their neighbors, the rooms had great soundproofing.

chapter
25

TAG WAS UP BEFORE ALEX THE NEXT MORNING, freshly showered and feeling antsy, judging by the path he was wearing in the carpet. Alex watched him from the bedroom doorway and knew exactly how he felt.

The assignment was about to be over; they could both feel it, and along with the anticipation dancing along Alex's nerve endings was a little uncertainty and a little sadness. There'd be regret, too, when she and Tag parted ways, regret for what might have been if they hadn't wanted different futures. But she'd resigned herself to that.

At least Harper would be out of her life, too. She'd made up her mind to see it done. If he didn't come after her, she was going after him. That was what she needed to concentrate on. Tag didn't make it easy.

She stepped into the suite's sitting room; he stopped pacing and took up staring. Alex let herself enjoy it. After all, she'd gone to a lot of trouble. She wore blue this morning, a bold bright blue that made her gray eyes softer, and she'd buffed and moisturized until her skin glowed like pearl. Her blouse was sheer with a lace-edged camisole beneath, both tucked into a raw silk skirt that hugged her body and ended just above the knees.

Thanks to her mother, she was Miss USA from the crown of her perfectly styled head to the tips her dainty little spike-heeled sandals, the kind that only covered the toes. And when she went to the bar to pour a cup of coffee, she made sure to pass close enough so Tag could catch the smoky, subtle scent she'd dabbed on—not overpowering, just enough to enhance.

"You're making it hard," he said.

She looked over her shoulder at him, her gaze dropping around belt level.

"To concentrate," he elaborated with a grin, not bothering to hide the fact that her interpretation wasn't wrong, either. "This is what pushed me off track the last time. I was thinking about you instead of concentrating on Harper, and it got us both in trouble."

"So stop thinking about me," she said, not quite managing to suppress a pleased little smile. "I can take care of myself."

"Not in those shoes. Not that I'm complaining. I like what they do for your . . . legs."

"I have another pair. You can try them out if you like."

"I was thinking more along the lines of getting you out of them."

"Funny, I was thinking the same thing." She turned her foot this way and that, studying the shoes. "They're completely useless if I have to run. But I have to admit it's nice to wear something besides jeans."

"I'm all for that," Tag said, stuffing his hands in the pockets of the hotel robe he'd put on after his shower. "Jack Mitchell is supposed to be bringing me some clothes—"

Right on cue there was a knock on the door. Tag checked the peep, already grinning as he opened the door.

A hulk of a man walked in, looking like the stereotypical secret agent. Or a mafia hit man. He was dressed in muscles and black—black jeans, black shirt, black bomber jacket with a shoulder holster underneath. The muscles were everywhere. He tossed Tag a duffel, but he made a beeline for Alex, enveloping her hand with his and shaking it carefully. "Jack Mitchell," he said, then turned to Tag, completely dismissing her.

"Don't mind him."

Alex had no idea who was talking until Mitchell shifted aside and she spotted a waif of a woman behind him. She was as slender as a supermodel and as cheerfully dressed as Jack was somber. She wore a floaty Missoni-print dress with heels Alex would have sworn were Jimmy Choos, and she was flawlessly made up. Otherwise she was a pleasant-looking, completely forgettable woman—probably not a bad quality for an undercover agent—but her twinkling eyes and bright smile made her plain features come alive.

"Aubrey Sullivan," she said, sending Jack a teasing side-long glance, "the brains of this outfit."

"By brains she means mouth," Jack said.

"I mean brain, singular, since the jury's still out on what's inside that thick skull of yours."

Jack grinned. "It's not my brain that keeps you hanging around."

"You're right, and it only took you six months to figure that out."

The sarcasm was thick enough to keep a fleet of psychiatrists busy for years, but the way the two looked at each other was so intimate it was almost too uncomfortable to watch.

"So where's this map I've heard so much about?" Aubrey asked, changing subjects like a light switch.

"The map really isn't an issue anymore," Tag told her. "It was just a decoy Bennet Harper used to con people into investing money, and then to lure Alex out in the field so he could hang the theft of the treasure on her and get his mystery investor off his back."

"I think I can help with the mystery investor part." Jack took a piece of paper out of his inside jacket pocket and tossed it on the table.

Tag unfolded it and smoothed it with his hands, bending over to read it.

Alex was getting an eyeful. So was Aubrey. The robe was barely knee-length when he was standing straight. "Ummm . . . maybe you want to go get dressed, Tag."

He bolted upright, the expression on his face so comical Alex had to hold back her laughter. He grabbed the duffel and nipped into the bedroom. Alex thought it was an excellent opportunity to find out who Harper's investors were. If Sappresi was one of them.

Jack, however, wasn't in a sharing mood. He picked up the list and held it behind his back, one eyebrow inching up.

Alex took it as a challenge. She was considering her options when Aubrey strolled over and stepped between them.

"Don't mind him," she said to Alex. "Jack's a black and white kind of guy. If you're not on his side of the line you must be the enemy."

Jack narrowed his eyes at the top of Aubrey's head. She rolled hers up at him. "While we're waiting for Tag, why don't you show me the map?" she said to Alex.

Alex sent Jack a look, but she really didn't have a choice, so she retrieved the map from Tag's pack and handed it over. "We checked two of the sites and didn't find anything."

"Is this Mike's idea of a joke?" Tag asked.

They all turned around and saw him standing in the open bedroom doorway. "This" was a pair of khakis over scuffed brown boots, a khaki shirt, a worn brown leather bomber, and a gray fedora. All he was missing was the whip.

Alex and Aubrey burst out laughing. Jack crossed his massive arms over his massive chest and grinned from ear to ear. Alex was glad he was on their side.

"Mike said you were on a treasure hunt," Jack said. "I thought you oughtta look the part."

Tag looked over at Alex. "You wanted Indiana Jones, I guess you got him."

"It takes more than clothing. Indiana Jones always found what he was looking for."

"I wasn't really looking for treasure," Tag reminded her. He crossed the room and bent over the list.

Jack joined them, the two men head to head and shoulder to shoulder, no room for civilians. So Alex went to join Aubrey where she was sitting at the bar with Juan Amparo's map.

"There's not much here, is there?" Aubrey said, her pixie face puzzled.

"No. We searched these two sites." Alex indicated the areas she meant.

"*La Cruz de Piedra,*" Aubrey read.

"It means Cross of Stone."

"I know. I read a Spanish-English dictionary the other day." She looked up, caught Alex staring at her. "Photographic memory. Trust me, it's not as great as it sounds. Anyway, I wonder why Juan used that word. *Cruz.* He had to be a devout Catholic. I'd expect him to use the word for crucifix."

Alex took a second to process the lightning-fast shifts in the other woman's thought patterns. "Isn't a cross a crucifix only when the figure is there?"

"See? The memory didn't tell me that. This second site, Smith's Creek, sounds like a man named Smith lived there."

Alex nodded. "We found the remains of a corral but nothing else. The third site is just like the second, grassland with no discernible features unless you count hills. And now that I know it was all a hoax, I'm glad we didn't waste any more time."

Aubrey fingered the paper, bent closer to study the little burlap bag. "Pretty convincing for a hoax."

"Harper wouldn't chance using a fake. His investors are wealthy people, they'd have the means to authenticate it if they wanted to."

Aubrey sat back. "I did some research."

"I told you not to waste your time with that," Jack said

from across the room. "Mike said it wasn't important anymore."

"I was intrigued," Aubrey shot back, rolling her eyes for Alex's benefit. But there was a fond smile there, too. "Jack wouldn't let me help him with the list, so I had some time on my hands. If the Lost Spaniard had been found it would have been in some newspaper somewhere, which means it would be on the Internet, and it's not."

"Unless Juan dug it up himself."

"That's possible, but the story is that he was killed in Casteel, for the map." Aubrey held up a hand. "I know it's just a story, but a lot of times those word-of-mouth tales turn out to be pretty accurate. And I did find something interesting. His name, Alejandro Domingo Augustin Amparo de Tallavera."

"That's a mouthful. How do you get Juan out of that?"

"Who knows? But it means he was somebody important in Spain, and this notation at the top of the map, *la salvacion de Amparo*, Amparo's salvation, supports that. I'm betting Juan lost his lands or went broke or something, and he came to America to find enough gold to put himself back on top."

"Which means he wouldn't have dug up the treasure until he was ready to go home. And since he was killed here—"

"The treasure is still out there," Aubrey concluded, "maybe at one of the other sites."

"The only other sites marked are Mount Rosalie, Casteel, and Denver, and we figured those are just reference points," Alex said. "There's no way Juan climbed a mountain to hide his gold, not without something more definite to remind him where it is. And I don't believe he'd have hidden anything close to a populated area. Too much chance he'd be followed, or someone would stumble across it."

"And that's everything?"

"Except for the directional notation to the right—*este*, east. Probably just an orientation point."

"Even in the 1800s north was generally used as an orientation point," Aubrey said, "and the map is drawn so that north is at the top."

"Juan wasn't a cartographer."

"Then he should have drawn a big *X* or written something like 'dig here.' "

Aubrey kept talking. Alex wasn't really listening because a thought was dancing at the edge of her mind, like a word on the tip of the tongue. She nearly had it when Aubrey shoved the map away and flounced out of her chair in a distracting swirl of color and energy.

"Oh well," she said with a flip of her hand, "Jack might be able to make sense of it, if we could convince him it's worth his time. Of the two of us, he's the problem solver—and if you tell him I said that I'll deny it."

Alex smiled. She couldn't help it. "Can I ask you something? You and Jack met on a case, right?"

"You could put it that way," Aubrey said. "Jack kidnapped me out of the Library of Congress and dragged me from DC to Miami where he thought it was a good idea to confront Pablo Corona in his own home."

"Ouch." Corona was the biggest drug lord in the western hemisphere, and he was reputed to be crazy. "But it all worked out, and you two got together."

"And you want to know how, right?" Aubrey smiled. Her eyes cut to Jack, softened. He'd looked at her the same way. They might be verbally at odds, but the emotions ran deep. "He's irritating, macho, pig-headed, stubborn, and a major pain in the neck. But if there's enough good stuff under all that, you just have to train them."

Alex sighed, her gaze going to Tag. "That would probably take years and I'm pretty sure our future can be measured in hours."

"Yeah, I felt that way about Jack, too, but he grew on me."

"Let's see, fungus, warts, boils . . . None of the stuff that grows on you is pleasant."

"True, but you're stuck with it," Aubrey said.

"Not if you have a good doctor."

"Would that be medical or psychological?"

Alex laughed. "It wouldn't hurt if he was both."

"YOU JUST HAVE TO TRAIN THEM," JACK SAID TO TAG, both of them watching the women sitting at the bar, their heads bent together over Juan Amparo's map. "It's like a puppy. When you first bring it home, it's yappy and excitable and out of control. You just have to be patient and firm and in no time it comes right to heel when you call it."

"You don't say things like that to Aubrey, do you?" Tag asked, still looking at Alex. She'd probably shoot him if he compared her to a dog. She liked animals better than people, but she'd shoot him anyway, just on principle. "Alex is pretty steady—for a woman—but she doesn't trust me."

"Can you blame her?"

"It's not like I didn't have a good reason for everything."

"Jeez, you tried logic on her?" Jack shook his head, severely disappointed. "I'm telling you, there's no use trying to reason with women. They're too emotional. It's best if you just give in to stop the chatter or tears or whatever noise is coming out of them, do things your way, and then deal with the fallout later."

He sounded like it was a hardship to be stuck with Aubrey, but Tag had seen the way Jack looked at her. She might not have him wrapped around her finger, but there was definitely a partnership there, and Jack wasn't the one in charge, even if Aubrey let him think that.

"You want to talk about women or criminals?" Jack grumbled.

Tag focused on the list again, shaking his head at the names of several well-known businessmen, all of whom should have known the first rule of investing: if it sounds too good to be true, it usually is. "Thomas Warren, Congressman; James Hadley, Secretary of the Interior," he read off the list. "They'd be the ones with the clout to get a complaint to the bureau."

"Yeah, but I think this is the guy you're going to want to talk to." Jack flipped the page over and pointed at a name—which was unnecessary since it jumped out at Tag.

"Anthony Sappresi," he said, clamping down, hard, on the mix of excitement and hatred coursing through him. "Tony the Sap."

"You don't sound surprised."

Tag bumped up a shoulder. Jack was probably aware of his history with Sappresi, but even if he took it to Mike, it wouldn't go any further. Tag knew he wouldn't be pulled off the case, not after he'd been put on it for just this eventuality. Sappresi was his, a gift from Mike, end of story. End of Sappresi.

But the takedown wasn't all he had to worry about. He'd spent six months on his own trying to pin Zukey's murder on Tony the Sap, and that was on top of the year spent by other agents and sanctioned by the bureau. "Nothing sticks to Tony Sappresi."

Jack shrugged. "Nothing illegal about putting money into a treasure hunt."

There was if you tried to kill the person who allegedly found it. Not that Sappresi had made an attempt on his or Alex's life. Yet. But Sappresi had finally made a mistake. Its name was Bennet Harper.

"What you need to focus on here is getting him off your back," Jack said. "Fast, before he finds out you're in town, and he comes after you. Or her." He jerked a thumb in Alex's direction.

Not advice Tag needed, and not just because of his thirst for justice. Sure, he wanted Sappresi to pay for killing Zukey. He wanted Alex safe more.

"What would you be willing to do to get him before he gets you?"

Tag didn't have to think very hard to get Jack's point, not when he knew the other agent's recent history. "You're suggesting I take the fight to him, like you did with Corona."

"I'm saying sometimes you have to throw out the rule book," Jack said. "Zukey knew that."

"That's what got him killed."

"Tom Zukey was a pro. He had good reasons for what he did and how he did it." Jack pulled his chirping phone out of his coat pocket, looking at the readout while he finished his thought. "Something went down he wasn't ready for. It can happen whether you're following the rules or not."

Jack answered his phone, listened for a half a minute, then disconnected without speaking. "We have to go," he said to Aubrey.

"Really?" She streaked across the room, squealing as she threw her arms around Jack's neck. She was positively glowing.

Jack looked like he'd had a bad plate of oysters.

"She's not pregnant, is she?" Tag asked.

Jack went from green to white, ample payback for the Indiana Jones outfit.

"It's my first assignment," Aubrey said.

"Don't get all worked up." Jack unfastened her arms from around his neck. "It's a small case, and I'm not letting you carry a gun." He looked at Tag. "She has a tendency to wound me. All the time."

"I don't need a gun," Aubrey said. "I have a backpack."

Jack rolled his eyes, but there was that ever-present sparkle of amusement.

They took off without more than a quick good-bye, leaving Tag and Alex alone, staring at one another, both with their own thoughts.

"So what were you and Aubrey talking about?" Tag finally asked Alex.

"The map, but we already know that's a dead end. Did you find out who the mystery investor is?"

"I think so."

"And?"

"It's a matter for the FBI."

"It's revenge." She walked over to him. He couldn't have missed her disgust if she'd hit him over the head with it. "You're going after Sappresi."

"You were listening."

"I heard enough."

"That was the important part."

"No, the important part is what's going on in there." She tapped his forehead. "Sappresi killed your partner and tried to kill you, and you're going back for more."

He started to deny it.

"Don't fall into your old habits," Alex said.

"Okay. I'm going to deal with Sappresi. Alone."

She crossed her arms, one eyebrow inching up to her hairline. "You know what, Donovan? That's exactly the kind of idiocy I'd expect from you."

chapter
26

"YOU'RE GOING TO CALL ME STUPID AND JUST walk away?"

Halfway to the bedroom, Alex turned back. "That's what you're doing."

He started to deny it, but she came back and drilled a finger into his chest. "How would you take it if I expected you to sit here doing nothing while I went after somebody who wanted me dead?"

"He killed my partner, Alex."

"Yeah, I know that. What I don't understand is why you're in such a hurry to take him on. All the ducks are ready to quack, Tag—"

"And while we're waiting for them to line up in a nice, neat row, what's to keep Sappresi from coming after us? Once he finds out I'm back in town it'll be open season, Alex."

And there, in his eyes, was the real reason he wouldn't wait. "You're afraid he'll come after me." It might have given her a warm little glow, if he hadn't been putting his life on the line to save hers.

"He thinks you found the treasure. By now your mother has put the word out. That means Harper knows you're in Boston, and if Harper knows Sappresi knows."

Something skittered along Alex's nerves, something that burned off her temper. This must have been how Tag felt when he found out Sappresi was within his reach, she thought, excited, nervous, anxious to get the show on the road. There was a healthy dose of fear mixed in, too; probably not something Tag was suffering from, but she didn't do this sort of thing on a daily basis. And she wasn't afraid Bennet Harper would actually harm her. She was afraid she'd never get a chance at him.

"I'd think you were speechless," Tag said, "but I know you better than that. What's cooking upstairs?"

Alex shrugged. "You're right, I just didn't want to say it."

"You're not going to try to talk me out of going after Sappresi anymore?"

"What good would it do me?"

"None."

"Then good luck."

"That sounded final," Tag said.

"I won't be here when you get back. If you come back."

"I will, Alex, and when I do you'll still be here."

"We'll see about that." She whipped around, heading for the bedroom. She made it three steps before it hit her. She closed her eyes and took a few seconds to let some of the pain and anger settle in so she could keep her voice steady. She wasn't strong enough to face him. "You have agents downstairs," she said without turning around.

"You're staying put until all the loose ends are tied up. Even if I have to put you in custody to do it."

"I'm already in prison," she said, her heart feeling like lead in her chest.

"This is a nicer cell than we usually provide," Tag said, "but you're right about the men downstairs, and their job is to keep you in, just as much as it is to keep the rest of the uncollected players out."

"You're going to lock me up while you go out and finish this thing, after everything we've been through?"

"You're not FBI, Alex."

She did turn then, and she didn't give a damn what he saw on her face. "Now you want to make me into a victim because it's convenient for you? After all your big talk about not living my life that way?"

He strode across the room, took her upper arms in a grip that was sure to leave marks. She couldn't feel anything but the wounds he was leaving on her heart.

"Do you think I could stand it if you got hurt? Do you think I could even concentrate on what needs to be done, knowing you were in danger?"

"It doesn't matter what I think." She brushed his hands off and stepped back. "You've made that perfectly clear."

"Alex . . ." He stuffed his hands in his pockets, looking every bit as miserable as she felt. But he wasn't changing his mind. "I'm sorry."

"So am I."

TAG WALKED OUT AND LEFT HER THERE. SHE'D GIVEN him no choice. But it was eating at him.

Jack Mitchell was right. Tag had to go after Sappresi before he came after them. Tony the Sap hadn't gotten his nickname because he was an idiot. He'd started his career of crime as a hit man, one who'd taken a great deal of pleasure out of beating his victims to death with a lead-weighted bag—a sap. He didn't do his own dirty work anymore, but he was still a dangerous guy. Too dangerous for Tag to leave him walking the streets when he had a vendetta to settle, and Alex was on the other side of it.

Tag knew she understood what he was doing and why. She was only being difficult about it. Because he'd hurt her, and he'd let her down. She wanted to see this thing ended as much as he did, and he'd cut her out. In her shoes, he'd be pissed, too—hell, he was pissed. Anger had gotten him to the lobby, but the anger was gone, and now he was at war with himself.

Now would be the best time to go after Sappresi. Tag knew that. Sappresi worked out of his home in Savin Hill. Usually his wife or his kids would be around, except they'd flown out a couple of days before on their annual school's-out vacation. That meant there'd be one, maybe two of Sappresi's guys in the house. Because he wouldn't be expecting any trouble.

All Tag had to do was go in, throw the truth in his face, and sit back and wait for Sappresi to make a move on Harper. It was going to stick in Tag's craw to rescue the guy who was setting Alex up to the homicidal mobster. But it had to be done.

Better, anyway, than Tony fleeing the country, which was what would happen if Tag waited for Mick and Franky to be picked up and sweated for their statements, and Sappresi got wind of it. Not a chance he could take. Sure, he'd be risking his life, but Zukey would have understood.

And anyway, Alex was safe—burning mad, but safe. The sooner he walked out that door and did his job, the sooner he could get back and talk her out of her bad mood, just like he'd always done.

So why was he standing in the middle of the lobby, staring like a lunatic at the bank of elevators, instead of walking out the front door? Alex, he thought, and Sappresi.

She'd left him feeling . . . guilty, he decided. Unsettled. Sappresi had undermined Tag's self-confidence months before. And here he was, mooning over Alex's hurt feelings when he should be running out the door to finish something so important to him he'd nearly died trying to take care of it the first time.

Again, no contest, and since running would be overkill, he glanced at the elevators one more time and walked away. He made it to the sidewalk before he stopped again, the late morning pedestrian traffic flowing around him like a logjam in a river. He rubbed a hand over his chest, not liking the way it felt. Tight, a little painful, but the real source of wrongness was lower in his gut. And then it hit him, and he was racing back inside, punching the elevator button even as he decided not to wait for it and slammed through the door to the stairs. He took them two by two, but it wasn't fast enough. He was all but passing out, black spots dancing in front of his eyes, chest burning with every breath he dragged in. His effort wouldn't be enough, though. Alex was going to die.

NOT FIVE MINUTES AFTER TAG LEFT, THE DOOR TO THE hallway opened again. Alex's heart jumped, settling back to flutter in her chest and leave her nervous, breathless. Hoping. But she wasn't running back to Tag. He'd walked out, he could make the first move.

She finished tossing the rest of her things in her mother's Chanel bag, including the Miss USA outfit she'd worn that morning. She'd changed back into her jeans and T-shirt, beating herself up for using what few feminine wiles she possessed to keep Tag from walking away. The only thing worse would have been if they'd worked.

Whether she wore couture or denim, she was the same woman, and that woman had never been able to keep up a pretense for long. She was pretty good at torturing herself, though, which was what she was doing by putting off the inevitable.

She turned, took a deep breath, and headed out of the bedroom. She got as far as the doorway before she stopped.

She'd had some half-baked idea of trying to sneak out of the hotel and having her own reckoning, just like Tag was doing. The man standing in the suite's sitting room made it unnecessary.

"How'd you get in here?" she asked him.

"I charmed the maid into believing I forgot my key," Bennet Harper said with a smile that proved his claim. But the maid wouldn't have known him well enough to see the jittery edge in his eyes.

"Did you charm the guards downstairs, too?"

"They were pathetically easy to elude," he said. "All it takes is a bit of self-confidence and a delivery man's uniform."

"While they're looking for a guy in a suit." For the first time she noticed his clothing: cheap blue workpants and a blue shirt with an oval name patch on the breast pocket. His attitude of entitlement hadn't lessened one bit, but it was slicked over with a thin sheen of panic.

Alex leaned against the door frame, hoping she looked a hell of a lot more relaxed than she felt. "You didn't go to all this trouble because you couldn't wait to see me again."

"Actually, I did." Bennet jerked forward half a pace and stopped, running a hand back through his hair. "I knew you'd be here, in this hotel. Your mother's precious reputation demands it."

Absolutely, Alex thought, she'd chosen the Colonnade on purpose, but not for her mother's sake.

"It was a mistake, Alex."

"Was it?" she asked him. But it wasn't the question that got to him, it was the confidence in her voice when she asked it. And it was her smile. She could see the puzzlement and the worry. For the first time Bennet was beginning to wonder what he'd walked into.

He swore with a foulness that surprised her—she hadn't thought he'd known words like that—and then he tore through the suite. Alex took a seat at the bar and waited for him to finish his tantrum.

"There's no one here but the two of us," Bennet said.

"Did you think I needed help to take you down?"

Bennet reached into his pocket. "I've got the gun," he said, pulling it out and pointing it at her.

"So you have," she said, a little zing of satisfaction mixing in with a healthy dose of fear. Having a gun pointed at her was nothing to scoff at, even if she'd wanted exactly this. "Now what?"

"Your mother, Alexandra. She's ruining me."

"Good. I asked her to."

"Then you—you can make her stop."

"It's too late for that," Alex said. "Gossip has a life of its own. You know how word of mouth works, you use it whenever you can. The only difference is it's not working in your favor this time."

"It will be," he said, some of the nerves backing off behind his sneer. "First you're going to call your mother and tell her to stop spreading lies about me. Then we're going for a short drive."

Alex snorted softly. "You going to shoot me and throw my body into the bay?"

"I'm not going to do anything to you."

"Maybe not personally, but you're going to hand me over to Anthony Sappresi." He bobbled the gun, and she smiled. "You didn't know we'd figured that out, did you, Benny?"

"Don't call me Benny," he snapped, his whole body shaking now, vibrating with a mixture of rage and fear.

"You used to like it when I called you that."

"I tolerated it, just as I tolerated you."

"Yes, I caught on to that. It took me a while, but then I was young. And stupid. I'm not anymore." She cut her gaze to the door, and he jumped to exactly the conclusion she was going for.

"You're stalling," he said, "waiting for that nobody who's fucking you to come back and save you."

"That nobody is an FBI agent, and he didn't fuck me, Bennet, you did. And quite a few other people while you were at it. It wasn't the first time, and it wasn't the last, but your little run of fraud is over. The FBI knows all about you and your latest treasure scam. They know about Anthony Sappresi, and they know you set me up so he'd kill me instead of you."

Alex eased off the bar stool and took a step toward him, then another. "And what makes you think I need anyone to save me? I live in a place where everyone carries a gun. I've learned to know who's dangerous and who's not."

Bennet swiped a hand over the back of his mouth, a hand that shook. "Stay away from me," he warned, "I'll shoot."

"No, you won't. If you were capable of doing your own dirty work, you wouldn't have needed to set me up to get Sappresi off your back."

"I don't want blood on my hands," Bennet shot back, "I'm too smart for that."

"You don't have the guts for it. Or should I say the balls?"

"You've gotten crude since I dumped you."

Alex laughed. "I can be as crude as I choose. I've still got the pedigree you'll never have, no matter who you marry or how much money you accumulate. You'll always be the kid who grew up in a trailer because you can't let it go. Just like you couldn't let go what happened between us. That was your mistake, Benny."

She stepped forward again. "And I dumped you, remember? After which I left town, but that wasn't enough for you, was it? You shoved into my life again, you tried to get me killed, and you left me no choice but to come back here. For you."

"Another mistake," he snarled, jerking the barrel of the gun toward the door, then again, and when she still didn't move, it was clear he wasn't quite sure what to do.

"That always worked in the movies, didn't it," she scoffed.

His eyes darted around the room then back to her face, and a bead of sweat dripped from his temple down to the collar of his shirt.

Alex walked toward him again. "Shoot me," she dared him. "You can go to Sappresi and tell him what a big man you are. You won't have the money, but you can find a whole new flock of sheep to fleece and pay him off with the proceeds."

"D-don't Alex," he stammered, "I'll pull the trigger if you make me."

"Go ahead," she said, her voice getting louder, her tone more belligerent. "If you can find the balls to pull that trigger, do it."

And he did.

chapter 27

WHEN TAG HEARD THE GUNSHOT HIS HEART stopped beating, his feet stopped moving, and he swore time stood still. The only thing still ticking along unhindered was his imagination. Worrying about Alex getting hurt was nothing compared to the possibility of her getting dead. Because he hadn't gotten there in time. Just like Zukey.

Harper shrieked something unintelligible, and Tag knew Alex had pushed him over the edge. He had the key card in his pocket, but he went through the door, going in low and fast, not so much worried about his own safety as aware of the fact that he wouldn't do Alex any good if he was shot trying to get to her.

In the split second he had to assess the situation, he saw Alex standing by the bar, Harper leveling a small pistol at her. Tag threw himself at Harper just as he fired the gun again. There was a split second of breathless pain, under his left arm, a phantom that disappeared as soon as he identified it. It was all about Harper, then. And Alex.

Tag caught movement out of the corner of his eye—

Alex getting to her feet. But Bennet still had the gun, not to mention the strength of the truly desperate. Tag couldn't afford to split his attention. If he had, he'd have seen Alex coming, and he'd have seen the fire of righteous fury in her eyes before she wedged herself between them, gun be damned, and proceeded to kick the shit out of Bennet Harper.

Tag wouldn't have bet on Alex to be passive, exactly, but hand-to-hand combat with Bennet Harper hadn't been high on his list of predictable scenarios. And he definitely wouldn't have expected her to be winning.

Just as Tag was getting over the disbelief that she was getting the better of a man who had her by at least sixty pounds and was a couple miles past sane, Alex took Harper down with a swift knee to the crotch.

"Imagine that," she said to a retching, groaning Bennet Harper, "you do have balls after all. You just needed someone to find them for you."

"You finished?" Tag asked her.

She whipped around. She didn't look happy to see him, and she didn't say anything, just bent, bracing herself on Bennet's stomach while she retrieved the gun lying half beneath him. He groaned and retched some more. Or maybe he was sobbing.

Alex walked over and stood with Tag—but not too close—both of them taking in the pathetic picture Bennet made, curled into a fetal position and moaning like he was at death's door.

"Yeah," she said, "I'm done."

"You didn't, by any chance, work off all your anger on him?" Tag wondered out loud.

She handed over the gun and gave him a look that told him to be grateful she wasn't armed anymore. "Not hardly."

THINGS MOVED FAST ENOUGH TO MAKE ALEX'S HEAD spin after that. Tag made a couple of calls, and they trooped down to the U.S. attorney's office. Bennet Harper, cuffed and looking satisfyingly miserable, was trundled into an interview room. Alex made her statement as well, and by the time she was done, Tag was waiting to talk to her.

"Mick and Franky were picked up in Denver," he said right off the bat. "They rolled over on Harper, and Harper rolled over on Sappresi, just like we figured he would."

Alex took a deep breath, holding on to her temper. "And?"

"Harper won't be charged for cheating his investors—"

"Or for trying to get me killed? Or shooting at me himself?"

Tag's jaw worked a couple of times. "For anything."

"So you can put Sappresi away for killing your partner." Alex didn't know why that surprised her; it had been Tag's goal all along.

"Nothing sticks to Sappresi," he said. "This is the first time we've had anything to charge him with. Junior is being picked up as we speak, and once his testimony is added to everything else we have, Sappresi won't see a sunrise for the rest of his life."

"And what about Bennet? He goes back on the street to find more people to cheat?"

"Um . . . yes and no." Tag rubbed at the back of his neck. "He'll be placed in witness protection," he finally admitted. "If it's any consolation, I'm doing my best to see that he winds up flipping burgers in some small town in Iowa, surrounded by cows and corn fields."

"Great, throw in a trailer park and it'll all be good."

"Alex . . ."

She got to her feet and moved out of his reach.

Tag stood and stepped in front of her before she could make her dramatic exit. "I know you're angry," he said. "I know it doesn't feel like enough, but Harper is losing his life. Not literally, but someone from the FBI will be watching him at all times. He won't be able to run any cons, and trust me—"

Alex popped up an eyebrow at that turn of phrase and Tag had the grace to look abashed.

"The point is," he continued, "his life as he knows it is over. There's nothing he can do but work a nine-to-five job for a nine-to-five salary. He's going to be ordinary, Alex, and you, more than anyone, know that's the worst punishment he can get."

"You're right, Tag." It wasn't just an empty comment, either. Living a blue collar life would be worse for Bennet Harper than prison. So why did she feel this soul-sucking emptiness? And why didn't they have anything else to say to one another? Or maybe Tag looked so uncomfortable because he did have something to say to her. Odd, but she hadn't thought he'd have trouble with good-bye. Or that she would.

Before either of them could find the words, a man came out of the back hallway. Tall, dark, handsome in a rugged way, a man with the kind of presence that had every head turning his way. Tag gestured him over, and he obliged, walking with a slight limp.

"This is Daniel Pierce," Tag said, "the U.S. attorney."

"Nice to meet you." Daniel shook Alex's hand, lingered over it.

She managed to dig up a smile from somewhere. Daniel didn't smile back. His eyes searched hers, deep brown, compelling, drawing conclusions she didn't want a complete stranger drawing. She wanted Tag to draw those conclusions, but he was working overtime to turn a blind eye to everything that didn't pertain to Bennet Harper and Anthony Sappresi.

"I've heard a lot about you," Daniel Pierce said, leaning in just a bit, making the connection intimate and giving her the impression she could confide her deepest secrets to him.

"I'll bet you're hell in court," she said. And she bet he stacked the jury with women whenever possible. A man like this had to know his effect on the opposite sex. A man like this would use it.

"I am hell in court," he said. "I'm hell out of it, too, so I've heard a time or two."

"I was just telling Alex that Harper gave up Tony Sappresi for the murder of my partner," Tag said, not so subtly easing Daniel aside.

"And for the attempted murder of another FBI agent," Daniel added, not so subtly refusing to budge, "namely, you. At the moment, I'm not too happy about the attempted part."

Pierce was smiling, but Alex got the impression it was the competition with Tag more than attraction to her. Daniel Pierce didn't strike her as a man who opened up easily, to anyone. That kind of emotional distance would challenge some women and have others pausing, considering, and probably cutting their losses early. Alex did neither. She didn't feel like she'd ever consider another relationship in her life. And that included one with Tag Donovan.

"So it's over, then?" she said to Daniel. "You don't need me anymore?"

"Not in connection with the case, I'm glad to tell you. Your testimony may be necessary later, but all you need to do is leave a number where you can be reached, and you're free to go."

"I think Alex should stick around until Sappresi's in custody," Tag put in.

"That's not really necessary," Daniel said. "You should feel free to call me, Miss Scott—"

"Alex."

"Alex," he repeated with a smile. "Like I said, feel free to call me any time you want a progress report." Or anything else, his tone said.

"I think we need to talk, Pierce," Tag said. "In private."

The two men went off a little way and conferred, not bothering to control their expressions, or keep their voices down low enough for her to miss the gist of the conversation, if not the actual wording.

Tag was adamant she stay in Boston; Daniel calmly disagreed. Alex didn't give a damn what either of them thought.

And she wasn't letting them decide what she was going to do and where she was going to do it. So she headed for the exit.

"You can't leave yet," Tag said, putting himself between her and the door.

"The U.S. attorney doesn't agree with you," Alex pointed out, "and I'd think it would be his call at this point."

"She's right, Donovan. The FBI has done their part by closing the case. Alex has agreed to come back and testify if we need her, and I don't think it's a good idea for her to be in the building when Sappresi is brought in. It's bad enough he's got her name, no point in giving him a face to go along with it."

"See, you're going to be in danger when you walk out that door."

Alex ignored him, looking to Daniel again.

"Actually, once Sappresi hears the facts I don't think he'll want anything to happen to you," he said to her.

Because he'll be blamed for it. None of them felt a need to say it out loud, but that didn't make it any less true.

Daniel limped over and took her hand. "It was nice to meet you," he said. "I hope I have the pleasure again soon."

He sent Tag one of those male-to-male enigmatic looks and walked away.

Alex gave Tag a look that contained a message, too. He got it, but he didn't budge from in front of the door.

"What are you going to do now?" he asked her.

"I'm going home."

"Good, I think that's the best thing. Sleep in, let your mother pamper you for a couple of weeks while you decide what to do next."

Alex smiled, but even she knew it was shadowed with sadness. After all they'd been through together, that he knew her so poorly, well, it was heartbreaking. "I mean Colorado. I need to get my files from Matt, write my report, and decide what to do next." Because what she found—or didn't find—in Colorado would be a huge deciding factor. But she wasn't saying as much to Tag. He'd think she was a fool, and she'd been close enough to that to be sensitive.

"I have to finish up here," he said.

"You have to go get Sappresi."

"I'm going, but I won't be alone."

"It doesn't matter, Tag, you're back."

She could see she'd surprised him, that he hadn't had the time to think it through. "Why did you come to the suite after you left today? Because your gut instinct is back," she answered before he could. "Your confidence is right up where it was before your partner was killed.

"And I'm done running, so we both have our lives back." And those lives, those individual goals, would lead them in different directions.

Tag looked like he wanted to deny it, but after a second or two he slipped his hands into his pockets and nodded. "I have a report of my own to write, but once I'm done, I'm coming to Casteel."

"Why?"

He opened his mouth, then shut it again. "We still have some things to settle."

"You've got my number," Alex said. "Just give me a call once you've made up my mind for me."

"You're still mad," Tag said, and had to agree when Alex rolled her eyes, as it was the understatement of the century. He took her arm, but she yanked it loose and walked outside, away from the rest of the strike team that was assembling to go out with Tag to pick up Sappresi.

"You've done your part," Tag said to her once they were outside, away from any audience. "You brought Harper down. The case is over as far as you're concerned—as far as I'm concerned, too, once Sappresi and Dussaud are in custody. That doesn't mean that you and I . . . that we . . . You don't belong in Colorado, Alex."

"I don't belong in Boston, either."

"You could have a job with the FBI. Aubrey Sullivan, Jack's friend—"

But she was already shaking her head. "Getting tossed out of airplanes and shot at isn't for me."

"Then take a job as an analyst."

"And sit in an office all day?"

"It wouldn't be an office at first. More like a bullpen, lots of desks, brainstorming with other analysts and trying to make sense of intelligence . . . Not helping, huh?"

"I like my own company," she said simply.

"I thought you liked mine, too."

"I do, but I can't live the way you do, Tag. I wouldn't be happy locked up inside an office, and I'm not cut out to sit in my mother's parlor and wait for you to drop by between cases." She met his eyes. "And wonder if you were going to make it back at all."

Tag ran both hands back through his hair. He paced a couple of steps away, then back. "This isn't going the way I imagined it."

"You mean you thought this through? If you'd considered my feelings—"

"I thought I had."

"Not all of them."

"Does the word compromise mean anything to you?"

"Yeah. I learned it in the eighth grade just like everyone else. It means two sides of any conflict giving ground so they can meet somewhere in the middle. So how are you budging?"

"I said I was in love with you."

Her temper shifted down long enough for Tag to see the unhappiness in her eyes, to hear it in her voice. "That was just adrenaline talking, us against the world, the heat of the moment."

"No, it wasn't."

She sighed, lifting her gaze to his. "I love you, too. But how long do you think it would last if I stayed here and took a job with the FBI? How long would you love me if I talked you into walking away and living in some forest or other with me? You'd miss the danger, the rush. You'd get bored. And you'd begin to resent me."

"You're wrong about that."

"Am I? What if I asked you not to go after Sappresi?"

"That's different. He killed my partner."

"So this one is personal. What about the cases that came before?"

"They were bad guys. They needed to be taken off the streets."

"There are a lot of bad guys out there, Tag, and they're not all going to grow consciences suddenly."

"Somebody else can deal with them."

She snorted softly. "Real convincing, Donovan. I especially like that little stutter when you said s-somebody else."

"Doesn't mean I wasn't serious. I'll quit, right after I bring in Sappresi."

"Really? You're volunteering to go with me?"

"Absolutely." He stuffed his hands in his pockets. "Where are you going?"

"Colorado. My report. Then . . . I don't know."

"Well, that sounds like an adventure." A tame one. "I could—"

Alex shook her head. "Give it up, Donovan. You know you'll be climbing the walls inside of two days."

"You asked me to quit my job—"

"No, I didn't," she said. "I asked you what you'd do if I wanted you to walk away from Sappresi, and you answered all my questions."

The strike team came out of the U.S. attorney's office, along with Daniel Pierce. Whatever Tag had been about to say, he'd changed his mind, now that five of his coworkers were in the vicinity. Alex figured they'd said everything there was to say, but then, she didn't have to face anyone the next day. Except herself.

She stepped up to Tag, rested a hand on his chest, and leaned in for a short, bittersweet kiss. She felt his heart kick under her palm, just like hers did. And when she stepped back, she moved her hand to her own heart, a vain attempt to ease the ache there.

"Good-bye, Tag," she said, and went back inside to call

a cab because she didn't want her last memory of him to be walking away from her—knowing that where he was going he might not come back alive. Better to remember him vital and excited, heading off to do the job he loved. More than he loved her.

chapter
28

ALEX SCOTT EASED THE BINOCULARS UP TO HER eyes an inch at a time, barely drawing breath. She made no sudden movement, there was no glint of reflected light off the lenses, no sound, and still her quarry whipped around. Wild, piercing golden eyes, magnified a thousand times, seemed to stare directly into hers.

Excitement shivered down her spine, mixed with a healthy dose of fear. A full-grown African lion was nothing to mess with, especially half-starved from a brutal dry spell that should have been relieved by the yearly rains a month ago.

Good thing she was a mile away, and there was a herd of zebras milling around the nearly dry water hole between the two of them.

Alex waited until the cat went back to stalking its prey, then she carefully hung the binoculars from the rearview mirror of her open-top Jeep, fielding the look her dog sent her from his guard post on the rear seat. Canine impatience. "Just a couple of shots," she said, her hand moving over the rifle scabbard and stopping at the camera bag nestled between the seats, "then we'll pack it in for the day." Stupid whined, but he did it softly.

It was the plane that set everyone off. It wasn't unusual for a small plane to fly through that part of the Serengeti, but the sound carried for miles. So did Alex's curse. The zebras scattered, and the cat took off in pursuit. Alex was pretty much frozen in place, shading her eyes, watching gravity invade her life for the second time.

Facing a hungry lion was nothing compared to realizing that whoever it might be was aiming, unmistakably, for her. Her heart was pounding a mile a minute, and the term "fight or flight" would only have applied if she'd been steady enough to drive. Or run.

If it wasn't Tag Donovan hanging from that parachute, she'd eat one of those zebras herself. The question was why. It was the possible answer that had her all worked up. Stupid wasn't too happy about it, either.

He crossed the seat to where Alex stood by the driver's door. She scratched absently behind his ears and, reassured, he paced to the other side of the Jeep. As the parachute dropped lower, though, he started to whine, his hackles went up, and his attitude switched from doggie perplexity to defending his territory. Alex knew from firsthand experience that his territory included her. Stupid might be a mutt, but he was smart, he was loyal. And he was protective.

She stowed the camera bag she was still holding, systematically packing up the rest of her gear, and studiously ignoring the parachute, even when she heard the distinctive thud of a touchdown way too close for comfort.

Stupid went into full pre-attack mode, snarling, growling, poised to spring. Alex brought him to heel with a hand movement.

"It worked out so well the first time, you decided on a repeat performance?" she said when the footsteps she'd heard stopped not far away. She didn't look up. She couldn't.

"They let me have a parachute this time," was the response she got, in a voice that made her heart jump into her throat and her stomach drop a couple of feet.

She didn't know whether to cry or throw up, but either option was unacceptable. Turning around and keeping her expression absolutely blank was what the situation called for. Seeing Tag, standing there, *alive*, in all his mouth-watering, muscular, irreverent . . . maleness didn't make that easy.

The heartbreak she'd managed to hold off ratcheted up to excruciating. But at least she didn't have to worry about crying anymore. Getting her Winchester and shooting him, that was a real possibility.

And he'd take it as a sign she wasn't over him. "They?" she asked with a nonchalance that might have been convincing if it hadn't been so studied.

"The guys I hired to bring me out here."

She closed her eyes, took a few seconds to let the relief wash through her.

"What, you thought I was on a case?"

She shrugged. "What else?"

"I missed you in Colorado."

That brought her head up, her eyes finding his.

Tag sauntered around the Jeep, Alex turning to keep him in sight with the kind of wariness and suspicion she'd have shown toward one of her cats. It wasn't exactly misplaced. She had no idea what Tag was going to do next, but there was a good chance it wouldn't be healthy for her.

The dog didn't like it either.

"Stupid," Alex said, sharply enough to have him sitting back on his haunches. He never took his eyes off Tag.

"Stupid? First Jackass, now Stupid. And of course he's a male."

"Of course, but that's not why I named him Stupid," Alex said, relaxing marginally. "I never told you Jackass's original name was Benny, did I?"

"Benny. Bennet Harper. So Stupid—"

"Didn't really have a name. He was a stray that just sort of dropped into my life and refused to leave. He's smart as a whip. Somebody already had him trained on simple commands, and it didn't take me long to teach him to obey me.

But he has a stubborn streak a mile wide, and he can't quite get it through his hard head that I can take care of myself."

Tag grinned. "Sounds like someone I know."

Alex felt that grin sucking her in, taking her back to the times they'd worked together, laughed together, and . . . She pulled herself back from memory lane before the inevitable next step.

Recovering from Bennet Harper had been child's play compared to getting over Tag Donovan. Nearly two months had passed since she'd walked away from him at the U.S. attorney's office in Boston. But she hadn't left him behind. Not really. She'd fallen in love with Tag Donovan. Not the superficial, starry-eyed kind of puppy love she'd felt for Bennet. This was the real thing, the warts-and-all version of love that didn't blind you to a person's faults but made you jump in heart-first anyway.

There was only one way to fight that kind of stupidity. Work, lots and lots of work. She didn't think of him every waking moment, and she didn't lose sleep over him anymore. But he snuck up on her at odd times, crippled her thoughts, ached in her heart, exhausted her with the battle to banish him again. Now he was invading her in person, and she felt all those things, but if she backslid into their old relationship, that would be her fault.

"I know that look," he said. "You're building a wall, Alex."

"Damn right, I am."

"You said you were done running. Hiding's the same thing."

"Don't spout that psychobabble at me," she snapped. "I made my choice. So did you." She dug out her trusty old satellite phone, flipping it to him. "The battery is fully charged. I suggest you get in touch with someone who can take you to the nearest airport."

Tag put the phone down. "You don't want to know what I'm doing here?"

"I want to see the back of you, walking away."

A muscle in his jaw worked, and his expression went

stony before he smoothed it out. "Okay, let's talk about you."

"Let's not." She started to step into the Jeep, but he reached in and snagged the keys from the ignition.

Alex made a wild grab. Stupid lunged for him. Tag jumped back, which might have been comical if he hadn't snagged the prize.

"I nearly lost a couple of fingers there," he said.

"Give me the keys or you'll lose a lot more than that."

"If I give you the keys, I'll lose everything."

Alex held out her hand, palm up, pretending she hadn't heard his comment. Or that she was reading anything into it.

"If you want them," Tag said, slipping the keys into the front pocket of his jeans, "come and get them."

Her eyes on his the whole time, she walked over and reached into his pocket as shallowly as possible, just until she could curl her finger around the key ring. "You can't talk your way around me anymore, so now you're playing cheap tri . . ."

He dropped his mouth to her neck, cruised his lips up to her earlobe, and all the breath wheezed out of her lungs. She closed her eyes for a second, just a second while need rushed through her on hot and prickly feet. But when she felt her heart begin to trip, felt him move in closer, she jerked away and climbed into the Jeep, a clean, quick break before the pounding and throbbing inside drowned out any shred of reason.

"Alex, don't run," he said, his voice as unsteady as her hands fumbling with the keys. "I still love you. Isn't that worth a few minutes of your time?"

She fought with herself briefly, then sat back, defeated by a combination of desire and logic—both her own. Tag was right. She'd have cut her tongue out before she admitted it to him, but he was right. If she was ever going to put him behind her, she needed to finish this once and for all.

"I didn't run away from you in Boston, I didn't run away from Colorado, and I'm not running now." Stupid whined, still nervous about Tag and probably picking up on her mood. She reached back and ruffled her fingers through his mangy fur, letting her eyes roam around to remind herself why she was there.

The Jeep was completely open but for the windscreen and a roll bar, so she could see the land stretching away to the horizon in all directions. The sun was a huge yellow ball sinking into the west, the sky around it a pastel watercolor, the air before shimmering with heat waves. It was so different from a Colorado sunset where the shadows of the mountains raced out to drop the land into darkness before the sky followed. It was different from Colorado in every aspect, but just as wild and beautiful in its own way. She took a deep breath of the dusty air and knew again that she'd made the right choice. She didn't belong in any one place. She belonged to the world.

"I'm changing careers," she said, "going into photojournalism. Conservation projects mostly."

Tag had let her have her moment, now he came over to lean against the side of the jeep, just by the windshield where he could see her face in the deepening twilight.

"Photojournalism doesn't pay very well."

"It won't pay anything until I establish myself."

"And yet you're rebuilding your cabin—"

"With indoor plumbing and a darkroom."

"No stable?"

She smiled fondly. "Jackass decided to stay at Dee's. With Angel. I'm using the cabin as a home base between assignments. It's free, doesn't cost anything to maintain, and I can get there on my dirt bike just as easily as I can on horseback."

"Dirt bikes aren't cheap." Tag leaned a forearm on the top of the windscreen, grinned over it at her. "The treasure was bigger than you thought, wasn't it?"

Alex popped up an eyebrow. "What treasure?"

"You took the map when you left Boston. Interestingly enough, some gold coins showed up recently for sale on the Internet. The claim is they came from Juan Amparo's gold mine, the Lost Spaniard."

"I'm not selling anything on the Internet."

"Citizens for Casteel is—that's a newly formed charitable corporation."

"I've heard of them," she said. "I understand they're planning to build a school in town."

"Nice of you to cut them in," Tag observed.

"They had to put up with the invasion of crazies every few years," Alex said, "they deserve it."

Tag looked like he wasn't entirely convinced of that, but he let it go. "How did you figure it out?"

"Aubrey did, actually." Alex climbed out and went around to the old but still sturdy strongbox bolted behind the Jeep's rear seat. She didn't have much of real value, but she'd learned if she wanted to keep it at all, she needed to keep it close. She worked the lock and pulled out her satchel, removing the map as she walked around so she could spread it open on the hood. The fact that it would be an unspoken invitation to Tag escaped her until he came to hover over her shoulder.

She did her best to ignore him. She managed it mentally. Her body was a different story, but she could get past the heat and tingling and heart palpitations. She just had to concentrate on something else. Conveniently, she had the perfect distraction right in front of her.

"Aubrey did some research and figured out that Juan was probably a wealthy man in Spain who fell on hard times," she began. "This notation at the top of the map means Amparo's salvation, and she thought he was trying to accumulate enough money to get back on top."

"But he was killed for the map, right?"

"Right. Aubrey couldn't find any report of the treasure having been found, and we know it wasn't at any of the sites marked."

"We didn't check the third site."

Alex waved that off. "It wasn't there, and the only other place we never managed to identify is Mount Rosalie, so I did some research before I left the Colonnade. Turns out Mount Rosalie was renamed Mount Evans in 1895, after

Juan's time. At first, I thought it was just another landmark, like Denver, but why choose Mount Evans? Why not something more well-known, like Pikes Peak?

"The notation for east at the side of the map kept bothering me, too," she continued. "Aubrey passed it off as Juan being an amateur mapmaker, but why would he point out east instead of north, especially since the north is at the top of map? None of it made sense, until I fell asleep on the flight back to Denver, and all the stuff about crosses and salvation and Juan being religious connected up in my brain." She drew an imaginary line between Casteel and the stone cross due north of it, another between Mount Evans and the right side of the map. "The fourth point of the cross is Castile in Spain, which is what the east notation means, and my cabin is right at the intersection." She looked up, met Tag's eyes. "No one ever knew exactly where Juan lived."

"Until now."

"Yep, and I wouldn't have found it if Bennet hadn't burned my cabin down. There were heavy rains while we were back East. Part of the ground that was protected by the cabin floor for the last hundred and fifty years washed away. Sticking out of the mud and mess I saw a corner of that," she pointed to the strongbox where she kept her satchel.

She'd hoped Tag would want a closer look at the box, but he stayed where he was, so close that if she took too deep a breath she'd rub against him. Alex braced herself and deliberately stepped back into him. He moved, but only far enough for her to open her satchel and take something out, something that sparked light from the rays of the setting sun.

Tag reached over her shoulder and took the gold coin, holding it up. A woman's head was on one side, the date 1860 below and stars around the edge. The obverse was the American eagle, olive branches in one claw, arrows in the other. Around the edge it read "Pikes Peak Gold, Denver, Five D."

"That was made locally in Colorado by Clark, Gruber and Co., who later sold their mint to the U.S. government."

"More Internet research?"

Alex smiled, handing him another object, which he took in his other hand, so he had both arms around her now.

She should have moved away; he wasn't holding her there. He was barely touching her, but she didn't have the strength to deny herself the breathless moment of pleasure, remembering how it felt to be wrapped in his arms for real.

But a moment was all it could be. She concentrated almost desperately on the hunk of rock Tag held, the size of his palm, veins of pure gold threading through quartz.

"Alex—"

She slipped out of his arms before he could tighten them, and to hell with letting him see that he'd gotten to her. "I found everything from gold dust to minted coins to raw ore in the box," she said when she'd put enough space between them. "Juan was a thief. That's why we didn't find a claim. He never filed one. He just robbed everyone else."

"So simple," Tag said, his voice as husky as hers.

Alex refused to let it mean anything. He was aroused. So was she. Sex had never been a problem for them. Commitment was, and it appeared her luck with men hadn't improved in that area. "If Bennet had actually looked for the treasure, he'd have been richer than he could have dreamed. But he never had any imagination, never believed in anything but the quick, easy score."

"He took a shortcut," Tag said. "Sometimes they don't lead where you expect." He stuffed his hands in his pockets. "So . . . you haven't asked me any questions."

Because they were all loaded, she thought. They started off harmlessly enough, but they all seemed to lead somewhere emotional, and her emotions had been her enemies for the past couple of months. It didn't help, knowing Tag was trying to take her off guard, talk his way around her.

But she was curious—which she hid behind a one-shouldered shrug. "The case was all but closed when I left Boston."

"Hasn't gone to trial," Tag said, "but yeah, it's closed. Harper wound up pretty much where we figured. Sappresi was brought in, and he won't be able to slither out of the charges this time. Guys are lining up to rat him out."

"I thought the mafia frowned on that."

"He was getting to be a problem. I imagine they find it ironic that for a change the bureau is solving a problem for them. Junior got off pretty much scot-free, but he didn't do anything wrong. And he's probably burning that you found the treasure. Kills his perfect record."

"What makes you think he knows?"

"I'd imagine somebody told him by now."

"Somebody?"

"Trust me, he'll get over it in no time." Tag shifted from one foot to the other, crossed his arms, then uncrossed them. "Once everything was tied up I came looking for you."

"Took you a while to find me, especially since all you had to do was call my mom."

"Your mom wasn't exactly cooperating."

Alex flashed him a grin. "She learned her lesson with Bennet Harper."

"Yeah. If I'd been thinking straight I would have used the FBI's resources to locate you before I quit." After a couple of beats, Tag smiled slightly. "It's your turn to talk. You know that, right?"

"Yeah." But suddenly there weren't any words in her head. There wasn't anything but a dull roaring sound.

"You're not saying anything."

"I know that, too."

"Go ahead, let me have it. I rehearsed."

Alex leaned a hip against the Jeep's front grille. "You rehearsed?"

"I didn't stand in front of a mirror practicing facial expressions and different inflections or anything, but, you know," he spread his hands, "kind of running scenarios in my head."

"How did they end?"

He bumped up one shoulder. "I don't know, but they all started the same way." He lifted his gaze to hers. "I love you."

Alex put her things back in the satchel, walked to stow it in the strongbox, then came around to the driver's side of the Jeep.

Tag stepped in front of her waiting until she lifted her gaze to his.

She sighed, shook her head. "Love isn't a magic pill, Tag. We want different things out of life."

"Do we?"

"I'm going to be on the road most of the time."

"Then I'll go with you."

"You going to hold my camera for me? Be my gofer?"

"I'll go wherever you go, do whatever." He said it without hesitation, with absolute certainty that he could leave behind a life that had so clearly defined him.

Alex was still afraid to take that final leap of faith. "You'll get bored," she said.

"First, you're underestimating yourself. Second, I'm not completely without options. I think I can find something to keep me busy while you're working."

She narrowed her eyes at him. "Is that supposed to be an argument in your favor? Because the last time you kept me busy, there were people trying to kill me."

"Afraid I'll get you in trouble again?"

"Actually, yeah."

"Not on purpose, and not for a long, long while." He took her in his arms, took her mouth.

She tried to hold it back, but tears started leaking from her eyes. She'd been fighting for so long, herself more than anyone else, and she didn't even know why anymore. "I don't have to travel all the time," she said. "You could get your job back, and—"

Tag scooped her up in his arms, whirled them both in a circle, then set her on her feet, hugging her so hard she swore she felt her ribs rubbing together. "This isn't going to be a long-distance relationship, Alex."

"But—"

He kissed her again, and this time she went with it, wallowing in the fast burst of heat and the soft glow of warmth sliding with it into her system. She wasn't foolish enough to believe love could solve all their problems, but she figured it would give them a pretty good common ground to build the foundation for a life together.

Tag dropped his mouth to her neck, peeling the shoulder of her T-shirt down as far as he could to get to bare skin.

Alex was all for bare skin. "God, Tag, I love you."

"Yeah, me too," he said, fumbling with the hem of her T-shirt and then giving up to run his hands beneath, palming her nipples right through her sports bra.

Alex moaned, finding some bare skin of her own. When Tag boosted her onto the hood of the Jeep, and she had to open her eyes to catch her balance, she realized how dark it had gotten. "We can't do this here," she gasped, fighting the deep, drugging pull of his hands and mouth rushing over her.

"Okay." But he took her mouth again and helped her slide to the ground, slowly, full frontal contact the whole way. And he kept his hands on her for the short walk to the driver's side, laying his mouth on hers when they got there, sinking into her until he knew if he didn't let her go they were going to wind up on the ground, and probably serve as a snack for the local predators.

"There are a couple of problems we have to deal with," Alex began breathlessly, leaning on the side of the Jeep while she caught her breath, "before we take this any further."

"Fine." Tag kissed her again. "Let's discuss them on the way to your place. How far is it?"

"Too far to walk. That's Problem Number One."

Tag gave a pained and breathless laugh. Making it to the other side of the Jeep was probably too far to walk in his current state. "I can make it if you can. What's Problem Number Two?" he asked as he started around to the passenger side.

Stupid snarled, teeth bared, hair on end, keep-your-distance-or-lose-an-arm serious.

"Convincing him to let you in the Jeep," Alex said.

Tag eyed the dog, and Stupid eyed him back. After a minute or two the dog gave a little whine and lay down, nose on his front paws. He was still watching every move Tag made, but he was apparently prepared to postpone his final opinion.

"I'm impressed," Alex said, climbing behind the wheel. "Where'd you learn that, the FBI?"

"Jackass." Tag slid into the passenger seat. "But don't tell him I said so, it'll only go to his head."

Don't miss the page-turning
suspense, intriguing characters,
and unstoppable action that keep
readers coming back for more from
these bestselling authors...

Tom Clancy
Robin Cook
Patricia Cornwell
Clive Cussler
Dean Koontz
J.D. Robb
John Sandford

Your favorite thrillers
and suspense novels
come from Berkley.